W9-BZW-075

Praise for Tawni O'Dell's "Riveting" (*Publishers Weekly*) Novels

Angels Burning

"O'Dell does a stellar job of depicting the despair of those who live in a blighted rural community, while providing a complex study of the human soul and the fragile line that's crossed when someone chooses to end another person's life."

—*Publishers Weekly* (starred review)

"Compelling, fast-paced . . . O'Dell's latest is character-driven fiction at its best."

—*Library Journal* (starred review)

"In *Angels Burning,* Tawni O'Dell ratchets up the suspense with stunning twists and turns that send the unsuspecting reader careening toward a shocking ending. *Angels Burning* is a no-holds-barred, page-turning, perfectly crafted thriller that kept me reading long into the night. I can only hope that this is not the last we hear of O'Dell's feisty and complicated protagonist Dove Carnahan."

—Heather Gudenkauf, *New York Times* bestselling author of *The Weight of Silence*

"O'Dell returns with a captivating mystery . . . Filled with surprising twists and turns, this whodunit in a sullen town is a page-turner."

—*Kirkus Reviews*

"With a writer as insightful as Tawni O'Dell, and a protagonist as fascinating as Dove Carnahan, from the first page you brace yourself for the hard truths of the town of Campbell's Run. *Angels Burning* lives up to every bit of its promise. This is a terrific book."

—Jamie Mason, author of *The Hidden Things* and *Monday's Lie*

"Impossible to put down."

—*Booklist*

"Without doubt, *Angels Burning* is the best mystery I've read all year. Tawni O'Dell's characters are at once brutal and tender, baffling and wise. They will hold you transfixed while this story sneaks up and breaks your heart."

—Carla Norton, *New York Times* bestselling author of *Hunted* and *The Edge of Normal*

"[An] intense psychological thriller . . . O'Dell tells her dark tale with assurance and a talent."

—*Bookpage*

"A feast of a story. O'Dell handles family, friendships, and toxic love with a ferocity reminiscent of Pat Conroy."

—Stella Cameron, *New York Times* bestselling author of *Trap Lane* and *Out Comes Evil*

"Tawni O'Dell's Appalachian mystery is vividly set."

—*The New York Times Book Review*

"O'Dell's language is as beautiful as her setting is bleak, and her characters live and breathe as they struggle over the defining line between victim and survivor. *Angels Burning* is a fine mystery, but O'Dell is also working on a broader canvas: the rust belt of the human heart."

—Matthew Guinn, *New York Times* bestselling author of *The Scribe* and *The Resurrectionist*

"A darkly compelling look into how the past colors the present, this psychological thriller will linger with readers."

—*RT Book Reviews*, 4-star review

"This book had me on the edge of my seat. I promise—you won't be able to put it down."

—Brenda Novak, *New York Times* bestselling author of *Blind Spot* and *Hello Again*

"O'Dell shows why she is among the bestsellers. Her magic is powerful."

—*Suspense Magazine*

One of Us

"A fearless exploration of the line between mental illness and true evil, a place many thriller writers visit but without the kind of fearless insights O'Dell reveals in this powerful novel."
—*The New York Times Book Review*

"[A] searing, tragic vision of working-class people . . . Powerful and uncompromising, yet radiant with love, this one's pretty close to a masterpiece."
—*Kirkus Reviews* (starred review)

"Riveting storytelling and genuine emotional punch . . . excellent."
—*Publishers Weekly* (starred review)

"A well-written psychological thriller that will appeal to fans of Gillian Flynn and Daniel Woodrell."
—*Library Journal*

"An evocative novel about murder and intrigue in a small mining town . . . compulsively readable."
—Christina Baker Kline, #1 *New York Times* bestselling author of *Orphan Train*

"A masterfully unfolded, absolutely engrossing story as smart and sassy as it is wise . . . love [is] at the heart of it all, in crisp, insightful prose that sweeps the reader along. A knockout."
—*Booklist*

"Rich, compassionate storytelling."
—*Entertainment Weekly*

ALSO BY TAWNI O'DELL

One of Us

Back Roads

Coal Run

Sister Mine

Fragile Beasts

angels burning

Tawni O'Dell

POCKET BOOKS

New York   London   Toronto   Sydney   New Delhi

The sale of this book without its cover is unauthorized. If you purchased this book without a cover, you should be aware that it was reported to the publisher as "unsold and destroyed." Neither the author nor the publisher has received payment for the sale of this "stripped book."

Pocket Books
An Imprint of Simon & Schuster, Inc.
1230 Avenue of the Americas
New York, NY 10020

This book is a work of fiction. Any references to historical events, real people, or real places are used fictitiously. Other names, characters, places, and events are products of the author's imagination, and any resemblance to actual events or places or persons, living or dead, is entirely coincidental.

Copyright © 2016 by Tawni O'Dell

All rights reserved, including the right to reproduce this book or portions thereof in any form whatsoever. For information, address Gallery Books Subsidiary Rights Department, 1230 Avenue of the Americas, New York, NY 10020.

This Pocket Books paperback edition May 2021

POCKET and colophon are registered trademarks of Simon & Schuster, Inc.

For information about special discounts for bulk purchases, please contact Simon & Schuster Special Sales at 1-866-506-1949 or business@simonandschuster.com.

The Simon & Schuster Speakers Bureau can bring authors to your live event. For more information or to book an event, contact the Simon & Schuster Speakers Bureau at 1-866-248-3049 or visit our website at www.simonspeakers.com.

Manufactured in the United States of America

10 9 8 7 6 5 4 3 2 1

ISBN 978-1-9821-7211-4
ISBN 978-1-4767-5597-7 (ebook)

For my beloved little sis, Molly Meghan

chapter one

THE LAST TIME I was this close to Rudy Mayfield he was leaning across the seat of his dad's truck trying to grope my recently ripened breasts.

I close my eyes, and for a moment I smell a teenage boy's sweaty, horny desperation barely masked by Dial soap instead of the sweetish smoky reek of charred flesh mixed with the acrid odor of sulfur always present in this poisoned ghost town.

"Who does something like that?" Rudy asks for the tenth time in the past minute.

It's become his mantra, a numbing chant to help him cope with the impossibility of what he encountered this morning on his daily trek down this deserted road.

His dog, Buck, a shaggy, white sheepdog mix, raises his head from where he lays at Rudy's feet and gives him a sympathetic look.

"You're absolutely sure you didn't see anyone?" I ask again.

We both glance around us at the buckled driveways leading to the crumbled foundations of a dozen missing houses, and the gnarled leafless trees clawing their way out of the softly simmering earth like giant hands of the undead. The bright orange rust coating of a child's toppled bicycle fender is the only speck of color anywhere in the desolate landscape.

"My grandpa's the only one who stayed at the Run who's still alive. Aside from me checking on him, no one comes here. You know that."

"Well, obviously someone came here," I point out. "That girl didn't show up on her own and light herself on fire."

Rudy's face turns the same shade of gray as the faded blacktop beneath his feet. He swallows and stares hard at his impressive beer gut straining against an old undershirt spattered with various colored stains like countries depicted on a great white globe.

"We had a few good times back in school," I say to him in as light a tone as I can manage under the circumstances.

The distraction works and he gives me a lopsided smile, the same one he used to give me in health class whenever our teacher said something obvious or useless, which was most of the time. He still has the same pretty green eyes half hidden in the shadow cast by the brim of his ball cap; the years haven't dulled them.

"Yeah," he says. "I never understood why we didn't go out. I liked you."

"Maybe you should've told me that."

"I thought us doing it in my dad's truck told you that."

"That just told me you liked doing it in your dad's truck."

I still remember his surprise when I didn't stop him. He probably thought it was my first time, and it should have been; I was barely fifteen and too young to be fooling around, but my mother's robust sex life had aroused my curiosity at an early age. It had the opposite effect on my sister, Neely, who felt she knew everything she needed to know about the act from the many times we couldn't avoid hearing it and the few times we peeked. She never seemed to have a desire to explore it on her own, but I wrongly believed my mom did it because she enjoyed it, and I wanted to know what made it so great that she'd prefer rolling around with naked, grunting men instead of playing with her kids or feeding them.

I hear a car approaching. Buck raises his head.

The road through Campbell's Run has been closed for as long as I've been alive and is so shattered by potholes and overgrown with weeds, it's impossible to see from a distance. We left the gate open for the coroner, but it's a state police cruiser and two unmarked cars that arrive first.

"I have to get back to work," I tell Rudy as I bend down to give Buck a scratch behind his ears. "But don't go anywhere. We might have some more questions for you."

Corporal Nolan Greely comes walking toward me. He looks like the kind of big, solid, humorless trooper that makes a motorist's heart sink when he sees him in his side-view mirror. He's actually a detective in the state police Criminal Investigations Division and no longer wears a uniform but he doesn't need to. From his iron gray crew cut and the slow, purposeful pace of his steps, there's no denying he's a cop.

He stops in front of me and looks me up and down with a face set in stone and a pair of mirrored sunglasses hiding his eyes.

"Hello, Chief," he greets me. "You on your way to have tea with the queen?"

I'm in an iris blue skirt and blazer and a new pair of taupe patent-leather pumps I just bought at Kohl's with a 30 percent–off coupon. The blouse I'm wearing is a bright floral print in honor of the sunny summer day.

"I'm supposed to be at a Chamber of Commerce breakfast at the VFW."

His expression doesn't alter. I can't tell if he admires, pities, or envies me.

"I have to admit I was surprised you called me right away," he tells me. "There was a time when we would've had to pry this case away from you."

"I've decided not to waste my time and energy fighting the inevitable," I reply.

"You mean me specifically?" he asks. "Or the entire state police force?"

I give him a slight smile.

"You, Nolan," I joke. "If you were a superhero, that would be your name: the Inevitable. And your superpower would be always showing up, even when you're not wanted or needed."

"I'm always needed," he says without smiling.

"Well, I'm not reluctant to ask for your help this time," I explain. "I have a good bunch of guys working for me, but none of them are prepared to deal with this."

"That bad?"

"Worst I've seen. I think she's a teenager."

I reach down and slip off my shoes.

"I can't walk back there in heels," I explain, "and I don't have a pair of practical shoes with me."

Again, I can't tell if Nolan admires, pities, or envies me.

We start walking toward the site. Nolan motions at the two crime scene techs that arrived with him. They head toward the body in their duty uniforms of cargo pants and polo shirts with the state police badge embroidered over their hearts carrying their cameras and evidence kits. I motion at Colby Singer and Brock Blonski, the two officers on the scene with me. After initially examining the body and waiting as they stumbled away and threw up, I sent them off to look for bloodstains, footprints, or any other kind of evidence.

Blonski and Singer are rookies to police work and life in general. They're in their early twenties and both still live at home, although Blonski recently made the bold move to an apartment above his mom's garage. I hired them about a year ago. The only dead body Singer's ever seen prior to this girl was his grandmother who was dressed in her Sunday best lying peacefully in her white-satin-lined casket. Blonski was first on the scene at a traffic fatality a few months ago. It wasn't pretty, but it was nothing like this.

"Have you ever been here before?" I ask Nolan.

"Once on a dare when I was a kid."

We stop next to a snarl of fallen barbed wire.

"You can't get over that in your bare feet," he says to me.

"I did it before."

Without saying another word, he grabs me around the waist and swings me in the air over the wire.

"That was humiliating," I comment once I'm on the ground again.

"I would've done the same for a man," Nolan assures me, "only I rarely run across one performing his duties without shoes."

I ignore his dig. I've been in a male-dominated profession for my entire adult life. I've experienced every kind of alienation, sabotage, and harassment the Y chromosome has to offer. Most of it isn't sincere; it's simply expected. I save my disgust for the true misogynists.

The mine fire that destroyed the town of Campbell's Run began several miles belowground more than fifty years ago before finally making its presence known on the surface ten years later when a sinkhole opened up in a backyard, releasing a cloud of steam rife with the rotten-egg stench of sulfur. The hole turned out to be three hundred feet deep and the temperature inside it turned out to be almost twice that number. Soon afterward, a little girl's rabbit hutch was swallowed up, then a birdbath. One morning the handlebars of a prized Harley were found poking out of a ten-foot-long ragged slash in the owner's driveway.

All of the town's residents were relocated except for a few holdouts like Rudy's grandfather, who refused to go and somehow managed to remain living here while all around him his neighbors' empty houses were torn down, roads were barricaded, and warning signs went up.

The only other building left standing was the white clapboard church. The government didn't have the nerve to tear it down. From where I'm standing now, it's hidden around a bend in a road and I can glimpse only the weathered gray cross at the top of its spire, but I can picture the rest of it clearly: a simple forgotten sanctuary, the once bright red paint on the front doors almost completely worn away except for a few stubborn strips.

I was out here a dozen years ago when Rudy's grandfather called to tell us someone had stolen the church's stained glass windows. I worked that case hard while everyone around me considered it a waste of time. I was more successful than I imagined I'd be. I discovered the thieves were professional antique scavengers working out of New York, but I was never able to come close to an arrest or track down the property. Here those windows were miraculous bursts of color and faith in the midst of bleakness. Now they're in the summer homes of the filthy rich and go underappreciated. I feel personally violated every time I think about it.

I step gingerly over the scorched ground, fully aware of the dangers beneath my feet, while Nolan stomps heavily behind me, daring it to give way.

Where the fire burns hottest, more than a dozen

smoldering gashes have opened up. Dead trees have broken loose from the weakened soil and fallen over. Their exposed roots remind me of the tangled legs of dried-out spiders that Neely and I used to find in our attic.

In one of these fiery holes in the ground, someone has stuffed a dead girl.

Nolan and I stare down at her.

The top portion of her body has been badly burned. Her eyes are open and staring in surprise out of a face that looks as if it's been slathered in barbecue sauce and overbaked until it's begun to crack and flake. Most of her hair is gone, and the damage to her skull is obvious. I highly doubt she survived those blows. Hopefully they were inflicted before she was lit on fire.

"We've searched the area and the road. There's no sign of blood from those head wounds. She must have been killed somewhere else and brought here," I tell him, needing to fill the silence. "It's been dry lately, so unfortunately, no footprints, no tire tracks."

Nolan kneels down to get a closer look.

"I think whoever put her here thought she'd burn up and disappear," I go on, "and when she didn't catch on fire, he doused her in some kind of accelerant. Then there's this."

I gesture at a comforter streaked in bloodstains and black burn marks we found in a bank of weeds.

"Chantilly pattern in corals and oranges with a turquoise medallion overlay. I'm pretty sure that's from the Jessica Simpson Sherbet Lace collection. You can find it at Bed, Bath and Beyond."

Nolan looks up at me with his unreadable reflective eyes.

"I was shopping for some new bedding recently," I explain. "I didn't get *that*," I further justify myself. "It doesn't look like she was allowed to burn long. Maybe someone tried to put out the fire with the blanket."

"Could be the killer felt some remorse, or could be someone was with him who couldn't stand to watch," Nolan contributes. "How'd Mayfield find her?"

"His dog."

He doesn't say anything else. My officers and I stand by while he continues to stare intently at the dead girl from behind the black depths of his glasses.

Even eerier than the landscape is the absence of any noise. It's a perfect June day and not a single bird is chirping, not a fly is buzzing, dogs aren't barking and children aren't calling out to each other. No one is mowing a yard or playing a radio or wielding a power tool.

"How do you want to get her out of there?" I ask Nolan.

She's only a few feet down, but there's no way of knowing how fragile the earth is around her and how deep the chasm might be beneath her. There's also no way to know the extent of her burns and the resulting condition of her body. If we try to pull her out, she might come apart.

Nolan finally stands back up.

"One of us needs to get down there to help hoist her up," he says. "We can tie a rope around whoever goes. I've got two troopers with me, but they're big guys."

He sizes up Blonski, who has a stocky, no-neck weight lifter's build, then Singer, who's tall and lanky, then me.

"Do you weigh more than him?" he asks me.

"No," I reply sharply.

"You sure? He's skinny as a stick."

"He's six-two and a man. I weigh the least. I'll do it."

"You're wearing a skirt, Chief," Singer ventures hesitantly. "And you don't have any shoes."

"Yeah," Blonski chimes in. "Shouldn't we wait for someone with the proper clothes and equipment who knows what they're doing?"

"Who knows what they're doing?" I repeat in a tone that puts an end to any further argument.

I take off my jacket and slip a rope under my arms while the men hold the other end. I'm not worried for my safety, but I am worried about my blouse. I hate the fact that I've been caught off guard unprepared to do my job, but in all fairness to me, this is not my job anymore. I have an office now with a comfortable chair and a Keurig: I'm a coordinator, a schedule maker, a form filer, a public relations maven, a handshaking figurehead. I'm the first female police chief in the county. I cling to this knowledge in an effort to maintain some dignity as I descend into a muddy hole to retrieve a corpse.

I try not to think about the girl or to look at her until I absolutely have to. The hole is hot and steamy, and I also try not to think about the earth around me falling away, exposing the leaping flames of hell a mile beneath my dangling feet.

I wedge myself against one side and reach out to

grab the body around its midsection. It looks as if the fire didn't spread below her hips.

The sight of her young bare legs sticking out from a pair of cutoff shorts makes my throat tighten. Miraculously one of her flip-flops is still on one of her feet. Her toenails are painted neon pink, and an anklet made of sparkly hearts glimmers in the black dirt.

I gently pull her toward me, ignoring the sound, smell, and feel of seared flesh and bones, and try to imagine the girl she once was before her heart stopped beating and her soul fled. Did she like school? Did she have a lot of friends? What did she want to be when she grew up? Did she ever get to do it in a pickup truck?

None of us speak once we have her laid out on the ground. We stand around her in a protective circle and silently share our individual grief. Tears are acceptable in even the most hardened police officers in situations like this. They're all thinking of sisters or daughters. I'm the only one who sees myself.

I'm the first to look up and away from the dead girl and this dead town to the lush green waves of rolling hills on the blue horizon, and I feel the familiar ache that always comes over me whenever I'm faced with ruined beauty.

One by one, the men turn away, too, consumed for a final moment by their private tortured thoughts before returning to the practiced numbness that enables them to do their job but unfortunately can't shield them from their dreams.

Our sleep will be haunted tonight by those legs that even in death look like they could get up and run away from here.

chapter two

SINGER AND BLONSKI arrive back at the tan brick municipal building that houses our department well before me. I had to stay and talk to the coroner and strategize with Nolan. Campbell's Run is a no-man's-land when it comes to police jurisdiction since it doesn't exist as a town anymore according to the state of Pennsylvania. The road going through it doesn't exist either. Buchanan is the nearest community with its own police force, and I've been the chief here for the past ten years.

Nolan has all the resources of the state police at his disposal, including their forensic lab. I have six officers (two on vacation), four vehicles, and a frequently broken vending machine. The investigation is his, but we'll assist. The arrangement would be the same if the girl had been found on my doorstep. The crime is too heinous to risk failure due to our inexperience with homicides and a budget that can barely put gas in our cruisers and ink in our printer.

It doesn't hit me until I pull into my parking space

and realize I'm still in my bare feet because I wouldn't put my new shoes back on, that I forgot to go home and shower and change. I think about turning around and leaving, but we have a single shower in our locker room and I have a pair of sweats in my office. I have a lot to tackle this morning. I'll go home and get some real clothes on my lunch hour.

Singer and Blonski are deep in conversation with Karla, our dispatcher, and Everhart and Dewey, my two other available officers. This was their day off, but I need all hands on deck. Dewey has four kids out of school for the summer and seemed happy to be called into work. Everhart's wife is pregnant with their first child, just past her due date, and is driving him crazy; he seemed even happier. All talking ceases when I enter the building.

"I realize I'm a little dirty," I say, and walk past quickly without allowing any commentary.

I motion at Singer and Blonski.

"You two. A word, please."

They follow me into my office. This ten-by-twenty-foot enclosure painted the color of khaki pants with one window overlooking a parking lot and no central air is the closest I come to having a nest, and the vigilant fondness that comes over me once my officers enter here is the closest I come to feeling maternal.

"How much do you weigh?" I ask Singer as I open my window and perch on the sill, hoping for a breeze.

"One sixty," he says.

"No way," Blonski cries out, plopping down in a chair the same way he might land on a buddy's chest during a backyard tussle. "And you're six-two? You're a freak. You need to bulk up."

"It doesn't matter how much I eat. I don't bulk," Singer replies, lowering himself into the other chair.

"I didn't appreciate your comments in front of Corporal Greely," I tell them.

"We were trying to protect you," Singer replies.

"You're an idiot," Blonski informs him, shaking his head.

"If I were a man would you have felt the need to protect me?"

"If you were a man you wouldn't have been wearing a skirt and a—"

"Do you know why I'm dressed like this?" I interrupt Singer.

"I like your blouse," he says.

"Because I was on my way to eat tasteless scrambled eggs and soggy bacon with town officials and concerned citizens and discuss the potholes on Jenner Pike and the new dog-barking citation. Next time you want to protect me, protect me from that."

"Yes, ma'am."

Blonski grins. The chastisement was meant for both of them, but Singer has taken on all the blame and this means Blonski won.

The first time I saw BROCK BLONSKI written across the top of a job application, I pictured a linebacker from Fred Flintstone's favorite football team, and when I met him, aside from the fact that he wasn't a cartoon character wearing a loincloth, he fit the bill: square-jawed, broad-shouldered, competitive, with a deceptively lumbering large-primate gait.

He spoke in grunts and monosyllables and ate entire rotisserie chickens for lunch. I was beginning to think the fact that his first name was only one swapped vowel away from the word "brick" completely summed up his personality until I overheard him explaining the latest developments in neuroscience nanotechnology to the mother of a boy who had just suffered a head wound after wrecking his dirt bike. He only pretends to be dumb.

"I wanted to thank you for volunteering," Singer says to me. "I was afraid the detective was going to ask me to do it."

"I wanted to do it," Blonski says.

I look at them sitting side by side: one with thick dark hair parted fastidiously on one side, long limbs folded into his seated body umbrella-style, a live-wire jumpiness about him; the other a human ATV, head shaved, leaning back in his chair with eyes half-closed like he's about to nod off. They're two seemingly very different young men, physically and mentally, but to someone my age all that matters is they're both twenty-three, which means they're exactly the same.

"Were any missing-persons reports filed recently for a teenaged girl?"

"Nothing in our county," Blonski responds.

"Too bad it's summer and school is out. An absentee list from the high school would be a good place to start looking."

"Won't the state police be doing all that stuff?" Singer asks.

"I'm sorry, Officer, would you like the day off?"

His face reddens.

"No, it's just that . . . " he begins.

"We're going to conduct our own investigation. We know the area and the people living in it better than they do. Corporal Greely welcomes our help."

"Welcomes?" Blonski wonders skeptically.

"Feels obligated to accept our assistance," I correct myself. "I'm going to take a shower. When I'm done, we're going to brainstorm."

Singer gets up from his chair and heads for the door. Blonski lingers.

"She might not be from around here," he says.

"Only someone from around here would think to dump a body out at the Run," Singer counters.

"Maybe the killer is from around here but the girl is from somewhere else?"

Singer disagrees.

"How would he have found her? Have you ever run into anyone around here who isn't from around here?"

Blonski gets up and leaves. I stop Singer as he's heading out my office door and hand him one of my new pumps.

"Can you get out that scuff?" I whisper to him.

"Sure thing, Chief," he says.

I NEVER USE the locker room. I'm surprised to find that it's neat and clean. I realize immediately that I don't have a towel, soap, or a comb. There's a faded blue beach towel with a picture of a shark on it, fangs bared, folded and sitting on the end of the bench. I pick it up and inspect it. It's dry and it doesn't smell. Wrapped inside is some kind of bodywash.

As I walk past the mirror, I stop and stare dumbly at my reflection. I can't believe I just had a conversation with two of my men in this condition and they were able to keep straight faces. I look like a chimney sweep.

I can't help thinking about my mom and what her reaction would have been to my appearance. She was obsessive about personal cleanliness to the point where she named her first child after her favorite soap. She took at least two showers a day and set aside a full hour every evening for her religiously observed bubble bath complete with lit candles, soft music on the radio, fizzy pink Mateus wine in a plastic gold chalice from a Renaissance Faire, and an altar set with shiny glass bottles, tubes and ceramic pots with metallic lids, and sparkly silver lipstick cases.

Her desire to be immaculate didn't extend past her body, however. I can't ever recall seeing my mother run a vacuum or wash a dish. Our grandmother used to stop by sometimes and tidy up until I got old enough to do it, but her visits weren't often enough to combat the filth, piles of clutter, and soiled clothes that accumulated everywhere.

I always wished Grandma would get mad at Mom and tell her she needed to be a better mother and a better housekeeper, but she thought her daughter's refusal to attend to such mundane domestic tasks was perfectly acceptable because she was beautiful.

"Your mother shouldn't have to worry about

things like this. It would be a crime for a girl that pretty to do dirty work," she'd say as she attacked our sticky kitchen linoleum, her hair covered with a knotted bandana, wearing a colorless housedress and clunky rubber-soled shoes.

Anyone seeing Grandma would've never known she had produced an offspring too lovely for mopping.

The ever-practical Neely finally piped up one day and asked, "If being pretty is such a big deal, why doesn't Mom use it to make money? She could be a movie star, or Miss America."

Grandma looked like she was about to scold Neely, then her face softened like she was going to say something kind. She ended up not saying anything.

What we didn't realize was that Mom *was* using her looks to make money. Various boyfriends bought her clothes, paid our rent, gave her spending money. When times got desperate, she'd work for a little while as a waitress or secretary in town, but each job would quickly lead to finding a new sugar daddy.

I step into the shower and turn on the water, making it as hot as I can stand. I watch it turn black as it hits my muddy skin and streams off my body before swirling down the floor drain. No matter how much I scrub and dig, I can't get the grit out from under my fingernails.

I wonder if the dead girl was pretty. Probably. Most teenage girls are some kind of pretty simply by virtue of their youth, even though almost all of them think they're ugly.

I make the water hotter until I can't stand it anymore, knowing it's still not anywhere near as hot as the flames that had begun to consume the girl's face.

I've managed to keep the details of her at bay, but standing here naked and exposed on a concrete floor, I lose my resolve. The image washes over me along with the steaming water: patches of burned skin the amber brown of pipe tobacco crisped tautly over her face and bare arms; her skull, caved in on one side, scattered with straggly shocks of singed hair; her hands clutching at nothing, the fingers like strips of jerky. It suddenly strikes me that her hands were burned worse than any other part of her body. I file this away in my head as possibly important.

I know this is the moment when I should finally cry for her, for the life she didn't get to live and the horror of her final moments, for her family and the anguish they will never be able to escape for the rest of their days, but the tears don't come until I abandon my thoughts of the murdered girl and begin to concentrate on the monster who could do something like this. It's familiar territory for me, and the rage and righteousness I find there warms and comforts me. They're not tears of grief but of relief.

Back in my office, still in bare feet, with my unruly dark hair pinned to the top of my head, wearing gray YMCA sweatpants and a pink sweatshirt from a breast cancer fund-raising fun run, I sit at my desk and reach for my reading glasses with a sigh.

I started wearing them last year. At first I kind of liked them. I convinced myself I was rocking the sexy librarian look. That delusion ended fairly quickly.

I just turned fifty a couple of weeks ago. The number on its own doesn't bother me. I didn't even get upset when Singer unthinkingly proclaimed with sincere admiration, "Wow, fifty! That's half a century."

I'm in good health. Aside from a little bit of gray in my hair that I cover, a few lines on my face, and the beginning sag of certain body parts, I still look good. I'm okay with my age, but nobody else is. Especially men.

I bristle at the thought of Nolan hurling me over that fallen barbed wire back at Campbell's Run this morning like I was a sack of road salt. He would've never done that when I was younger, because the same act would have had the sensual connotations of a romance novel lover swinging his sweetheart over a babbling brook.

He also would have never asked me about my weight with the dispassionate scrutiny of a farmer passing by a penned hog at the county fair.

Maybe this is my comeuppance for spending so much energy during my life trying to make men in my profession ignore my face and figure and take me seriously as an equal. I didn't want them to treat me like a girl; now I do, and all they see is a sexless blob.

Singer knocks on my door even though it's open. He pauses and sniffs the air.

"I smell Axe bodywash," he says.

"Never mind."

"There's a guy out here who insists on seeing you."

"Something to do with our girl?"

"No. He won't give his name, but he says he killed your mother."

He let's the weight of this statement sink in. I'm

sure he expects a reaction from me, but I have none to give.

"Are you okay, Chief? Do you think this joker is serious? Should we check on your mom?"

"My mom was murdered when I was fifteen."

He drops his eyes to the floor.

"I'm sorry. I didn't know."

"It's okay. Show him in."

I'm perfectly calm. I don't have to force it. I really feel nothing, and I wonder fleetingly if that means there's something wrong with me.

I assumed I'd never see him again, but I never ruled out the possibility. He's an old man now but still vain about his looks. He hasn't lost his hair. It's completely gray but thick. He's put an oily gel in it and slicked it back from his forehead. He's wearing a faded but clean short-sleeved checked shirt with fake pearl buttons and an enameled American flag belt buckle as big as his fist. His bare arms are covered with tattoos in heavy black ink. He didn't have any when he went in, so they must be the work of a prison artist who seems to have randomly scribbled on and slashed at him. I can't make out a single image or word.

"Hi there, Dove."

He smiles at me. His teeth haven't fared as well as his hair. They're stained, and he's missing a few.

"You're all grown up. Well, you're past grown up. You're way on the other side of grown up."

"I get it. You've made your point," I say.

"Though you weren't exactly a little kid when I went away. You already had a good-size rack on you. Nice ass."

"Still the charmer, I see."

I fold my hands on my desk.

"What do you want, Lucky? Or did your nickname change to something more accurate in prison? Is it Pathetic Loser now?"

"No need to make personal attacks," he replies, taking an unoffered seat. "It's still Lucky. Compared to a lot of guys where I just come from, I am lucky. And I got a few years shaved off my sentence for good behavior. What could be luckier than that?"

"I was notified you were being released."

He sizes me up in the covetous way he used to look at Mom and me and Neely but also cases of beer, our neighbor's Trans Am, and our TV before he turned it on and sat down to watch a ball game. He had two expressions: a sullen bored pout for things he didn't care about or didn't understand, and a greedy groping gaze for everything else.

"How's that little sister of yours? I hear she's a lesbian."

"She's not a lesbian."

"That's not what I heard. I heard she's a real man-hater."

"Lots of heterosexual women hate men. Thanks to men like you."

"Too-shay," he exclaims, flashing me another hay-colored smile. "I hear she's a dog trainer now. Some kind of dog whisperer or, in her case, more like a dog shouter."

He laughs, highly amused by the sputtering spark of his own dim wit.

"You've heard a lot for a guy who's spent the past thirty-five years behind bars," I say.

I'm as amazed as I was in my youth that my mother had anything to do with him, but this was common musing for me back then. As far as I could tell, my mother's only standard for men was that they could afford her. Young, old, handsome, homely, muscly, portly, blue-collar, white-collar, married, single, educated, and dumb as dirt: we watched all kinds come and go.

Very few appealed to Neely and me, and those who did initially always proved to be jerks in the long run. Lucky had been a jerk from the start, although we both agreed he was good-looking. He worked in a factory that made parts for mining equipment and drove a black Harley with a dazzling electric blue stripe. He drank too much, but so did our mom, and he treated my siblings and me like we were the hired help or naughty pets depending on his mood, but so did our mom.

"Maybe I'll go see her."

"Stay away from Neely."

"Hit a sore spot," he cries, grinning. "Come on. You aren't still mad over that pop I gave her that one time for talking back to your mom? If you'd had a dad, he would've done the same thing."

"What do you want?" I repeat.

"I think you know."

"I have no idea."

"How about your little brother? What was his name? Spot? Fido? Bandit?"

"Champ."

"Yeah, right, Champ."

"He left the state when he graduated from high school."

"Running away from his sisters, huh?"

He was running away from something. Definitely not his sisters. At least Neely and I have always prayed this wasn't the case.

I'm not about to allow this conversation to turn to Champ.

I look at Lucky over the tops of my glasses.

"I've got a lot to do today. I need you to leave."

"So you're not going to be nice about any of this? Even after all these years?"

"Good-bye, Lucky."

"Not good-bye. I'll be seeing you around. Your sister, too."

He stands up and stares down at me. I know he's trying to rattle me, but he has no idea what he's up against.

I'm suddenly struck by the vivid image of my mother as I saw her before I left for school the day she died. She was standing in front of Gil's big bay window in her shorty emerald green bathrobe sipping a cup of coffee and playing with her mane of Farrah hair. She was studying the neighbors' trash as the garbage men tilted their cans into the masher at the back of the truck. She said you could tell a lot about people by what they threw away.

Since she had married Gil and finally attained the respectability of a shared last name and a big house in an upscale part of town, she had begun spying on the neighbors, a pastime she had never indulged in when we were poor. Then, she had been content to be the object of everyone else's prying eyes. Grandma called her new habit being a nosey parker until Gil taught her the word "voyeurism." She preferred it, saying it sounded classy.

Those acquainted with my mom's past would go on to say that Cissy Carnahan dying on trash day was perfect timing.

Lucky turns to leave and I begin to let my guard down, but he stops in the doorway.

"All I want to know is why you and Neely lied and sent me to prison for something I didn't do."

I don't flinch. I stare him down, saying nothing, until he finally gives up and leaves.

I will never tell him that I've often wondered the same thing.

chapter three

MY MOM'S MURDER is something I keep hidden most of the time; when I have to bring it out, I wear it like a crown or a noose, depending on my mood. After talking to Lucky, I've slipped it over me like a Kevlar vest.

Her violent end happened thirty-five years ago, and even though it was the most heinous crime this town has ever seen up until today, it has been largely forgotten except by her children, her mother, and, of course, the man who unfairly paid for it.

I like to think the man she was married to at the time remembers, too, as he continues to float around Europe on a cloud of family money serving out his self-imposed exile. At the time I wanted Gil as far away from my siblings and me as possible, but now I think I could finally deal with him properly. I wouldn't mind if he came home again.

However, I realize I'm not ready to deal with Lucky. I may have seemed tough and detached when I talked to him, but my conscience was wringing its hands inside me. My actions against him seemed inarguably necessary at the time; now I'm not so sure. One of the worst aspects of growing older is the lengthening of hindsight. As it stretches, it becomes thinner and more transparent and we see things more clearly.

I drive home around noon to change my clothes. I'm still shoeless, and the feel of the gas pedal beneath my bare foot conjures up memories of Lucky giving me driving lessons. It was summer. He'd come roaring up on his motorcycle on a Saturday morning relishing the disapproving scowls on the faces of Gil's neighbors peering out from behind their fancy drapes the same way Mom watched their garbage. I'd grab Gil's car keys and run out to meet Lucky, usually forgetting to slip on my Dr. Scholl's.

Lucky's relationship with Mom had ended five years earlier. After they broke up, a parade of men came and went before she finally took the plunge with Gilbert Rankin. I had begun to think that Mom was not only too beautiful for housework but also for marriage. I could imagine Grandma's reasoning: "It would be a crime for a girl that pretty to only be able to manipulate one man for the rest of her life."

Mom had entered her thirties not seeming the least bit interested in a commitment, but I think Gil's money and availability had been too much to pass up.

Gil came from one of Buchanan's wealthiest families. All small towns have a few who no one knows exactly where their money originally came from, but in Pennsylvania it can almost always be traced back to something dark or invisible that's been dug, blasted, or piped out of the ground. His father had given him a department store and two restaurants to keep him busy. He also appeared to have an active love life, but despite constant rumors about possible potential spouses, he had never married or had any children.

One day I came home from school to find Lucky lolling on Gil's avocado-green-and-sunflower-yellow paisley-swirled couch with his steel-toed biker's boots propped on the Lucite coffee table that looked like a gigantic ice cube made from lemonade. He had a can of beer in one hand and the other hand on Mom, who was laughing at something he'd said. They didn't try to cover up anything when I walked in. It occurred to me fleetingly that they might be doing something they shouldn't, but I had learned a long time ago not to judge my mother's actions, since nothing productive or satisfying ever came of it. Mom was as oblivious to moral censure as Gil's constantly yapping terrier was to shouts of "Shut up!"

Lucky happened to drop by one day while I was asking Mom to take me driving. I was going to be able to get my permit soon, but I didn't have anyone to teach me.

Lucky volunteered. I don't know if he did it thinking it might earn him points with Mom or if he wanted to be near my nice ass and already good-size rack, but I think the main reason was that before and after my lessons in the empty high school parking lot he got to drive Gil's big, shiny, cranberry Buick Riviera, and he drove it way too fast.

Learning to drive was one of those rare moments where I missed not having a dad. As far as I could tell, no one needed a dad. I didn't feel this way because Cissy had been one of those impressive single moms who stepped up and admirably performed the roles of both parents; she barely showed up for her own part. It was because my siblings and I had survived without one, and we couldn't miss what we didn't have.

However, society dictated that there were certain milestones in a daughter's life that required a father. A dad taught you how to ride a bike, took you on your first camping trip, walked you down the aisle, and gave you driving lessons.

I had never known my father, but at least I knew his name: Donny McMahon. He denied he was my father from the moment Mom informed him she was pregnant. This was back in the days before blood and DNA testing. They weren't married, and Mom already had a bit of a reputation. There was no way to make him or the rest of his family accept me, although Grandma told me he came to see me when she was babysitting me and we were alone. My mom's pride prevented her from allowing me to have a relationship with a man who spurned her and, more important, refused to pay up. Grandma insisted my dad loved me as long as no one was looking.

He died two years after my birth, on a sleety day in March in the first Pontiac Sunbird our town had ever seen. The accident left him too mangled for an open casket. I have two photos of him that were taken before his face would become unrecognizable to his loved ones: a wallet-size senior picture from high school where my resemblance to him is painfully obvious, and a faded Polaroid of him grinning and posing next to the car that would be the instrument of his death a month after its purchase.

Neely's father was "passing through." This is the only information we were ever given about him. We used to come up with all kinds of scenarios for who he was and how he and Mom met. Our favorite was to paint him as a masked hero along the lines of Zorro, or the Lone Ranger, or Batman. He broke into Mom's bedroom one night, got her pregnant, and continued passing through before she was able to discover his identity.

Champ's father, on the other hand, was someone Mom knew well. He was a respectable guy with a wife and kids, or so Mom told us one drunken dateless night when she was stuck at home feeling sorry for herself. She went on to say she could never tell Champ his father's name because she had promised him his bastard son would never try to contact him.

Unlike Denial Donny and Passing Through, Champ's principled father gave Mom a stack of ten-dollar bills once a month. It was hush money and that meant it was more reliable than traditional child support because he would've never dreamed of missing a payment. We called him the Envelope.

I always felt bad that Neely and Champ were saddled with an added burden that I had been spared. Throughout their childhoods they were forced to wonder about their dads and knew they could see them in the street and never know. It could have even happened to Neely. If her dad had passed through once, he could pass through again.

I didn't have these lost-father worries. I had a name, two photos, and I knew exactly where mine was at all times: the cemetery behind the Buchanan Methodist Church.

After I change and make a sandwich, I drive to Neely's before I head back to work. I don't know why I feel the urgency. Even if Lucky was ambitious enough to try and find her, he'd never get anywhere near her unless she wanted him to. I don't think he'd try to physically hurt her, and if he did, it would be bye-bye Lucky or at least good-bye to Lucky's balls. I'm also not worried about any potential emotional damage he could cause her. Neely put away her feelings about Lucky a long time ago. I envy her that ability.

I need to tell her now because otherwise I'll spend the rest of the day thinking how wrong it is for me to know something big that Neely doesn't know.

The drive to her place raises my spirits and helps turn my thoughts away momentarily from the dead girl who's lying on cold stainless steel in the county morgue waiting to be given a name. Neely's compound is deep in the woods off a gravel road that runs through state park land past Laurel Dam, a lake fed by freezing mountain springs with a sandy beach area populated this time of year with picnicking families, blasé teens stretched out on blankets, and shrieking, blue-lipped children.

No one would ever be able to find Neely's place if it weren't for the totem pole of warning signs at the bottom of her mile-long driveway that leads back through more dense forest to her home and office.

She doesn't advertise her business at all. Starting from the bottom, they read: NO TRESPASSING, NO SO- LICITING, NO HUNTING. At the top is a gift from a grateful bichon frise owner who came to her all the way from Pittsburgh with a nippy, piddling, chronic yapper and left with a calm, quiet accessory she can now tuck confidently away in her designer tote; it's a handcrafted sign that reads: BEWARE OF DOGS BUT BE TERRIFIED OF ME.

Both of Neely's pickup trucks are parked in their usual spots along with a car I don't know. She must be with a client.

I get out of my car and close the door and wait for the woods to come alive.

I'm sure the dogs hear any vehicle the moment it turns up the drive, but they wait until it arrives at Neely's log cabin office, parks, and the occupants get out before they appear. Neely never trained them to do this. It's something they've developed on their own.

No matter how many times I've experienced their greeting ritual, my heart always races and my mouth goes dry partly from an instinctual fear that dates back to our Neanderthal ancestors and partly from the thrill of watching these animals patrol their land.

One moment, I'm alone. The next, I'm sur- rounded by five German shepherds. They materialize out of thin air without making a sound and stand evenly spaced around the edges of the tree line.

When a newcomer notices one, he or she might smile or even call out to it. After all, they wouldn't be at Neely's place if they weren't dog lovers. Then they spy another and another. Their eyes begin to dart nervously. They turn around and check behind them and what do they find? Oh, yes. Another one.

The dogs don't bark. They don't rush forward. They stand perfectly still and watch. There's Kris and Kross, identical red-and-black littermates with impeccable bloodlines brought over from Germany; the dignified Owen, a retired police dog from the Bronx; Maybe, a coal black shepherd mutt Neely rescued; and her beloved Smoke, an enormous ten-year-old pure white that I'm convinced not only understands the human language but can read our thoughts as well.

Besides Neely and the boy, Tug, who works for her, I'm the human they know the best. They recognize me instantly but take their time acknowledging my right to be there. Maybe always breaks rank first and trots over with his tail waving happily behind him. Kris and Kross see this as their release cue and come galloping toward me. They're only three years old, the youngest of the group, and want to play. I keep a couple tennis balls in my glove compartment for this very reason. As they approach, I hold one up in each hand. They both stop at the same instant, their eyes fixated on their quarry. I throw both balls at the same time in opposite directions and they tear off after them.

Owen arrives next and walks the perimeter of my car before he lets me pet him. Smoke disappears back into the trees.

Kris and Kross are back already.

I throw the balls again.

Neely's office door opens and she walks out along with a man and a pit bull.

It's a hot day but she's in her usual jeans, work boots, and a plaid flannel shirt over a T-shirt. Her long blond hair, sugared with strands of silver, is pulled back in a ponytail and hidden beneath a state police K-9 unit ball cap.

Over the years, I've come up with the theory that stunningly beautiful women can only deal with their affliction in one of two extreme ways: they can embrace it wholeheartedly at the expense of everything else about them, or they can deny it and try to hide from it.

Neely has gone the second route. It hasn't worked in my opinion. She can cover herself up in men's clothes and shun makeup, jewelry, and blow-dryers all she wants, but unless she were to put on a mask like we used to theorize her dad wore on the fateful night of her conception, her exquisite face is there for all to see.

Strangely enough, even though she's the attractive female offspring of an attractive female, she and Mom never bore any resemblance to each other except for sharing the same wide-set, pale blue topaz eyes. I told Neely once in a burst of sisterly ego-boosting that they looked just like the December birthstone ring behind the Woolworth's jewelry counter she wanted so badly. She told me my eyes looked like melted brown sugar. This is one of the nicest compliments I've ever been given.

Neely's dogs all start toward the pit bull that begins to bark menacingly and strain on its leash. Neely calls out in a stern voice, "Stop!" She doesn't repeat the command. She doesn't deliver it as an angry shout or a wheedling request. All of her dogs do what they're told. They stand at attention, panting. Smoke reappears, slipping silently out of the trees.

The pit bull goes nuts.

Neely tilts her head and gives the man an expectant look.

He immediately begins yanking upward on his dog's leash and yelling, "Stop! Stop! Stop! Stop!"

"Make her heel," Neely says. "In a circle. Like I showed you."

"Heel!" the man shouts. "Heel!"

"Say it; don't scream it."

"Heel," he says.

The man starts walking in a tight loop while continuing to yank on the chain. The dog falls into step but doesn't stop barking and lunging. The man's arms move up and down like pistons. His neck turns a dangerous shade of red, and patches of sweat form under his arms. I'm beginning to think he might have a stroke when the dog finally begins to obey. By the time Neely releases them and allows them to get into their car, the two of them are walking well together. The dog is focused on the task at hand, not the other dogs.

"Was that Lucy?" I ask Neely when she joins me.

She nods.

"How's she doing?"

"Fine."

"Did the cat live?"

"It did."

"Free," she calls out to her dogs, and they head to the spot where Lucy last stood with their noses to the ground.

"Do you mind taking off that flannel shirt? You're making me hot."

Smoke has silently shown up next to Neely's side. He watches her closely as she slips off the offending garment without saying a word and ties it around her waist. The T-shirt beneath it is gray.

"It's summer, Neely. Lighten up. I'm going to get you a bunch of colorful tank tops. Yellow, orange, pink, purple . . ."

"Great," she says. "I could use some new rags. I want to wash the trucks this weekend."

"You'll be happy to know my new blouse got ruined this morning."

"The drapey floral one that looked like a seat cushion from an old lady's wicker porch furniture?"

"It's a trend."

She gives me a small, quick smile. It's gone almost before I see it. Neely smiles only slightly more often than Mom used to clean.

"How'd you ruin it?"

"Climbing into a sinkhole out at Campbell's Run to retrieve a dead girl's body."

The information doesn't seem to surprise her. This isn't because I'm constantly dragging around dead bodies but because not much surprises her.

"That's terrible," she says. "Do you know who she is?"

"Not yet. You won't believe who found the body. Buck the dog."

"I know about thirty Buck-the-dogs."

"I don't think you know this one. He belongs to Rudy Mayfield."

She ponders the name while shooing away Kris and Kross, who've shown up for more fetch. She takes the tennis balls from me and returns them to my car.

"Rudy Mayfield," she begins. "He had green eyes, and sat next to you in health class, and was always telling you about his latest project in metal shop."

"I think it was a form of foreplay for him," I add to the description. "You have an incredible memory."

"How'd he look?"

"Not good. He's gained a lot of weight."

We've started strolling toward her office, where she's going to grab a can of Coke from her vending machine, the only extravagance in her life.

Smoke remains at her side. The four other dogs follow behind her in pied piper fashion.

"You know," she says, "a lot of people in other depressed areas of Appalachia have turned to crystal meth to help them cope with the destruction of their economy and way of life. Around here our drug of choice seems to be carbohydrates. I suppose that's the lesser of two evils."

"I never thought of it that way."

Tug appears from behind the office before we reach it. A huge bag of dog food is flung over one of his shoulders, and I'm amazed he's not staggering beneath its weight. He's one of the skinniest fourteen-year-olds I've ever seen; a boy made of pipe cleaners with hands and feet too big for the rest of his body like a puppy's oversize clumsy paws. He has on a pair of long, baggy camouflage shorts I bet are held up with a belt that's been looped around his nonexistent waist three times.

He stops when he sees the dogs. Maybe runs up to him first.

Tug and Maybe came into Neely's life on the same day. She received a phone call from a boy who wouldn't tell her his name. He asked her if she only trained dogs or if she saved them, too.

She told him she could put him in touch with the local ASPCA or animal control or even the police but he insisted this was a top secret situation that couldn't involve any official agency, or as he put it, "I'll get beat." The matter-of-fact way he stated his possible fate along with the tremor that came into his voice when he spoke about the dog convinced Neely to help him.

The dog belonged to Tug's uncle, who kept him penned outside and went for days without feeding him because he believed a hungry dog would make a more vicious guard dog. To this day neither Neely nor I have been able to figure out what the man owned that needed guarding.

Tug's uncle also liked to kick the dog, and when he got drunk, he liked to take wild potshots at him with his rifle while shouting, "Maybe I'll kill you; maybe I won't."

Tug explained to us after we got to know him better that his uncle also used to do this to his ex-wife.

The plan was remarkably easy to carry out; it just required the right heroine with the right skill set.

Neely showed up with a leash, a muzzle, and a bag of liver treats while Tug's uncle was at work and stole the dog.

Tug was with her, and when they arrived back at her home and she put the newly christened Maybe in one of her kennels with a bowl of food and a promise to Tug that she would be able to erase all the suffering he'd endured and soon he'd be able to love again, the boy burst into tears.

She offered Tug a job on the spot. I think for her the rescue mission was a package deal.

"Hey, Chief Carnahan," he says to me with a teenager's verbal shrug of forced unenthusiasm.

"Hi, Tug. How are you?"

"Good."

He continues on his way with the dogs trailing after him, except for Smoke, who waits to see what Neely will do next.

I can't stay. I need to get back to work. There's not going to be an easy way to bring up what I want to tell her, so I just say it.

"The reason I stopped by was to let you know Lucky's out of jail. He stopped by to see me this morning."

Neely shows exactly the kind of disinterest I hoped she would except that she unthinkingly rubs her jaw where he smacked her hard enough to send her toppling out of her chair at the kitchen table, where we were doing our homework and Champ was diligently working on a sticker book.

Neither one of us will ever forget Mom's reaction. She flew over to Neely and scooped her up in her arms. She kicked Lucky out of the house. She tended to Neely all night, even running to the grocery store to get her favorite ice cream and to the newsstand to buy her a *Mad* magazine that she would've never approved of under normal circumstances. The next day, Neely had a bruise on the side of her face and her lip was puffy where she'd bitten the inside of her mouth. Her jaw clicked when she opened and closed it. Mom let her stay home from school for two days, and both nights she provided slurpable dinners: Campbell's Chicken & Stars soup, Snack Pack pudding, mashed potatoes and gravy from Kentucky Fried Chicken, applesauce, and more ice cream with gobs of Cool Whip. We joked afterward that the way to get Mom's attention was to have someone hurt us. It stopped being funny, though, when we realized we actually believed it.

"What did he want?" she asks casually.

"I think he wanted to rattle me, but he didn't succeed. He said he's going to see us around. Both of us."

Neely snorts.

"Yeah, well, he's welcome to come see me anytime. If he can get past my dogs, I'll talk to him."

"He's an old man now," I tell her. "He's not going to cause any problems."

"What about Champ? Did he ask about him?"

"He could barely remember his name."

We fall silent as we always do when the topic of Champ arises. Our sibling love for him has placed us in a special kind of hellish limbo: we're not allowed to be part of his adult life, which we choose to imagine as a kind of heaven, yet our earthly childhood ties to him are too strong to ever let him go completely. Modern technology has made our plight worse, not better. We could be texting daily. We could be friends on Facebook. We could be following his tweets. Instead, we hear from him once a year on no particular date. One of us will get a text from a number we don't recognize with a random area code hundreds of miles away: I'm doing good. I hope you are, too.

No matter how we respond, he never replies.

When he left all those years ago, I was twenty-three, already a state trooper, and already looking for another job. Two years later a position opened up in my hometown police department, and I've been there ever since.

Champ had become a man seemingly overnight. His teen gawkiness was gone. He was tall. He had muscles and facial hair. His once chirpy voice was now low and slow. He had a mop of almost black hair and dark eyes the color of tea that's been left to steep too long. The Envelope's genes had apparently prevailed when it came to Champ's coloring.

He stood next to the beat-up Chevette he was planning to drive across the country. All his belongings in the world didn't even take up half the trunk space.

Neely and I didn't have a serious heart-to-heart talk with him that day. The taboo subject from years earlier remained as inaccessible to each one of us as it had always been, but for the first time since our mother's demise he cracked that particular closet door just enough that the rancid smell of an improperly stored trauma wafted out.

"It's nobody's fault," he said.

I knew it was definitely somebody's fault, but if he needed to think this way, I wasn't going to correct him.

"What are you thinking about?" Neely asks. "You've got a funny look on your face."

I don't want to talk about Champ.

"I was just thinking about how Singer and Blonski had never heard about our mom," I reply instead. "It happened long before they were born, but still . . . something that big happens in your life, you feel like it's written on you somewhere. That it's the only thing people see when they look at you."

I make brackets with my fingers against my forehead where the words would be spelled out. "My mom was murdered," I recite.

"I remember feeling that way."

"Especially in a small town like Buchanan. It was all anyone talked about. Now it's about to start again. People aren't going to be able to forget about this murder for a long time. A teenage girl. What was done to her."

"You have no idea who she is?"

"There was no ID on her and her face and her hands . . ." I decide not to finish this part of the description. "She had pink toenails and a glittery anklet."

I notice Tug standing behind Neely. He has the same ghostlike ability to sneak up on people unobserved as Smoke.

He's pulling on his left ear, which is sticking out from beneath his ball cap. This habit is the source of his nickname. He tugs on his ear whenever he's nervous or afraid; he told Neely he's been doing it since he was a baby.

"What is it, Tug?" I ask him.

"My sister Camio has one of those ankle things. It's got hearts on it," he replies, staring at the ground. "She wears it all the time. Her boyfriend gave it to her."

He continues to furiously yank his ear lobe as he adds in a broken voice, "She didn't come home last night. She ain't never done that before."

Smoke takes inventory of the three humans with his head tilted to one side. He lets out a solitary, clipped bark. He knows what we're thinking.

chapter four

I'VE NEVER PAID much attention to the Truly family. They're too noxious and pervasive to ignore entirely, but like the colony of red biting ants that have taken up residence in the crack in my back stoop concrete, I've found I can usually step around them.

Miranda Truly, the matriarch, gave birth to eight children during her union with chain-smoking, hard-drinking, overeating, diabetic Walt, who died tragically but not surprisingly in his fifties from the failure of too many body parts to bother listing. Of these children, six lived to adulthood, five stayed out of jail, four stayed off crack, three worked from time to time, two were sober, and one found Jesus. All six would procreate many times over.

Clark Truly, the baby of the family, has managed to avoid prison, drugs, and religion, but not the bottle. He's in his forties, married to Shawna Ridge, employed by a trucking company, and the father of five, including Tug and Camio. One of his older brothers, Eddie, is the former owner of Maybe.

I called Nolan and we discussed our best course of

action regarding the victim. We agreed that we didn't want to bring the parents of the girl to the morgue and have them try to identify her. Due to the condition of her face, we're not even sure her own mother would be able to recognize her. She doesn't have fingerprints anymore. We decided I should visit the family and ask them to release Camio's dental records.

I'm sure there was a time when this house was clean and pretty, none of its parts sagging, faded, or warped from neglect or misuse, a classic American symbol of hope and possibilities. The same could be said for Shawna Ridge Truly, whose lovely, fresh face atop a willowy body wrapped in lacey virgin white smiles out from a yellowed wedding photo on a shelf behind the large, listless woman she's since become. She sits in the middle of a once-blue velveteen couch now covered in a soot gray patina of worn-at-the-knees shininess. Her long, lank hair is the color of potato peels, and she has a dark, dull gaze that keeps wandering away from me to the plasma TV taking up most of the wall next to me. She hasn't offered to turn it off or even mute the sound.

The coffee table in front of her is covered with stacks of tabloids, overturned soda pop cans, rank gym socks, crumpled tissues, a clear plastic container empty except for a few smears of blue cake frosting, a plate encrusted with swirls of hardened ketchup, and a baby bottle half-filled with something brown and fizzy.

The curtains are drawn against the bright sunshine. An overhead lamp has been turned on, but little light can shine through the powdery layer of dead insects accumulated at the bottom of the fixture. The room has a fried food, dirty diapers, damp dishrag odor to it. The carpet made a spongy squish when I crossed it a few moments ago. The feel of it beneath my feet made me think of tromping through a field of mushrooms. I had no problem taking my shoes off to walk around Campbell's Run, but I'd never do it inside this house.

Shawna's eldest daughter, Jessyca, stands off to one side of the couch loosely holding a baby on one hip while expertly navigating an iPhone in her other hand. A substantial roll of aggressively tanned flesh spills out between her cropped T-shirt and a pair of denim cutoffs. The baby's tiny fingers grasp the fabric of her top and try to bring it to her mouth. She gives the child a quick glance full of maternal affection and I have no doubt they belong to each other.

Shawna doesn't appear to be the least bit interested in why I'm here. I don't think Jessy is either. The difference between them is that the first one couldn't care less if I spent the rest of the day sitting here with her watching moronic daytime TV while the second one wants me gone. Jessy watches me closely, her eyes shiny with distrust.

"Is your husband around, Mrs. Truly?" I ask.

"He's on a job. Been gone for two days. Be back in two more," Shawna replies without looking away from the TV.

"What do you care about my dad?" Jessy asks, the suspicion in her eyes hardening into outright hostility. "Is he in trouble?"

"No. This isn't about him. I have a few questions about Camio."

"Camio? That little bitch better not show up around here anytime soon."

"Jessyca Lynn, shut your fat face," Shawna snaps, again without tearing her gaze away from her program.

"You're the one who's been calling her that," Jessy shoots back, sounding a little hurt.

"Is there a problem?" I ask.

"No, there ain't no problem," Jessy says to me in a mocking tone. "She didn't come home last night, and she was supposed to do a bunch of stuff for me and Mom today. We're just mad at her, that's all."

She leans over to put the baby down on the floor.

"Don't do that!" I cry.

She gives me a funny look. Even Shawna glances in my direction.

"I mean, can I hold her?"

I reach out my arms.

Jessy plunks the baby in them. Apparently her dislike of me doesn't extend to a need to protect her offspring from me.

"Have you talked to Camio today?" I ask her sister.

"Tried texting earlier. She's not answering."

"It's almost two o'clock. Could you try contacting her again?"

She taps out a quick text.

"Might as well call her, too," Shawna adds.

Jessy holds the phone to her ear.

"Camio, you stuck-up little pig. Where the hell are you? You had a lot of shit you were supposed to do for Mom today. Call me when you get this."

"She's with that boyfriend of hers," Shawna volunteers.

"You know this for sure?"

I get no further reply.

"Could we try to contact the boyfriend or his family?" I ask Jessy.

"No way. We don't have nothing to do with them."

"Why not?"

Her inability to provide an answer for the amount of animosity suddenly blazing up in her eyes makes me instantly suspect this is one of those baseless hatreds akin to racism: an inarguable prejudice rooted in nothing concrete or rational, just the insistent whispers of your tribe that shunning particular others is a requirement of membership.

I heft the baby a little higher on my shoulder and try a different route.

"Is it normal for Camio to disappear like this and not check in for this length of time?"

"No," Jessy says, dropping her petulant posturing for a moment. "This ain't normal for Camio at all."

"What's going on here, Shawna?"

I turn at the sound of a forceful female voice, and I'm surprised to find its source is an elderly woman who at first glance looks like the proverbial wind could blow her over.

She's skin and bones, but there's nothing remotely frail or sickly about her. On the contrary, her gaunt stare and emaciated frame give her a formidable aura of impossible survival, as if she stepped out of a post-apocalyptic landscape in a science fiction film.

"Nothing, Miranda," Shawna answers her.

"Nothing?" her voice rings out, and I half expect the TV to turn itself off. "The chief of police is standing in your house holding your grandbaby because of nothing?"

I quickly scan through my mental contacts file trying to remember if I've ever come face-to-face with Miranda Truly before. It doesn't matter if we've ever actually met; women like her know everyone in town and all their family histories.

"You're one of the Carnahan girls," she says to me.

"Yes, ma'am."

"You're smiling."

"Am I? It's just I haven't been called a girl in a long time."

"Does it feel good?"

"I'm not sure."

"Your sister was in the same class as my Marty."

I remember. Martin James Truly, sixteen, fell off an abandoned railway bridge into the sluggish Crooked Creek after a night of drinking and raising hell. No one ever knew for sure if he was alone when it happened or if he had help taking the header.

A couple of years later his brother Ross was killed running a red light on his motorcycle. The state police surmised that when he saw the semi beginning to cross his path, he tried to avoid it by going underneath it but only ended up going beneath its back tires. It came as no surprise to anyone to learn he'd been an avid fan of *The Dukes of Hazzard*.

Families like the Trulys make me think of the sea turtles I've seen on wildlife documentaries and the almost insurmountable odds against the babies surviving into adulthood. They're picked off by birds when they hatch unprotected on the beach and then the ones that make it to the sea become easy meals for countless fish and aquatic creatures. In the case of the Trulys, their main predator is their own bad judgment.

"What can we do for you?" Miranda asks me, and I sense the shift of power in the room.

I wasn't exactly in command before she arrived, since neither of the other women in the room paid much attention to me, but it was tacitly understood that I was an authority figure. Now I've been reduced to a well-groomed interloper in a summer-weight pantsuit and wedge heels peddling unwanted justice for all.

It would be a waste of time to ease into any conversation about brutal, senseless death with this woman.

"We've discovered the body of a teenaged girl," I begin, "and we've received some information that has led us to think that she might be your granddaughter Camio. I'm sorry to put you through this, but we need to check out all possible leads."

"What makes you think it could be Camio?" Miranda asks.

I hand the baby back to her mother and take a crime scene photo out of my purse.

"Do you recognize this?"

Jessy and her grandmother stare at the close-up of Camio's feet, at the neon pink toenails and the strand of fake diamond hearts circling her slender ankle.

"Oh my God," Jessy gasps.

She instinctively holds her own child tighter to her chest.

"Oh my God," she says again. "Mom!"

Shawna doesn't even glance our way.

Jessy grabs the photo out of my hand and rushes to her mother. Tears are streaming down her face.

"Mom! Look! It's Camio."

She shoves the photo in front of Shawna, who darts a look at it.

"It's feet. So what? You know how many girls paint their toenails pink and have crappy little anklets? And don't you start telling me again that that Massey kid bought it special at Kay Jewelers. It's a piece of shit you can get at Walmart. I seen 'em."

"It's Camio. Look at the scar on the side of her foot. Remember when she was little and stepped on that nail and it went right through? It got infected."

"Why the hell do you know so much about your sister's feet?"

"Mom!" Jessy screams, shaking the photo at her. "What's wrong with you?"

Shawna slaps her daughter so hard, the sound makes the baby start to cry.

"Don't you talk to me like that," she hisses.

I take a step forward, but I'm stopped by Miranda laying her hand on my arm.

"What happened to her?" she asks.

"I'm afraid I can't give you any more information at this time. We'd like to have access to her dental records so we can make a positive ID."

"Where is she?"

"The county morgue."

She motions at Jessy and Shawna.

"Come on. We're going."

"Mrs. Truly," I try to stop her. "I don't think that's a good idea. She's in very bad shape."

"Worse shape than having her head ripped off by a tractor trailer or spending two days dead at the bottom of a crick? Marty had crayfish in his eye sockets."

I don't know what to say to this.

"Shawna. Your child is dead," Miranda announces. "Get up now."

Shawna rises in slow motion and shakes crumbs out of her shirt.

On her way past me, she jabs a finger in my face and spits, "Don't you say nothing to me. You can ma'am Miranda but don't you ma'am me."

I want to tell her that I'm not the enemy, that we're the same, that I know what it's like to be poor, to live in squalor, to wonder why others have it better but that these unpleasant realities didn't make me turn inward and blame and dislike the bigger world; they made me want to be a part of it.

Aside from the presence of my siblings, my mother's house depressed and frustrated me. I came up with the plan that I would sleep and eat there out of necessity but do all the rest of my living somewhere else.

I loved school. I loved activities and events. I loved having friends. I loved having boyfriends. I loved my town. I loved community involvement.

I loved my mom, too, and this is why I was constantly cutting her breaks. I knew she was bad at mothering, but I was never sure if this was the same thing as being a bad mother. Neely and I were convinced that deep down Mom loved us; otherwise, why would she have kept us?

"I'll have an officer meet you there," I tell them.

Neither Miranda nor Shawna make sure that I leave before them. They pull out while I'm standing beside my car. I briefly entertain the idea of going back in the house and poking around, but I know I can't.

I'm about to go when I see a little boy crawl out an upstairs window and scurry across the front porch roof with the agility of a squirrel.

He stops precariously close to the gutters and produces a Slim Jim from his jeans pocket. He tears off a piece with his teeth.

"Who are you?" I call up to him.

"Derk Truly. Who are you?"

"Dove Carnahan."

"That's a stupid name. We shoot doves."

"I'm sure you do. How old are you, Derk?"

"Eight."

"Is it okay for you to be home alone?"

"I'm alone all the time."

I wait to see if he's going to venture any closer on his own. Like the woodland creature he reminds me of, I'm certain he's skittish and easy to frighten away.

He sticks the meat stick back in his pocket, lies down on his side, grabs the edge of the roof, rolls off, then swings onto the porch in one fluid motion. He lands on his feet with a resounding thud.

I stay where I am. He's an adorable boy: big brown eyes with long lashes, a sprinkle of freckles on his cheeks, ears a little too big for his head. His close-cropped hair has a baby seal appeal to it, and I'd like to grab him and stroke its silky softness.

"Do you know Camio's boyfriend?" I ask the little angel.

"Zane Massey," he answers me. "He's a cocksucker. His whole family's a bunch of cocksuckers."

I'm not the least bit surprised by his language, but I can tell from the defiance on his face and in his stance that he expects me to be.

"Really? Do you know what a cocksucker is?"

"Yeah," he replies, unconvincingly.

"The only Masseys I know are Terry and Brie and their kids. He's a CPA and she's a secretary in an orthodontist's office. Now you could say they're a bunch of Presbyterians, or a bunch of brunettes, or a bunch of animal lovers, or a bunch of Ford-Explorer-driving, Old-Navy-shopping, Olive-Garden-dining Taylor Swift fans, but I highly doubt this family sits around sucking cocks together."

He stares back at me saying nothing. At least I've got his attention.

"Know what you're talking about before you open your mouth," I tell him. "It's a good rule to follow."

"I don't follow rules."

"I see. What do you think about your sister Camio?"

"She's a bitch."

"Why's that?"

"She wants to leave."

"With Zane?"

"Don't know. She wants to go to college."

"You think that's a bad idea?"

"College is for cocksuckers."

"Well, that's partially true. And what about your brother Tug?"

"He's okay."

"He works for my sister, the dog trainer."

"Tug says she's okay."

I get into my car.

"It was very interesting talking to you, Derk," I tell him through the open window. "You have a nice day."

I pretend to be busy writing down something in a notebook.

Out of the corner of my eye, I see him leave the porch and start to approach me while trying to look like he isn't.

I take a candy bar out of my purse, break off a piece, and wait for him to arrive outside my window. He does.

"Don't you have another brother?" I ask him.

"Shane's in jail. He stabbed someone."

I extend the rest of the candy bar to him. He grabs it without hesitating and shoves it into his mouth.

"Any cocksuckers in jail?" I wonder.

"Nope," he says through a mouthful of chocolate.

chapter five

I CALL NOLAN and tell him the girl is almost certainly Camio Truly and her family is on their way to the morgue. Nolan rarely swears but he lets loose with a few choice words that Derk would have admired. He didn't want the family at the morgue yet. He says he'll drop everything and meet them there.

I decide not to tell him the name of Camio's boyfriend. Let the big man figure it out on his own.

Nolan wouldn't approve of me talking to Zane and his parents yet. He'd want us to wait until we were sure of her identity and go at them with the shocking news that his girlfriend was dead but if she was dead then we'd be conducting a murder investigation and Zane would be a potential suspect because boyfriends always are and his parents would immediately circle the wagons. I know them, not well, but well enough to assume they can't be happy about their son dating a Truly and that, like most parents, they'd do anything to protect their child.

. . .

SINCE IT'S A SATURDAY, I might find one or both of Zane's parents at home. During the era when I grew up, there's no way a kid would be inside on a day like today, but nowadays there's a good possibility he's embedded in the basement rec room playing video games.

Terry Massey's mowing his yard. He holds up a hand to shield his eyes from the sun and to get a better look at who's pulling into his driveway.

I'm in my own car and wearing street clothes. I shouldn't be a scary presence, but I smile brightly and wave cheerily at him when I get out of my car just to assure him that everything is okay.

I know Terry because he helped Neely with some tax problems related to her business a few years ago. He's the antithesis of his profession's milquetoast stereotype. He's a big, bluff guy, gregarious and loud, who gets up from his desk and eagerly comes at you across his office for a handshake like a linebacker heading for a fumbled ball.

The roar of his mower subsides, and he makes his way across his perfect carpet of vivid green grass. I'm reminded that I need to tend to my own yard, then wistfully recall my fantasy to let it revert back to its natural state of weeds and wildflowers where birds and animals can cavort freely, but we have strict guidelines for lawn maintenance within the borough; outside of it residents can grow their grass three feet tall, cover their property with no longer functioning household appliances and disabled vehicles on cinder blocks, and dispose of anything unwanted—from a chipmunk carcass to an old recliner—by lighting it on fire in their front yard. From what I saw earlier, the Truly family seems to have wholeheartedly embraced this look.

"Hey, there, Chief Carnahan."

Terry draws a forearm across his face to wipe the sweat away.

"I've told you before to call me Dove."

"Okay, Dove. What can I do you for?"

"I was hoping to talk to Zane."

The welcoming grin falls off his sunburned face.

"He's not in any trouble," I tell him. "I just have a few questions for him. Is he home?"

He takes a moment to decide how he's going to answer me.

"No, but he's only a block away at a friend's house. I can text him."

"That would be great. Is your wife home?"

"She's out back."

I follow him around the side of his two-story, mocha brown, vinyl-sided house with barn red trim, marveling all the while at how some people manage to keep their yards cleaner than I keep my kitchen.

I've met his wife once in passing at the Olive Garden. My memory of her is of various elements, not of an overall impression: shiny hair cut in a swingy pageboy, a forced cackling giggle, a distracting multi-strand necklace made of silver-dollar-size red metallic discs. I would have been able to pick her laugh out of a lineup but not her.

We find her kneeling on a plastic mat next to a flowerbed. I'm certain she took the time to pick out her outfit rather than throw on just anything to dig in the dirt. She's wearing a pair of orange capri pants, matching Crocs, a sleeveless yellow blouse, and a blindingly white baseball cap. Her work gloves are covered in a butterfly pattern and are amazingly clean.

She sits back on her heels and flashes a warm smile at her husband and me.

"Honey, you remember Chief Carnahan. Dove," he adds with a wink.

She pulls off a glove one finger at a time and extends her hand to me while Terry walks over to a patio table and picks up a cell phone.

"Nice to see you again," she says, and hops to her feet.

"She wants to talk to Zane," her husband explains while texting.

"Zane?" Her smile widens and tightens. "Why? Zane never gets in trouble. He's almost too good."

I try to make my smile equal hers in size, but the muscles in my face won't comply.

"That's refreshing to hear about a seventeen-year-old boy," I say. "He's not in trouble. I want to ask him a few questions about his girlfriend."

I leave the statement hanging in the air, waiting to see if she'll supply a name.

"Camio?"

"Yes. What can you tell me about her?"

"She's a nice girl. Polite. Straight A's from what Zane tells us. A little on the shy side. We have no problems with Camio."

She darts a look at her husband.

"But . . . ," I urge her.

"It's her family."

"You've met them?"

"Well, no. But we don't really have to meet them to know what they're like."

"How's that?"

"Half of them are dead or in jail," she says.

"But the other half isn't," I offer.

Terry laughs. His wife smiles at him, uncertainly.

"I've met her mother," she continues.

"And how did that go?"

"I don't want to sound mean," she lowers her voice to a conspiratorial level. "I understand some people have no willpower. It's an addiction, you know. Overeating. Just like being addicted to drugs or alcohol. The only difference is that you can stop eating like a pig. I mean, just stop it. Put the Twinkie down. Drugs and alcohol are much harder to quit. Not that I would know firsthand, of course."

"When you met Mrs. Truly did you have any kind of interaction with her other than realizing she's overweight?"

"She was extremely rude. It was a school function. I introduced myself. I said, 'I'm Zane's mother,' and she said, 'Do you want a medal?'"

A laugh leaps to my lips, and I clear my throat to cover it up.

"Are Camio and Zane serious?"

"No," she says automatically, shaking her head, while her husband simultaneously nods and says, "I think so."

Before I can question them further, Brie pulls her husband aside and attacks his ear with tiny hisses that I can't quite make out.

"Were they together last night?" I try.

Again, I receive two different answers. A "no" from Zane's mother, and another "I think so" from his father.

Brie fixes Terry with a glare, and he turns suddenly serious.

"What's this about?" he asks me.

"Camio is missing."

I carefully watch their faces: Terry looks a little shaken, while Brie appears almost pleased.

"From what you know of her, do you think she might have run away?" I ask.

"If she has run away, I wouldn't be all that upset," Brie replies. "I know that's a terrible thing to say, but I can't help myself."

I nod my understanding.

"It's almost as if you have an addiction to saying terrible things."

Terry lets loose with a guffaw.

"I told you she's got a great sense of humor. For a cop."

"I thought you said you didn't have a problem with Camio?" I continue.

"I don't. She's a nice girl and I wish her well, but I don't want her to be the mother of my grandchildren."

"I thought you said they weren't serious?"

Her frustration gets the better of her, and she explodes into one of her shrieking giggles I remember from the restaurant.

"You're twisting my words." She laughs.

I can tell Zane has arrived by the sudden transformation in her expression; the brittle panic melts into fuzzy fondness, then two stark lines of worry appear on her forehead and dip toward her nose.

I look over my shoulder and see a teenage boy loping toward us with the easy, loose-limbed gait of an athlete leaving the field after a satisfying practice. He's cut through a half dozen backyards to get home. Even if Zane is not too good—as his mother believes—he's good enough to earn the tolerance of his neighbors.

He arrives in front of us. His mother immediately puts an arm around his shoulders. He allows it to rest there for five seconds before shrugging it off. I can almost hear the two of them ticking off the countdown in their heads: the mother thinking it's better than nothing, and the son thinking it's the least he can do.

He's dressed in shimmery red basketball shorts that fall to the knee, a dark blue tank top, and a pair of rubber white Nike sandals. No piercings. No visible tattoos. No outward signs of rebellion. I'm impressed at how quickly he obeyed his father's call.

Terry makes the introductions. Zane doesn't seem intimidated or surprised by my presence. He takes the fact that the chief of police has shown up at his house on a Saturday afternoon wanting to talk to him as a matter of course. Either he's an authentically nice kid who's utterly innocent or a sociopath who's completely guilty.

"Could I have a moment alone with Zane?"

The parents have become uneasy. I don't expect a teen to sense this, but he does. Zane smiles at them.

They're a smiley, attractive family. I've yet to meet the younger daughter, but I'm sure she fits in snugly with the rest, completing them like the last piece of a puzzle. I know there's a professional portrait of them in color-coordinated sweaters posing on a rustic footpath on a wall in their house somewhere, along with photos of both children documented at every milestone age.

Shawna Truly didn't have a single photo of any of her five children displayed anywhere that I could see, just her own faded wedding picture.

"What's wrong, you two?" Zane asks his mom and dad, and they relax at the joshing quality of his voice.

"They're totally paranoid I'm going to fu . . . I mean, mess up someday in a major way 'cause I haven't so far," he says to me, and laughs. "Sometimes I feel like doing it just to get it over with."

"This will only take a minute," I say to everyone.

Brie clenches her mouth shut. Terry holds his hands out to me, palms up, as if he's giving me the memory of his son's long-gone infant body.

I want to tell them that I won't hurt their baby, but I can't make that promise yet.

"Where were you last night, Zane?" I ask, once his parents are safely inside the house, each pressed up against a different window watching us.

"I was out with some friends. Then I was home."

"You have a girlfriend but you weren't out with her?"

"We were supposed to go out, but she bailed on me."

"Did she say why?"

"She got in trouble or something like that."

He pulls his phone out of a pocket and starts scanning through his text messages.

"We were going to go catch a movie, then she texts me and says she needs to see me right away. She wanted me to meet her at Laurel Dam. We hang out there a lot in summer at the bonfires. I drive all the way out there, and she's not there and no one's seen her. I text her and she says she got in trouble and she's not allowed to leave the house. Then she stopped answering my texts."

"When was that?"

He checks his phone again.

"Eight twenty-four p.m."

"Was it unusual for her to stop communicating with you?"

"Camio could be real secretive. It kind of bugged me at first. I even got jealous sometimes. Then I decided it was just her being weird about her family."

"Weird how?"

"She's embarrassed by them, but at the same time she sticks up for them like crazy. It's hard to explain. I've only been out there twice, but I'll never go back. I mean, I've been around families who say shitty things to each other when they're mad, but I've never been around people who are mean to each other all the time. When Cam's with them, she's just like them. I hardly recognize her."

"Do you have a picture of her on your phone?"

He goes through his photos until he finally comes to the one he wants to show me.

It's a summer picture. A lovely dark-haired girl with a slightly sunburned face. She has a sprinkle of freckles across her cheekbones like her brother Derk.

She's holding an orange Popsicle to her lips and smiling around it.

I can't help but think about the way we found her, and vomit rises in my throat. In my head I hear Rudy Mayfield's voice: *"Who does something like that?"*

"I took this last weekend," Zane says.

He beams down at the place where he holds her in his hand. He doesn't notice that I have to turn away from him.

"She's pretty," I say while composing myself.

"Yeah, she is."

"Would she run away?"

"Cam? Never. She wants to go to college more than anything in the world, so she has to finish school. She already got a 2350 on her SATs this spring but she's planning to retake them in the fall. She wants to get a perfect score. People like that don't run away."

"Why is she so motivated?"

"She doesn't want to end up like her sister or brother. Jessy got pregnant in high school, and Shane's in jail. She wants out of here."

"What about her two younger brothers?"

"She thinks if she can show them a different life maybe they'll want to get out, too."

"And what about you, Zane? Do you want to get out of here?"

"I got nothing against this town, but I'll probably move after college just 'cause there're no good jobs here. I want to make some money."

"Doing what?"

"I don't know. Something in business probably.

I'm going to Penn State and party my ass off while I can, then I'll take my degree somewhere and get serious."

"No offense, but Camio sounds very focused and driven. You . . . not so much."

My words don't bother him. On the contrary, he flashes me more of the Massey pearly whites.

"It's not like I'm dumb or something. I think I'm pretty typical; Cam's the one who's extraordinary."

I smile back at him for using that word.

"You're definitely not dumb," I tell him. "So what do you think she sees in you besides your obvious good looks?"

He shrugs away my compliment the way he shrugged away his mother's affection: accepting it but thinking he doesn't need it.

He gives my question serious thought. Not a lot of kids his age would do that.

"We didn't go to prom," he begins. "She'd never tell me why she didn't want to go, but I knew it had something to do with her family. I was really pissed at first. It's just junior prom but still, all our friends were going. Plus my mom went ballistic. She wanted to take a million pictures of me in a tux and post them all over Facebook. She's really into all that sappy mom bullshit."

We both glance back at the house to see his mother and father openly watching us from their separate windows.

Brie starts to raise her hand in a wave, then realizes she doesn't want us to see her and disappears behind a ruffled curtain.

"I figured if we weren't going to go Cam at least owed me an explanation, but she wouldn't give me one," he continues. "We got in this fight and I told her I was going to take someone else. She said she wouldn't be mad at me if I did. That made me feel even worse, so I told her we'd just skip the stupid junior prom. And she smiled and said that's why she loves me, because I'm on her side."

My phone beeps. It's a text from Nolan: +ID. Camio Jane Truly, 17.

When I look up from it, all of Zane's youthful nonchalance is gone, replaced by the adult tenseness that comes from a premonition of tragedy.

The break in our conversation gave him a chance to finally wonder what's going on.

"Why are you asking me all this stuff? I haven't heard from Cam since last night. I'm starting to worry about her. Do you know where she is?"

"Yes," I tell him.

The relief on his face breaks my heart.

chapter six

WHEN WE WERE GROWING UP, Neely, Champ, and I lived in a leaky, creaky, flaky, cobwebby, moldy, sweltering in summer, barn cold in winter, slightly left-leaning structure on Springfield Street that from a distance looked as if someone had plunked down a weather-beaten birdhouse in the middle of a row of beloved but rarely played-with dollhouses.

We spent our childhood there until we moved to Gil's mansion when we were fourteen, twelve, and nine. His wall-to-wall-carpeted four bedrooms, two bathrooms, formal dining room, living room, eat-in kitchen, and even a rec room enclosed behind a pink brick façade, two white columns, and sparkling clean windows we could actually see out of wasn't really a mansion, but compared to Chez Cissy it certainly was, and we always referred to it in an English accent as Rankin Manor.

We were even able to get Grandma in on the game. She's ninety-two now and in a nursing home, but to this day if our conversations turn to her daughter's brief, ill-fated marriage, she raises her voice to an imperial croak that would make Dame Maggie Smith proud and reminisces about Rankin Manor and Lord Gil.

On the surface Gil's house certainly seemed better suited to our freshly scrubbed, expertly made-up, flashily dressed mother than our previous one, but she never seemed as comfortable there as she did in the pseudo-shack. None of us were. This was through no fault of Lord Gil's. He did his best to accommodate us. He decorated one of the bedrooms in marshmallow Peep yellow and teal for Neely and me. We both found the room too alarming for sleep and took our bedding into the walk-in closet that was bigger than our old room anyway.

He did better connecting with Champ. Neely and I weren't offended. We chalked it up to them both being male and the fact that little kids are easier for adults to deal with than older kids. I was a teen and had the feeling Gil looked at me as a piece of adolescent pottery that had already been fired in the kiln. I was hard and set, whereas Champ was still squishy and malleable and his wide-eyed, frisky presence cried out for caresses and shaping.

Neely was only twelve, but she was an intense, eerily observant, uncompromising kid who wasn't to everyone's liking. She wasn't shy or standoffish. Timidity stems from fear, and aloofness comes from a feeling of superiority; neither applied to my sister.

I've never known anyone else like her, and lacking anyone to compare her to, I was never able to come up with an adequate summation of her personality in my mind until she began her work with service dogs and subsequent love affair with German shepherds in particular. Neely is just like her dogs. Her silence is louder than most people's shouting.

The house I live in now is on Springfield Street. A psychologist might have something to say about my deciding to live a few blocks down from my childhood home, one that wasn't necessarily bursting with good memories, and he'd probably have even more to say when he found out that it was torn down and replaced by a beer distributor long before I moved here.

I wanted to live in this house when I was a kid, and I can't think of a better reason for purchasing a home as an adult than this. The attractions were many, but what drew me to it the most was that it looked like a bunch of houses thrown together. The bottom half was constructed of pale gray rock and set into a slight rise in the yard that gave it the appearance of having been excavated right out of the ground. The top half was wood and painted an outrageous shade of sea foam green with windows and eaves trimmed in flamingo pink that screamed cheap Miami motel. An all-glass sunroom overflowing with potted plants took up one side; *If we ever live in this house*, I'd tell Neely, *we're going to call this the jungle room*. An exposed set of stairs clung to the other side of the house leading to a tiny third-floor room in the shape of a turret. I called it the grotto until I said the name out loud one day and Neely corrected me, explaining that a grotto was a little cave. She was pretty sure I meant garret.

I'm always happy to see my house. I did eventually

replace the original trim with a more respectable white, but I've changed nothing else.

After my visit to the Massey residence, I spent the rest of the day back at the station being ignored by Nolan while having to deal with the media he sent my way. He knows I have a knack for placating the public, plus this allows the state police to stand behind their usual wall of reticence. If I say something they don't want said, they can blame the incompetence of yokel law enforcement while secretly hoping what I let out might help the investigation. Nolan counts on this. He knows I'm a strategic leaker.

Two of my officers are on vacation: one in the Outer Banks with his family, the other in Canada somewhere hunting bears. I've rallied the other four and explained the best thing they can do right now is circulate and talk to everyone they can without seeming to care what answers they get. Small-town gossip is 95 percent unreliable but the 5 percent based on fact is pure gold, and usually the people who know something relevant don't realize they do and are willing to chatter away.

I pull into my garage but walk outside before going inside for the sake of my next-door neighbor, Bob, who's always standing in his driveway in a pair of sweatpants cut off below the knees, unlaced gym shoes, and a faded concert T-shirt, talking on his cell phone, and smoking a cigarette. The only variation in his appearance is a parka thrown over the outfit in winter.

He's been on disability for the entire fifteen years

I've lived here. I don't know how he was disabled or where he was working when it happened, but I do know he has a mousy wife named Candy who holds down two jobs and rarely talks except on a few occasions when she's had one too many Bud Lights during a family cookout. Each time this has happened she shared her two favorite fantasies with me over the fence: that Bob dies in his sleep and that he dies while he's awake.

Bob always greets me in the same manner, and I fear if I don't allow this ritual to occur in our driveways, he will try to get into my house.

"Catch any bad guys today?" he calls out.

"Not today," I reply, smiling.

I walk back into my garage.

My house is mostly books, shoes, a few sentimental knickknacks and souvenirs, lots of color, and lots of polished hardwood floors, the only element of my living space that I fastidiously keep clean. I have a well-organized but still seemingly messy kitchen where I spend most of my time if I'm not in my den, which doubles as my office with overflowing bookshelves, a TV, a big desk, and a comfy old couch where I end up sleeping more nights than in my own bed.

All the rooms are painted a different color. My kitchen is the deep blue of the sky on a perfect autumn day. My den is the reddish-brown of fallen pine needles carpeting a forest floor. My bedroom is lilac, my favorite flower that grows on a bush. My guest room is Tastykake Butterscotch Krimpet, my favorite food that comes off a factory assembly line. I've forgotten the colors of the living room and dining room; I never go in there. The jungle room is still a jungle and the grotto is barren except for a beanbag chair, a minifridge stocked with beer, and a reading lamp.

Once I was on my own as an adult and I had a dependable income, I discovered cooking could be rewarding and a lot of fun if a person could actually afford to buy the necessary ingredients. As a kid, I had no choice but to construct meals for my siblings and me from what was around and what we could afford, and for the most part this included boxes of dried macaroni, cans of cat-food-grade tuna, Wonder Bread that turned to a sticky paste the moment it hit our tongues, slimy bought-on-the-day-of-expiration bologna, ketchup and mustard packets Mom brought home from dates, Chef Boyardee's entire repertoire, and when life was good, hot dogs; sometimes I was even able to wrap them in Pillsbury crescent rolls.

Now I love to cook. It relaxes me.

I kick off my shoes, change into a pair of shorts and a tank top, and head for the kitchen, where I flick on the small TV sitting on my countertop and grab a beer out of the fridge while perusing its contents for tonight's supper.

Behind me I hear my own voice and turn around to see me on the local news telling a reporter that this is a terrible tragedy and our department will be working diligently with the state police to bring the perpetrator to justice.

I squint at the screen, then pull open a drawer looking for a pair of glasses.

I've never been to an eye doctor in my life, and I

don't intend to start now. I refuse to accept that I might need serious, all-day-long eye assistance. Instead, I've become an enthusiastic proponent of reading glasses. I have them scattered throughout my house, my car, at work. I was relieved to discover they're cheap and can be bought anywhere from drugstores and grocery stores to T.J.Maxx, where I found a boxed set of three pairs with gaudy, designer frames for $12. My favorite is a pair that looks like green apple and watermelon Jolly Ranchers have been melted together.

I find a pair with leopard-print frames and plunk them on my face.

The camera really does add ten pounds, because there's no way that extra ten pounds around my middle is my fault, I assure myself while I take another swig from my beer and rip off a chunk of the crusty bread I picked up on my way home from Zuchelli's Bakery.

My image dissolves into one of the Truly family standing outside their home. Jessy's holding her baby in one arm and has the other around a miserable-looking, raw-eyed Tug, who's taken his cap off and holds it respectfully in his too-big hands as if he's already mourning in a church. Shawna's holding Derk by the shoulders and has him placed directly in front of her like a shield. He twists and fidgets, fighting his captor, and I watch her fingers dig into him.

There's a man with them I assume to be Clark Truly. Bad teeth and a bad mullet are his only distinguishing features. He looks a good twenty years older than the forty-two he has under his belt. I attribute this to the booze, but some of it could also be due to the instant aging that occurs when a man's called home from the road to face the brutal murder of his daughter.

He's got a good sway going on and his words are slightly slurred.

"We got nothing to say except whoever done this better hope the cops get to them first."

The reporter wisely decides not to pursue the family interview any further, but before the spot returns to the safety of the news desk, I notice the words of his father jerk Tug out of his grieving stupor for a moment and a flash of hot rage dances across his guileless features before settling in at the tips of his ears, turning them bright red.

I look away from the TV and concentrate on cooking instead. I chop up a bunch of garlic cloves and tear up a few slices of prosciutto and toss them into a pot with simmering olive oil, then go outside to pick some basil out of my garden and put a sliced eggplant on the grill. Back inside, I add what's left of my last bottle of red wine to the pot and reduce by half, then a can of crushed tomatoes, a little water, and a jar of my homemade sauce I put up every summer after my tomato harvest.

The sauce is simmering and the water's boiling for pasta when I hear a knock at my front door. It's a cop knock. *Boom, boom, boom.*

Nolan's standing on my front porch, preliminary autopsy report in hand.

"It could've waited until Monday, or you could've faxed or emailed it to me like I asked a hundred times today," I say to him.

"I was busy," he says in lieu of a greeting. "You cooking something? Smells good."

"Come in."

He heads straight for the kitchen. I retrieve my eggplant from the grill. He's already helped himself to a beer and taken off his tie and his shoulder holster by the time I return.

"Make yourself at home."

"Nothing too interesting," he begins.

Nolan doesn't believe in small talk.

"The blows to the head killed her."

"So she wasn't . . ."

"No. She was already dead when she was lit on fire."

I chop up the eggplant and throw it into the sauce and dump a box of penne into the boiling water.

"So it was unnecessary. It was something personal for the killer."

"Or he was trying to get rid of the body like you said out at the site and changed his mind or someone else changed it for him.

"Two distinct wounds made from the same weapon as yet unidentified," he continues. "There were rust particulates in the wounds. Could be from the weapon or where she was killed or how she was transported. No sign of sexual assault. Initial blood work looks clean. No alcohol or drugs."

"Who are you bringing in besides the family?"

"The boyfriend."

"He has a name. Zane."

"Don't start getting mushy."

"You're not bringing him in as a suspect already?"

I feel a little protective of Zane. In my gut, I know he didn't do it.

"I told you I talked to him earlier," I remind Nolan.

He leans back in his chair and assesses me from behind his shades.

"He came across as a nice, normal kid who seemed genuinely in the dark and then genuinely devastated. I think he loved her."

"Loving their girlfriends is the number one reason boyfriends kill them," Nolan replies.

I put together two plates of pasta, top them with fresh basil and pieces of buffalo mozzarella that immediately begin to melt into the sauce, and signal at Nolan to join me outside to eat on the deck.

He grabs the bread and his beer and follows.

"I wish I had some wine to go with this," I say, sitting down.

"I don't," he says.

"How's the wife?" I ask to piss him off.

The correct response would've been, *Let me run to the State Store that's only a five-minute drive away and get you a bottle.*

"Visiting the grandkids in Colorado," he says with his mouth full.

"Isn't that what she was doing the last time I saw you about a year ago?"

"I think she was visiting the other grandkids in Ohio then."

"Does she ever visit you?"

"Not anymore. What did you think about her mother?"

I take time to savor some of my dinner knowing the pause won't derail Nolan. He has one topic of conversation: work.

"Everyone deals with grief differently," I finally respond.

"Don't give me that TV-shrink bullshit. We both know there's only one way a mother deals with losing her child."

"So maybe Shawna Truly has some issues. It doesn't mean she had anything to do with her daughter's death. How were Miranda and Jessy at the morgue?"

"The sister was inconsolable. Miranda Truly is a tough old bird, but she shed some tears, too. Frankly, the mother looked bored."

"Maybe she's just completely shut down. She's got one child in jail, one who got pregnant at eighteen, now one dead at seventeen."

"Kind of makes you wonder what's going through the heads of the two that are left."

"Hey, Chief?" I hear someone calling out.

Singer comes walking around the side of my house carrying my taupe pump.

"I knocked but nobody answered."

He stops when he sees Nolan and our dinner on the table.

"I'm sorry. I didn't know you had company."

"He's not company."

The two men eye each other up and down. Singer's

in a pair of cargo shorts, brown leather loafers, and a yellow-and-gray-checked oxford shirt over a yellow T-shirt with the sleeves rolled up to his elbows. Even though Nolan's still in his suit from work, his missing tie and jacket make him seem obscenely under-dressed.

"Good evening, Corporal Greely," Singer says with a little formal dip of his head.

"Singer," Nolan grunts.

I'm amazed he remembers his name.

"I brought you your shoe," Singer announces.

I take it from him. It looks brand-new.

"This is fantastic. Thank you."

I beam at him; he beams back.

"Would you like to stay for dinner?"

"I don't want to intrude."

"You wouldn't be intruding."

"You'd be intruding," Nolan says.

Singer laughs nervously.

"Okay. I'll see you at work."

Nolan barely waits for the boy to depart before asking, "What's wrong with him? Is he gay or does he have the hots for you?"

"Which would bother you more?" I wonder. "There's nothing wrong with him. Stop being such a backward redneck."

I know I've hit his sore spot. Nolan's family is only one step up from the Truly family, but it's an important step.

He stands up from the table and I think I may have crossed the line. He comes toward me, then stops short, leans down, and kisses me.

I throw my arms around him, and he pulls me roughly from my chair. I have a sudden pounding desire to have him crush me into bits too small to even be collected let alone be put back together.

There's nothing like witnessing the savagery of the human animal firsthand to make our bodies ache for a reminder from our species that we're also capable of exquisite acts of mercy.

I break free from his embrace only long enough to pull off his glasses. I always make him look me in the eyes when he's using me for redemption.

chapter seven

IT USED TO BE if I saw a little sneaker on the side of the road, I'd think a kid lost his sneaker. Now I think a mother lost her kid.

I never had any children. Their creation has to be either accidental or intentional, and I was too careful to risk the first and too carefree to attempt the second. Now that I've wrapped up my procreating years, I get an occasional twinge of regret, but on days like today, I comfort myself with the knowledge that by not having a child I won't ever have to face the kind of devastation that would come from losing one.

Shawna Truly still isn't exhibiting any signs of grief, but, unlike Nolan, I'm not convinced this means she could be involved in her daughter's death, although I will admit it's hard to feel sympathy for her. Camio's murder has hardened her mother's malaise into a wall of anger impossible to scale, while it's appeared to have the opposite effect on her sister.

Jessyca has been more open during this visit than she was the first time I met her. She's taken me upstairs to see Camio's room, an oasis of self-respect in the Truly home.

The space is neat and clean, not purposely sterile but a little empty. It reminds me of the room I shared with Neely in the Springfield Street house. We slept, changed our clothes, did our homework, and shared our secrets there, but we never bothered to personalize it. This wasn't a conscious decision; we just sensed we shouldn't settle in, and even though we lived there for almost ten years, we never lost this transient feeling. Like Neely's father passing through her conception, we passed through our childhoods hopefully on our way to a better place.

Camio's room could belong to any teenage girl or to anyone of any age. The only area that shows any real use is her desk, where books, pens, folders, and notebooks are scattered.

A few of the books are about psychology, checked out from the school library, vague, dated, pedantic treatises explaining the field to laymen. Jessy confirmed that Camio wanted to be a psychologist someday. I found it heartbreaking that this smart, ambitious girl had to read useless, dog-eared texts wrapped in crinkly cellophane jackets when there was an endless amount of up-to-date, snappily written information on the subject that was only a purchase click away on Amazon.

She had a laptop that Jessy told me she bought used two years ago with money she earned from an after-school job. Nolan confiscated it and has techs going through it. So far nothing has popped up. She had a few close girlfriends. Nolan has already talked to them and got nothing out of them. He wants me to interview them later today hoping I'll have better luck because I'm a girl, too.

Jessy's sitting down and picking at a loose thread in what looks like a homemade patchwork quilt folded at the end of Camio's bed. Her long butter yellow hair hides her face. She has about two inches of brown regrowth visible at the top of her head, and her fingernail polish is chipped, two of my mom's biggest pet peeves. She insisted you could tell the quality of a woman by how perfectly painted she kept her nails and how well she concealed her dark roots. Jessy has failed miserably at both.

The baby is on the floor busily gnawing on something that occasionally squeaks. I stoop down to get a closer look. It's a long flat strip of brown plush with a fox's head on one end and a tail on the other. She's chewing on a stuffing-free dog toy. They're very popular, according to Neely. A dog can destroy one without scattering the filling all over the house and yard, but the Trulys don't have a dog.

"What's your baby's name?" I ask as I scoop her into my arms and stand up again.

"Goldie."

"I like it," I say. "Is there any special meaning behind it?"

"It was partly Cami's idea. She said I should name her after something precious like diamonds. I thought of a Gold Card."

I smile at her. "I guess that's a step up from calling her plain old Visa."

She doesn't smile back. I realize attempts at humor

aren't going to go over well with this girl. I try sharing instead.

"My little brother's named after a puppy my mom had when she was little."

I don't tell her that this same puppy was tied up outside because no one would take the time to house-break or train him and he eventually bit a neighbor boy and was put to sleep.

"That's kind of cute," she says dully.

"So Camio was happy for you when you had your baby?" I ask.

"For the most part. She was kind of jealous, too."

"I thought Camio wanted to go to college and have a career. Why would she be jealous of you having a baby right out of high school?"

"'Cause she was crazy about babies. She wanted to have a whole bunch. And now I already got one."

"What about you? Did you want a baby?"

She breaks the thread on the blanket with a snap and moves on to another one.

"Goldie was an accident."

"You mean you were using birth control but still got pregnant?"

"I mean I got pregnant 'cause I wasn't using birth control."

"Then Goldie's not an accident. She's a conse-quence."

She gives me a blank look.

"Whatever," she says.

"I know this is a sensitive question, but did you ever think about not having the baby?"

"Are you kidding? Grandma would've skinned me alive."

"What if she didn't know?"

"She knows everything. You can't lie to her. Mom thinks she's part witch."

"They don't get along?"

"Everybody gets along with Grandma, 'cause we have to."

Goldie drops the dog toy to the floor and reaches for my necklace. She stuffs the beads into her mouth.

"So Camio has her own room?"

"We used to share. Derk and Tug got the one next door."

"Where do you and Goldie live now?"

Jessy stops picking at the quilt and falls back on the bed. She reaches her hands over her head and begins to move her arms up and down like she's making a snow angel.

"The basement," she replies, closing her eyes rapturously. "I sleep on a couch."

I wonder if acquiring a bigger bed can be a motive for murder? Who knows with this family?

Goldie gets tired of my necklace and realizes she's lost her fox strip. She starts whimpering, and Jessy lunges for the toy. She hands it to her baby before she can begin to wail.

"She loves this thing. Can't live without it," Jessy explains.

I feel it would be tacky to tell her it's a dog toy. To my surprise, she tells me.

"It's a dog toy," she says. "Derk picked it out for

her. Tug took him to get her a gift and he hated all of the baby stuff. He got her a rabbit, too. It's around here somewhere."

"I heard Camio didn't go to her junior prom even though Zane wanted to go." I try to get her back on the topic of her dead sister.

"She would've had to take so much abuse about it. Just easier not to go."

"What abuse?"

"My folks hate Zane."

"Why?"

"Don't know. They hate most people."

"Did you go to your prom?"

"I dropped out already."

"You didn't finish high school?"

"Cami was helping me get my GED."

The words are barely out of her mouth before she bursts into tears and plops back down on the bed.

Goldie turns her little curly blond head in her mother's direction at the sound and begins crying, too.

I shift the baby to a hip and sit next to Jessy. I put my arm around her shoulders and try to comfort her, but she's stiff and unreceptive. She holds her arms straight out in front of her, and I notice the chipped nail polish on the tips of her fingers is the same color as what was on Camio's toes.

"I was mean to her," she sobs.

"Sisters say mean things to each other sometimes," I assure her while clutching her tighter to me and bouncing her bawling infant. "I'm sure she knew you loved her."

A movement outside the window grabs my attention. We're on the second floor and my first assumption is a large bird must have flown by, but then a head pops up over the sill. I think it might be a bear cub or a chimp before remembering the first can't climb a house and the second doesn't live on this continent. A pair of aware dark eyes, like tiny reverse flashlights that absorb instead of illuminate, meet my own for a split second before they disappear along with the head. Derk.

I do my best to calm down Jessy and her baby. The two of them are still crying when I leave but not as hysterically. Jessy holds Goldie to her chest and rocks her from side to side while she clutches her fox.

I make my way back downstairs. A bunch of extended family has descended on the Truly house today. They mill around, smoking and trying to converse over the blare of the TV, many of them clutching beers even though it's only 10:00 a.m.

Tug is absent. He went to work. Jessy explained that he was too upset to stay in the house and her parents didn't care if he left.

Shawna, draped in sleeveless regal purple polyester, sits on the couch where I talked to her two days ago. She seems to have grown bigger, both figuratively and literally. Her bulk takes up half the couch but her presence takes up the entire room. She's become even more detached and this somehow makes her even more insurmountable, the immensity of her expected agony matched only by the terrible size of what she doesn't seem to feel.

She refused to speak to me when I arrived earlier

and she wasn't the only one. No one would talk to me about Camio. I felt like I couldn't be more unwelcome here if I was the murderer.

Nolan interviewed all the key family members yesterday except for Miranda, who considered it sacrilege to discuss her granddaughter's murder on the Lord's day. He also talked to Zane and his parents, Camio's coworkers at Dairy Queen, and a few friends, and so far hasn't been able to determine where Camio was between the hours of 5:00 p.m. and 8:42, when she sent Zane the text.

We know she got home from her job around five and handed over the car to Jessy, who left with Goldie to go to a friend's house. The only other working vehicle on the premises was their father's pickup, and neither of the girls were allowed to drive it. When Neely dropped off Tug after work around six, he says Camio was already gone again. Even though her mother never left the couch during this entire time period, she claims to have no idea when her daughter came and went or if she heard a car outside picking her up. Her father was on the road, and her grandmother was at her own home two miles away.

Camio's purse was found in her room, but her phone was not and is still missing. Her girlfriends exchanged a couple of messages with her while she was at work, but they all confirmed, along with Zane, that Camio wasn't a big texter, rarely posted on her Facebook page, and didn't participate in any other kind of social media. Unlike most kids her age, she could electronically disappear for days at a time except to stay in touch with Zane by phone. It wasn't strange not to hear from her.

"You find anything in her room?" Clark asks me when I join him and the rest of his extended family again.

I've encountered hard drinkers who have been jolted sober by tragedy; Clark Truly isn't going to be one of them. His eyes are bloodshot, his language slurred. His hands, holding a red Solo cup and a cigarette, tremble uncontrollably. This man makes his livelihood driving very large trucks; I don't feel good about this.

"I wasn't looking for anything," I tell him. "I was just trying to get a sense of who she was. You must have been proud of her."

"Why's that?"

"She was a hard worker. Got good grades. She was heading for college."

"Why would we be proud of that?"

The words are a challenge daring me to suggest that an education is a positive thing thereby implying that everyone in this room is a failure; this is certainly not what I would be implying, but these are people with skins as thin and brittle as an onion's outermost layer.

"Oh, I don't know. A lot of people would be proud of that. Apparently, you're not one of them. What makes you proud? Teen pregnancy? DUIs? Bar stabbings?"

Twenty pairs of close-set predatory eyes, eager for a confrontation they can blow out of proportion and add to their endless catalog of unforgivable slights, land their hot gazes on me. Weak chins, thin lips, puffy cheeks, blotchy complexions: they all suffer from the same special kind of malnutrition that doesn't come from not getting enough calories but from getting the wrong kind.

Before Clark or anyone else can respond, a familiar knife-edged voice rings out.

"You'll have to forgive Chief Carnahan for her disrespect," Miranda says. "She never had anyone to teach her any manners."

I turn and find the small, bony woman, already dressed in funereal black, standing behind me with the proprietary air of a crow perched on roadkill.

"Her mother was the biggest whore this town's ever seen and her own daddy wouldn't claim her. I knew his mother, Betty McMahon. Good, God-fearing Christian woman."

She looks directly at me.

"She used to refer to you as slut spit."

Everyone watches me, waiting to see how I'm going to react. Will I get angry, or flustered, or burst into tears and beat a hasty retreat? Clark leans so far forward, I'm afraid his bloated belly on top of his two spindly legs might pull him forward and topple him to the mushy floor where his impact would undoubtedly make a loud squish.

I know the ugly insult to my mother and me should bother me more but what bothers me most is the knowledge that this woman would never dare speak this way to Nolan or any other male officer.

"And just think," I reply conversationally, "right now Betty's son, Donny, is probably hanging out with your son Ross in that special place in heaven set aside for reckless idiot boys who drink too much and drive too fast without giving any consideration to the kind of corpses they're going to leave behind for their God-fearing mothers. Yet the slut spit lives on."

"You better get out of my son's house," Miranda warns me in a low voice.

"Go on and arrest that boyfriend," Clark shouts, lifting his cup in the air as if toasting the idea.

"We'll arrest whoever killed your daughter," I say.

Shawna's eyes flicker toward mine. For a moment, I see bright, intelligent pain there before they go dead again and return to the TV screen.

"I promise you," I add for her benefit, but it's impossible to know what she hears when I speak.

ONCE I'M OUTSIDE, I take a deep breath away from the eyes and wonder what life was like for Camio as a member of this family. Zane said she was just like them whenever she was here, but she was a different person away from them. Surely this other person slipped out occasionally while she was inside this house.

I understand her desire to leave; I had the same one, except mine was simply to get out of someone else's house—my mother's, Gil's, my grandmother's—and have my own life here in Buchanan, but if I had been part of a huge, difficult, extended family, maybe I would've felt the need to flee much farther away, too. When I finished high school, there was just Grandma, Neely, and Champ in my life, and I loved all of them too much to leave.

I also know what it's like to have a mother who doesn't care about you. This isn't always the same thing as having one who doesn't love you. Love is a highly subjective concept; everyone has different standards for what qualifies.

I'll never forget canvassing witnesses at Laurel Dam back when I was a rookie trooper after a jilted husband showed up at the Grover's Candy company picnic and put three bullets in his estranged wife's belly. He would've done the same to her boyfriend, but he was off taking a leak somewhere.

"He couldn't stand to see her with another man," one of her coworkers told me while peering over my shoulder at her friend's remains being carted off to the morgue. "That's how much he loved her."

Huh? I thought.

My mother's idea of love was equally confounding to me. She either gave us no attention or way too much, and ironically her slavish fawning left us feeling empty and cold while the days she ignored us were jam-packed with molten emotion.

She was always in love with some random man and was constantly saying how much she loved her babies and I think she thought she meant it, but for our mom, love had nothing to do with surrender or providing comfort of any sort; it didn't involve sacrifice or concern. It was an honor she bestowed on others and like a soldier receiving a metal trinket to make up for the loss of a limb, I felt like a hero—and also a fool—for taking it from her.

Shawna might love her children very much, but for some reason she's decided not to let them know.

I make my way through the maze of cars and pickups parked at senseless angles in the front yard that's already crowded with discarded vehicles, a few dented major household appliances, a rusted swing set, equally rusted bicycle frames with no tires, a heap of bicycle tires, and a stained, shaggy couch sprouting foam and the occasional quivering nose of some kind of rodent.

I marvel as I always do at this very specific kind of American poverty. The Trulys by most people's standards would be considered poor, yet they were able to buy everything here that has ended up as trash in their front yard. They have a $3,000 TV and the latest phones, and I can't imagine what they spend monthly on beer and cigarettes, but they couldn't afford a laptop for their daughter to help her with her schoolwork or a copy of *Psychology for Dummies*.

Derk is sitting cross-legged on the roof of my car. Upon my approach, he lunges forward and rolls down my windshield in a kind of sideways somersault that propels him off the hood and onto the ground, where he continues to roll several more times before springing to his feet and dashing to the nearest truck. He swings himself up into the bed and disappears.

I walk over and look down at him. He's lying flat and rigid on his back with his eyes squeezed shut.

"I can see you," I tell him. "Are you part squirrel?"

His eyes click open.

"I'm part woof."

"You're too fast and coordinated to be a wolf. You remind me more of a mongoose."

"What's that?"

"It kind of looks like a ferret. It lives in Africa and Asia and kills cobras. Big, poisonous snakes with huge fangs."

He sits up.

"Tug killed a copperhead once."

"Cobras are bigger and deadlier than copperheads."

"Tug knows a pack of woofs."

"They're dogs, but they look like wolves. Not woofs."

"How do you know?"

"I know them, too. They live with my sister."

"He's gonna take me to meet them someday."

"You want to meet them right now?"

He leaps out of the truck and gallops back to my car, darting in and out and over and under the obstacle course of junk and junk-in-waiting.

I follow knowing I probably shouldn't drive off with someone's eight-year-old child without obtaining parental permission and that it might not be exactly ethical to buy him a Zuchelli's cupcake and pump him for information about his dead sister, but I'm not feeling particularly by the book today.

I get these flashes of irrational passion where I'm willing to risk everything I've worked for in order to accomplish one thing I can't control. I know I didn't inherit this tendency from my mother, who accomplished all things by risking one thing.

I've always assumed this trait came from Denial Donny. He risked his life for the freedom of a few bourbon-soaked hours on an icy night behind the wheel of a fast car and lost, but in doing so, he may have done me a favor.

By the age of fifteen I had the best kind of parents: ones who were dead and couldn't hurt me anymore.

chapter eight

DURING MY TWENTY-SEVEN YEARS in law enforcement, I've been involved in the investigations of three homicides, not including the death of Camio Truly. Each was committed by a family member, spouse, or significant other. If you're going to be murdered around here, it's going to be by someone you know well, trust, and probably love. For reasons I've never been able to understand, this makes the locals feel safe.

There are a lot of Trulys and that makes for a large suspect pool. I'm not a big fan of the family, but so far no alarms have gone off in my head when I've talked with any of them. The same can be said for Camio's boyfriend, Zane, and his parents. I haven't talked to her three best friends yet, but Nolan has. They all have strong alibis and he says none of them pop.

People can be scummy, desperate, lazy, and sleazy. They can be liars and cheaters, manipulators and users, thieves and bullies. They can use verbal and even physical abuse to dominate others, but murder is a special act that requires a big push. In my opinion, motive is the most important piece of the puzzle. Most people don't run around killing other people; they have to have a good reason or, more accurately, they have to think they have a good reason. At the moment, I have no idea why anyone would want Camio Truly dead, but someone has the answer to this question.

I glance down at Derk standing next to me in Zuchelli's Bakery staring wide-eyed at the kaleidoscopic trays of cupcakes and individual-size pies topped with meringues or whipped cream or berries bursting out of the sugar-dusted crust.

He's filthy. I shouldn't let him eat anything without washing his hands first, except I'm sure he always eats without washing his hands first.

The milk blue tissue-paper-thin tank top he's wearing is baggy on him and ripped under one armhole. The decal on the front has faded into a white patch of cracks. His shorts are cutoff jeans. The legs are different lengths and ragged; I'm sure he made them himself. I didn't realize until he got out of the car that he isn't wearing shoes. I'm hoping the other customers won't notice or won't care, since he's with me. "Official police business," I'll tell them if asked.

Practically nothing has changed about this place since I was a kid. The floor is the same red linoleum. The tables and chairs are still elaborately scrolled whitewashed iron with fake red marble tops and thick plastic cushions that sigh when someone takes a seat. The walls are covered with poster-size lurid photos of moist, glistening cakes, pies, doughnuts, and fruit tarts. Pastry porn, Neely calls it.

The owners, Sal and Mary Zuchelli, are devoutly patriotic to their adopted country when it comes to their sweet side; a croissant, biscotti, Napoleon, or scone will never be found here, but they put no restrictions on their bread. They bake all kinds and they sell it by the loaf or served one warm slice at a time with a small cup of homemade whipped butter from Sawyer's Dairy.

Lena is working this morning, one of a seemingly endless supply of pretty, young, female, doe-eyed extended family members who take turns working here. Without asking she slices me a thick slice off a round garlic Tuscan loaf and slides it to me on a plate with a side of butter and a coffee to go. I also order two dozen jelly-filled and glazed doughnuts. I have a meeting with Nolan and his team later.

Derk didn't say a single word to me on the drive over here. I hadn't seriously been planning on bribing him with food, but I'm afraid I have no choice.

"What do you want?" I ask him.

"Six cupcakes and a pie."

"Six cupcakes?"

"And a pie."

I dig in my handbag for a pair of reading glasses, pushing aside my diaphragm I no longer need and my gun in its purse holster I probably won't ever need. I rarely wear it anymore.

I peer at the prices written on the board over the counter.

"Fine," I say to Derk. "Tell the girl which ones you want and have her put them in a bag. You can eat them on the way to see the dogs."

"Woofs."

"Wolves."

"Woofs."

Before I can pay, Derk snatches the bag out of Lena's hand and bolts for the door.

"Go to my car," I call after him.

"Is that your illegitimate kid, Chief?"

Chet Shank, the eldest grandson of the original Chester Shank, Esq., who used to be one of our most prominent attorneys, has come up behind me. He's fixated on his iPad and isn't looking at me. I know he thinks he's made a hilarious joke. His humor is the obvious, observational, personal-attack kind favored by second graders and fraternity brothers. I can easily picture him pointing and saying, "Look at that guy's nose! He has a big nose!" before bursting into uproarious laughter.

"No, Chet. He's not mine."

He smiles while still not looking at me. He likes to give the impression that he's never encountered anyone important enough to capture his full attention.

I usually deal with him by walking away.

"You sure? I can't believe you never had any kids, an attractive woman like you."

"What does that have to do with childbearing? In case you haven't noticed, there's a lot of unattractive people out there having kids right and left."

He laughs at this and finally tears his gaze away from his notebook screen.

I don't add, "Like you, for instance."

Poor Chet: overweight, insecure, already losing his

hair in his thirties, a second-rate undergrad and a third-rate law degrees; the kind of guy who checks out his reflection in the backs of spoons and gives animated interviews in his car to invisible reporters about the cases he'll never have.

To make matters worse, his younger brother turned out to be whip-smart, good-looking, and a natural-born litigator. He went to Cornell Law School, then came back to Buchanan to make his folks happy and brought with him a Jewish wife, who's also a lawyer and who kept her maiden name and added it to the Shank shingle.

"I just had a consultation with a Frederick Dombosky," Chet informs me while giving Lena some sort of elaborate hand signals. "He wants to hire me to sue you for defamation of character."

"Lucky?"

"He says you and your sister lied in court. What was it? Thirty-five years ago?"

He shakes his head in disbelief.

"I wasn't even born yet. Anyway, he says he's innocent."

"What a shocker."

"I know. They all say they're innocent. But to hire a lawyer *after* you've served your sentence? You've got to admit that's rare. He's really serious about this."

"Why would we have lied?"

"He seems to think you did it so the cops would stop looking for the real killer. He thinks you were protecting someone."

"Who?"

"Gil Rankin."

His answer startles me into swallowing a gulp of hot coffee too quickly and I start coughing.

"He said you kids really liked Gil," Chet goes on, not noticing my discomfort or surprise.

"We didn't care about Gil one way or the other," I say once I can speak again. "We certainly wouldn't have lied to protect him if we thought he killed our mother. Besides, he had an airtight alibi."

"He also fled the country."

"He didn't flee the country. He went to Europe to get away from all the publicity. He cooperated with the police before he left. He came back for the trial. That's not fleeing."

And if he was fleeing anything it was his dead wife's three kids. I don't tell Chet this. We went to live with our grandmother.

"Lucky says the alibi was flimsy," Chet explains with a shrug, his attention wandering back to his iPad. "He says Gil could've left and come back. His employees would've lied for him."

"What was Gil's motive?"

"His wife was having an affair."

"Gil didn't know about the affair. Lucky was the one with the motive. Mom was dumping him once again and he was crazy about her. Tons of witnesses heard them fighting the day before and his threatening her. He had a history of violence with women. He had no alibi. His fingerprints were all over the bathroom."

"Whoa." He holds up one hand and gives me his insufferable, placating smile again. "Are you trying to convince me or yourself?"

"I don't need convincing. I saw him do it."

"Don't get mad at me. He was convicted. He paid his debt to society. Nobody cares anymore except him. He's saying you lied, that's all. He says you didn't see him do it because he didn't do it."

"Did you say he hired you?"

"He's planning to as soon as he can come up with my retainer."

"If you take him on, haven't you violated some kind of attorney-client privilege by telling me all this?"

"I'm not sure. Let me Google it."

Now I do walk away.

Zuchelli's is located on our main thoroughfare named Glencora Street after the wife of our town's founder, Harold Buchanan—not James, our country's fifteenth president and the only Pennsylvanian to hold the office—who owned practically half of Laurel County at the turn of the last century, made a fortune from mining, sold his company to the mammoth J&P Coal, and ran off into the sunset with his wife's younger sister, the much prettier Annabelle, who also has a street named after her but in a seedier neighborhood.

Even though a major coal company was based here and at one time employed most of our male population, Buchanan survived the collapse of the mining industry. In large part this was due to the fact that we're also home to a small college, a large medical center, Grover's Candy, and AAA baseball franchise, the Buchanan Flames, with their own midsize stadium and adjoining fairgrounds.

The inhabitants of the surrounding towns consider

our burg to be a bustling city. It's true that we have our own bit of urban sprawl, including chain stores and chain restaurants, six car dealerships, and a hillside checkered with Monopoly-marker low-income housing, but I do most of my living in the heart of town not only because the police station is here but also because I like the feel of continuity it gives me. Our downtown has managed to remain relatively unscathed by progress. A few businesses have fallen victim to the passage of time. The travel agency with its glossy posters of exotic destinations and a life-size cardboard cutout of a hula dancer in its front window is now an insurance office. The newsstand where I used to buy Mom her fashion magazines and hide in a corner with racy paperbacks became a video rental store and is now a coffee shop with Wi-Fi.

The Woolworth's where Neely and I used to go after school to buy our forty-fives, watch hamsters run mindlessly on their wheels in the pet section, gaze longingly at the cheap paste jewelry that for some reason was locked up in a glass case, and share an order of greasy fries at the lunch counter is now an Antiques and Collectibles Shoppe, which is a more upscale way of saying permanent indoor flea market.

Rankin's, the swanky department store Gil owned, is now an American Eagle. The tattoo place became a cigar shop and is now a tattoo place again.

The law office of Chester Shank, Esq., is now the law office of Shank, Shank, and Goldfarb. My department car, a white Ford, is parked in front of it and as I step out of Zuchelli's, I notice Singer and Blonski's cruiser is parked behind it.

Derk is standing on the roof of my car, brown paper bag in one hand, the other shoving a cupcake in his mouth. Singer is trying to reason with him while Blonski is trying to grab him, but Derk deftly dodges his swipes at his feet like he's a small cowboy being showered by bullets from a Wild West villain telling him to "Dance."

"What's going on?"

Singer turns, red-faced from frustration. Upon seeing me his blush deepens. I know he's thinking about Nolan and me having dinner two nights ago.

"This child was sitting on the roof of your car, Chief," he starts to explain. "When we told him to get down, he said he's a friend of yours and if we don't piss off he's going to have us fired."

I step up to the car.

"So we're friends, Derk? I'm glad to hear it. But that doesn't give you an excuse to be disrespectful. If you don't get down I'm going to arrest you."

"You can't arrest kids," he tries to shout, his words muffled by the cake and icing in his mouth.

"Officers," I say.

Blonski needs no other encouragement. He heaves himself onto the trunk of my car and lunges at Derk, barely missing him. The boy takes a flying leap onto the sidewalk, where Singer nabs him. If he were willing to drop the goodies, he might be able to wriggle free and make a run for it, but his concern over them throws off his balance and his judgment.

Blonski pulls his handcuffs off his belt and dangles them in front of Derk.

"You want us to cuff him?"

"That won't be necessary. Put him in my car. He's Derk Truly. Camio's little brother," I tell the two of them before they can ask.

I don't provide any other information. They don't seem to care. They do as they're told, shut Derk inside my car, then turn back to me practically bursting with something important to tell me.

"We just took an interesting missing-persons report," Singer eagerly informs me.

"Do you remember that sick rat bastard we arrested last year for domestic abuse? Broke his wife's jaw and almost put her eye out?" Blonski begins. "And when we looked through the house we found all that teen schoolgirl porn?"

"Britney Spears the early years kind of stuff with even less clothes," Singer further elaborates.

"Lonnie Harris," I answer them.

"Right," Blonski confirms, with a nod. "His wife came into the station this morning and said he's been missing since Friday night."

"Why'd she wait until Monday to report it?"

"He's been known to go on weekend benders, but she says he always stays in touch by phone. No matter how drunk he gets, hardly an hour goes by that he doesn't text her something nasty, but she hasn't heard from him this whole time."

"She said she wanted to report it because she knew she'd be the number one suspect if he turned up dead," Singer adds. "This way it would show she has nothing to hide. Pretty smart."

"She's not that smart," Blonski throws back at him. "She stayed married to the guy."

He turns to me.

"What do you think, Chief? You think he could be the killer and he's split town? We know he's violent and we know he likes teen girls."

"We also know Camio wasn't sexually assaulted," I remind him.

His face falls. Singer looks dejected, too.

"But you never know. We have to follow all leads. You should take this seriously."

They brighten up a bit.

"Check out his residence. His phone records. See what he was up to these last few months. Talk to everyone who knows him. If you come up with any tie to Camio or any member of the Truly family, no matter how tenuous, let me know right away."

Blonski heads for their cruiser. I touch Singer lightly on his arm before he can follow.

"Can you get those muddy footprints off the roof of my car?" I ask him.

He nods.

"Sure thing, Chief."

Singer originally put Derk in the back but he's already climbed into the front, leaving smears and fingerprints of yellow, blue, and brown frosting all over my seats.

"Why do they call you Chief?" he asks me once I'm settled behind the steering wheel.

"Because I'm the chief of police."

"No, you're not," he snorts.

I toss a bunch of napkins at him. He ignores them.

I'm suddenly hit by a memory of Champ: he's the same age as Derk, sitting next to Gil in the front seat of his big Buick looking lost and small but smiling because Gil has just handed him a big chocolate cupcake out of a red Zuchelli's box that also held a coconut cream pie he had picked up for dessert, Mom's favorite.

I remember the pang of jealousy I felt when Gil gave Champ the treat and wondering why I cared. I didn't want a cupcake. I was too old for that. And I didn't want Gil's attention. Like most of Mom's boyfriends, he creeped me out. I didn't care about letting my little brother have the front seat. It was summer, and Neely and I had just spent the afternoon at the public pool and were happy to sit together in the back, smelling of watermelon Lip Smacker and chlorine, where we could whisper about the older girls' bikinis and the older boys' developing muscles, and giggle over Gil's outdated pompadour.

Later, when I came upon Champ and Gil watching TV together while sharing a plate of Oreos, something Champ usually did with his sisters, I wondered if maybe I wasn't jealous of what Champ was receiving from Gil but what Gil was giving Champ.

I knew it was a good thing for him to finally have a dad even if the dad in question wasn't his real one. The important thing was he would have a man in his life to teach him stuff, to care about him, to play with him, and set an example. Next Father's Day, while I was putting flowers and a Hot Wheels car on Denial Donny's grave and Neely was reading her *Encyclopedia of Dogs* for the thousandth time while musing about the limitless glamorous identities Passing Through might have—astronaut, captain of industry, European

royalty, rock star, Olympic athlete, dog owner—
Champ would no longer have to content himself with
a drawer full of empty envelopes.

I was happy for him, but Neely and I had always
been the center of Champ's universe, and maybe I
was a little worried that he didn't have enough love in
him to share with all of us. Whenever I'd spot a cupcake paper in the kitchen trash can, I'd wish Gil
would dump Mom like all the others. Sometimes I'd
wish he'd disappear altogether.

After Mom died, Champ wouldn't go near cupcakes. Grandma used to bake dozens for him because
she knew how much he liked them, and he'd pale at
the sight of them. Grandma took it in stride as she did
everything and chalked it up to one more strange
manifestation of the grief we were all experiencing:
boy misses murdered mother who was too pretty to
die; can no longer eat cake.

By then I knew the reason must be something
stomach-turning, but I never made him talk to me
about his sudden cupcake revulsion or anything else
about Gil. At the time, Neely and I thought we were
doing him a favor. If we didn't make him talk about
it, he wouldn't think about it, and maybe it would go
away. We were kids, too. We didn't know any better.
We didn't know living nightmares don't ever go away
because you can't wake from them. The most you can
hope for is to dilute them by spreading them around.

"When's the last time you saw Camio?" I ask Derk
after ten minutes of driving in silence during which
time he's eaten two more cupcakes.

I'm amazed when he replies, "Couple days ago."

"Which day?"

"Don't know."

"What was she doing?"

"Going for a walk."

"Where did she go?"

"Don't know."

"Did she go for lots of walks?"

"Don't know."

He reaches inside the bag and pulls out a mini blueberry pie.

"Let's save that one for when we're out of the car," I tell him.

He smashes it into his face.

I comfort myself with the knowledge that Singer probably knows how to get blueberry stains out of car upholstery. I don't know how or why Singer is so accomplished at cleaning. He seems both proud and embarrassed whenever I ask for his assistance in this area and I get the feeling the reason behind his expertise is highly personal. This is why I haven't pried but I will eventually. He hasn't worked for me long enough yet.

"You never followed her? Come on, Squirrel Boy. I know you did. I bet you followed her, hiding in the woods the whole time and she never saw you."

He eyes me through a mask of blue-black goo.

"She goes to the main road and her boyfriend picks her up. She goes to Grandma's house. She goes to Uncle Eddie's."

Eddie Truly is the former owner of Maybe and the eldest of Miranda's children. He'd be in his late sixties now. He was drafted right out of high school, did one tour in Vietnam, and headed straight for a bottle, a needle, and a dangerous crowd of bikers when he came home. To my knowledge he's never stopped using the booze or the drugs. He did stop hanging out with his old gang when a couple of members broke into his house one night and stabbed him twenty-two times. Drug deal gone bad was the final verdict the police gave at the time. No arrests were made. Eddie wouldn't talk. His survival into a sixth decade is nothing short of a miracle. I can't imagine smart, pretty, Popsicle-loving Camio with the sparkly heart anklet and outdated psychology books having anything to do with him.

"Why does she go to your uncle's house?"

"Don't know."

"Does your uncle have kids, a wife?"

"He lives by his self."

"Himself."

"His self."

"What does she do there?"

"Goes inside, then goes back out. Sometimes she's crying."

"You're sure about that?"

"I told Tug."

"What did he do?"

He falls silent. I know I'm pushing this. He's probably said more words to me today than he's said to his entire family all year.

"He asked her," he answers me while staring bewildered at his already empty hands covered in blueberry filling and golden flakes of crust. "She got real mad and told him it was none of his business. Then she started crying again and said people are bad and he was right to spend all his time with the woof dogs."

I watch him watching his hands, trying to decide what to do with them.

"There are napkins sitting right beside you," I tell him.

He darts a glance at the pile, then wipes his hands down the front of his shirt, his shorts, and ends at his kneecaps before bringing them back to his mouth and licking between his fingers.

We finish the rest of the drive in silence. He pushes his face up against the window and watches the town flash by, sits back and stares at his feet once we're out in the country again, but perks up when we turn onto Neely's road.

The flickering bits of sunlight filtering through the leafy netting of the treetops towering over us gives the shadowy green air a hazy, rippling, underwater effect. I ask him if he likes to swim. He says nothing.

I don't see Tug and Maybe. The four other dogs and Neely are standing with a man and a boy.

I park and get out of my car. Upon seeing me, Neely throws her arms wide and runs toward me, beaming, something I haven't seen her do since before our mother died and our acceptance of the reason why.

She gestures behind her at the dark-haired duo, carbon copies of each other from their matching outfits of cargo shorts, polo shirts, and sandals to their uncertain smiles and right hands raised stiffly in awkward waves.

Of course my sister provides the explanation in dog terms.

"Champ found his way back home," she calls out to me.

chapter nine

I HAVE PLENTY of friends with children, grown children at this point. Some—like Nolan—even have grandbabies. And I've been told by them time and again how I can never truly understand what love is since I don't have kids.

Although I should qualify this statement by mentioning that it's always women who tell me this. Men don't seem to share the same belief; usually when I run across one of them crying in his beer over the greatest love of his life, it's a woman who's not his wife, a car, a sports team, or sometimes even a power tool.

From what I've observed over the years, romantic love is largely situational. You fall in love because you're sixteen, or because he has nice abs, or because he offers to put you on his health insurance. It's based on moods, superficial whims, and the needy psychological mess that accounts for human personalities combined with basic lust. Once the romantic love dies out, if a couple is lucky, an enduring companionable partnership continues on. If not, it's splitsville.

A mother's love for her child is something altogether different. It's a force of nature: primal, unrelenting, depthless, inflexible. It can't be bought or taught, replaced or reasoned with. Mothers will put their own happiness and welfare behind that of their children every time.

Well, maybe not all mothers.

Champ was not and is not my child, but I can't imagine loving anyone more than I did him and still do. When we were growing up together, it was an unforced, senseless kind of love as easy and gratifying as the taste of a drippy soft-serve cone on a summer's day or the unconscious warmth I felt when Grandma tucked an extra blanket over me on a winter's night.

Watching Champ sitting in the plank of sunlight on the staircase landing intently playing with his Matchbox City or hearing the yank of his See 'n Say cord come from another room followed by a barnyard animal sound and his delighted laughter, I'd feel an electric hormonal jolt I was too young to understand. It was a sweet sting, full of pleasure and ache, like the release of finally, secretly scratching a chicken pox scab even though everyone has promised the act will leave a scar.

I've never been upset at him for cutting me out of his life. It would've been too difficult and exhausting to maneuver around each other. We would have always been walking a tightrope between too much to say and too much not to say.

He knew Neely and I knew, and even though he also knew we loved him and would do anything for him, every time he looked at us, he saw something in our eyes we couldn't hide. Not pity. Not anger. Not even shame over not being able to save him from Gil. We could control these emotions. What we couldn't control was the pain. Our pain. The pain someone feels for someone she loves who she can't help, can't heal, can't restore.

I'm not prepared for how bad it hurts to see him again.

"Dove," he says, and all the years fall away as completely and perilously as an avalanche.

I'm left teetering on a precipice of unwelcome memories and the equally unwelcome discovery that time does not heal all wounds. It may have taken the edge and shine off but the blade has remained permanently plunged in the flesh of my soul, a dull, rusty, eternal reminder.

I try to say his name but nothing comes out.

"It's Champ," Neely explains, calmly and kindly, like I'm awash in senility.

Champ gives me the goofy, bug-eyed, grandma-without-her-dentures smile he used to make whenever he thought I was taking too long to understand something that was glaringly obvious to him and Neely.

I bust out laughing and give him a hug.

"And this is your nephew, Mason," he tells me once we break our embrace.

I glance down at the slight little boy dressed exactly like his dad except he's wearing traffic-cone orange socks with his sandals. The tips of his ears and his nose are sunburned and peeling, both knees have Batman Band-Aids on them, and his hair is shaved into a crew cut similar to Derk's except he has scabbed-over nicks and cuts on his scalp like he's been at the mercy of a drunk army barber.

He has a purple Trapper Keeper clutched possessively to his chest; he shifts it to his left side while extending his right hand to me and says, "I'm named after the jar."

"He's not named after the jar." Champ sighs. "He recently discovered mason jars and now he tells everyone this is where we got his name from."

Mason gives my hand a quick shake.

"Dad's right," he admits. "My mom wanted to name me Jason, but Dad said every guy named Jason he ever met was a jerk. Dad wanted to name me Milo after Milo in *The Phantom Tollbooth*. That was his favorite book when he was a kid and now it's mine. But Mom said Milo was a nerd name, and Dad said, yeah, all the Jasons would probably beat me up, so they mushed the two names together and got Mason.

"I wish I could be named Thor," he finishes.

"Who doesn't?" Neely concurs.

"Mason and I decided it was time to take a trip and see the country," Champ explains while placing his hands on the boy's shoulders, "and he wanted to see where I grew up and meet his aunt Dove and aunt Neely."

"He got fired," Mason says, jerking a thumb in his father's direction.

Champ gives the shoulders a squeeze.

"I didn't get fired. I quit."

"That's not what Stevie said."

"Stevie doesn't know what she's talking about."

"Who's Stevie?" I ask.

"His last girlfriend," Mason replies. "She dumped him."

"We broke up."

"She was pretty nice," Mason goes on with his description. "She never ordered mushrooms on her half of the pizza even though she liked them, 'cause she knew I was afraid they'd touch my half."

"He doesn't like mushrooms," Champ explains.

"They're fungus," Mason supplies, wide-eyed. "Like the stuff the scrubbing bubbles kill in the bathtub."

"It's not the same thing," Champ says in a tone that lets us know this isn't the first time they've had this conversation.

"Fungus is fungus," Mason asserts.

"Hey!" he calls out, jabbing a finger around my side. "There's someone in your car."

I forgot all about Derk.

Kris, Kross, and Owen are standing next to the passenger-side door licking at ten little blueberry stained fingers wiggling at them through the cracked window.

"It's okay. You can come out," I tell him. "They won't hurt you."

"I ain't scared of 'em," he yells back at me.

"Then why are you staying in the car?"

He doesn't have an answer for me. He throws open the door and pushes his way into the middle of the three large dogs, and they start licking him all over.

He holds his hands up over his face and I think I

hear a giggle, but I have a hard time imagining this particular child is capable of feeling glee.

A whistle rings out and the dogs look at Neely, who tells them, "Stop." Owen and Kris do what they're told, but Kross—her problem child—continues doing what he wants.

She walks over to Kross with Smoke at her heels, slips off the leash she wears draped around her neck the way a doctor wears a stethoscope, clips it onto his collar, and gives it a sharp yank.

"Stop," she says again.

Kross sits back on his haunches and looks pathetic.

"I'm Neely Carnahan. This is my place, and these are my dogs," she tells Derk. "Who are you?"

Derk crosses his arms over his chest.

"Derk Truly."

She looks down at him from beneath the brim of her ball cap, sizing him up like she might a potential new member of one of her obedience classes.

"Are you Tug's brother?"

He nods.

"Tug's on a walk with Maybe. He should be back soon."

She turns her back on Derk and returns to us. The dogs follow her. Derk watches them go, then decides he should do the same.

He stops a short distance from Mason. The two of them eye each other suspiciously. They look to be about the same age. Mason might be a little older.

"Your socks are stupid," Derk blurts out.

We three adults turn our heads in unison toward

Mason to see how well he'll return Derk's serve. He seems smart and capable but also a little awkward. He could choose not to participate in a volley of insults and take refuge behind his dad or start to cry.

"You're stupid," Mason fires back. "You're covered in frosting and blueberry pie. Don't you know how to eat?"

Derk isn't prepared for Mason's smash. He sends back a wild shot that veers out of bounds.

"The chief's a cocksucker!" he shouts, and takes off running.

Neely motions for the dogs to follow him, then she and Champ look at me with varying amounts of curiosity and condemnation in their eyes. I'm flooded with déjà vu. When we were kids they were always looking at me this way, always wondering what I was up to and assuming I wasn't going to tell them the whole story. I have no idea how many times I said to them, "It's better if you don't know."

"He doesn't know what the word means," I tell them.

"And that makes it okay for him to use it?" Champ asks.

"He wanted to meet the dogs," I explain to Neely. "I guess Tug talks about them all the time. But I was only planning on dropping by for a minute. I have a meeting with Nolan and his team."

"The dogs will stay with him until he realizes he's lost, and then they'll lead him back here. I can take him home when I take Tug," she volunteers.

"Are you sure?"

"In return, you can make dinner for all of us to-night at your place." To Champ she says, "Dove's a great cook."

"She always was," he says. "Just no Chef Boyardee, please."

"Don't worry."

We drop into a clumsy silence, the unexpectedness and enormity of our reunion sinking in for all of us. I never said it out loud to Neely or Grandma, and I rarely said it to myself, but I never expected to see my brother again.

"Okay. Great. I don't know what else to say. I'm overwhelmed."

Champ gives me another hug. I was too shocked by the first one to notice details, but this time I'm only too aware of how thin and frail his body feels be-neath his shirt.

His color isn't good. His eyes are sunk deep into bruised sockets. I guiltily glance at the insides of his arms as he pulls them away looking for track marks. He didn't do drugs in high school, but his demons could have driven him to anything during the years since then.

"It's okay. I'm sorry I stayed away so long. I just couldn't—"

"Enough," Neely cuts him off. "We'll have plenty of time to talk about serious stuff later if we want to."

"I don't want to," Mason pipes up.

"Me neither," Neely agrees.

She hasn't stopped grinning the entire time I've been here. I'm starting to be concerned. Like any ac-tivity a person has avoided for great lengths of time, I wonder if too much of it all at once can harm her. I think of the disclaimers at the beginning of workout videos: anyone considering taking part in vigorous physical exercise should consult a doctor first.

Has anyone ever stroked out from smiling?

"I'll call you later," I tell my sister.

I start heading to my car and realize Mason is trotting along beside me, holding his binder against his chest again.

"What kind of chief are you?" he asks.

"A police chief."

"That's cool, but it would be way cooler if you were an Indian chief like Crazy Horse."

"I agree, but I couldn't pass the physical."

"Are you really a good cook?"

"Yes."

"No fungus please."

We reach my car and I'm suddenly consumed by a need to get away from here. It takes everything I have not to push Mason to the ground, throw open my door, and tear out of here with squealing tires spitting out gravel behind me. I don't want to revisit my past. I don't want to be crippled with rage and regret again. I don't want to hate. Neither does Neely. She wasn't smiling; her face was contorted with pain. She's wearing a mask.

"Anything else you don't like?" I ask Champ's little boy.

The binder flips open with a small ripping noise and I'm transported back in time to Champ's first day of high school and his excitement over his first Trapper Keeper. We had been living with Grandma for four years by then. I was a commuting sophomore at a nearby college and Neely was starting her senior year of high school, something she did to fill the hours when she wasn't volunteering at the local animal shelter or working at the Greenview Kennels. I had taken Champ out a few days earlier to get school supplies, at which time he informed me that everyone had one of the cool, relatively new binders filled with folders and if he didn't have one, he would be a social outcast. The original design with a snap had been updated to Velcro. By the time he graduated, it would be changed back to a snap again after numerous teachers complained to the manufacturer about the noise. That morning he sat at Grandma's kitchen table ripping it open and closing it again until I shouted at him to stop and tried to pull it out of his hands. We got into a spirited tug-of-war. I let him win.

The Velcro means Mason's Trapper is vintage, but it's not one of Champ's. He covered his with doodles and stickers. This one is bare except for the carefully lettered name across the top: Mason James Carnahan.

Mason glances inside and reads from a list, "Onions, dippy eggs, mayonnaise, olives with the red slimy things in the middle, coffee, fish unless it's in a stick, Go-Gurt, pork chops, coconut, and fake cereal."

"Fake cereal?"

"They say it's the same as the real cereal and you buy it 'cause it's cheaper and it's not the same."

He rustles through some papers in one of the folders and pulls out a small, colorful square of paper. I can't tell what it is from a distance. I don't have on my glasses.

"Got it," I say. "Anything else?"

He looks at the ground while considering my question. The back of his exposed neck glows pink and is dusty with tattered skin from a sunburn peel. Champ always had the same burn. His came from spending hours on end sitting in our tiny patch of a backyard hunched over his toy cars and trucks, or his plastic soldiers, or his farm animal set.

I'm suddenly awash in memories of my brother at that age. They end with a thud outside a closed bedroom door where I hear Gil's husky promise and Champ's whimper, then I find myself standing in my mother's bathroom looking at her lifeless hand at the end of a slim bare arm hanging limply from the tub and her big diamond solitaire engagement ring sparkling prettily in the candlelight. I almost took it. I had a moment born of reading too many novels as a kid that romanticized running away where I thought I could sell it and Neely, Champ, and I could take the money and head west. Runaways always headed west. But I was too responsible even back then. We were going to have a roof over our heads, dinner on the table every night, and go to school like normal people did. It was very important to me that we seemed normal.

Eventually Champ would run away, but he waited until after he was eighteen so it wouldn't seem like running away; it would simply be leaving.

Why has he come back? Why do runaways return? To settle a score? To get answers? To borrow money? Not to visit two sisters he hasn't needed for more than two decades and definitely not to try and start over.

Mason raises his head and our eyes meet. His are filled with too much worry for someone his age; I'm afraid mine are filled with too much recklessness for someone my age.

He hands me a coupon for Cinnamon Toast Crunch cereal.

"No cupcakes," he says gravely. "They make my dad cry."

chapter ten

THERE'S NOTHING like standing in the middle of a large conference room bathed in unforgiving fluorescent lighting with a bunch of men, decades younger than you, staring at your backside while you study photos of a burned, bludgeoned dead girl tacked onto a dry-erase board to make you forget about your own problems.

In the span of forty-eight hours Nolan has already covered a lot of ground. I'm not surprised. He's a tenacious investigator. Once a case falls into his lap, it's as if he puts on a pair of blinders and becomes one of those Central Park horses pulling tourists around, his head down, no distractions, only able to see the strip of pavement in front of him, which in his case is the trail leading to a killer.

Unfortunately for his wife and children, they became part of the noisy traffic he found it necessary to ignore in order to do his job, and he continually plodded right by them, never giving them a second thought but expecting them to be waiting for him in the stable afterward ready with praise, affection, and a trough full of food.

His wife has stayed with him all these years, but I can't imagine she's been happy. They spend most of their time apart. I guess they both decided it would be easier to have separate lives than go through a divorce. It's none of my business. I'm not the other woman and never have been. During the twenty-seven years I've known Nolan we've probably had sex maybe thirty times, our hookups never planned and never talked about afterward. Like our latest, they've come out of nowhere, the surprise adding almost as much excitement to the act as the lusty comingling of body parts.

I was sexually active throughout my forties but not necessarily sexually satisfied. The other night with Nolan was the first non-self-inflicted orgasm I've had in five years.

I was so pleased that while I was online looking up the Jessica Simpson bedding collection to identify the comforter that had been wrapped around Camio Truly, I Googled traditional anniversary gifts, found out five years is wood, and ordered myself a coffee table.

Nolan dismisses his team. They grab up the remaining doughnuts along with their notes and cups of coffee and give me nods and growling mutters of gratitude.

Nolan invited me to this briefing as a courtesy, but I know he also values my input. The same can't be said for the men working for him who are either young, ambitious go-getters hoping to be a detective of his rank someday, or experienced cops confident in their abilities and possessive of their testosterone-fueled, by-the-book world. They may have a bit of respect for my title and a few might even think I earned it through merit and not because of some type of political feminist maneuverings, but none of them have the slightest regard for my domain. They consider small-town cops to be glorified babysitters. I don't take offense at this. In a way I am the day-care equivalent of law enforcement. I've spent my twenty odd years as a cop cleaning up after the residents of Buchanan, teaching them basic manners and social skills, putting them in grown-up time-out when their behavior becomes destructive or distracting.

What I do is just as important as what they do. If I do my job right, people might not end up getting to a point in their lives where they commit the offenses that make them the problems of these troopers.

Standing this close to the murder board with everything written in big block letters, I don't need my glasses, but I get tired of taking them on and off. I've learned to slide them down my nose and look over the tops of them.

Nolan obviously doesn't wear his shades when he gives a briefing to his fellow officers. Without them, it's immediately obvious why he does wear them during every other aspect of his job. He's built a career on being a hard-ass but he has gentle eyes, a comforting shade of baby-blanket blue couched in a crinkly web of kindly old-uncle creases.

He's looking at me.

"Your glasses aren't terrible," he says. "I thought

they'd make you look old, but you don't look any older than you are."

"Here you go with the sweet talk again." I sigh.

He's moved the family members out of the suspect category. I notice with a heavy heart that Zane Massey is still there.

"The immediate family members all have alibis," he tells me while jabbing a finger at each blown-up DMV photo in turn. Camio's incarcerated brother, Shane, is represented by his mug shot.

"Father was out of town on a job. Sister was at a friend's house. Older brother has two hundred inmates and a dozen guards who can account for his whereabouts."

"And Shawna?" I wonder. "You seemed to think she was a possibility the other day. What happened?"

"This crime required effort. I can't imagine her getting off the couch."

I shake my head at this.

"Why is it brass won't let you talk to the press?"

"You think the same thing," he grunts at me.

He's right. Whoever killed Camio swung a heavy object at her head, rolled her up in a blanket, drove her to Campbell's Run, lit her on fire, and stuck her down a sinkhole. Even so, I don't have as much trouble imagining Shawna doing any of that as I do picturing her cleaning up afterward.

"We've been through the house and their vehicles. There's no sign of blood anywhere, and a head wound like that would've bled like crazy. Would've been a helluva mess to clean up. Nearly impossible to erase all traces," Nolan goes on. "You're positive the comforter didn't belong to them?"

"I can't be a hundred percent sure," I answer, "but like I told you, it's definitely not their style and it's also pricey. I can't see Shawna blowing a hundred twenty dollars on a comforter, plus then you feel obligated to get the shams and bed skirt, maybe a few throw pillows—"

"I get it," he cuts me off, moving away from me and puckering up his face like the mere mention of a bed skirt might make him start lactating.

He throws himself back into discussing the case.

"You've got a drunk for a father, a mother who checked out a long time ago, a son in prison, and a dropout daughter who got herself knocked up in high school. On paper it looks like the ideal family environment where something like this could happen."

"I know what you're saying," I join in his analysis, "but I think they're too messed up to do something this messed up."

"Come again?"

"They all seem more concerned with self-destruction than anyone else's destruction. Even Shane's knife fight. Witnesses say the other guy started it and it might not have happened at all if they both hadn't been three sheets to the wind. Accidents do happen, but otherwise, where's the motive? This is one tight-knit clan, and even though Camio might be a little different, she was still one of them, and I think they all loved her in their own highly dysfunctional ways. Zane told me when she was around her family she became just like them. I don't know exactly what that means but I have a pretty good idea. Her number one loyalty seems to have been to her family even if she wanted to get away from them."

I walk over to Zane's most recent school photo, enlarged and posted at the top of the suspects list. He's not stone-faced or staring belligerently trying to prove he's too tough or too cool for this yearly ritual. He's smiling for the camera, probably thinking about all the relatives who are going to end up with a copy of the picture compliments of his mother.

She flashes through my mind. I see Brie Massey running around riffling through drawers and pulling open photo albums looking for a photo to give to the police believing if they just had the right one, they'd see the same wonderful, innocent, clean-cut boy she saw instead of seeing someone capable of murder.

Nolan comes up behind me.

"He admits he went out to meet her right around the time of her death but claims she didn't show up."

I turn to him with my hands on my hips and look at him in exasperation over the tops of my glasses, then quickly take them off altogether when it occurs to me I might very well look like some reviled teacher from his youth.

"Why would he admit that if he did it?" I ask.

"To throw us off."

"Did that kid strike you as the kind of kid who'd try to throw off the police? And he wasn't gone from the house long enough."

"We don't know that. We still don't have a straight answer from the parents about how long he was gone.

Dad says he thinks he was gone for about an hour. Mom originally said he wasn't gone at all. Once we told her Zane admitted he went to meet Camio, she changed her tune and said he may have been gone. Either one of them would lie to save him."

"What about his car?" I challenge him. "Came up clean didn't it?"

"All the Massey vehicles are clean," he admits.

"And what about his motive?"

"It's possible they were breaking up. Last time they were at the house together, Miranda Truly said she overheard them fighting. Camio told Zane she wanted to break up and he got very angry."

I think about this revelation for a moment and my chat with Zane about Camio's family and his two visits to their home. If they needed to have that particular fight, I can't imagine he'd let it happen in a house full of Trulys. Camio wouldn't want that either. Maybe Miranda heard what she wanted to hear.

I look away from happy-go-lucky Zane to Lonnie Harris's glaring mug shot taken the night he put his wife in the hospital. His face is pale and soft but his eyes are hard and flat.

Singer and Blonski called me on the way over here. During their search for a connection between Harris and Camio, they showed his photo to her co-workers at Dairy Queen and one of the boys who worked there recognized him. The kid couldn't remember if Camio had ever had contact with him, but the coincidence combined with his history of violence against women and his pornography preferences was enough to get Nolan interested.

Next to Harris is a photo of a skinny, skittish-looking guy with a lot of messy hair: the brother of the man Shane knifed. He vowed revenge at the time, verbally harassed Shane at his hearings, and threatened his family, but his brother recovered, Shane went to jail, and nothing had been heard from him for the past two years. For him to suddenly decide to seek vengeance now in such a horrible way against Shane's sister seems unlikely but has to be checked out.

Finally I come to Uncle Eddie. Nolan doesn't have anything written next to his photo yet except a big question mark.

He's invited me to go with him to talk to Eddie after this meeting. Now that we know Camio spent time alone at his house, not only does it raise questions about him but it also opens up endless possibilities for her running into sketchy characters Eddie knew, including drug-dealing bikers.

I haven't told Nolan my source for this lead was a cupcake-stuffed eight-year-old. He trusts me enough to know I wouldn't give him a lead without good cause, but he's not happy about the mystery surrounding my information. Eventually I'll have to come clean.

I put my glasses back on and skim through the autopsy report again.

She was a seventeen-year-old girl of average weight and height in good health. No drugs or alcohol in her system. No signs of sexual assault. No signs of recent sexual activity at all, wanted or unwanted.

Cause of death was a blow to the head with a heavy, flat object that left rusted iron particulates in the wound, or the miniscule flakes could have been picked up from the floor or ground where she was killed.

I reluctantly glance at the close-up photo of the wide, jagged laceration at the back of her skull with splinters of bone poking out among flyaway strands of singed hair.

The coroner determined the first blow would've immediately knocked her unconscious and been sufficient to cause her death, and considering the placement of it, she probably didn't know it was coming. These two bits of information are the only remotely tiny bright spots in this tragedy. Camio was alive one minute, dead the next. Hopefully she didn't know she was about to die. She didn't experience any physical pain or terror.

"We've talked to her teachers," Nolan interrupts my thoughts. "They all say she was an excellent student. Straight A's. Advanced-placement classes. Her relationship with Zane was common knowledge. They were thought of as a cute couple."

The same sour look comes over his face when he says "cute couple" as when he heard the word "shams."

"I told you that I talked to her three best friends, but I thought you might want to do it, too."

I don't look up at him. I pretend to be immersed in the report. I want him to beg.

"Teenage girls are not my thing," he adds.

"I'm relieved to hear that."

The accelerant was gasoline. It was haphazardly thrown over her body but her hands were saturated with it.

"What about the burning of the hands?" I ask him. "Any thoughts on what that's about? Do you think it was done to conceal her identity? No fingerprints?"

"Doesn't make much sense. There are still dental records. DNA."

"Something symbolic, then?"

"Possibly. Will you talk to the girls, too?"

That's the closest to begging he'll ever come.

"Yes."

"I also wouldn't mind you taking a shot at Shawna in an official capacity. Bring her into the station for questioning. I've already talked to her. I don't think she did it, but I think she knows something."

"Wow. Okay. I'm looking forward to *that*."

I toss the autopsy report back on the table and pick up the transcript of Camio's text messages. Her phone still hasn't been recovered. It's either been switched off or destroyed.

For a seventeen-year-old, she didn't text that much. The majority of her messages during the week preceding her death were between her and Zane. There were some to her sister and friends but none to unidentified contacts. From what I can see, the conversations were banal.

I focus on the final exchange between her and Zane the night she was killed. The texts were sent during the thirty-minute window surrounding her time of death. It's possible she was killed right afterward.

Camio: I need to see you.

Zane: ??

Camio: Please meet me at laurel dam.

Zane: U ok?

Camio: Yes. It's important.

Zane: More UAW shit?

Camio: Please.

A half hour later Zane texts: Where r u?

Camio texts back: I'm sorry. I got in trouble.

I look through their earlier conversations and I get a prickly feeling at the back of my neck. I'm not sure if it's from the excitement of making an important discovery or the creepiness over what I think I've discovered.

"Something's wrong with these texts," I tell Nolan. "Did you look at these yet?"

He comes up beside me.

"Not yet. One of my guys is supposed to be on it."

I point at a flurry of texts between Camio and Zane the day before and then at the final ones.

"Camio's texting style has changed," I exclaim. "She's suddenly writing in complete sentences. She sounds almost formal: 'Please meet me.' And look. They always refer to Laurel Dam as 'the dam.' Here she writes out 'Laurel.' And she always uses the letter 'u' for 'you.' Look. Here she writes out 'you.'"

"You're right," he says. "And what's this? UAW? United Auto Workers?"

I burst into laughter. I can't help it.

He gives me a profoundly dirty look.

"UAW," I explain between giggles. "Us Against the World.

"And here's another thing. Look at the amount of time between texts. Once a conversation was initiated, their responses to each other were instantaneous. But with this final conversation, Zane replies instantly to her but look at Camio's responses."

We both stare at the numbers.

"It takes her several minutes. That's an eternity by teen texting standards," I say.

"What are you saying?"

"I'm saying Camio didn't send those texts."

I reach into the Zuchelli's box for the lone surviving doughnut, take a bite, and smile at him with powdered-sugar lips. I deserve it.

chapter eleven

NOT LONG AFTER Neely rescued Maybe and gave Tug a job, I swung by Edward Truly's house to get a feel for the guy. I didn't anticipate any trouble from him. He'd have no way of finding out who took his dog. The trip was motivated purely by my notorious nosiness.

Then, as now, I was struck by a sense of isolation that made me think of a lone homesteader's cabin on a windswept prairie with nothing to see in any direction except the sway of tall grass.

I don't know where this feeling came from. His house is small and sits alone on the side of the road with no visible neighbors, but a mile over the hill in one direction is a trio of slapdash-constructed yet much-loved houses with frilly curtains in the windows and well-tended flowerbeds lining the front walks; in the other direction is Sawyer's dairy farm and a few miles beyond that is Buchanan. He doesn't live in the middle of nowhere, yet the starkness of his property gives off an air of forlorn separateness that makes it seem banished. His sheared yard is devoid of any vegetation: not a tree, not a bush, not a single burst of dandelion yellow or a sprinkle of violets. The house itself is a study in the absence of imagination: an old, aluminum-sided ranch painted entirely white, even the trim, with an attached one-car garage; except for its lack of potential mobility, it could easily be confused with a double-wide trailer.

Nolan and I stand on the concrete front stoop. Eddie's house address numbers are missing. I notice the reverse shadows of a six, two, and seven dangling beneath three rusted nails; clean white symbols against the weathered, grayish white. Somehow I know he removed them on purpose.

The man who opens the door bears only a passing resemblance to the man in the photo on Nolan's murder board who was scruffy and unwashed with belligerent eyes and long, lank, greasy hair. The hair is still long, but it's been recently washed and with the filth removed, it's turned out to be the bright silky white of a mall Santa's beard. He's freshly shaven and wearing a clean blue T-shirt. The only signs of his biker past are the tattoos on his arms and a skull earring.

"Mr. Truly, I'm Corporal Greely with the state police. We spoke on the phone," Nolan introduces himself and nods at me. "This is Chief Carnahan, Buchanan police."

"I know," he says, and levels a searching gaze on me I find a little unnerving. "I was there when Miranda gave you your dressing-down. You held your own," he adds with a tinge of amusement in his voice that sounds almost like admiration.

"Come on in," he urges.

The room he leads us into isn't particularly clean or picked-up, but the dusty furniture and muddy footprints, the dirty socks and an empty pizza box on the floor don't seem to be so much signs of poor housekeeping as they do evidence of someone once living here who abandoned the house suddenly and completely.

I look around for any signs of personal expression. Photos. Books. Some kind of hobby or just something he likes: a sports team, motorcycles, hunting, fishing, jigsaw puzzles, carpentry, naked women, his country.

Nothing. It has even less warmth and individuality than a doctor's waiting room, and I realize that's the vibe this house and this man give off. Eddie Truly is waiting. But waiting for what? True love? The grass to grow? His big break?

"You said you wanted to talk to me about Camio."

He takes a seat in a recliner, the only other furniture in the room besides the couch, coffee table, and an old-fashioned entertainment center with a TV, DVD player, and shoebox-size speakers he probably bought in the nineties housed inside it.

Nolan and I are forced to sit side by side on the sofa. He's more than a little peeved at me right now. As we were pulling into Eddie's driveway I finally revealed the identity of my witness against him. Nolan almost turned the car around and left. For some reason, he seems to feel the combative, potty-mouthed, half-feral eight-year-old youngest brother of the victim who hates everyone as far as I can tell isn't a reliable font of information. I think those same qualities make him an incorruptible source.

"Don't know what I can tell you," Eddie claims.

"How well did you know her?" Nolan asks, prescription Ray-Bans firmly in place across the bridge of his nose.

The sun is streaming through the front window, keeping him from looking completely ridiculous. We're talking to Eddie Truly after all, not guarding the president.

"That's a funny question," Eddie replies. "She was my niece. I knew her as well as men know their nieces."

"That's a funny answer," Nolan says.

Eddie looks at him, trying to get any sense of the deeper meaning behind those words, but all he sees is a blank set of features and two black holes where the windows to Nolan's soul should be.

"I'd see her at Clark's house now and then," he further explains, "but I don't hang out with my family much."

"Those were the only times you saw her?"

He runs his hands through his hair, falls back against the recliner, and let's out a defeated sigh. For a moment I think we're going to skip nervousness, denial, defensiveness, and anger and get right to the confession, but he gives Nolan a smirk of disappointment.

"Okay. I get what this is about. I wondered how long it would take till the cops started coming down on me considering my past. I don't hang out with any of those people anymore. Haven't for a long time. I'm clean, sober. I got a job."

"And you're a liar," Nolan comes back at him. "We've already caught you in your first one. We know Camio came to visit you here at your house."

This is the moment of truth. Even I don't know if Derk made up everything he told me.

A brief spark of defiance runs through Eddie. He clamps his hands on the armrests and rises up in his chair but quickly changes his mind and crumples back against the cracked faux leather upholstery.

"I didn't have nothing to do with her dying," he says quietly. "She was a sweet girl."

His word choice is interesting: not *I didn't kill her*, or *I didn't have anything to do with her "murder"*; he said he didn't have anything to do with her "dying." With these words, all the violence, shock, and outrage had been removed. Her death was no longer an act of aggression but something visited upon her; not something someone did to her but something that happened to her. Something expected. Maybe even something inevitable.

"Why did she come to see you?" Nolan persists.

"Hell," he says, shifting uncomfortably in his chair.

He gets to his feet and starts rubbing his hand over his mouth and chin while his eyes dart around the room searching for the bottle of booze he would have run for in the past.

"She liked to talk to me. Wanted to know about some stuff in my past."

"What kind of stuff?"

He shoves his hands into the pockets of his jeans and shakes his head.

"You know."

"Know what?" Nolan prods him.

"Know all about me. I'm sure you've checked me out. You know my criminal record and my service record."

I came here fully expecting to dislike this man because he mistreated an animal and because he's a Truly, but I'm beginning to wonder if the first could have been a regrettable mistake he made in his past like many others and the second might be a reason to feel sympathy for him instead of contempt.

He's the oldest of Miranda's children. What was that like? He survived a war only to return and watch two younger brothers cut down in their prime by their own recklessness mere miles from their home. What did that do to his head? His own little patch of the American dream turned out to be more dangerous than the killing fields of Vietnam.

"I'm sure Corporal Greely knows everything about you from your favorite song down to the last time you had a prescription filled," I say to him.

Both men turn and look at me like they're surprised I have a voice.

"All I know is your niece used to walk all the way over here from her house in order to talk to you. That's a couple of miles isn't it? And sometimes when she left she was very upset, even crying."

"What?" Eddie says, concerned.

"Corporal Greely, being male and being highly suspicious, jumps to the obvious conclusion that you must've hurt her in some way," I go on. "But as a female who wants to think the best of everyone, I'm wondering if she was upset *for* you and not *by* you. I think she cared about you very much."

He walks back to his chair and falls into it like he's just arrived home after a hundred-mile march.

"I spent some time in and out of VA hospitals. If you asked anyone in my family, they'd tell you I had ongoing complications from a couple of bullets I took in 'Nam. But that would be a lie. They were through and throughs. Healed just fine. I was in the psych ward."

He pulls up his shirt and shows us his scars, two tiny, pink, puckered mouths on his lower left side.

Nolan was shot in the line of duty twelve years ago. It happened right after I'd started looking for the church windows stolen from Campbell's Run. I think this is one of the reasons I threw myself into that case. It provided a distraction, first from wondering if Nolan was going to die, then from wondering if he was going to walk again, and then from wondering if he was going to be able to be a cop again. To this day every time I see a stained glass window, a spasm of fear clutches at my heart.

Nolan came here wanting to dislike Eddie Truly as much as I did and wondering if he might be our killer; now he has to give him begrudging respect and accept that on one level, he has more in common with this man than he does with anyone else he knows.

"It started out with her wanting to talk to me about Vietnam. She was always trying to find out what makes people tick. She wanted to be a psychologist when she grew up. She didn't know I'd been in a loony bin when we started talking, but eventually I told her and that's what we ended up talking about most of the time."

We all fall silent.

"So there's your big mystery solved. She felt sorry for me, I guess. There was a time in my life where that would've offended the hell out of me and I would've kicked her out the first time I got an inkling of it, but now"—he pauses, leans forward in his chair with his forearms on his knees, and stares hard at the floor—"I gotta tell you it felt good to have someone finally care. I talked her ear off. Told her things I've never told anyone, and while I was doing it I realized no one ever asked. Not a single goddamned person my entire life. No one wanted to know about 'Nam, and no one sure as hell wanted to know about the hospital."

"Can you think of anyone who would want to harm her? Anyone she had a problem with?"

"Like I said, she was a sweet girl," Eddie replies. "Far as I know, everyone loved her."

"What about the boyfriend?"

"I know the family's all up in arms saying he did it. There's no way. Cami was crazy about him and vice versa. She was so excited over that sparkly anklet thing he gave her."

My thoughts jump to the piece of jewelry and how alive those legs looked attached to a body that had been grilled like a piece of meat. I feel like I might be sick.

"Your mother said she heard them have a heated

argument about breaking up," I provide as a distraction, even though it's Nolan's claim.

Eddie gives me the same look he gave me earlier when he mentioned Miranda, a strange mix of something playful and defeated.

"Then it must be so," he says, rising to his feet. "Now if you don't mind, I got somewhere I need to be."

Nolan and I stand up, too, both of us knowing this isn't true. There's no place Eddie Truly needs to be. This fact could be considered liberating, but I think it's become his private prison.

I suddenly understand what he's waiting for. He's been doing it since he stepped off that army plane into the sweltering heat of a jungle that must have hit him like an oven door thrown open in his face. He's waiting to die.

From where I'm positioned, I can see through a doorway into his kitchen and through a window into his backyard, where there's an empty kennel.

"Do you have a dog?" I ask him.

He follows my gaze.

"I did. Afraid I didn't treat him too well."

"What happened to him?"

"Don't know. He might've been able to slip off his collar, but I don't see how he cut through the lock on his kennel door."

He looks me square in the face and I know the question he's asking me. He must know who Tug started working for after his dog went missing.

"I've been to some dark places in my mind," he says, turning away from me and staring at the empty pen. "Sometimes you mistreat the thing you love best just 'cause it's there.

"Wherever he is now, I hope he's okay. His name's Hòa Bình."

"Hoban?" I repeat uncertainly.

"Hòa Bình. It's Vietnamese."

He leans down, tears off a corner of the empty pizza box, and writes it out for me.

"It means 'peace.'"

He hands me the scrap of cardboard. I take it from him and nod. Tears spring to his eyes. Loss and shame flicker there, then relief.

chapter twelve

EVERHART'S WIFE went into labor while Nolan and I were chatting with Eddie Truly. This is his first child, a boy already named Jacob, already nicknamed the Jakester, already photographed more inside his mother's uterus than I was ever photographed outside of Cissy's, and already the proud owner of an NFL regulation Steelers football helmet and a sandbox shaped like a NASCAR Sprint Cup Series Gen 6 complete with real tires.

Dewey, my thirty-six-year-old senior officer, has four kids who have all been extensively documented at every stage of life and the proof printed out from digital photos and tacked onto our communal bulletin board. He's taken Everhart under his wing these past months, training him and filling his head with parental tales ranging from adorable to terrifying.

Singer and Blonski are too young and too single to have more than a polite passing interest in the procreating of their coworkers. I'm not sure Blonski has even noticed that among our schedules for DUI classes and flyers urging everyone to wear a bike helmet are endless candids of little Deweys blowing out birthday-cake candles and dressed up for Halloween.

I know Singer has noticed. For all his domestic qualities, raising children doesn't seem to be something he's eager to do. When he walks past the board, he eyes the photos the way a shellfish-allergy sufferer regards a plate of shrimp salad.

Welcoming a new life into the world has provided a temporary distraction from the thought of the life that has been taken too soon. My men may not officially be part of the active investigation surrounding Camio's death but a murder this brutal and inexplicable brings with it a host of other problems to small towns. Everyone is suddenly on edge, hearing suspicious noises in the night, glimpsing threatening strangers, noticing cars parked where they shouldn't be, and we have to check it out. People call and drop by with unsolicited insights into the victim and those who knew her, and we have to listen patiently to all of it in the slim hope that we might hear something useful.

People don't want to believe someone living in their town could kill a young girl and light her on fire. They want the perpetrator to be an outsider so they can continue to believe evil doesn't bloom in their own backyards. However, if they are forced to acknowledge that an unsavory element exists right under their noses, a family like the Trulys is an acceptable choice. Not only do they have a track record of less heinous but disreputable behavior, they also don't have any allies. The Trulys don't go out in the world and make friends. They bring carefully culled individuals into their tribe for reproductive purposes and create their own network of support and assistance. This works fine for them most of the time until they need something one of their own can't provide, like a communal benefit of the doubt.

As I explained to Nolan earlier, I don't think a family member did it. He's not completely convinced yet. He wasn't even won over by the reformed Uncle Eddie.

He asked and was granted permission to send a team to search Eddie's house and vehicle. I don't think he's going to find anything and that includes Camio's cell phone, which has taken on new importance since I discovered the discrepancy in her final texts to Zane.

Nolan agrees with me that those texts have provided two important probabilities about the killer. Whoever sent them might not be too familiar with smartphones, but this fact doesn't help much. Even my grandmother, who's in her nineties, has one. Her arthritic fingers make it difficult to use the keypad, so I got her a stylus that she's constantly misplacing; when she does use it she taps with the capped end of a pen instead. She loves to send me messages that are made up entirely of emoticons. I've become an expert at deciphering them.

Birthday cake / microphone / sleepy face = We did karaoke for someone's birthday at the home today and now I'm tired.

Soup bowl / thumbs-up / revolver / angel = Thank God the soup's good today or I was going to have to shoot someone.

Face with eyes X-ed out / monkey with eyes covered = Someone died and I know nothing.

Face with eyes X-ed out / monkey with mouth covered = Someone died and I'm not saying anything.

A line of ten birds = Lots of birds outside my window today.

The English flag / bag of money / clock = Can't talk now; *Downton Abbey*'s on.

More important, the other clue the texts provide is that the killer seemed to be trying to frame Zane. Why else pretend to be Camio and get him to meet her around the moment she was murdered? This all but rules out the psycho-stranger theory since the killer would have had to know about Camio's relationship with Zane even to the point of knowing where they liked to hang out. It doesn't completely rule out someone like Lonnie Harris, who, although not closely acquainted with Camio, could have stalked her.

But why frame Zane of all people? The ruse could be personally motivated: the killer hated Zane and wanted to get him in trouble. If this is the case, then every member of the Truly family is back at the top of the suspect list, since they all disliked the boy. Or it could be because he's an obvious choice. Boyfriends and husbands are always the first suspects in a female's murder. If this is the reason, our killer is not only vicious and resourceful but smart, too, an unfortunate combination for those of us trying to catch him. Or her.

There's a chance two people were involved. It

would've been difficult for one person to move the body although not impossible, but Nolan and I both find it strange that parts of the comforter were burned and bits of the synthetic elements of the fabric were found melted onto her skin. This almost certainly means someone covered her with the blanket again after the fire started. Could the killer have changed his mind and decided leaving her in a sinkhole out at the Run would be concealment enough, or begun to feel some sort of remorse and decided he should just let her be? Or was there a second person who never wanted Camio dead in the first place and couldn't stand to see this final atrocity visited upon her? We don't have anything to back up our hunch about an accomplice, but if he or she exists, he or she might have been the one who sent the texts to help cover up for the one who did the actual deed.

Chet Shank told me Lucky thinks I accused him of killing my mother to protect Gil. He couldn't be further from the truth.

I wasn't prepared for this teenage girl's murder to bring up so many memories of my mother's. I suppose it only makes sense that thinking about one should make me think about the other, but I've investigated a few homicides before and dealt with many accidental and natural deaths on the job and I've never been affected this way.

As I've been obsessively mulling over the facts of Camio's case today, each one has brought me back to some long-forgotten detail of my mother's crime scene: her perfume bottles and jars of lotion gleaming and glittering in the sputtering candlelight; the bloody bathwater tinting the clouds of white bubbles pink like cotton candy; her one lovely naked arm wedged against the side of the tub rising out of the water like a swan's neck.

The cheap Renaissance Faire goblet was long gone. Since she'd married Gil, she drank her wine out of crystal. The glass lay shattered on the tile floor. She must have been holding it when she was struck.

I stood there in the Dove-scented air looking down at the unharmed features of my mother's perfect face partially submerged beneath the sticky red water and knew Grandma would be pleased that the killer had struck her from behind and she could still look pretty in her casket.

One of Lucky's empty beer cans had missed the mark when he tried to toss it in the wastebasket and had rolled beneath the radiator. I was only fifteen and had no interest in police work at that time but I still remember thinking, *Fingerprints*. Neely was nowhere to be found. Grandma arrived too quickly. "I Will Survive" by Gloria Gaynor was playing softly on the radio; I remember thinking, *Not this time*.

I LEFT WORK as early as I could and ran to Shop 'n Save. I tried to concentrate on my grocery list for tonight's dinner but my mind was full of lifeless human limbs—Camio's bare legs, my mother's bare arm.

I'm relieved to get home. I almost expect to see reporters outside my house—they've been popping up everywhere these last few days—but no one's out except for Bob standing in his driveway, talking on his phone, and smoking a cigarette. His mildly annoying presence is somehow comforting in its constancy.

"Hey, Chief," he calls out while I unload the groceries from my trunk. "Did you catch the guy yet?"

His switch from the all-inclusive "bad guys" to the specific "the guy" disappoints me. I'd like to think there's at least one person around here who isn't caught up in Camio's murder, and if there could be anyone that oblivious it would be Bob, but no such luck.

"Not yet," I call back.

I suddenly realize part of the reason why Camio's case is reminding me so much of my mother's might be the notoriety attached to it, although Camio's is a much more public crime because of the times we now live in.

This town hasn't seen a scandal to compare to my mother's death until now but no matter how horrible and lurid the circumstances surrounding her demise, it remained Buchanan's private business. She was murdered in 1980, back before the Internet and social media existed, before twenty-four-hour TV news channels and reality crime shows. Hers was a sleazy, bloody tale motivated by rage and lust, yet news of her death didn't even spread as far as the other side of the state.

Camio's death has already gone viral. Forget Scranton and Philadelphia, people in Beijing and Dubai have heard about the girl who was torched and left to burn in a town that's been on fire for more than fifty years.

People have been showing up at Campbell's Run

to see the place where she was found, so I've had to start sending a cruiser by every now and then because the area is dangerous. All I need on top of everything else is for some meddling interloper snapping pictures with a phone to go plummeting three hundred feet into a smoldering mine tunnel.

An LA graphic artist has whipped up a poster of a charred zombie girl with glowing green eyes wrapped in chains made of sparkly hearts crawling out of a flaming ditch and captioned it: *Coal Town Cutie*. Singer and Blonski found it online and showed it to me. The guy's selling it framed for three hundred dollars.

This unwanted spotlight has made not only the Trulys and the Masseys defensive but the whole town. We've started circling our wagons, trying to protect our good name along with Camio's memory.

This didn't happen with my mom's murder. People didn't want to own it; they wanted to shoo it away.

"A lot of people are saying it was her boyfriend or her dad," Bob calls out to me.

This is the most he's said to me since I got my promotion and had my deck put on. Bob thinks he's an expert at home improvement even though I've never seen him attempt any.

"Really? And why are they saying that?"

"Because that's who usually kills teenage girls if it ain't a psycho."

He pauses.

"It ain't a psycho, is it?"

"I'm pretty sure it wasn't a psycho," I assure him, and note the relief that passes over his face.

He gives me a big smile and raises his cigarette in a salute before going back to his phone call.

Once inside my house, I'm able to put aside all thoughts of either murder and think about something almost equally troubling: my brother, Champ.

I'm happy he came back but also worried. A person doesn't disappear from his hometown and cut all ties with his family for twenty-five years, then suddenly return for no reason other than a flimsy claim of wanting to take a cross-country road trip with his son.

I put on the brightest piece of clothing I own to balance out my somber mood, a sleeveless sundress of smiley-face yellow with big orange daisies splashed across it. The skirt has a little flare and hits midthigh. I suppose I'm too old to wear something this short and skimpy. I never questioned my clothing choices during my forties, but now that I've rounded the bend into my fifties I second-guess everything. I don't want to look my age, but I also don't want to look like I'm trying to look some other age.

I give a quick twirl in front of the mirror. If I had a giant lollipop and a pair of patent-leather Mary Jane tap shoes with lace ankle socks I could pass for an oversize Shirley Temple. It's not a dress I'd wear out, but I'm entertaining at home.

Along with steaks and some steamed green beans from my garden, I'm making homemade mac and cheese and my world-famous potato salad. Mason can't object, since I don't use a mayonnaise-based dressing. Mine is white wine, olive oil, white wine vinegar, Dijon mustard, minced shallots, and lots of fresh parsley tossed with diced boiled red potatoes and Jarlsberg cheese.

I made sure to avoid everything on Mason's list. Especially cupcakes.

He and his dad and Neely arrive at my front door looking exactly the way they did when I left them. One more red flag goes up in my assessment of Champ. The first thing I'd want to do after driving hundreds of miles for many days is take a shower and change my clothes and I'd make my child do the same but Champ and Mason remain rumpled, battered, and bleary-eyed.

Neely's still in jeans and a gray T-shirt, but she's shed the old, faded brown work shirt she was wearing over it earlier and traded her navy blue K-9 Training Corps ball cap for a red one advertising a dog food brand. This is about as dressed up as she gets.

She stops short when she sees me and eyes me up and down.

"What is wrong with you?" she asks exactly the same way she would if I were one of her human students who has just revealed she lets her dog sleep on her bed instead of crating him.

"I feel festive," I reply.

"Wow," Champ laughs.

He takes me by the hand and spins me around.

"I feel like I should take you salsa dancing."

Champ still has the same infectious smile he had as a kid. A few good nights' sleep and a little fattening up and he'd be what I'd call a good-looking man. I study his features anew. I've lived my entire life in this town, and I have a very public job and personality. I know everyone, but I've never been able to track down Champ's father. I've searched the faces of every man I've ever met who would be the right age, but I've never found a resemblance to anyone.

"I like your dress, Aunt Dove," Mason chirps up.

I glance down at him standing next to Neely, holding his binder under one arm.

"You remind me of the ladies painted on the walls in a Mexican restaurant we went to in Arizona," he goes on. "They had good tacos. Remember, Dad?"

"I sure do, bud."

He rips open his binder, rustles through his folders, and comes up with a cheap paper menu for Manny's Mexican Food. He hands it to me.

"Dad tried to talk to the waitress in Spanish," he goes on, cracking a big smile. "It was a disaster."

"What do you mean?" Champ teases him. *"¿Dónde está el baño?"*

Mason dissolves into giggles.

"She was from Cleveland," he can barely get out.

I skim through the menu and give it back to him.

"What's for dinner here?" he asks. "I'm starving."

"Steaks, mac and cheese, potato salad, and green beans."

"I love all those things!" he gushes, his big dark eyes growing even bigger and darker. "I'm so happy to meet you."

He sticks out his hand. I shake it, then he takes off to explore my yard.

"How old is he?" I ask Champ.

"Nine going on sixty-two."

"He's a nice kid. You've done a good job with him," Neely says.

"Yeah, well. What can I do to help?" he abruptly changes the subject.

"How are you at grilling?"

"I'm a master griller."

"Great. Then you're in charge of steaks. I'll bring them out. Neely can come with me and get you a beer. Go ahead and start the grill."

I lead them through the house and onto my deck. Neely then follows me into the kitchen. We're barely inside before I start pumping her for information.

"So where's his wife or ex-wife?"

"I don't know."

"What do you mean, you don't know? You've just spent the entire day with a brother you haven't seen in twenty-five years who has a son we never even knew existed and you didn't bother to ask him about the boy's mother?"

She opens the refrigerator and brings out three beers.

"I'm not you," she says, handing me one.

"What is that supposed to mean?"

"I didn't interrogate him."

"I repeat, what is that supposed to mean?"

She opens her bottle and takes a swig.

"From the sound of things they've been on their own for a while, but Mason quotes his mom a lot like he's just talked to her and it doesn't seem to bother Champ. Wherever she is, I don't think they're on bad terms."

I check on my mac and cheese in the oven. About fifteen more minutes. Perfect.

"What *did* you find out? Where are they from? What does he do for a living?"

She shrugs, reaches for a fork, and starts eating potato salad out of the serving bowl.

"They've moved around a lot. He's had a bunch of different jobs. Nothing good."

"You mean he doesn't work with dogs."

"Nope."

I swat her hand out of the bowl.

"Did he . . . ?" I toss back my head and make the motion of drinking at my lips.

"Or?" I follow it by pantomiming popping pills, shooting up, and taking a hit off a joint.

"He slept," she answers me. "I never saw him take anything, although I saw him smoke a cigarette and he definitely has the shakes."

"What kind of shakes? Drug shakes? Booze shakes?"

She raises her hands and waves them wildly at me.

"Shakes," she whispers dramatically, and frowns at me.

"What happened with Derk?"

"Nothing. He came back with the dogs like I said he would. Have you ever seen him climb a tree?"

"I know. He's part squirrel."

She waits until my back is turned while I'm salting the steaks and she eats more potato salad.

"He played with Mason for a little while. I was surprised, but they seemed to get along. I took him home with Tug. I'm really worried about Tug. He's so angry."

"What do you expect? His sister was just murdered."

"That should make him sad, not angry."

"Stages of grieving," I say. "Anger's one of them."

I pick up the plate of steaks. She grabs the beers. We head outside.

"You know Tug won't get any help," she tells me. "He has no one to talk to."

"We didn't get any help."

"But at least we had each other. And Grandma."

"He has a family."

I say the words, but I know Tug's family isn't going to be any help to him at all.

I've decided I'm not going to tell Neely about Uncle Eddie and Hòa Bình aka Maybe for now. Neely doesn't forgive and she doesn't forget. Eddie could sell everything he owns and donate it to the ASPCA and spend the rest of his life washing baby penguins pulled out of oil spills and tracking down poachers in Africa, and it wouldn't make a lick of difference to her. He mistreated a dog: end of story.

We have a nice meal together. Even the bugs cooperate and leave us alone. It's a softly warm night, and as the sun begins to set and the sky turns from azure to lilac, the few clouds break apart and drift away, leaving behind a twinkling spray of stars and a bright white crescent moon.

During dinner, I reassess my earlier criticism of Neely's inability to get any information out of Champ. He's surprisingly adept at avoiding all topics related to his personal life. Even I have a tough time uncovering anything meaningful.

She was right about the shakes. He's a drinker. He

drinks most of my beer, and after he and Mason wash the dishes, he asks if I have anything harder. I lie and tell him no, but when he says he'll go out and buy a bottle, I miraculously find some whiskey.

The subject of sleeping accommodations comes up. Champ insists they can stay in a motel but Neely offers them my home. She has just as much room as I do, but her need for privacy borders on insanity.

When I ask how long they're staying, Champ announces that he thinks he's going to look for a job here. I glance at Mason to see how he takes the news, but he's digging into a bowl of ice cream and doesn't seem to care one way or the other.

"That's great," Neely exclaims. "We'd love to have you back home. Wouldn't we, Dove?"

"Of course. You guys can have the guest bedroom or maybe Mason would like to sleep in the grotto."

"The grotto?" Champ wonders.

"It's not a grotto," Neely explains. "It's a garret. The little room under the roof. When we were kids living in the old house with Mom, Dove used to like this house and would talk about living in it someday. She accidentally called the top room a grotto. And it stuck. She still calls it that."

Mason looks up from his bowl with his mouth ringed in chocolate syrup.

"What'd you say about Garrett?"

"It's a little room at the top of a house."

He bursts into laughter.

"Do you know what's so funny?" I ask Champ.

"I think so."

Once Mason calms down enough to be able to talk, he gulps, "My best friend's named Garrett. Wait'll I tell him he's named after a room."

"He's not named after a room any more than you're named after a jar," Champ tells him.

"Your dad's named after a dog," I volunteer.

"I know, but that's not as funny."

"Your aunt Dove's named after soap," Neely says.

This sends Mason into another fit of hilarity.

Since he thinks this is so hysterical, I get up and go to the bathroom and come back with a cake of Dove soap.

Champ takes it from me and smells it through its wrapper.

"Reminds me of Mom," he says simply.

He sets it down on the table in front of Mason, whose giggles are starting to trail off.

"This was the only soap our mom used," Champ further explains. "And she was obsessed with being clean."

Neely picks up the soap and examines it like she's never seen it before.

"That's for sure," she comments. "You ever wonder why?"

"What about Aunt Neely's name?" Mason asks.

"Neely's named after a character in a book called *Valley of the Dolls*," I answer him. "Our mom read it when she was pregnant with her. It was a big best-seller at the time."

"What was the character like?"

"She was a feisty song-and-dance girl from the

wrong side of the tracks who became a pill-popping, alcoholic movie star who destroyed everyone she loved on her relentless climb to the top."

He looks over at Neely.

"Why would your mom name you after her?"

She plunks down the soap.

"She had high hopes for me."

Apparently I have to take matters into my own hands if I want to unearth any personal information about my brother or my nephew.

I signal at Neely to take Champ and his drink outside on the deck.

"How would you feel about moving here?" I ask Mason once they've gone.

"I don't care. We move a lot. I'll miss Garrett."

"What about your mom? Do you mind me asking? Where is she?"

He takes a few bites of ice cream, then sets down his spoon and reaches across the table for his Trapper. I wait for the rip of the Velcro.

I think maybe he's going to show me a picture of her, but he pulls out a copy of a death certificate and hands it to me.

"My mom died of a very bad disease called AIDS. She was an intra venus drug user."

He breaks the word "intravenous" into two words and I wonder if he knows the actual meaning of it or if he thinks it has something to do with the planet and maybe believes that her addiction was a science fiction experiment that got out of hand.

"But she loved me very much," he finishes.

I look down at the piece of paper. I can't read anything, not even her name. My vision is blurred with tears I don't want to inflict upon this little boy.

"I'm sorry, Mason."

"I'm not sick," he says, going back to his ice cream. "I've never been sick a day in my life. Dad loves to tell people this."

"Dove!" Neely shouts from the deck. "Your work cell's ringing."

"Answer it for me."

I take a seat across from Mason and try to figure out what I should say next. I've settled on asking him if he's seen any good movies lately when Neely bursts into the room, my screen door banging shut behind her.

She has the pallor of a corpse and the hot stare of an escaped convict with baying hounds on his trail. I've never seen this amount of despair on her face, not even when I told her about Gil and Champ.

"Tug's at the Masseys' house," she says. "He has a gun."

chapter thirteen

THERE ARE VERY SPECIFIC police guidelines for dealing with an armed someone threatening to blow the head off an unarmed someone who he believes has wronged him in a despicable and utterly unforgivable way. They exist for a reason. They usually work, and the instances where they don't, it's a fair bet nothing could have saved the situation.

As I'm about to step onto the Masseys' immaculate lawn glowing an emerald green beneath the street lamp, I know I'm not going to apply a single one of them. I'm about to leave all my experience and training at the curb, along with my job title and several knots of panicked neighbors, and become nothing more than a foolish, middle-aged woman in a gaudy sundress with a Glock.

I can hear Tug's shouting from outside. He and Zane are in the Masseys' living room standing only a few feet apart. The windows are open. The curtains are parted. An overhead light and a floor lamp are on, and I can clearly see the rifle he has resting against his shoulder pointed at Zane, who has his hands held up in front of his chest, palms out, like he's frozen in a game of patty-cake.

Under no circumstances should I try to enter the home. I should try to communicate with Tug from outside. I should wait for backup. Other officers will be here momentarily. I can hear the sirens in the distance.

Brie Massey is standing in the middle of the yard, her face contorted and tear-streaked, raptly watching the scene playing out in the window as if the boys were putting on a particularly heart-wrenching performance of a beloved play.

She turns at the sound of my car door slamming. I notice her knees and forehead are bloodied, and I immediately know she was with Zane when Tug arrived. Once she realized what was about to happen, she would've grabbed on to her son, trying to make herself into something more than a shield, a maternal protective coating. Tug would've had to peel her off him and throw her out the door. She stumbled and fell onto the front walk.

She forgets about the window and comes running at me, the wild desperation in her eyes making me think she's planning to knock me to the ground, already blaming me for what's about to happen to her son, but she drops to her injured knees in front of me and throws her arms around my legs.

"Save him," she sobs. "You have to save him. Please save him."

I look back at Neely, who insisted on coming with me. I know she wants the same thing, only she's thinking about the other boy's life.

Our eyes connect and she nods at me.

Where is Terry? I wonder as I head for the house. It's a little after nine. Does he have a bowling night or a weekly poker game with the boys? Is he running an errand? Did the missus send him out for ice cream before settling down to watch TV, or is he on a beer run? Is he putting a case of Yuengling in his trunk right now, singing an eighties tune he just heard on the oldies station that reminds him of summers when he was a kid, while his son is about to be murdered in his own living room?

Where's the younger sister?

From inside I hear Tug screaming, "You killed her! Why can't you say it? We all know you did it. You killed her!"

"I didn't do it!" Zane moans, his denial broken up by weeping. "I loved Cam."

"Shut up!" Tug shrieks. "You're a liar!"

I don't try to talk to him through the open window. I go directly to the front door and have a perverse moment where I think about ringing the doorbell.

I'm armed with my gun and two important pieces of information. One, Tug's had plenty of time to shoot Zane and he hasn't. This means he's conflicted. And two, he used the word "we." This is not a decision he made on his own. He's been put up to it even if he doesn't realize it. Deep down Tug doesn't want to do this, but that doesn't mean he won't.

Before I push open the door, I become remarkably calm and aware. I hear one of our cruisers arrive and hear Blonski shout, "Chief! Wait!" I notice a crack in the walkway where a few weeds have poked through, and considering the fastidious care Brie and Terry give to the rest of their yard, I know it must drive them both crazy and I wonder why they haven't fixed it yet. I look down at my feet in a pair of sandals I threw on and notice my toenail polish is beginning to chip. The memory of Camio's polish, vivid pink against her cold white skin smudged with warm black earth, pops unwelcome into my head and I feel like I've been sucker punched in the gut.

I call out Tug's name and step inside.

I never stopped to think how Zane would react to my entrance.

Upon hearing my voice, Tug turns toward me and Zane dashes for the nearest doorway. Tug catches the movement out of the corner of his eye and his hunter's reflexes whirl him back around, shooting.

It's over that quickly.

Zane falls to the floor.

I scream at Tug. It's enough to distract him.

He whips back in my direction with his rifle poised to shoot me. I stand braced with my handgun pointed at him knowing my chance is over.

My own life doesn't flash before my eyes. I think of Camio again and how she was helping her sister get her GED and how she helped her uncle deal with his demons and how she wanted to grow up and join a profession where she might have helped countless troubled, unhappy people. I see them stretched out before me on a country road waiting patiently in line for relief that will never come to them.

"What would Camio want you to do?" I ask him quietly and evenly, trying to keep my voice steady, which is proving easier than keeping my gun steady.

"She loves you, Tug. That love doesn't die with the person. Getting revenge for her isn't loving her back. Being a good person is loving her back."

He's shaking just as much as I am: his gun, his skinny adolescent arms, his chicken legs in his baggy jeans. His lips, nose, and eyebrows twitch crazily like separate living creatures trying desperately to get off his face. If ever there was a stressful time when he needed to act out his nickname, it's now. I want to tell him, *It's okay, go ahead, put down the gun, and grab an ear.*

Behind me I hear other officers enter the house. Planks of red and blue lights slice through the darkness outside.

He falls apart. He could've just as easily shot me, then maybe even shot another cop before he was gunned down himself. But he didn't. I don't know who gets credit for this miraculous save, but it certainly isn't me.

The rifle hits Brie and Terry's polished hardwood floor with a loud clack and Tug follows, crumpling into a heap, covering his face with his oversize hands he hasn't grown into yet, convulsing with loud, ugly, braying sobs.

I don't secure the prisoner. I don't remove his gun from his reach. I don't do anything I'm supposed to do. I run for Zane.

He's been shot once in the right side. He's unconscious but still has a pulse.

The room suddenly fills with noise. Rushing footsteps, men shouting, radios squawking, sirens wailing. I'm putting pressure on Zane's wound when Brie Massey comes up behind me and all other sounds are extinguished as completely as a small fire beneath a heavy blanket.

I never want to hear a scream like that again in my life. Ever.

TUG TRULY IS OUR COLLAR. The shooting of Zane Massey occurred in our town. My officers have taken him back to our station to get a statement and process him with my sister acting as a de facto parent until his own can be notified.

I can't shake the creepy feeling that his parents know exactly where he is and what he's done, that they sent him out to do it without a single thought about what might happen to him. Did they actually think he could get away with it? Didn't they realize he could end up dead or in jail for the rest of his life? Losing a child should make a family draw the others nearer, not sacrifice another in the name of vengeance.

Nolan was on the scene instantly. It turns out he was at the Dairy Queen going through surveillance footage looking for Lonnie Harris. The shooting impacts his case, since both Zane and Tug are still persons of interest in Camio's murder, and as I'm sitting in his car with his siren screaming and light flashing, driving ninety-five miles an hour on our way to Children's Hospital in Pittsburgh where Zane has been taken in a helicopter, I'm telling myself this is the only reason he showed up. I don't want him to care about me. I don't want anyone to care about me. I don't deserve compassion.

I'm not cold, but I can't stop my teeth from chattering or my hands from shaking. He's wrapped me in his suit jacket and given me his thermos of hot coffee that I set between my knees and occasionally clench like a Thighmaster.

He hasn't asked me a single question about what happened. I guess on some level he doesn't have to. He survived being shot twelve years ago, but his best friend didn't. A survivalist who was very vocal about his hatred of cops was wanted for questioning regarding a bomb that was found by a much-lauded janitor in a county courthouse basement before it went off. Ten troopers were sent to the suspect's home. They thought the property was secure. They were wrong. The guy's wife snuck up behind Nolan and shot Trooper John Jankewicz in the back of the head before he could react. Nolan got off three shots that killed her but not before she put one in his chest.

It's just as well he's not grilling me, because I can't remember anything. My thoughts are jumping all over the place.

My dress is covered in Zane's blood, but I don't know how it got there unless I laid down on top of him. My mother's blood was all over the bathroom. The killer had smashed in her head with Champ's bat, and head wounds bleed like crazy. I couldn't get over how much was on the walls and floor yet how much was still left inside her to slowly ooze out and turn the bathwater crimson. Camio's head would've bled the same way. Whoever killed her had an almost impossible task trying to clean up. Grandma tried to clean up Mom's bathroom. The next day after the police had been in and out what seemed like a hundred times, we'd all been questioned, and Mom's body had been moved from the coroner's morgue to the funeral home, Grandma descended on the bathroom armed with a bucket, mop, sponges, steel wool, and a whole host of soaps and solvents. Gil had to forcibly take a scrub brush out of her hand and explain to her that he'd pay someone to clean. I remember Neely asking me how much that would cost. I thought it was a strange question.

We arrive at the hospital and Nolan maneuvers me down corridors covered in colorful murals of dinosaurs, rainbows, and cartoon characters, in and out of elevators playing songs from Disney movies, past quiet, dimly lit rooms I don't want to look into.

"Is Children's the best hospital for a gunshot wound? Getting shot isn't exactly a common childhood affliction," I ask him as we round a corner and almost plow into a dad taking a walk with his bald little girl in pink fuzzy slippers and a matching satiny robe wheeling an IV stand.

I've noticed how no one even looks twice at the old lady covered in dried blood.

"It's not the bullet you have to worry about anymore; it's the internal damage," he explains. "He's past needing a good ER doctor; now he needs a great surgeon."

Brie and Terry Massey are standing in front of a nurses' station talking to an older couple. Grandparents, maybe. A woman who resembles Brie and I assume is her sister hands her a paper cup of coffee. Everyone looks awful, but they're talking. They're not crying or collapsing. A girl with braces and long dark hair in a ponytail clings to Terry's side. I recognize her as their daughter from the family portraits I glimpsed in their living room before I let their son get shot in front of me.

Terry notices me first. He calls out my name. Brie sees me and waves weakly.

They don't realize they should hate me. They see me as a hero: a plucky small-town police chief who left a family cookout to go barreling into harm's way to try and save their son. I may not have succeeded but I tried.

I pull Nolan's jacket closed over my dress.

"Any news?" I ask them.

"He's in surgery. They won't tell us anything."

"That's normal," Nolan assures them.

"This is our daughter, Courtney," Terry makes the introduction.

"What happened?" she blurts out.

She's the first person who's asked me this.

"Why didn't you stop him?"

And this.

"Chief Carnahan did her best," Terry answers for me. "She could've been shot, too. She was very brave."

This is more than I can handle. I excuse myself and walk away. Nolan catches up to me just as I start to cry.

"I can't do this. I can't be here. I shouldn't be here."

"Calm down."

He puts his hand lightly around my shoulders and the feel of this innocent gesture makes me want to do him. Right here. Right now. Up against the rows of sick little boy and girl self-portraits made from bits of yarn and dried macaroni hanging on the wall behind me. I want to be pounded again until I reach that rapturous release, then can collapse on this clean, cold floor with glitter-coated ziti in my hair.

"I'm sorry. I'm acting like a girl."

He doesn't comment. He takes me by the arm and leads me to an empty playroom. All the toys have been neatly put away for the night. I plop down on a stool. It's uncomfortable. I slide off it onto the floor. He takes a seat on a table after carefully checking it for traces of finger paints or Play-Doh.

"I'm going to lose my job," is the first thing that comes out of my mouth.

I'm stunned by my selfishness. A boy may by dying. His family will be destroyed. Another boy is going to jail. And all I can think about is how I make a living and Nolan's big . . . hands. But it's much more than that. Watching the Masseys through the playroom windows as more teary friends and relatives arrive, it suddenly hits me that my job is my life. I have no kids, no husband. I don't even have a goldfish.

"You're not going to lose your job," Nolan says.

"I should lose my job."

He gets up and starts throwing open tiny brightly painted cabinet doors looking like an ogre rummaging through a woodland cottage kitchen where a fairy princess is rumored to be hiding. He comes away with a roll of paper towels and rips off a couple for me.

I wipe at my face.

"I went barging in," I finally tell him. "I called out Tug's name, and when he turned toward me . . ."

"The Massey kid made a break for it," he finishes for me.

I nod.

"Then the Truly kid had no choice but to shoot him," he continues. "He wasn't allowed anymore time to think about what he was going to do. You took that away from him."

I nod again.

"And then. . . ?"

"I froze. I couldn't shoot Tug. I have no idea why I'm not dead."

I've known Nolan a long time. He won't tell me *Everything's okay* and *We all make mistakes* any more than he'd tell a team of eight-year-olds who suck at soccer that everyone's a winner.

"What would you have done if you'd been stupid enough to get yourself in that situation?" I ask him.

It's a pointless question. We both know he never would have been in that situation. He would've proceeded by the book and Zane Massey might be sitting at home right now, shaken up but physically fine. After the initial shock passed, his mom would be all over Facebook.

"You know what I would've done," he says. "I would've shot that boy. He'd be dead."

A chill goes through me as much for Nolan as for Tug. How would Nolan have lived with that? Even knowing he had no choice? Maybe I knew I couldn't live with it. Maybe that's why I couldn't shoot.

"I lost my mind," I say.

"You lost your objectivity," he corrects me. "You took it personally. You went all mama bear."

I guess I must still seem pretty upset, because he comes and sits on the floor with me. This big man with his iron gray crew cut in his suit pants with his serious black shoes looks ridiculous down here.

He puts one of his hands over mine.

"I don't care how many years you have on the job, no one is ever prepared for a life-and-death situation. Everything you know goes out the window except your instincts. Your instincts wouldn't let you shoot that boy even though he had a gun pointed at you, and odds were he was going to shoot you and then turn around and put a couple more bullets in Zane."

"So my instincts are crap?"

"Maybe. But no one's dead yet. So maybe not."

My phone beeps. I've been in touch with the station and Neely all night, keeping up-to-date on Tug through calls, but this is a text.

I take out my reading glasses.

Nolan raises his eyebrows.

"You don't need those to shoot, do you?"

"I can see at a distance just fine."

I take a look and manage a tired smile.

"What could possibly make you happy at a time like this?" Nolan asks.

I show him the photo of Everhart and his wife holding a tiny blue bundle surrounded by a cloud of blue Mylar balloons with the caption: The Jakester's here!!

chapter fourteen

I WALK INTO my little brick police station with its drab waiting area and poorly stocked vending machine, past the scratched and dented filing cabinets and four communal desks with squeaky chairs housed in a room painted the same shade of gray as an eraser smudge, and into my office where I put a forearm against a wall and rest my head upon it. I'm overcome with a mix of relief and familiarity. I love this place. I love every stain on the putty-colored carpet and every spider that keeps diligently reweaving its web in the ceiling corners. I love the smell of burnt coffee and Pine-Sol, and the feeling of accomplishment at the end of the day, whether we helped find a lost pet, or mediated a dispute between a business owner and an irate customer, or stopped a man from beating his wife, or just gave out a bunch of speeding tickets.

I'd be lost without my job. And my men.

"Chief?" Singer knocks on my door.

Blonski and Dewey are with him.

"It's really late," I tell them. "You should go home. There's nothing more we can do tonight.

"And tell Matt congratulations," I say to Dewey. "I'll be by to see the Jakester once he's settled in at home."

"Okay, Chief," Dewey says, and starts to bolt like a kid who's been let out of school early, then catches himself and turns back to me. "Are you okay?"

I hold up my hands and do a fashion model pivot so they can admire the Looney Tunes nurse's scrubs I was given at the hospital.

"I'm fine. Our thoughts should be with the Massey boy."

Dewey leaves, but I motion for Singer and Blonski to take seats. They look as tired as I feel, but they're young. They'll look like a million bucks tomorrow after a good night's sleep. I won't.

I take a seat on the edge of my desk.

"Where's Clark Truly?"

"We took him to Rockland," Blonski replies. "We would've just let him sleep it off in the holding cells here, but he was a fighter."

He grins and jerks a thumb in Singer's direction.

"Singer maced him."

"He kicked me in the balls," Singer protests.

"I wanted to light him up," Blonski says eagerly.

I tick-tock a forefinger at him.

"No Tasers unless absolutely necessary."

"He fought dirty," Blonski continues. "Even before he started throwing punches at us, I wouldn't have felt comfortable taking him home to his family."

"And we definitely wouldn't have let him back in his vehicle," Singer adds. "We got him on DUI, resisting arrest, and assaulting an officer."

"Did you get anything useful out of him in regards to Tug?" I ask.

Blonski leans back in his chair and puts his hands behind his head.

"Nada. He was pickled. He may have known why he was coming down here when he left his home, but he didn't know by the time he got here."

"Tug's mother?"

"Never showed."

We all fall silent for a moment as we let the significance of this sink in. I know Singer and Blonski are very close to their mothers. They both still live at home, though Singer has been looking for his own place at his father's urging. Blonski's mom is a widow, and I know he wouldn't feel good about leaving her even though she, too, has given her blessing if he wants to move out of her garage apartment.

None of us can understand how a mother could find out her fourteen-year-old son is in jail for attempted murder and not rush to his side.

I make a mental note that it's time for me to have that serious talk with Shawna Truly.

"The sister came," Singer adds. "She even brought her baby with her. She was upset."

"Did she say anything useful?"

"Only that Tug didn't mean it. She said he's not the kind of kid who would hurt somebody. He was just crazy with grief."

"Did you get his statement?"

They exchange smirks.

"Your sister had Sandra Goldfarb over here so fast

I thought the woman had been hiding under my desk," Blonski says.

"Best defense attorney in the county," I provide. "Maybe the world."

I know the Trulys won't pay for her, and Neely doesn't have that kind of money. Maybe Sandra took the case pro bono, but why? Tug's not a sympathetic client except to Neely and me. My officers certainly don't feel sorry for him.

"Mizzz Goldfarb . . . ," Blonski continues, drawing out the "Ms." that Sandra insists on putting in front of her name.

Nolan does the same thing whenever he encounters these two abhorrent letters he insists are helping to undermine the domestic tranquility of our country.

". . . wouldn't let Tug say a word. She said he'd give a statement tomorrow."

"Is he still in holding?"

"We kept him like you said. We'll move him to juvie tomorrow."

Against my better judgment, I decide to have a word with him. I don't know what I hope to accomplish. I think I just need to see him looking like his regular self again and not leveling a gun at my head.

He's on the cell bench curled up on his side with his hands clasped under his bare head and his knees pulled up to his chest. This is the first time I've ever seen him without a ball cap. It was taken from him at booking along with his shoelaces and his belt. The same chill of desolate loneliness I felt at his uncle Eddie's house courses through me. Asleep in the dark, barely lit by a parking lot lamp shining through the small barred window, he looks half his age, and his age isn't much to begin with. He's too young to be facing any aspect of life on his own, let alone something this devastating.

I don't want to wake him. I'm about to leave when he asks, "Is he dead?"

I look back at him. He hasn't moved but his eyes are open.

"He survived surgery," I reply. "He hasn't regained consciousness yet."

"So he's going to be okay?"

"There was a lot of internal damage. He lost a lot of blood. He could still die."

Tug doesn't say anything.

"Do you want him to be okay?" I ask.

"He killed Camio."

"Who told you that?"

"Everyone."

"Who's everyone?"

He reaches a hand to his head to adjust the hat that isn't there. He doesn't answer me.

"Will you talk to me tomorrow?"

"What is there to talk about? I shot him. Everybody saw me do it."

There doesn't seem to be any anger left in him. He sounds defeated and resigned to his fate.

"I don't think you wanted to do it."

"What's that supposed to mean? You think I was hypnotized?"

"I'll talk to you tomorrow."

He flips over on his other side, turning his back to me.

A muffled, "No, you won't," comes from the heap of baggy clothes covering little more than skin and bones.

"I'll take that as a yes. Get some sleep."

BY THE TIME I make it home to my house it's almost two in the morning. Champ is asleep on my couch with the TV on. Mason is asleep on the bed in the guest room on top of the covers. It's a warm night, but I find a light blanket and put it over him.

I need to shut down my brain. This is one of those times when I wish I was a drinker or that I wasn't afraid of chemical sedation. I don't think a chapter of a novel or a *New York Times* crossword puzzle is going to do it for me tonight, but I'm wrong.

I settle into my bed after a hot shower, slip on my glasses, pick up my book, and fall asleep instantly.

In my dreams I'm wearing an even louder dress than the one I had on earlier along with a pair of bright red cowboy boots, a sombrero trimmed in a rainbow array of pom-poms, and two pearl-handled revolvers strapped in a silver-studded holster. A shiny gold star proclaiming me the "Sheriff of Mexico" glitters next to my impressive youthful cleavage (the stuff I had before things started going south). I'm in a shoot-out with a gang of young boys whose leader is a woman with a wolf's head.

I'm in the middle of the dream, holed up in a seedy cantina, down to my last bullet, when I'm awakened by a small voice and a large yank on my arm.

My eyes fly open. My reading light is on but the

sun is shining brightly now. Sometime during the night I rolled over on top of my book. My glasses are miraculously still on my face. I take them off and rub at the bridge of my nose.

"Aunt Dove! Aunt Dove!"

It takes me a moment to remember where I am and the identity of this little person. He's still in the same clothes he arrived in yesterday, even the glaring orange socks. His Trapper Keeper is securely under one arm.

"What is it, Mason?"

"My dad's gone."

I sit up straighter. My whole body aches.

"What do you mean 'gone'?"

"He's gone. The car's gone and all our stuff."

I reach out and stroke his buzz cut while glancing at my bedside clock. It's 7:23 a.m.

"He's probably running an errand or maybe getting some doughnuts for breakfast," I try to assure him but a sick feeling begins to spread through me.

He shakes his head.

"No. That's not it. He's gone."

"Has he ever left you with someone before?"

"No, but I've always known he's been preparing for this."

"What's this?"

"The big drop."

I hear the Velcro rip. He opens the binder and pulls something out of one of the folders.

"He left this."

He hands me an envelope. I fumble my glasses back onto my face so Mason won't see me tear up. I don't have to open it to know it's full of tens and twenties.

chapter fifteen

I STAND IN FRONT of my bathroom mirror examining my Morning Old Face or MOF as I've come to
think of it. It's a syndrome I've identified that occurs
when I first wake up and my face looks much older
than it is. My color is bad. I have dark circles under
my eyes. My cheeks sag. The lines on my forehead
pop out. Later in the day I improve, but until then
I wish I could wear a Cinderella false face. I actually
priced them at Walmart last Halloween. They're only
a couple of bucks. The ones with hair are a little more.

When we were kids, Grandma was always telling
us she was "about to have a come apart." It was one of
the few regional expressions from her own childhood
in Georgia she retained after marrying my grandfather, a Pennsylvania boy who was stationed at Fort
Benning before and after World War II.

Neely and I used to dig each other with our elbows and snicker as we imagined Grandma literally
coming apart, limbs dropping all over the kitchen,
hair falling out, eyeballs hitting the linoleum and rolling under the refrigerator.

I've always known what those words were supposed to mean, but today I believe they truly describe me. I've dealt with a lot of stress and high-pressure situations throughout my life but too much has happened in too short a period of time, and I have too much to fix and solve and protect today. I don't feel like I can cope. I want to crawl back into bed with my MOF, and a cream-filled Zuchelli doughnut, and watch bad TV.

But I can't. For starters, I have an abandoned little boy downstairs eating non-fake Cinnamon Toast Crunch who happens to be a nephew I never knew I had.

I also have dozens of missed calls on my cell, including one from the mayor and another from the president of the town council reminding me that I'm obligated to give a full account of any shootings at the next meeting. They only require this so they can hear the gory details firsthand and then dole it out one gossipy spoonful at a time to their friends and families.

Before I go back to the station and begin the endless paperwork and media song and dance resulting from last night's shooting, I'm going to swing by and see Grandma. She has this ability to help me conquer my problems without ever providing any useful answers to them. I also want to tell her about Champ and Mason. And I also want to pump her for information about the Trulys.

It occurred to me when Miranda was slandering my mother and me and mentioned her friendship with my grandmother who had refused to claim me that my grandmother who not only claimed me but practically raised me was a player in all this, too. She's lived in Buchanan since arriving here at the age of twenty already pregnant with the baby who would be too pretty for sandboxes and strained spinach. Miranda Truly is probably ten years younger, but they would know each other or certainly know of each other. Between Grandma and her circle of friends at the home, I can find out more about the Truly family in the time it takes to drink a pot of coffee than Nolan and his databases could ever uncover.

I put on one of my most serious summer suits, since I'll be giving interviews: a pale gray skirt and jacket with a tiny pink pinstripe. I usually wear an old broken-in pair of gray faux-leather pumps with a reasonable heel but as I stand in front of my shoe shelves today feeling overwhelmed and insecure, my hand seems to have a mind of its own and reaches for my new four-inch stiletto, blush suede, peep-toes. I'll be taller than just about every man I come in contact with today, and if that doesn't intimidate them, my fabulousness will.

I make Mason take a shower and change his clothes while I return phone calls. I begin by calling the hospital. Zane's still in ICU. There's been no change in his condition.

Champ remembered to leave Mason's clothes and belongings behind when he took off in his car this morning. The boy has a suitcase and a duffel bag. He won't let me look in either of them. I agreed as long as he promised me he had no animals or weapons.

"You look nice, Aunt Dove," he tells me as we meet near my front door.

He's changed into a pair of bright blue soccer

shorts with a silver stripe down the sides, a yellow Guns N' Roses T-shirt, and another pair of orange socks he promises are clean.

"Do you know who Guns N' Roses are?" I ask him.

"Dad likes them," he replies.

He scrunches up his face, grabs an imaginary mike, and launches into an Axl Rose falsetto.

"'Welcome to the jungle. We got fun and games . . . ,'" he shrieks.

"Okay. You've convinced me."

"I like their name," he says. "I like it when things go together that shouldn't go together."

"Like your socks and everything else in your ward-robe?"

He gives me an almost pitying look.

"Orange goes with everything."

I have no choice but to take him to Neely's. He says he can stay by himself, but I'm not comfortable with an unsupervised nine-year-old hanging out in my house. I don't tell her we're coming. She had a rough night, too. I decide it's better to tell her what Champ has done in person and then dump his off-spring on her. If I called her first, she'd say no, and if I showed up anyway, she'd send Smoke out with a note attached to his collar.

It's another beautiful day. Low eighties. Dry. Not a cloud in the sky. Our Junes are usually a mishmash of rainy, frustratingly cold days interspersed with bouts of freakish heat and humidity so high the air is almost drinkable. Boots with a parka over cutoffs and a tube top is common attire for a summer cookout around here. The weather's been almost too nice. People are being lulled into a false sense of Santa Monica perfection that's going to end badly for them when the temperature suddenly drops into the fifties and it pours for a week straight.

Neely's dogs come trotting out of the woods to greet us, tongues lolling, tails waving. They don't make a sound, but the trees all around us are filled with chirping birds and chattering squirrels jumping from branch to branch.

"Have they ever killed anybody?" Mason asks before getting out of the car.

"Of course not. Didn't you play with them yesterday?"

He nods.

"Then you know they're very friendly, very well-trained dogs."

"Yeah, but they look like they kill people all the time."

"Well, they don't."

"But they could."

"But they don't. Are you afraid of them?"

"No. But I might need someone killed someday."

This conversation is starting to concern me. I'm reminded again how little I know about him and his life with his father.

"Like who?"

"I don't know."

He turns away from me.

"A bad guy," he says, and opens the door.

Kriss, Kross, and Owen descend on him. They love kids and don't get to be around many. Maybe stays back. I wonder if he can sense telepathically that something terrible has happened to his buddy Tug and he's not feeling social. I'm sure he knew when Tug was here yesterday that he was a wreck.

Smoke waits for Neely, who comes strolling down the gravel drive with her hands in her jeans pockets.

"I'm glad you're okay," she says to me.

"I'm fine."

"Zane?"

"Too early to tell. Still unconscious. You want to tell me who's paying for Sandra?"

"I have some money stashed away."

"On top of what we pay for Grandma's home, you can afford Sandra? You realize there's no way Tug isn't going to jail for this unless Sandra is given the opportunity to razzle-dazzle a courtroom with a bunch of extreme emotional disturbance rigamarole, and those billable hours are going to add up to the cost of a house."

"Rigamarole?" she repeats with an amused cock of her head.

"I'm serious, Neely."

"Don't worry about me. I'm not going to do anything stupid."

"Hi, Aunt Neely," Mason calls out, waving from among a forest of swaying tails.

"Hi, Mason."

She waves back and says to me, "What's he doing here?"

"I need you to watch him."

"Where's Champ? Oh no. Don't tell me he thinks he's going to use us for babysitters all the time if he moves back here. I mean, Mason's a cute kid—"

I hold up my hand to cut her off.

"Sit down. I have something to tell you."

"Sit where?"

She gestures all around her at the trees, the gravel parking lot, the kennels behind her office.

I take a deep breath and blurt out, "Champ left."

"What do you mean he left?"

"He's gone. His stuff. His car."

I take the envelope of cash out of my purse.

She stares hard at it. I try to figure out what she's thinking and can't. I'm surprised when she finally looks back up at me and is obviously angry.

"He's become his dad. He's the Envelope now."

"That's not fair," I instinctively rush to my brother's defense. "Champ didn't abandon his son. He's been with him for nine years."

"And that makes it okay? What is the age where walking away from your kid is acceptable? Disowning him from birth is bad, but nine is okay?"

"We don't know he's abandoned him."

"What about his mother?"

"Dead," I tell her.

This gets no reaction from her. I know she won't ask for more information. She finds details annoying. She brushes them away on her quest for the big picture like raindrops from a windshield.

She plunges her hands back into her pockets and peers up at the blue sky through the treetops, shaking her head.

"I knew something was wrong. It was too weird for him to show up all of a sudden after all these years. He came here on purpose to dump his kid on us."

"We don't know that."

"Yes, we do."

The heat in her voice is unusual for her. Smoke cocks his head. His black eyes set in his white wolfish face have been fixated on her during our entire conversation.

"Listen to yourself," she chastises me. "You'd never defend this kind of behavior in anyone else. Stop making excuses for him. Something bad happened to him a long time ago. Something incredibly bad. But it doesn't give him a free pass to be selfish for the rest of his life."

"How has he been selfish?" I cry.

Smoke whines softly. She reaches down and pats his head.

"You, me, and Grandma," she explains. "People think being selfish means hogging the blankets or not sharing your french fries but the ultimate selfish act is hurting the people who love you. He cut us out of his life because it was easier for him. He never gave a thought about what it would do to any of us."

She's right, but I can't blame Champ for hurting us. I've never been able to blame him for anything. After what he's been through I do believe he's earned a free pass, but she's also right that I wouldn't feel this way if he were the brother of some random woman who walked into the station telling me he left his son with her. I'd be sympathetic to his past but I'd be adamant that he needed to put the welfare of his child ahead of his old wounds.

"Rules of behavior apply to people as well as dogs," Neely falls into her instructor voice. "A well-trained dog can be part of every aspect of your life while a dog that misbehaves ends up in the pound. No matter how much you explain this to people, there's still those idiots out there who equate training methods with torture and think making a dog listen to you is being hard on him."

"What are you saying? We failed to train Champ properly?"

"I'm saying he needed someone to help him and that should've been us, but he bolted the minute he was off his leash."

"And what would you do with that dog once you got him back?"

"First step, kennel him."

"Oh, great. We should've locked up our brother?"

"Figuratively."

"And how were we supposed to do that?"

Smoke raises his left paw, his sign he's distressed. He only shakes with his right paw.

She stoops down and wraps her arms around him.

"Make him explain himself to us instead of making him dinner," she replies, her tone softening. "You were right last night. I had him for a whole day and didn't ask him a single personal question other than 'Are you still a Steelers fan?' and 'What made you buy a Kia?'"

"The hamster commercial?" I ask her.

She nods.

"Now you're being selfish," I tell her. "Don't hog all the guilt. I want my share."

"Can't you find him?"

"I'm going to try, but I tried for years to find him

before. What makes you think I'd have better luck now?"

"Sneaky little bastard," she comments, getting back to her feet. "Remember when he disappeared for a day and it turned out he was hiding in different places all over the house, we just couldn't find him?"

"I wanted to kill him."

I can't prevent the words from coming out, and the fact that I wanted to stop them makes me realize how often I censor my thoughts about my brother. The trauma he suffered elevated him to some kind of saintly martyrdom in my eyes. It's a relief to feel something negative about him again no matter how small or fleeting. It restores his humanness.

Neely shoos Smoke in the direction of Mason and the other dogs. We both watch him trot away.

"I can't keep Mason," I say as much to myself as to my sister. "I don't know anything about kids."

"I don't know anything about kids either."

"I have a job."

"I have a job, too."

"But yours is more flexible."

"No, it isn't. I have four K-9s coming at the end of the month. That's a full-time commitment on top of my private lessons and classes. And my volunteer work at PAWS and the ASPCA. I'm busier than you. And besides, my job is more important."

"How can you say that? What's more important than maintaining law and order?"

"You think the dogs I train don't help maintain law and order? And they save lives."

After what happened last night, this last remark stings.

She's right. The dogs she's trained have pulled people from burning buildings and from under rubble after explosions and earthquakes. They've tracked down hikers lost in the woods, rescued drowning children, helped capture criminals, and sniffed out illegal contraband. She keeps scrapbooks documenting all of their careers, every commendation, every mention in the media. Every birthday is noted with an updated photo; they all look alike to me.

When the dogs retire from service, she sends each one a leather collar with gold studs and ten pounds of frozen marrow bones.

"You have a job with health insurance," she tells me.

"So?"

"He's going to need health insurance. Kids get sick a lot. They break bones. They stick things up their noses."

"You have health insurance, too."

"But I have to pay for mine."

"God, we sound like old ladies."

"Speak for yourself. I'm not old and I'm no lady."

She starts walking away.

"Go to work," she says without looking back at me. "The citizens need you. But so does this little guy."

She needs me, too, and I need her. Most days this is enough to see me through.

SANCTUARY RETIREMENT and Convalescent Home has been around long enough that it's still called a retirement and convalescent home, not an alternative living environment for mature individuals. Neely and I looked at a few of those, too, and Neely informed me if there ever comes a time when she has to be permanently kenneled, she wants me to have her put down. I promised I'd do the best I can.

Sanctuary is on the outskirts of town, handy for both of us. The main building is an impressive three-story redbrick farmhouse with dozens of windows trimmed in white that belonged to a prosperous family who woke up one day a hundred years after their farm was established to find the quaint country road the house faced was now a highway with a Walmart going up in full view of their front porch along with the inevitable strip mall that always accompanies the megaretailer like arms stretched out in a yawn of consumerism. They sold the house and land to a developer who hasn't done much with it except to tear down the old barn, attach a generic hospital-looking addition to the stately old house, and build a driving range next door. The back of the home has a spacious patio that looks out on a serene expanse of forested, rolling hills, but the residents prefer by far to sit on the front porch where they can watch the traffic on Jenner's Pike and the happenings in the Walmart parking lot. In summer, some of them drag chairs off the porch onto the lawn to watch the line of golfers whack away at buckets of balls.

Grandma isn't ill. She's old and brittle. She has severe arthritis in her knees and needs a walker to get around. During the course of two years she broke a wrist and a hip and cracked a rib. She recovered amazingly well for someone her age, but she agreed with Neely and me that it probably wasn't safe for her to live on her own anymore. She was approaching ninety at the time, but it was still hard for her to give up her independence. She mopily moved into the home and within a week, she was organizing *Downton Abbey* parties and leading walker aerobics. As often happens in small towns whenever people all of a certain age are thrown together, it turns out she knew practically everyone here, and of course, they all knew who she was, the mother of poor, beautiful, murdered Cissy Carnahan.

Time has been good to my mother's memory. More than three decades have passed. The town is full of people who weren't even born when she died, and if they are aware of her story, it's only the sensational headlines relating to her demise and not the details of her life. Her peers are in their seventies and Grandma's are in their nineties. Age has mellowed many of them, and society's views have softened. Unwed mothers are everywhere now, and my mother's wanton behavior and style of dress is tame compared to everything they see on TV and in the pages of the *People* and *Us Weekly* magazines littering the common area of the home. My mother may have been promiscuous and a lousy housekeeper, but she was well-mannered and respectful in public. Nothing like those Bad Girls or Real Housewives. Here, in Grandma's world at least, she's no longer thought of as an aggressive immoral temptress but as a victim of male lust, her dalliances merely surrendering to their constant hounding, and her three bastard children upgraded from untouchable trash to forgivable mistakes.

Three old men wearing ballooning shorts with skinny pasty legs sticking out of them ending in black socks pulled halfway up their calves and some sort of orthopedic sandals have formed a peanut gallery for the driving range today. They all have on ball caps and wraparound sunglasses that remind me of the goggles we used to wear in high school chemistry labs and are drinking mugs of coffee that look too large for them to lift. They represent a third of the male population here. Of the forty residents, only nine are men.

I greet them and the ladies sitting on the front porch.

"Your grandma's inside playing gin," one of them tells me.

"At eight in the morning?"

"Playing for buttons."

"Ah, serious stuff."

The women spending their final days at the Sanctuary with my grandmother are part of a generation and a class of blue-collar and farm families that made their own clothes. Most of them were very accomplished seamstresses in their day and accumulated treasured stores of unmatched buttons over the years. My grandma kept hers in a coffee can. When we were kids, Neely and I would dump them out on the floor in a kaleidoscopic spill of little discs and sort them into piles ranging from the boring white ones to the ones we were convinced were made of actual jewels and precious metals. I can still remember some of my favorites: a navy blue one with a silver anchor on it, a red one carved to look like a rosebud, a glass one that sparkled like a diamond, a coppery one shaped like an owl, a purple Lucite one shaped like a heart, one made from peach-colored taffeta, one from scarlet velvet.

The residents use them in place of money when they gamble. No one takes these stakes lightly. Everyone is sentimentally bound to their buttons.

I check in at the front desk. I can see Grandma from here sitting at one of the tables in the common area with her friend Marge, both of their heads bent over their cards, their cottony-white hairdos emanating a tinge of chrome blue underneath the fluorescent lights. Grandma's coffee can is sitting next to her elbow. Marge keeps her buttons in a shoe box.

The rest of the tables are sparsely occupied with other ladies having their morning coffee. Some are reading the local newspaper. Someone must have woken up the managing editor last night, because Zane's shooting made the front page. There's a picture of Tug being led in handcuffs to one of our cruisers and one of Brie Massey following her son's gurney to the ambulance. Thank God there isn't one of me, but I'm sure some of the neighbors got me with their phones. They might have even taken video. I'm probably getting a million hits on YouTube right now stalking across the Massey front yard in my fiesta wear clutching my gun. I've probably overtaken Grumpy Cat.

"Hi, Gram," I greet her, and lean down to give her soft, powdery cheek a kiss; it's like brushing my lips against a moth's wings.

She grabs my hand resting on her shoulder and gives it a quick squeeze, never taking her eyes from her cards.

I called and told her I was coming.

"Aw, don't bet the turquoise button," I tell her.

"It's fake."

"I know, but I love that one. Neely and I used to pretend it came from a real Indian."

"Let's take a break, Marge," she says, putting her cards facedown on the table. "This one won't let me bet anything. It will be nothing but, 'Oh, no. We used to pretend that one came from the moon, and not that one, we used to pretend it was real gold from a pirate's chest.'"

Marge smiles.

"Just a bunch of worthless old buttons," she says, surreptitiously unfolding a napkin and placing it on top of her pile.

I crane my neck to get a look in her box, and she quickly covers it with the lid.

"We saw you on the late news last night," Marge tells me as I take a seat between the two of them.

Great, I think to myself. There wasn't time for anyone from the nearest TV news station to get there. Someone did film it with his phone.

"What were you wearing?" Grandma asks.

"Ugh." I throw my head back and close my eyes. "I was almost killed, Grandma. Maybe you should ask me about that."

"There's no such thing as almost killed. You're either killed or you're not."

I feel her pat my thigh under the table.

"I'm glad you weren't killed."

I don't have much time. I should already be at the station. I'm not going to beat around the bush.

"So you saw Tug Truly was the shooter?"

"What a terrible, awful thing," she says, shaking her head.

Marge clucks her agreement.

"First the girl is murdered, then the brother murders someone else."

"The Massey boy is still alive. He made it through surgery. There's a chance he's going to be okay."

Grandma doesn't seem to hear. I've cleared center stage for her. All combined there are thousands of years of wisdom living under this roof and everyone is prepared to speak up on just about any topic, but my grandmother is the undisputed authority on murdered family members. Every ear in the room is tuned to our conversation, although everyone is acting like they're absorbed in something else.

This is exactly what I want. People sometimes clam up if you ask for information point-blank, but if you have a private conversation with someone loud enough for them to overhear and leave gaps in the story only they can fill, you'll have your answers in no time.

"There's nothing worse than having your child die before you," Grandma continues. "Cissy was so young and so pretty."

"I'm not allowed to talk about an ongoing investigation," I announce, "but I have to tell you, when I went to talk to the Trulys . . ."

I pause for a beat to let the wheels start turning.

"All I can say is they're a tough bunch of people."

Marge snorts but doesn't say anything else.

"They're not tough; they're mean," I hear a quavering voice behind me.

I glance over my shoulder and see a perfectly

round little woman, with round glasses and a round knot of gray hair on the top of her head, cutting a piece of jelly toast with a fork and knife.

She doesn't look up.

"I'd never met any of them before, and I was just doing my job," I continue, "asking questions about Camio, when Miranda Truly comes in the room and starts saying horrible things about Mom. I guess she knew Donny's mom, Betty."

Another snort from Marge.

"What did she say?" Grandma asks indignantly.

"The usual, Gram. You know. And she called me slut spit."

A communal gasp goes up around the room accompanied by a lot of head shaking.

"Mean as cat shit," the round woman mutters.

"I don't care. That stuff doesn't bother me. What I couldn't get over was how rude she was"—I look back over my shoulder again at the round woman who's now sipping her coffee and still won't make eye contact—"for no reason. I don't know this woman. I've never done anything to her. And I was in her son's house as the chief of police investigating her granddaughter's murder. Blew my mind."

I sit back in my chair and wait.

"Miranda Truly hates everyone," a woman in a high-necked yellow blouse covered in a bluebird print says from across the room. All her wrinkles seem to run vertically as if her face has been folded the way Neely and I used to make paper fans.

"Except for her own family," I provide.

"Ha!" the round woman explodes behind me.

This time I turn completely around and stare at her until she looks at me.

"She almost got her own sister killed from spreading hateful lies about her," she supplies.

"Sweet Jesus," the woman with the pleated face says with a laugh. "I haven't thought about Adelaide in years. Is she still alive?"

"Last I heard, Bev," Marge joins in the conversation. "She had to move away for her own safety," she says to me.

"What happened?"

Everyone grows silent. I think I may have asked too bluntly and missed my opportunity when the round woman says, "Ask Mary Jo over there. She was married to one of their cousins. She saw the whole thing with her own eyes."

I follow her gaze to a woman who doesn't appear to be all that much bigger than Mason. She's wearing a brown velour tracksuit, enormous tortoiseshell glasses, and a reddish-brown wig that I can only describe as a hair hat.

"I saw Eddie almost take his aunt's head off with an ax," Mary Jo says matter-of-factly, "but as far as the whole story behind it, I only know rumors and gossip like everybody else."

"Eddie?" I ask. "Miranda's eldest son Eddie? The one who served in Vietnam?"

"That's the one," Mary Jo says. "It happened not long after he came home. He was a mess back then. A scary, scary man."

"Addy was Miranda's older sister," Bev explains. "A

sweet girl. Pretty. Hardworking. Never complained. The best cook you ever wanted to meet."

"She could cook," the round woman concurs.

"Miranda hated her. Always did. No one ever knew why."

"Jealousy," the round woman says with a sigh. "Pure and simple."

"Miranda went around telling the most ridiculous stories about Addy," Mary Jo says. "We all knew they weren't true and we ignored her, but who knows how many people who didn't know Addy the way we did might have believed them?

"Long story short, Miranda told her own children the same twisted tales about Addy from the time they were little. And she had some doozies. One of her favorites was Addy locked her in a shed out back for three days and nights trying to starve her to death, and her mother didn't even notice she was missing 'cause she didn't care about her."

"I heard that one," a woman sitting in a wheelchair with a book in her lap pipes up.

"Then there was the time the girls were playing tag in and out of the house," Mary Jo goes on. "This was back when storm doors had real glass in them. Addy went running outside. Miranda was hot on her heels and reached out to push open the door, but it had swung shut and latched and her hands went through the glass."

"Ouch," I comment.

I've started picking through Grandma's buttons. She doesn't seem to notice.

"Her mother took her straight to the hospital. She got a couple of stiches in the palms of her hands. It wasn't Addy's fault, but she felt bad about it anyway. The version Miranda tells is Addy threw her out a second-story window and while she lay on the ground with shards of glass sticking out of her face and neck the rest of the family ate their dinner."

I look up from the coffee can of buttons.

"No way. She told people this?"

"Like I said, she told her own kids. And she also told them Addy hated them. She said, 'Aunt Addy may seem nice to your faces, but behind your backs she tells everyone you're ugly and stupid and not good enough to play with your cousins.' Of course they believed her. They were her children. She was their mother. Why on earth would she make up terrible things about her own sister?"

"It's absolutely diabolical," I comment, completely fascinated, repulsed, and slightly impressed.

"She wanted them to hate Addy as much as she did. But it goes deeper than that. She has the same attitude toward the whole world. Before Miranda married into the Trulys, they weren't a bad family. They weren't all that good either. But nothing like what they've become. She's created her own little country and everyone in it hates and distrusts anyone who isn't one of them."

I see a glimmer of colors I recognize buried in the button mix. I dig deeper and come up with Neely's favorite, a deep inky blue one swirled with green glitter. She used to call it the Earth button.

"So what about Eddie and the ax?" I wonder.

All eyes are on Mary Jo. No one is pretending not to listen anymore. Even some of the staff have drifted into the room and are spending an unnecessary amount of time wiping and straightening things.

"Family picnic," Mary Jo begins. "Too much drinking. I didn't see what went on between Miranda and Addy, but apparently Miranda was all upset over something Addy said and Eddie went crazy. He picked up an ax and went after her screaming about how she tried to kill his mom when they were kids and how he knew she thought they were all white trash and on and on.

"The other men kept him from hurting her, and that was the end of that. Addy moved away. She was already a widow by then. Her husband had died in a mine cave-in two years earlier. I think the only one of Miranda's who kept in touch with her and her kids after she moved was Clark. He was close to her youngest daughter, Layla."

"Wasn't that the one who died in the car wreck?" wheelchair lady asks.

"Yes."

"Where did Addy move to?" I need to know.

"Up around Altoona."

"And that made her feel safe? That's only a couple hours from here."

"Far enough. Eddie could barely get off a barstool back then. He wasn't going to chase someone over a mountain."

My phone rings. It's the station. I excuse myself and walk away to take it, then return to Grandma.

"I have to go," I tell her, "but I have some important stuff I need to talk to you about, so I'll be back soon."

"Let me walk you out," she says, rising to her feet, and maneuvering expertly into her walker.

"Thank you, ladies. You've been very helpful."

I get some smiles, some nods, some waves, and a salute from the round woman.

"So how reliable was that information?" I ask Grandma as we slowly make our way to the front door.

"Very. And it's amazing when you consider none of them can remember what they had for dinner last night."

"What about you? Can you remember?"

She smiles.

"Dry roast beef, lumpy mashed potatoes, gravy from a can, and succotash."

I put my arm around her shoulders.

"When I come back I'll bring you a pizza."

"Dove," she says, her tone and expression turning grave. "Lucky came by to see me."

"That fu—"

I stop myself.

"Did he upset you?"

"No. He just wanted to tell me that he's planning to make your life and Neely's life miserable until you admit you didn't see him kill your mother."

"And that didn't upset you?"

"You girls can take care of yourselves."

We've reached the door. One of the old guys is standing, yelling, and gesticulating wildly at one of the golfers who's brandishing a golf club from behind the protective netting and yelling back. I don't know what's going on, but I want to get out of here before it turns into something I might have to mediate.

"He says you lied to protect the person who did it," Grandma reveals.

I don't respond to this. She doesn't press me on the subject. She studies me from behind her glasses. Her eyes are alert and seem almost cunning to me. If they are the windows to our souls, then hers is thriving while its mortal home is rapidly deteriorating.

I wonder how Grandma would've dealt with watching her beautiful daughter grow old if she had been given the chance. I'm sure she believes it would've been a crime for a girl that pretty to wrinkle and fade.

My mother looked beautiful in her casket, she told me after the funeral. I was there, but I wouldn't go look at Mom's corpse. *Nothing dead can be beautiful*, I wanted to tell her, but I knew this would only confuse her, since she believed nothing beautiful could ever be dead.

Mom's face had been spared. Considering the rage behind the attack, some people wondered about that.

"Maybe I can understand that," Grandma says. "But why punish Lucky?"

"He hit my sister."

"A man should sit in jail for thirty-five years because he hit your sister?"

She eyeballs my purse. She knows.

"No," I tell her, as I put the button I stole into her outstretched hand, "but I'll settle for that."

chapter sixteen

LUCKY WAS DOOMED without Neely and me; all we did was save the jury some deliberation time.

The evidence against him was damning enough to convict him. He had motive and access. His finger-prints were all over the bathroom, although no one could say how long they'd been there. He had a history of violence, including two restraining orders taken out by old girlfriends, and a drunk and disorderly collar that involved punching the arresting officer.

If I had been Lucky's public defender, I would've put the victim on trial. It wouldn't have been hard to convince twelve Laurel Countians that Cissy Carna-han had it coming to her in the scarlet letter sense of justice. My mom wasn't a bad person as far as they knew. She didn't lie, cheat, or steal. She was friendly. She worked for a living between boyfriends and prior to marrying Gil. She was helpful when she felt like it, generous when it was convenient, and could be knee-buckling charming, but like all attractive women who flaunt their looks, she had a lot of haters— women who were jealous of her, men who wanted her and couldn't have her. Maybe she didn't deserve to die because she was an adulteress with a slutty past and three illegitimate children, they could have reasoned, but her lifestyle had certain risks attached to it, and one of them may have been the possibility of being beaten to death with her son's baseball bat by one of her jilted lovers while taking her nightly bubble bath. Lucky still would've been found guilty but maybe of a lesser charge with a lighter sentence.

Either way he would've ended up in jail whether he did it or not, with or without our testimonies.

I used to use this as an excuse to make me feel better; now the truth behind it is beginning to make me feel sick. Lucky was pushed in front of a bus. By me. It doesn't matter if he was already stepping into its path.

I arrive at the station still thinking about Lucky. At least it helped me temporarily forget about last night.

Our parking lot is full of TV news vans. A clump of reporters and cameramen, most of whom I recognize, are positioned in front of the station house listening to someone who's supposed to be me but I'm late.

I walk over, pausing to glance inside my department car I asked Singer to clean after my pastry-fueled extraction of information from Derk Truly yesterday. There's not a single spot of mud, icing, or blueberries anywhere.

As I near the crowd of reporters, I hear the voice of Bennett Sawyer, our illustrious mayor, local State Farm insurance agent, and cousin to the Sawyers who own the dairy.

Ben has been in love with me since the first grade. The feeling has never been mutual, but I still have the Valentine he gave me that year because it was one of the most beautiful things I had ever seen: a red-and-pink baby bird with wings made of real feathers sitting in a nest of silver glitter chirping teeny hearts from its beak. I thought it rivaled any of the gifts my mom had ever received from her boyfriends.

Now he has three grown kids, a wife who wears the pants in the family, and the biggest assortment of polo shirts I've ever encountered. These shirts are not flattering to his beer belly, which is technically a wine belly; he fancies himself a connoisseur and even converted his toolshed into a wine shed, since his wife flatly refused to let him turn her basement home gym she never uses into a wine cellar he might.

He sees me coming toward him and breaks off in midsentence to proclaim, "Here comes our hero now."

I'm not comfortable with being called a hero for a number of reasons but most notably because I didn't do anything remotely heroic. Zane Massey may die. Tug Truly is going to jail. Camio's killer is still out there. But I don't bring up any of this.

I smile, nod, greet the reporters I know by name, and field a few questions while Ben stands off to one side in a blue-striped purple polo and a military green Indiana Jones fedora. His hair started falling out a couple of years ago. He should just shave off what's left, but instead, he's taken to wearing a ridiculous array of hats. I can feel his eyes crawling all over me.

My ability to arouse passion in men who arouse nothing in me is the stuff of legends.

"I'm glad you're okay, Dove," he says as he follows me inside the station house.

Phones are ringing. The seats in the waiting area are full. Even Everhart, our new daddy, is here, along with Dewey, Singer, and Blonski, who I look at pleadingly as Ben and I pass. He knows what that means.

"Chief," he says, excusing himself from the woman he was assisting at one of the desks and rushing up to me. "We've got a situation you need to address. It's urgent."

Ben looks eagerly back and forth between the two of us, not showing any signs of leaving.

"Might be a matter of life and death," Blonski adds.

Amazingly, Ben takes the hint.

"Oh, then I should get out of your way."

"Yes, that's probably a good idea. I'll be in touch later."

"What a tool," Blonski mutters under his breath.

"What's going on around here?" I ask him.

"People are freaking. None of this has anything to do with the Truly murder or the Massey shooting. They're just upset by what's going on and want us to hold their hands and tell them it's going to be okay."

"Aw, that sounds right up your alley," I tease. "I have three girls on their way here. Camio's best friends. I'll need the interview room. But I want to talk to Tug first."

Everhart has wandered over. He gives me a cigar with a blue wrapper that reads: IT'S A BOY!

"Thanks. You know you can have today off."

He smiles a little guiltily.

"Nah. I got so many relatives at the hospital right now, I can't get anywhere near the Jakester.

"Tug's not here," he tells me. "Dewey and I moved him to Broadview already."

"Why?"

"Sandra Goldfarb," Blonski says, squinting his eyes and puckering his lips like he's just taken a gulp of a skunked beer. "She came breezing in first thing this morning and announced she's his lawyer. I told her you wanted to talk to Tug before he was moved and get a statement and she looked at me that way she does. You know. Like you're a bug."

"Or a mortgage payment," Everhart adds.

"She said he's not giving a statement and wanted him moved to Broadview and arraigned this morning. That we should have moved him last night. That we were derelict in our duties."

Singer joins us, wide-eyed and breathless.

"She didn't want you to talk to him, Chief, and get him to accept what he did," he says in a whisper. "She's planning on some big trial where she's going to argue he was out of his mind when he did it."

"Having a dissociative episode, probably," Blonski provides knowingly, folding his arms across his chest.

"Dammit," I say. "Well, she's going to have to let me talk to him, although now she's going to be in the room with us and not let him say much of anything."

"But we do have some good news," Singer says, practically bursting with excitement. "Corporal Greely sent us copies of the surveillance footage from the Dairy Queen. Lonnie Harris and Camio had an encounter."

I follow the three of them and sit down at Singer's computer. He plays the footage for me.

The images were captured in the drive-through. Lonnie's in his pickup truck. The girl in the window is Camio in a red-and-yellow Dairy Queen cap with her dark hair pulled back in a ponytail. The sensation of seeing her alive, smiling, talking, making change, handing over a bag of chili cheese dogs, fills me with an indescribable sadness. I'm the last person who held her in this world. She was dead already, but I pulled her body close and helped bring her out of the anonymous grave her killer intended for her. I never met her when she was alive. I've only seen frozen moments of her existence, a candid on Zane's phone and her DMV and autopsy photos on Nolan's murder board. Here she is in front of me, vibrant and cheerful, putting in her hours at work, looking forward to seeing Zane later, looking forward to the rest of her life, but then her expression darkens. Lonnie has said something vile to her. She closes the window and turns away.

The film jumps to three days later. Lonnie's back. Camio obviously remembers him. Her sunny smile doesn't surface. Her mouth is set in a stern line. She reaches to take his money, and he grabs her by her wrist. All of us watching the film flinch. She twists her arm and is able to wrench it free. Lonnie grins.

The footage is time-stamped three weeks ago.

"This is huge," I say.

"Chief," Dewey calls me. "There's some teenagers outside say they're supposed to talk to you but they won't come inside."

"Girls?"

"And boys."

Nolan must be doing backflips over this new information, I think to myself as I walk outside, although the acrobatics will occur only inside his head. I've never seen him outwardly express enthusiasm or happiness, but I like to think there's a mini Nolan inside him who jumps up and down like a cricket and shouts tiny, tinny "yippees" whenever something goes right.

He's probably at Lonnie Harris's home right now with a team of troopers tearing the place apart.

I recognize Camio's three best friends—Katy, Mindy Dawn, and Madison—from social media photos and the ones I looked up in their yearbook. All three of them are in cutoffs and skimpy tops with tiger-claw rips across the front. Their faces look the same to me: vague, almost drunken expressions on soft features that have gone straight from baby fat to couch-potato chubbiness. Footwear, hair color, and body shape are the only ways to tell them apart. Katy is busty and margarine-haired in clunky cork-heeled platform sandals. Mindy Dawn is a tall, lanky brunette with hoops in her upper lip, wearing scuffed white cowboy boots with fringe and silver beads. Madison is a heavy girl with crow black tresses streaked in electric blue in a pair of gladiator sandals that crisscross up her calves.

The two boys with them are interchangeable redneck spawn: jeans, black tanks, shit-kicker boots, empty wallets on chains, faded snuff can rings on their back pockets, camo ball caps. Their arms and shoulders are inked in bullets, bloody knives, and leering skulls, and their faces are carefully arranged in the sullen smirks of those who are proud of not trying. I know the armor well.

One of them stands possessively close to a Kawasaki motorcycle, the consolation prize for those who can't afford a Harley. It's in excellent condition, though. This boy cherishes his bike. The other leans against a black Ford Silverado that's seen better days. They both have chews in.

I was around the same age as these kids when my mother was murdered. For that reason and a few others, this time in my life has remained very clear and vivid to me. I remember exactly what it felt like to be them. Same town. Same school. Even though I had recently become the stepdaughter of one of the wealthiest men in town and now lived in a big house and wore much nicer clothes, I also knew what it was like to be poor, to be neglected, to have wants and desires that constantly went unmet.

I might not have been friends with this particular five standing in front of me, but I would've tried my best to be friendly with them. No matter how badly I was treated by others, I always tried to take the high road. I was a collector of people. I had friends from every clique: potheads, eggheads, meatheads, rednecks, no-neck jocks.

I was a caretaker, negotiator, organizer, and motivator long before I'd use these same qualities in my future profession, and I took my status seriously at the time. I even gave up my earlier sluttiness because I realized, as a popular kid and a leader, I had to set an example and be a role model no different than if I'd been a professional athlete or a congresswoman. I had a lot of boyfriends and went through them quickly but always one at a time, the same way I ate potato chips.

I'm going to give these kids the benefit of the doubt. The girls were friends of Camio's, and from what I know of her, I like her, therefore, I should like them.

"Hello, ladies," I say, smiling, as I approach them. "Thank you for coming in."

"We're not going to talk to you," Katy says.

"Why not?"

"We just don't want to. You can't make us, right?"

"By not wanting to talk to the police you make yourselves look suspicious," I explain, glancing quickly at all of them, trying to sort out the hierarchy and their relationship to the boys.

Mindy Dawn sidles up next to the boy with the bike. He flops an arm possessively around her shoulders. Madison glares at me, my shoes, the parking lot blacktop, the sky, Katy, her own fingernails; I notice they're elaborately, professionally polished in black and gold animal-print patterns.

Katy's in charge. She continues to be the group's spokesperson. I notice her nails are painted a rainbow tie-dye. Mindy Dawn's appear to be plain red.

"We already talked to that big dumb trooper," Katy says. "He knows we got alibis."

I secretly smile to myself wondering if the big dumb trooper is Nolan; he's been called much worse.

He told me they do have strong alibis and none of them have a motive, but they're teenage girls and I know everything that happens to a teenage girl can in some way be construed by her as something worthy of killing for or over.

"Don't you care about Camio?" I ask them. "About finding her killer?"

The boy with his arm around Mindy Dawn drawls, "You know who her killer is. Tug took care of him for you. For all of us."

All three girls look noticeably upset upon hearing his proclamation. There's no reason to think they didn't like Zane. He was a nice, good-looking kid and Camio's boyfriend.

"Zane didn't kill Camio," I correct him.

"Yeah, he did."

"And you know this how?"

He shifts his arm from Mindy Dawn's shoulders and wraps it around her neck in a chokehold. She leans back into him obediently. He's not going to answer me.

"Can you tell me this much?" I say, returning to the girls. "Did Camio ever talk to you about a customer at Dairy Queen who was giving her trouble? A scary-looking guy who harassed her in the drive-through?"

They all consider the question, look at each other to confirm, and shake their heads.

"Come on," Kawasaki says. "Let's get out of here."

"Just a minute, girls. If you weren't planning to

talk to me, then why did you come down here? Why didn't you call and say you changed your minds?"

Before any of the girls have a chance to reply, the boy tongues his wad of tobacco from one side of his lower lip to the other and says, "We thought it would be fun to come over and tell you in person just to piss you off."

His excessive, unwarranted dislike of me seems familiar, but the déjà vu moment passes. I can't remember when and where I felt this way before.

"I didn't catch your name," I say to him.

"I didn't give it to you."

His silent friend snorts a laugh from his post near the truck.

The girls shift around uncomfortably. Any bravado they arrived with has abandoned them. They look at their hero with awe and a little disgust. I'm sure he doesn't see the disgust.

I do the worst thing possible I can do to a kid like this. I ignore him.

"I really like your nails," I say to Madison. "Yours, too," I add, turning to Katy. "Did you get them done around here?"

I walk toward them and they reflexively hold out their hands and spread their fingers.

They tell me the name of the place. I know where it is.

"They did a great job," I say admiringly.

Not one to go unnoticed, Mindy Dawn untangles herself from Kawasaki's arms and comes over to our female powwow with her hands extended like a sleepwalker.

Her nails are a solid fire-engine red but with a tiny crystal glued in the middle of each tip.

"Those are so pretty," I say, taking her hands in mine.

"Camio had hers done like me," Mindy Dawn provides. "She loved anything sparkly."

"Only hers were pink to match her toenails," Madison pipes up, "and the crystals were heart-shaped to match the anklet Zane got her."

She barely gets out the last few words before she chokes up entirely.

A girl Madison's age with weight issues usually either succumbs to the abuse she receives from others and becomes timid and deferential or fights back by hating everyone before they can hate her. I had put her in the second category, but tears start streaming from her eyes and it's obvious she loved her friend Camio.

Mindy Dawn and Katy get misty-eyed as well.

I'm one step away from convincing them to come inside the station with me and plying them with free cans of pop and little bags of vending machine Cheetos when Kawasaki commands, roughly, "Stop talking to her. Don't you see what she's doing? She's trying to make you think she likes you so you'll talk to her. She doesn't give a fuck about your fucking nails."

"Why don't you stay out of this, Mouth?" I snap back at him.

"What'd you call me?"

"Mouth. Since you won't tell me your name I have no choice but to identify you by your most outstanding quality, and so far that appears to be your big mouth."

I watch rage cloud his face and fear replace the grief in the girls' eyes.

Bullies are cowards, and their cowardice usually originates from abuse they suffer at home. I bet he's used to far worse put-downs coming out of his mother's or father's mouth, but he's not conditioned to tolerate them from an outsider.

"He's one of Camio's cousins, Jared Truly," Katy reveals, her voice rushed and a little panicked.

Everything about this confrontation suddenly makes sense, especially my earlier déjà vu. I remember now. He reminds me of Miranda Truly and her attack on my mother and me.

"You don't have to talk to her," he goes on, never taking his eyes off me. "She can't make you. Cops got no power over us. We're minors. They can't do nothing to us."

He walks toward me. I wonder fleetingly if he'd be stupid enough to hit a cop, but he drops his head and spits a brown stream of snuff onto the toe of my right shoe.

"See that?" he says, raising his head and wiping a string of tobacco juice off his chin. "She can't hit me or spit back or even call me a dirty name 'cause then we cry police brutality and sue her fat ass."

When people find out about my mother's murder and the ensuing trial and everything my siblings and I went through, they often think this must be the reason behind my choice of law enforcement as a career. Maybe I wanted to emulate the police officers who helped me through the ordeal, or maybe I wanted to catch bad guys like the one who killed my mother. Nothing could be further from the truth. From beginning to end, the cops, the lawyers, the press were a bunch of self-serving buffoons. One of the mouth-breather local officers at the scene even made a pass at me. I guess seeing your mother beaten to death by her ex-boyfriend was supposed to make fifteen-year-old girls horny.

What did happen on that day is I fully accepted the fact that I had failed my little brother, that he could never be fixed, and I could never make that right. I had been living with evil and never noticed it. I had not been diligent enough.

From that day forward, I was on high alert and eventually wanted to do something productive with my suspicions. I know I can't save people or even change them. But I can make them behave.

"You're right. I can't do anything to *you*," I tell him.

I occasionally wear my gun. Depends on what my day looks like, what outfit I have on, how I'm feeling. Otherwise, I keep it in my purse holster. After last night, though, I'm going to have it on my person for a while.

I reach beneath my suit jacket and calmly take the Glock from my hip holster. It feels completely different than it did last night. Walking across the Masseys' front yard, it was heavy and cold in my grip. Now it's as light as a plastic squirt-gun party favor. I almost feel like giving it a Wild West gunslinger twirl before aiming it at Jared Truly's motorcycle.

I know what I'm about to do could easily cause me

to lose my job. Police officers aren't allowed to discharge their weapons unless they intend to use deadly force, and I don't want to kill this boy.

I shoot out his front and back tires. Nothing more.

One of the girls screams. Terror briefly wipes away Jared's practiced sneer of inferiority-bred superiority before his face darkens with rage.

He lets loose with a string of swear words and flings a savage stare at me before rushing to his bike.

My officers come charging out of the station house along with everyone else.

"Nothing to see here, people," I say as I stride in their direction.

I stop and watch Jared and his buddy load his disabled motorcycle onto the truck. He stays there beside it. Mindy Dawn joins him. Katy and Madison crawl into the cab with the quiet boy. They screech out of the parking lot.

"Officers," I say to Dewey and Everhart, "please follow that driver and ticket him for having passengers in the open bed of a pickup truck."

I turn to Singer and Blonski, who watch me with a mix of uncertainty and absolute trust.

"I've had enough of these people," I tell them, handing over my gun to Blonski. "Go get me Shawna Truly. It's time for us to have a talk. Here. In *my* house."

chapter seventeen

I GET OFF THE PHONE with Neely as Singer and Blonski escort Shawna Truly into the station. The timing is perfect, since the reason my sister called was to tell me Derk has shown up at her place with a backpack and a BB gun, wanting to play with Mason. The Trulys live a good ten miles from Neely. I have no idea how he got there: if a family member dropped him off; if he hitchhiked; if he traversed the route by leaping from treetop to treetop.

I wonder if his mother has any idea where he is.

I stand in the doorway of my office and watch her follow Blonski to our interview room. Everyone else watches, too. No one can seem to look away. I'm not sure exactly why. She's a large woman but we've all seen larger. She's wearing turquoise blue and yellow-striped capri leggings that wouldn't look good on a supermodel let alone a woman with a lot of bulk, and a voluminous sleeveless grubby white blouse that reveals upper arms the size of newborn Jakester, yet we've all seen plenty of bad outfits. She has a certain amount of notoriety now, but we all know it's not polite to stare at a woman who's just lost a daughter to the county morgue and a son to the state correctional system.

We all watch because there's something morbidly magnificent about her. Like a she elephant grandly walking through a group of deadly big cats to get to the water hole, she has a regal disinterest in her surroundings because she knows nothing can touch her. In her mind, she has reached a place where she is separate. She is above us all reveling in an enviable freedom because she doesn't care about anything anymore.

I'm about to make her care.

Our interview room is claustrophobically small, gray, windowless, stuffy, and has a metallic echo if someone speaks too loudly; it's sort of like hanging out in the drum of a washing machine.

I let her sit for a few minutes and watch her through our surveillance camera. People do some interesting things when left alone in this room. They pray, cry, sing, whistle, talk to themselves, drum their fingers, tap their feet, put their heads down on the table and nap. I've seen women touch up their makeup and men drop to the floor and do push-ups. One guy took out a pack of cards and started playing solitaire.

Shawna does nothing. She sits and looks straight ahead as motionless and permanent as a boulder.

She doesn't turn at the sound of me coming through the door. She doesn't focus on me when I take a seat across the table from her.

I slam down her high school yearbook and glance at the tobacco stain on my shoe as I cross my legs.

Singer offered to try to get it out, but I told him no. This is my brown badge of outrage.

"What the hell happened to you?" I ask her.

Her eyes flicker in my direction but don't stay stuck on me.

"I said, 'What the hell happened to you?' How much do you weigh? What do you think?" I pick a ridiculous number. "Six, seven hundred pounds?"

She looks at me again and quickly looks away, but the color's rising in her face.

"When's the last time you washed your hair?" I goad her.

I reach for a pair of reading glasses hooked to my jacket pocket and put them on while I open the yearbook and start flipping through pages.

Most people are helpless in the face of their teenage pasts. That time holds something they want to relive or finally bury, something they need to defend or praise, a long overdue apology or clarification they've been waiting for. Nothing can make them question everything about their present lives like that backward glance at all the self-doubt and lost possibilities.

I was everywhere in my yearbook, hamming it up in glossy candids, sitting on bleachers for team group photos, captured in sports action shots (I was the scrappy point guard of our district-champion basketball team and the school record holder in the 400 meters), posed in the library with the other student council officers (I was the president), smiling humbly on the football field in my strapless magenta dress with the handkerchief hem as first runner-up in the homecoming court. (I took the defeat well. I knew there was no way I was going to beat Lori Ann Van Cherry with her Heather Locklear hair.)

Still there's nothing in those pages that revealed who I was. It only showed what I did. I don't feel the need to explain this, but most people must. I'm counting on Shawna being one of them.

"You think you're going to be one of those people who has to be buried in a grand piano because they can't find a casket big enough?" I ask conversationally, returning to the subject of her weight. "I bet if they cremated you, you'd fill two urns. You know . . ."

I look up at her as if I've just thought of something important.

". . . your heart could give out at any minute. People your size drop dead all the time. Have you made your peace with Jesus?"

This last question seems to bother and confuse her. Her cheeks are burning a bright pink.

"Has Miranda helped you with that?" I wonder sweetly. "Ah, here it is."

I spin the yearbook around so it's facing her and point at an eighteen-year-old Shawna Ridge.

"That's a beautiful girl, right there. As pretty as Camio. Look at that smile, all that shiny blond hair, those big blue eyes."

She tries not to look but can't stop herself. Her lips droop in a pained expression, and her head is drawn forward and positioned tautly over the page as if an invisible hand has grabbed her by the back of the neck and is holding her there.

"A girl like that had big dreams, I bet. What were they? What did you want to do with your life? Be a movie star? You were pretty enough. How about a teacher? A doctor? A roller-derby queen?"

I pull the book back and flip to another page I looked up earlier. It's a candid of her and a couple of friends at a football game. She looks happy and alive, waving a cheap plastic pom-pom. I slide the book back to her.

She lifts one of her hands and touches the picture with two fingers.

"What were your dreams, Shawna?" I push her. "Did they include spending every minute of every day sitting comatose on a couch in Clark Truly's house, wallowing in filth, waiting for him to get home from his latest run so he can smack you around?"

She looks up at me again. She's paying attention now. Her eyes snap with wary alertness. I notice her throat convulse slightly as she swallows.

"Or is he afraid of you now?" I ask with a big smile. "Is he afraid you'll sit on him?"

Our eyes meet. I lower my glasses down my nose so she can get a better look at mine.

"I repeat, 'What the hell happened to you?' "

The next ten seconds seem to take an eternity to pass. I've tried to reach the girl in the yearbook who I believe is still alive somewhere inside the woman sitting across from me. Be alive, I silently will young Shawna. Don't be a tomb, I silently beg her older self.

"I don't know what you want from me," she finally speaks.

Her voice trembles, but I don't think from nervousness or grief. She's angry.

"I got nothing to say about Camio. And if you

think you can get me to turn on my family just by being mean to me—"

"Stop."

I hold up my hand, take off my glasses, and sink back in my chair disgustedly.

"Stop right there. Spare me the 'I pledge allegiance to the Trulys' bullshit. You're not one of them, Shawna. You married in."

She stands up, completely throwing me for a loop. I stand up, too.

"You don't know nothing about me or them!" she shouts.

"You want to get into this with me?" I shout back. "You really want to do this? Do you know who I am?"

Without realizing it, I walk around the table and get right into her face.

"Don't you dare give me any of your 'woe is me, downtrodden redneck, us against them' bullshit."

I push closer. We're nose to nose. Any closer and we'll be kissing.

"I see your drunk, wife-beating husband and witch of a mother-in-law and raise you one dead father, one whore mother, and a fucking pedophile!"

She's taken a step back from me and bumped up against the table.

I stick a finger in her face and hiss, "Now tell me why you don't care about your children."

Shawna's eyes go dark, and I hear a small intake of her breath. It's that moment in news footage when a building is about to be demolished—whether it be by a wrecking ball, an earthquake, or terrorists in a plane—when the destructive act has occurred but all there is to show for it is a puff of smoke before the structure suddenly, violently, swiftly collapses.

She falls back down into her chair and begins to sob.

I return to mine and watch her. She covers her face with her hands, and her shoulders shake. It's a noise like nothing I've heard before; the heartbreak behind it I recognize as human, but the unfettered pain is an animal's howling.

In the midst of her wails, she says something I can't make out.

"What, Shawna? What did you say?"

She throws her head on top of her arms on the table and continues to cry.

I lean so far forward to hear her response, our cheeks brush against each other and I feel her breath moist inside my ear, but she doesn't say anything more.

I sit up again.

"What did you say, Shawna?" I repeat.

She raises her head and slams her fists on the table.

"They're not mine!" she screams.

Her body is wracked with fresh sobs. She shakes so hard I fully expect the little room to start to crumble around us. Finally, her crying subsides and she takes a long shuddering breath.

She looks up at me and I see young Shawna shining in her eyes. She sticks out the tip of her tongue to catch a tear dribbling down her cheek and onto her upper lip.

"They're not mine," she whispers.

• • •

"CAN I GET YOU a glass of water?" I ask her.

I've let five minutes pass. I thought about leaving her alone again, letting her have some time to herself and collect her thoughts, but when I tried to get up, my legs wouldn't work. Shawna's revelation has left me stunned, shaky, and exhausted.

"Some coffee? Tea?"

She shakes her head. She blows her nose on one of the tissues she keeps pulling from her purse. Women sometimes keep one or two loose ones or one of those mini travel packets, but I've never seen this many coming out of one handbag like scarves from a magician's sleeve.

She takes the latest used one and places it in the snotty, tear-saturated pile mounting at her elbow.

"The children aren't yours."

I put it out there as plainly as possible. We'll see where it goes.

"Derk and Tug are mine," she sniffs. "The older three are Clark's."

"So he was married before?"

She shakes her head.

"So he wasn't married to their mother?"

She nods.

"This all makes a little more sense now," I tell her. "I didn't realize how much younger you are than Clark until I started checking you out and snooping around for your yearbook."

We both look down at the book. She's kept it open to the page of her and her friends and glances at it from time to time. I think the image is giving her strength.

"There's ten years between us."

"How old were you when you married him?"

"Nineteen."

I must make an unconscious sign of disapproval because she quickly follows with, "No one made me."

I smile at her. "That's kind of a strange piece of information to provide unsolicited."

"I just mean I wanted to marry Clark. He was good-looking and nice to me. And I needed to get out of the house."

She stops talking and looks guiltily at her hands clutching yet another tissue she's begun to slowly shred.

I don't let my mind wander into Shawna's childhood home. I don't want to know what went on there. It's enough to know she probably had no family support, no one to run to. On the contrary, she had a need to escape. The Trulys sniff out the weak and unprotected.

I feel bad now about asking her about her dreams earlier. She was probably so beaten down by the time she met Clark Truly, taking care of him and his three kids, that retiring to the couch at the end of the day may have seemed like a dream to her.

"I'm impressed," I say, trying to make it up to her. "Really, I am. That's a lot to take on. Three stepkids when you're just a kid yourself. How old were they then?"

"One, four, and six," she rattles off automatically. Her expression softens, maybe from recalling pleasant memories of them at that age or maybe secretly rejoicing in the fact that now one's dead, one's in jail, and one's saddled with a baby of her own.

"You must've really loved Clark," I say.

"I didn't know about them," she lets slip out.

She flashes me an embarrassed look.

"What do you mean?"

"When I married him, I didn't know he had kids. They were kind of presented to me afterward."

"Wow," is all I can think to say.

I sit back in my chair and take a moment to digest yet one more unbelievable ingredient in the steaming stew of Shawna Ridge Truly's life.

"How could you not know?" I ask her.

"He never talked about them. Nobody did. I never saw them."

"So what did you do when you found out? If it had been me I would've headed straight for divorce court."

She smiles. It's the first time I've seen her lips in any shape other than a scowling frown or an angry straight line, and the difference changes everything about her. Years fall from her face. When I met her I thought she might be in her late forties. She's only thirty-four. Now she looks it. Her posture even improves.

"I was kind of a hell-raiser back then," she says. "I had a temper. I said there's no way I'm staying. I can't take care of three kids. He lied to me and it was a big lie. I was getting out.

"We had a huge fight. Miranda was the one who calmed me down and convinced me to stay on for a little while and see if we could sort things out."

At the mention of Miranda's name she swallows her smile and the glimpse of a younger, livelier Shawna is gone.

I wait. At this point, she wants to tell me her story. I can sense it. We all want someone to know our worst secrets, even if it's only one other person. It makes them real. I wonder if she's ever unburdened herself before. I don't know who she could have possibly confided in.

She digs back in her purse. I'm surprised when she doesn't bring out yet another tissue. Instead, it's a wallet from which she extracts an old photograph hidden behind some credit cards. She hands it to me. It's a picture of a cat.

"The only thing I brought with me from home besides my clothes was my cat, Sugar. I named her that because she was all black except for white around her mouth and chin like she'd been eating sugar."

I get a sick feeling in the pit of my stomach; the tale of Sugar is not going to end well.

"I'd had her since I was little."

The tears begin. They're silent this time. They stream down her round cheeks.

"I woke up the next morning after the fight and she was dead. Slit wide-open from her little white chin down through her belly."

"Oh, God," I say.

I reach out and take her hand across the table.

"I'm so sorry, Shawna."

"I should've run," she says, her voice coming in hitching gulps, "but I didn't have anywhere to go. Police don't care about dead cats, and my family cared even less. None of them would tell me who did it. No one was sorry. They acted like it was no big deal."

I move my chair around the table until I'm sitting beside her and put my arm around her shuddering shoulders.

"I woke up the next morning and all my hair had been cut off. And my privates shaved."

"Jesus," I say under my breath.

"Miranda must've put something in my food and drugged me 'cause I'm a light sleeper."

I'm rarely left speechless, but this is one of those times. I don't know what to say to her. I try to imagine what would have been going through her mind back then, the combination of fear, disbelief, and isolation that would have allowed Clark and Miranda to control her and eventually own her altogether, body and soul.

"Other things happened, too," she continues but doesn't elaborate. "Anyway, I decided it was best if I stayed. Tug came along the next year and after a while I got used to Clark's kids. I came to love them."

"Where was their mother during all this?"

"All Clark would tell me was she's dead. Killed in a car accident."

The hair on the back of my neck stands on end, but I'm not sure why.

"You just told me you loved Clark's children. What changed?"

She goes back into her purse for another tissue and wipes her face.

"One day," she begins, "Miranda takes me aside

and tells me the mother of Clark's children was his cousin Layla."

This latest horrible piece of the puzzle doesn't arouse any kind of reaction from Shawna. I suppose by the time she discovered it, nothing could shock her.

"I guess they'd been doing it for years. No one knew. Layla kept having babies, and her mom kept helping her raise them. No one ever knew who the father was or if there was a bunch of fathers. No one cared. She said it was her business and everybody stayed out of it.

"After she died, Clark went and told her mother— his aunt Addy—everything and said he wanted the kids. I don't know what went on between them. Miranda and Addy are bitter enemies. I've never even met her. But I would guess Addy loved those three babies and wouldn't want to give them up. But under the circumstances what could she do? They were Clark's legal property. Then I found out for myself why she might have let them go."

She stops speaking and gives me a frank look with no emotion behind it like she's giving me the instructions to install some random appliance.

"She was repulsed by them after she knew," she says, " 'cause that's how I felt. I could barely look at them after that. And I hated myself for feeling that way. It wasn't their fault. But I couldn't love them anymore."

As much as I'd like to end this conversation, there's an important reason why I began it and I haven't reached my goal yet, although I'm not sure I can get there through Shawna alone. She's talking well now. I need to fire questions at her.

"Why would Miranda tell you this? She had to know it might affect the way you felt about the kids. You'd think she'd want you to love them and take good care of them."

"She knew I loved them. I think that's why she did it. She wanted to hurt me. She was always hurting me. Hurting everyone. It's what she does best."

"Do the children know?"

"They think their real mom was a nice lady who was killed in a car accident."

"They don't remember anything about living with her or Addy?"

"Camio was only a few months old when Layla died and they went to live with Clark and Miranda. Jessy would've been three. Shane five. They were too young to remember."

"And they've never wanted to find out anything about their mother? They've never wondered why they've never met any of her family?"

"Once Miranda tells you something's a dead topic, it's a dead topic."

I let the bomb drop.

"Could she have killed Camio?"

The same smile she showed me when she described herself as a hell-raiser returns but only for a second before it turns into something dark.

"Death would be a gift," she tells me. "An escape from her. She wants people alive so she can torture them."

"Is there anyone in the family you think might have done this?"

She shakes her head. "These are hard, mean people, but they seem to draw the line at killing. Besides, none of them had a reason to kill Camio."

That you know of, I think to myself.

"Who do you think did it?" I ask.

Her eyes fill with tears again, but they don't fall this time.

"A stranger," she says, running her finger over the photo of her cat. "I want it to be a stranger."

chapter eighteen

I LEAVE THE INTERVIEW ROOM with the intention of stripping off my clothes, kicking off my shoes, getting in my car, and driving naked until I reach the nearest ocean, then jumping in and swimming until I find a deserted island where I can live alone far away from all people and the things they do to each other.

But the feeling passes.

I run into Nolan and two uniformed troopers. I was right. They had been searching Lonnie Harris's house earlier. They stopped by on their way out of town after hearing shots had been fired at the police station.

"That was a great interview, Chief," one of the troopers says.

The other trooper smiles and nods his agreement.

Nolan stands behind them, hands in his pants pockets, his lower jaw working a piece of gum, his sunglasses hiding his eyes. He doesn't say anything.

Singer and Blonski are here as well. I motion them toward me and speak to them out of ear range of the others.

"Give Mrs. Truly a few minutes, then take her home. Be very polite and kind."

I look around the station. My eyes light on Everhart's desk. A bunch of his buddies who race in demolition derbies with him on the weekends thought it would be funny to send a big sissy bouquet of congratulatory flowers to his workplace.

"And give her those flowers," I add.

Blonski raises his eyebrows at me.

"Just do it."

I know Nolan will want to talk to me, but I don't return to him and his troopers. I head to my office.

I take a seat behind my desk and try to look as composed as possible.

I haven't done much to personalize this space other than put a few framed photos on top of my filing cabinet. There's one of Champ when he was Mason's age in a Pirates ball cap with a bat thrown over his shoulder grinning at the camera, freckle-faced from the summer sun. Gil would have already been molesting him but we didn't know. Or I should say some of us didn't know.

I've studied this photo hundreds of times looking for an outward sign I missed. I've tilted it from side to side thinking in a certain light at a certain angle it might react like a truth-revealing hologram and his dear face would turn into a screaming death mask of agony, or I'd spy Gil with devil's horns sprouting from his shellacked hair leering over his shoulder, but I've never been able to see anything in it but a normal, happy-go-lucky boy, and I guess that's why I like it.

Next to it is a photo of Neely and me, six and eight

years old, standing next to Grandma's old Plymouth on an Easter Sunday suffering the indignity of being forced to wear dresses to church, our skinny arms linked, our knobby-kneed bare legs ending in identical white patent-leather shoes we immediately scuffed up, me accidentally, Neely on purpose. My dress was navy, fitted, with a belt and Peter Pan collar that I wore like a uniform, and I had to restrain myself from directing traffic in the church parking lot or telling the little kids to slow down; Neely's was a pale yellow shift patterned with tiny daisies that she loathed.

Grandma used to call us Salt and Pepper. It wasn't a wildly original nickname, but it made sense for us: Neely with her light, almost Nordic good looks (Passing Through could have been a Viking, I used to tell her, or maybe a ski instructor) and me with Denial Donny's black Irish mop of tangled dark curls and dark brown eyes that Mom's genes had diluted slightly, like putting cream in coffee.

The final photo is one of only a handful I've ever seen of my mother and the three of us. We're sitting around a picnic table at the Lick n' Putt. We look completely normal. A lovely woman with three lovely children about to eat some lovely hot dogs and fries and play some miniature golf.

I've seen even fewer photos of my mother alone. For all her vanity, Mom didn't like to have her picture taken. Neely and I used to theorize while playing in the attic of our little crooked house amid the spider skeletons why this was true. Neely thought she was a wanted woman, on the lam from the police. I thought it was because she believed, like some tribes of Native Americans and Australian aborigines, that the camera had magical powers over her inner essence and she was protecting herself; it would've been a crime for a girl that pretty to have her soul stolen by Kodak.

These photos make me want to laugh out loud remembering the good times we had but also make me want to cringe.

"We're funny and sad at the same time," Neely once said to me while riding our bikes home from Laurel Dam, "like a turtle on its back."

I suddenly realize why the only picture Shawna Truly displayed in her house was her wedding photo to Clark. I thought it was a stroking of her ego recalling how pretty she once was, but it was self-flagellation, a constant reminder of the mistake she made that sealed her fate and made her what she'd become.

Nolan doesn't knock. If I were a man, he would knock. Even if he didn't respect me or like me or suspected me of murder, he would knock.

I'm mad at him. Not because he didn't knock but because he didn't take advantage of my vulnerability last night and have sex with me at a time when I clearly wasn't thinking straight but when I desperately wanted to be manhandled into a state of mind-numbing distraction.

He stops in front of our murder board. It's only the second one I've put together during my tenure as chief. The other two homicides that occurred during my career happened when I was a trooper and when I was an officer here.

"I always thought the purpose of a murder board was to be able to share information with your squad," he says.

"It has wheels. I move it back and forth. I like to look at it when I'm in my office."

He glances behind and sees there's a chalkboard on the other side.

"We borrowed it from the elementary school," I explain. "We don't have a lot of murders here."

He gives me a patronizing shake of his head.

"Did you borrow the markers, too? I like how every suspect gets his own color. Why does Eddie Truly get green?"

"Ex-military."

"The Massey kid, blue?"

"He's a boy."

"Lonnie Harris, brown?"

"Shithead."

"Shawna Truly, purple?"

"Royalty. The Queen of Crud."

"Miranda Truly, red?"

"Satan."

He shakes his head again.

"Did you find anything at the Harris place?" I ask him.

"A lot of porn. A loaded handgun in an unlocked closet, and he and his wife have three little kids running around."

"Lovely."

"But nothing that ties him to the Truly murder."

I take a pack of markers out of my top desk drawer and join him at the board.

Under Shawna's picture I write in purple: *Camio wasn't her child. Real parents were cousins. Could this be motive?*

Nolan studies it for a moment. He still has his sunglasses on. I can't tell what he's thinking.

I take out the black marker and in the center of the board I write: *Could this be THE motive?* I add arrows pointing from the question to each of the Trulys.

He doesn't comment.

He takes the green marker and writes under Eddie: *No alibi.*

Then he trades the green marker for my black one and writes on my timeline of Camio's missing hours: *TOD 7:30 p.m.*

"You have the definite time of death and didn't tell me? And it's over an hour before Zane received those texts?"

I was ready to tell him everything I learned about Miranda Truly this morning from my grandmother's friends and also that Eddie tried to kill his aunt Addy with an ax once, but if he doesn't feel the need to share, neither do I. I'm glad I didn't get around to writing any of it on my board.

He hands me the marker and takes a seat in the chair on the other side of my desk. I go sit behind it.

"You were worried what happened at the Massey house was going to cause you to lose your job," he begins the lecture I knew I was going to receive from him.

He jerks a thumb in the direction of the parking lot.

"That's going to cause you to lose your job."

"I appreciate your concern."

"I'm not concerned. I don't care one way or another what happens to you. You can keep on being police chief of Bumblefuck, USA, or you can retire and take your pension and open a little pink doodad shop and get a bunch of cats."

Nolan doesn't swear, so his description of Buchanan is out of character and means he's more upset than he's letting on.

"A doodad shop?" I wonder.

"You're a better cop than that," he goes on. "What you did. That was beneath you. You know better."

"If the next thing out of your mouth is I trained you better," I interrupt him, "I'm going to . . ."

He leans forward in his chair. "What? Shoot me?"

I lean across my desk.

"How many years ago was that?" I reply, trying not to shout. "I'm sorry I didn't follow in your footsteps and become some hotshot state CID detective. I'm sorry me and my ovaries let you down."

"You know your ovaries had nothing to do with it."

We're at a standoff. He sits back in his chair first. I take that as a sign of victory. I know he's taking it as a sign that he's more mature, more responsible, a better leader, a better cop.

"Did you surrender your weapon?" he asks.

I give him a quick salute. "Yes, sir."

"What'd this kid do to you?"

"He got to me. That's what he did."

"Is something going on with you lately I don't know about?"

I shift in my chair. I don't want to talk to him about my personal life. I certainly don't want to admit I'm letting anything in it affect my work. I'm definitely not going to tell him Lucky is running around threatening my sister and me and planning to sue us in civil court for lying in criminal court. But I have to tell him about Champ because I need his help. He is, after all, the Inevitable.

"There is something," I begin.

He stares at me until I think the hidden intensity of those masked eyes are going to make my head explode.

"My younger brother, Champ, who I haven't seen in twenty-five years showed up yesterday with a nine-year-old son I didn't know he had and left him with me."

He remains silent. He's not going to make this easy.

"I have very good reason to think he doesn't mean to come back or at least not come back for a long time. I also have reason to think he might have some alcohol dependency problems. Maybe chemical, as well. I'd like to find him. My nephew seems to be a very nice little boy, but I'm not mother material."

Nolan knows a little about my past. He was twenty years old, in college playing football, working on a criminal justice degree, and already planning to attend the state police academy when my mother was murdered. We met seven years later and he knew who I was. He remembered the crime, the victim's maiden name, and the names of her daughters. Even before he became a cop, Nolan followed accounts of all local crime like he already was a cop. He never asked me for any lurid details or pried into how my siblings and I survived; I appreciated this. It was enough that he knew this terrible thing had happened to us.

He knows nothing about what Gil did to Champ. He does know Champ moved away and I rarely heard from him.

He reaches underneath his suit jacket and brings out a pad of paper and a pen.

"When did he leave?" he asks.

"Last night. Or it would have been this morning. He was staying at my house and I got home around two a.m. I don't remember when I fell asleep. He was gone when I woke up."

"Why didn't you call when you discovered he was gone?"

"I don't know. I guess I was hoping he'd come back. He still might," I add hopefully.

Nolan ignores me. He knows I wouldn't be talking to him if I thought my brother would return on his own.

"Vehicle?"

"Green Kia Soul. California plates. I didn't get the number," I tell him before he can ask.

He frowns.

"Description."

"Forty-four years old, five-eleven, thin, maybe one seventy. Dark hair and eyes."

"Home address?"

"Don't know."

"Job?"

"Unemployed."

"Wife? Girlfriend?"

"None."

"Son's mother?"

"Dead."

He takes off his glasses and sighs.

"Do you know anything about him?"

"No," I admit.

"Criminal record?"

"I don't know."

He flips the notepad shut. "He's had a big head start. He's got to be well out of the state by now."

I want to say thank you, but he's being too much of a jerk.

"I've got the Truly case and four other active homicides. What do you have on your plate?" he digs at me further.

I think about all his favorite home-cooked meals.

"Tonight?" I reply in a snippy tone. "Stuffed pork chops with mashed potatoes and gravy. And lemon meringue pie."

He stands to go.

"Enjoy your pork chop," he says.

"Enjoy eating cold SpaghettiOs out of a can over your kitchen sink."

I know that even though he's ticked me off I'm going to feel bad for the rest of the day wondering if I hurt his feelings and if he really is going to eat cold canned pasta for dinner and it will be the last thing I think about tonight before I fall asleep. He'll forget I exist the moment he gets in his car and goes back to work.

A man can love a woman and still put himself first; a woman can put a man first she's convinced she doesn't love: this is why I never let myself get serious with Nolan.

He stops on his way out my door.

"Why's the victim's name written in orange?"

I look at Camio's eleventh-grade school photo tacked to the middle of the board. She's smiling sweetly but I know that proves nothing.

"The last picture taken of her when she was alive," I say quietly. "She was eating an orange Popsicle."

THE SHANK, Shank, and Goldfarb law offices are only a couple of blocks from the police station. The first opportunity I get, I call to make sure Sandra is there and then I run over.

Most of the people we arrest and process here in town don't end up employing Sandra. They can't afford her or they don't require someone of her abilities. They do fine with Chet.

I've been grilled by her on the stand a few times. She's sharp, precise, knows every detail of the case she's trying, and doesn't believe in long-winded opening statements or summations, whether they be pedantic or folksy emotional salvos that are supposed to appeal to a jury's desire to see justice done or tug on their heartstrings. She's all about the facts and casting reasonable doubt on them.

When she first breezes into a courtroom in one of her impeccably tailored dark pantsuits, with her short, spiky reddish-brown hair and guileless face without a trace of makeup, there's a moment when everyone thinks she's an overeager teenage boy intern who's arrived to stack folders and fill water pitchers. Once her identity is established, this feeling is quickly followed by a small-town instinctive dislike and distrust of her confident urban energy and androgyny that we assume must mean she thinks she's smarter, hipper, and better than us. But after watching her at work, we then start to think of her as the class brainiac, the one we make fun of and would never invite to a party but whom we cozy up to whenever we need help with some impossible homework assignment. The only difference is when Sandra helps you out it's not because she's a geek who wants you to like her; it's because you have or have not committed a crime that intrigues her and you give her a lot of money.

"Chief Carnahan," she says, looking up from her Mac for an instant. "I just got back from a hearing and my secretary told me gunshots were heard coming from the direction of the police station earlier."

Her fingers tap over her keyboard. She keeps her nails short but they're always polished, today in a flat coppery shade. It reminds me that I want to check out the nail salon where Camio's friends go.

"That's sort of the reason I'm here," I tell her. "I only need a moment of your time."

She motions to the chair in front of her desk. It's caramel leather and probably costs as much as all the chairs and the rest of the office furniture at the station house.

I slip off my stained shoe and place it on her desk: my desk is metal, the color of a tarnished spoon; hers is some kind of honeyed exotic wood that would make the Lorax cry, polished until it glows.

"Nice shoes," she says. "They look expensive."

"They're not. Kohl's. With my thirty percent off coupon and Kohl's cash they were almost free. I bought three pairs that day."

She picks it up and examines it with pursed lips.

"Sometimes they have good shoes. What happened to it?"

I give her an emotionless recap.

"During the course of the Camio Truly murder investigation, I was questioning a young man and his companions in the police parking lot when he spit chewing tobacco on my shoe in the hopes of provoking me into assaulting him. I responded by shooting out the tires of his motorcycle."

"Instead of shooting him?"

"Yes."

"I admire your restraint. Did you provoke him in any way?"

"No. He did it in order to show his friends that no matter what he did to me, I couldn't do anything to him because he's a minor."

"A minor? How old?"

"At least sixteen. And he's a Truly."

"Relation to Camio?"

"Cousin."

She puts the shoe down, folds her hands together, puts them against her lips as though she's kissing her knuckles, and stares at the framed copy of the signed verdict from a Supreme Court case she argued only three years out of law school hanging on the wall behind me; I have a scenic wonders of Pennsylvania wall calendar.

"I don't anticipate any trouble from him and his family," I also provide. "What happened in that parking lot will be embarrassing to them. They won't want to call public attention to it."

I know this doesn't mean they won't deal with it privately and if they do, it might result in something unpleasant happening to me or my property. It will most definitely lead to something unpleasant happening to Jared. I almost feel bad about this.

"But some concerned citizen might have a problem with what I did," I finish.

"And this is why you're here?" she asks.

"I decided I should retain a lawyer. Just in case."

She reaches for a yellow legal pad and pen.

"If asked, how would you defend your actions?"

"Let's blame it on menopause."

She doesn't bat an eye.

"Although I haven't gone through it yet," I add.

Perimenopause she writes on her legal pad and looks back up at me, waiting for me to go on.

Our town council is composed of Ben, six other men, and two women who are twenty years apart in age but both are a prim personality type that would leave a room if the inner workings of their police chief's withering reproductive organs and her raging hormones came up at a meeting. The men would leave the building.

"I've given it some thought, and if there's one thing that would make our town council want to wrap up an investigation into my conduct as quickly as possible, it would be the word 'menopause.'"

"It's brilliant," Sandra confirms.

"Thank you."

She stands and extends her hand to me.

"Ruined pink suede pumps. Perimenopausal mood swings," she says while we shake. "I think that's all we'll need. I know where to find you if I have any more questions."

"I'm going to talk to Tug tomorrow," I think to add.

"As long as I'm present. Let me walk you out."

She takes her suit jacket off a hook behind her door and slips it on over the cream silk shell she's wearing with her charcoal gray pinstripes even though she's only going to walk me to the elevator at the end of the hall. It must be automatic for her, the same way Grandma always reached for a bathrobe whenever she got out of bed to check on us even though she was already wearing a long, heavy nightgown even Superman's X-ray vision would've had a hard time penetrating.

"About your retainer?" I begin.

"Forget it. I don't think this is going to go anywhere, and besides, your sister has agreed to pay all of Tug's legal fees. I think it's enough that one Carnahan sister is going to buy me a new Mercedes."

We're about to pass Chet's office across the hall. The door is open. I'm pretty sure I hear a TV, some female shrieking, shouts and cries from a studio audience.

"I like the baby blue one you have now," I tell her.

"It's six years old and I want one in champagne."

Chet erupts into his distinctive snorting guffaw followed by a rousing cheer of affirmation for Jerry Springer's decision to let the catfight continue.

Sandra walks over and closes the door.

chapter nineteen

THE REST OF MY DAY doesn't improve. Most of the headaches have nothing to do with Camio's murder. The regular responsibilities and duties of my department don't cease because of one girl's death. The paperwork isn't reduced. Our constant accountability isn't eased. The concerns and crises of our citizenry don't disappear.

I try to be my usual accommodating self, but my concentration is shot and my patience worn thin. My thoughts keep bouncing back and forth between all these boys, past and present, suddenly dominating my life; one clinging to life in a hospital bed, one pointing a gun at my head, one with a missing father, one running wild, one being molested right under my nose, one making an unwanted baby and driving his car into a tree.

Their needs have become my personal burden, even the ones of my long-dead father, although I'm not sure what his could be. I'm angry with all of them. They seem to be purposely taking my energy away from the dead girl.

Typical men, Neely would tell me if I explained the phenomenon. *They always expect to come first.*

Typical woman, Nolan would tell me. *Always blaming men for your own problems.*

Just thinking about Nolan and anything he'd have to say on any topic makes my blood boil.

I was on my way out of the station when a woman passed me on her way in to make a complaint. Everyone else was out on a call or sitting at a speed trap. I explained nicely to her that she could have saved herself a trip and phoned, then tried to direct her to Karla to fill out a form, but she insisted she needed to talk to someone in person.

I've been listening to her for twenty minutes and as far as I can tell she still hasn't arrived at her official complaint.

I don't like whiners. My philosophy regarding a problem is fix it, and if you can't fix it, find a way to live with it that is least destructive to yourself and others. Whatever you do, don't talk endlessly about it while you do nothing.

Small-town cops listen to a lot of whining.

I went through a phase about a year ago when we were investigating a string of small arsons and ended up interviewing what seemed like everyone in town, where I could often be heard espousing the wish that people would, "Shut up and deal with their shit."

Apparently I said it so often, my men came up with the acronym SUDS for "Shut up and deal with your shit." It was a quicker way for us to communicate our feelings about someone and also to do it secretly without offending anyone.

We could pass each other in the station with a potential witness or suspect sitting at a desk and say in front of him or her, "I know someone who could really use some SUDS right now." For all anyone else knew, it merely meant we wanted beer.

Singer made us gold-trimmed laminated official membership cards to the SUDS Club and gave them to us for Christmas to put with our creds. We all laughed. It was something only Singer would do. I don't know if anyone else kept his card but I did.

I reach into my purse, take out my wallet, and open it while the woman continues to talk. She doesn't seem to notice. I find the SUDS card tucked behind some credit cards. My gold Visa makes me think of little Goldie Truly sucking on her dog toy, but then I immediately start to think about Derk and Tug buying it for her. Again, the males triumph.

I also find a scrap of a bar napkin from ten years ago. I don't have to look at it to know what's written inside its folds. Nolan took me out for a drink to celebrate when I was hired as chief. We had a good time, one of those nights where I could almost believe we could have an actual relationship if it wasn't for the fact that he had a wife and kids and I had an aversion to actual relationships. I was looking forward to a little Nolan-rollin'-in-the-hay. I figured it should be part of the congratulatory package along with the free drinks and nachos, but he got called in on the job. I went to the ladies' room while he was still on his phone. When I came back he was gone but had written on the napkin, *You're the best man for the job.*

My insides start to turn mushy, but another memory of Nolan pushes the first one aside and they harden back up again.

Not long after I left the state police and started working in Buchanan I went out on a call with another officer who is long gone now. A horse had fallen into an icy, half-empty in-ground pool and broken its leg. There was no way to get him out. In hindsight, we should've called animal control or a veterinarian, but the other officer, who had seniority and a penis that he was constantly assuring me was on the large size, insisted that we should shoot him and put him out of his misery.

The only times I had ever seen a horse being shot was in movies or on TV where a cowboy put a bullet in the animal's head because he'd gone lame. The horse would instantly fall down dead without any blood being shed.

This was not an accurate depiction.

Our horse's head shattered. Even standing several feet away we were both bathed in blood. I was picking out pieces of brain and splinters of bone from my hair for the rest of the day. But worse than this was the fact the horse wouldn't die.

The other officer was the shooter and he shot again, this time in the horse's chest. The animal stumbled to his feet. Now on top of being shot twice, he was going to drown.

I jumped in with him. It was irrational and pointless. I couldn't help him, but I couldn't bear the thought of him dying without someone comforting him.

I stood in the freezing water cradling his big ru-

ined head, whispering in his ear, until his one remaining eye stopped staring crazily and went blank. I
don't know how long it took. Five minutes? Two
hours? It wasn't until I knew he was finally dead and I
crawled out of the pool that I realized holding him
might have scared him even more than if I had left
him alone. I might have made his terror worse.

Sometime during the midst of all this, Nolan had
arrived. He'd been in the area, an occurrence that was
soon to become an unwelcome habit. The Inevitable
would inevitably show up whenever it was most in-
convenient for me.

I was soaking wet and slick with blood, trembling
from shock and the beginnings of hypothermia, my
eyes red from crying.

"Oh, God," I croaked, my voice raw from the cold.
"That's the worst thing I've ever seen."

He gave me a quick once-over. He was mad at me
because I had recently banged his best friend and left
his precious state police.

"Quit whining," he said.

So far the woman across my desk from me has told
me that her kitchen sink is backed up. Not completely
clogged but it drains slowly. Her ex-husband's sister
lives across the street from her and even though they've
managed to stay on civil terms after the divorce—she
accredits this to the fact that his own family realizes
what a worthless pile of crap he is—she's always coming over, walking in without knocking, helping herself
to food out of her refrigerator, drinking her booze, and
borrowing her clothes without telling her when she's
at work. The air pressure in one of her tires is really

low. She keeps filling it with air and it goes flat again. She has a friend who told her if you pour water over the tire and there's a hole, the air coming out will make the water bubble. She tried this and didn't see any bubbles. She's been dating this guy she kind of likes but he talks too much and she's not really that attracted to him, but he has a good job, treats her well, spends money on her, and is nice to her kids.

I leave my SUDS card in my wallet and take out one of my business cards instead, flip it over, and write on the back:

Drano
Lock your doors
Pep Boys on Jenner Pike
Marry him

I stand up, hand it to her, and leave.

NEELY MAKES THE BULK of her living through contracts with the state police and other agencies training service dogs, but she also has a thriving private business. She gives individual and group obedience classes and agility classes and also works with the ASPCA and PAWS when they have a problem dog that has special behavior issues that must be corrected before adoption.

From the amount of cars parked at her compound and the fact that her sentries are nowhere to be seen, I know she's conducting a class. She kennels her dogs except for Smoke, who assists her.

I'm late picking up Mason, but she won't notice. I wonder if she's even aware he's still here.

I walk around back to the practice ring and find Mason sitting on a bench with his binder on his knees. I don't see Derk, but he could be up a tree or he could've disappeared the same way he showed up.

Neely's working with twelve students: six human and six canine.

Mason hears my approach and looks up, smiling. I feel all the air go out of me.

"Hi, Aunt Dove," he says. "How was your day?"

"Okay. How about yours?"

"Okay, I guess. Aunt Neely says you're trying to find a murderer. She says you're going to catch him because you're a good detective. Are you?"

"Pretty good."

"Are you like Sherlock Holmes or Magnum, P.I.?"

"You watch *Magnum*, *P.I.*?"

"Dad likes the classics."

I take a seat on the bench next to him.

The six dogs in Neely's class are all in the down position. Neely weaves in and out among them, stepping over them, leaning down and squeaking toys in front of their faces, trying to get them to break the command. They're all behaving admirably.

"What are you doing?" I ask.

"I'm trying to figure out who's going to quit."

"Ah," I say. "So you heard Aunt Neely's welcome speech?"

He cracks a big smile.

"I filmed her with my phone. I'm glad I did. This stuff is pure gold."

He finds the video and holds up his iPhone for me to see.

Neely and Smoke stand in the middle of a circle of dogs and their owners. She makes Smoke lie down by barely glancing at him. A few of the dogs are bothered by him. They break their sits. One lets loose with a couple of high-pitched yips that make her owner cringe and yank harshly on her leash.

"All of you want to have a dog as well trained as mine," Neely begins. "None of you will succeed."

"'None of you will succeed,'" Mason repeats, chuckling. "That kills me."

"Yes," I chime in. "She's quite the motivational speaker."

"I know from the statistics derived from the countless classes I've taught that two of you will do very well here," she goes on. "You will work hard with your dogs at home and will end up with exceptionally well-trained dogs and live happily ever after."

She begins to pace back and forth in front of the owners and their dogs. Smoke stays put with his head raised and his paws stretched out in front of him. His color and position make him look like a marble statue crouched at the top of a museum's staircase.

"Two of you will end up with dogs who are trained well enough to be functioning members of human and dog society and will be wonderful life-long companions for you," Neely continues, "and one of you will end up with a dog that jumps up on visitors, yanks tirelessly at the leash when you go on walks, and forgets all his obedience commands except the occasional sit you make him do at the dinner table, where he shouldn't be in the first place, in order to give him a table scrap you shouldn't be feeding him. Despite his behavior, you will love him. He will be the one who suffers because you'll be constantly yelling at him and locking him up, which will make him a nervous wreck."

She returns to Smoke and tells him to heel. He jumps up and trots by her side as she breaks through the circle and walks its perimeter with Smoke mere inches from the other dogs, making all but two of them go nuts, barking, growling, straining at their leashes. Smoke ignores the commotion he's causing. He and Neely return to the center of the circle and he immediately sits.

"And finally," she says, "one of you will give up and stop coming to these classes altogether. You won't even email me to tell me you're quitting, which will be just one more example of your weak, wishy-washy personality and inability to see things through to the end that is going to make it impossible for you to train your dog. Look deep inside yourself. You already know who you are."

Mason looks up at me, grinning.

"'Look deep inside yourself,'" he says, and puts his phone down. "Pure gold."

"Can I ask you something about your dad?"

He sighs.

"I know what you're going to ask me. Does he play a lot of video games? The answer is yes. I like some of them, too. I don't think there's anything wrong with it."

I smile at him.

"I don't think there's anything wrong with video

games either. That wasn't what I was going to ask. Does your dad drink a lot of alcohol?"

"Sometimes."

"Does he . . ."

I can't find the right words. I don't need to. Mason has obviously been asked these questions before.

He hangs his head and says very softly, "He doesn't do anything intra venus."

I don't have the stomach for this. At the very least, maybe I can find out their most recent address.

"Where's the last place you were living?"

"Colorado somewhere. With Stevie. I didn't pay much attention. Dad said we wouldn't be there long."

"So you moved around a lot?"

"Dad says it's good to move around. He says if you sit still for too long you become easy pray."

He puts his hands together as if he's about to pray.

"I think he means prey like what a hunter chases," I correct him.

"I think he means someone who's easy to pray for because they got so many problems but you still like them. My mom was easy pray."

"Did you and your dad go to church?"

"I pray to Thor."

We both focus our attention back on the class.

Neely's making the dogs heel one at a time around the circle. A young woman in pink-and-black work-out clothes, matching gym shoes, and a ball cap, with a miniature dachshund is first. She walks at a normal pace; her dog's tiny legs are nothing but a blur trying to keep up.

"Her?" Mason asks. "Do you think she's the one who's going to stop coming?"

I pull a small bag of Doritos out of my purse. I stopped by the vending machine on the way out of work.

"You'd be amazed. Most of the time it's the men who wimp out."

A portly man with a white beard is next. I'm sure he's a big hit with everyone around the holidays. He starts talking the moment Neely gestures at him. I can't hear what he's saying from this distance. Neely stands with her hands on her hips and stares at him. I know she's gone someplace else inside her head and is only seeing his mouth move.

"I know this guy," I groan to Mason, offering him some chips. "This is the fourth session of group classes he's enrolled in. His dog, Maggie, is ten years old. No one starts training a dog at that age."

"She seems trained already," Mason says, through of mouthful of chips.

"She is."

"Then why's he here?"

"In search of a captive audience?"

The man finally shuts up and takes Maggie around the circle. She's a cute, perky little dog, snowy white with a black nose, mouth and eyes that look like they've been drawn on with a Sharpie. She heels perfectly.

Neely makes a point of praising the dog, not the human.

Next she motions at a middle-aged woman with a

golden doodle. He comes up to her hip and seems to be all legs and pale fluffy fur. A wave of nervous anticipation sweeps through the other owners. They seem to be collectively holding their breath.

The woman's face grows tense with pained concentration and determination but her eyes are full of fear, making her look more like someone who's about to swan dive off a cliff into a kiddie pool than walk her dog in a loop.

"Sammy, heel," she calls out, and takes a few steps.

Sammy immediately bolts.

She plants her feet and pulls on his leash with all her might.

"Sammy, heel!"

His forward momentum is interrupted briefly. He looks back at her, his tongue lolling out, his big furry tail waving, before lunging again.

"Stop, stop, stop," Neely holds up both hands. "I don't see a prong collar on Sammy."

"I can't do it," the woman responds. "I know you told me I have to start using one, but I can't do it. They're cruel."

"Uh-oh." I grab Mason by the arm excitedly. "Watch. You're going to love this."

I hold out the snack bag. We each pop a chip into our mouths.

"What's a prong collar?" Mason whispers.

"It's a training collar that has metal spikes on the inside of it that pinch the dog's skin. Some breeds are too powerful in the neck and chest for a choke collar. They don't feel them and that makes their owners yank even harder and this can damage their tracheas.

So continuing to use a choke can actually end up hurting the dog more than if the owner used a prong, but because the prong looks nasty, some people don't want to use it."

"Prong collars are effective training tools. They're not cruel," Neely explains in a deceptively amiable tone. "Is it cruel to make a child do homework that is difficult for him and he doesn't want to do?"

"Yes," Mason whispers fervently to me.

The woman hesitates. Neely knows this means she's considering the possibility that it is in fact mean to make a child do his homework. Neely can't stand this particular type of nice person: the ones whose supposed kindness doesn't stem from genuine benevolence but from their own selfish desire to avoid effort or confrontation.

She takes Sammy from her owner, leads him a few feet away, and makes him sit. When she returns to the woman, Neely takes two twenty-dollar bills out of her jeans pocket and tosses them on the ground at her feet.

"Forty dollars," she announces. "Would you like to have it?"

The woman gives her a quizzical smile.

"It's not a trick question. Yes or no?"

"Yes."

"I don't want you to have it but go ahead and try to pick it up."

As the woman kneels down, Neely nudges her in the arm. She looks up at her surprised.

"Go ahead. Take it," Neely says, continuing to prod her with two fingers.

The woman glances up at her again but doesn't let Neely's annoying poking stop her from grabbing the money.

She stands up and Neely takes the money from her and drops it on the ground again.

"Let's try it again. Do you want that money?"

The woman nods.

"Then take it."

This time when the woman leans down, Neely pinches her upper arm. Hard.

"Ouch," she yells, and covers the spot with her hand.

"Do you still want the money?" Neely asks.

The woman thinks about it. She's about to bend down again, her hand still covering the red mark on her arm, watching Neely warily the entire time, then thinks better of it.

"The difference between a choke collar and a prong," Neely summarizes. "Which one is going to make the dog learn?"

"Sweet," Mason exclaims. "I get the lesson, too. Sometimes you have to hurt someone to show them you love them. Like what my dad's doing to me."

The same winded feeling comes over me that I had when Mason greeted me earlier.

"Are you a good enough detective to find him?" he quickly adds.

Our snack bag is empty. He turns it upside down and shakes a few remaining crumbs onto the palm of his hand and licks them up.

"I might not be, but I know someone who is and I've asked him to find your dad," I reply.

I notice one of his Batman bandages is barely attached. I tug it off his leg. The wound underneath is still a little bloody.

"Okay," he says, not sounding very convinced.

I open my purse and take out one of the clear Band-Aids I keep handy for whenever a new pair of shoes gives me blisters.

I peel off the backing, place it gently over his knobby scraped knee, and give it a squeeze.

AT HOME WE MAKE CHEESEBURGERS on the grill for dinner and watch reruns of *The A-Team* (another classic) before I suggest we go out back and make some s'mores in my fire pit before bedtime.

Mason's roasting a marshmallow on a stick when I hear my front doorbell ring.

I ask him if he's old enough to leave alone with a fire and he makes a face at me.

I flick on my front porch light and Camio's friend Madison appears out of the black night. I don't think she wants to be seen. She glances nervously behind her.

She looks younger than she did earlier in the parking lot. The blue streaks in her hair don't seem trendy or even trashy tonight but something a child would do as part of a space-girl Halloween costume.

She's holding a backpack against her chest the way Mason holds his Trapper Keeper.

"Can you turn the light out?" she asks.

I comply then open the door and step outside.

"You're Madison, right?"

"Yeah."

"Would you like to go in?"

"No. I . . ."

She whips her head around as if she's heard someone sneaking up behind her.

"Here."

She shoves the backpack at me.

"This was Camio's. She kept it a secret from everyone except me. She even wrote out everything instead of putting it on her computer because she was afraid someone might get on and read it when she wasn't home."

"What is it?" I ask, taking it from her and unzipping the top.

I peer inside and see a three-ringed binder.

"It's a book she was writing. Something psychological." She lowers her voice. "About her family."

"Thank you. This might be helpful."

"She's hardly written anything yet. It's mostly just photos, but I don't want to have it, seeing as how she's dead and all."

I zip the backpack closed.

She's still wearing the gladiator sandals she had on earlier. Her skin bulges out between the leather cutouts and has turned a painful pink. I want to tell her to take them off.

"I really do like your nails," I offer instead.

She looks down at the gold animal prints at the end of her fingers like she's noticing them for the first time.

"The day we got them done I got in kind of a fight with Camio. Mindy Dawn wanted to get the same as

me and we got into a fight about it 'cause I didn't
want us to have the same nails, and Camio told us we
were acting like spoiled brats. And I told her she was a
bitch who thought she knew everything and thought
she was better than us."

I wait for what I know must be coming next. She's
going to be remorseful. She's going to tell me how
much she regrets saying something mean to her friend
who was going to die a few days later.

"Camio was going to leave," she states flatly. "She
was going to go to college and get a job and move
away and forget all about us. I'm really sad she's dead,
but this way she can be my friend forever."

"I guess that's one way to look at it," I say. "Can I
ask you something about Camio that's been kind of
gnawing at me?"

"I guess."

"Her sister told me she was crazy about babies and
that she wanted to have a whole bunch of them. I
don't know many teenage girls who are crazy about
babies. Plus Camio sounded like she was more concerned with school and a career than having children.
Did she ever talk about babies with you?"

A sly smile creeps across Madison's face. I'm not
sure about the meaning behind it. I hope she's going
to explain.

"Cami liked to mess with people," she volunteers.
"You know. See if she could get them to do what she
wanted without asking them to do it. Make them
think it was what they wanted when it probably
wasn't. More psychological bullshit.

"One night she got in a wicked fight with Jessy about this same shit you were just talking about. Cami was going to leave and have a great life and Jessy was going to be a loser living in a double-wide with a bunch of snot-nosed brats and a husband who beat on her. You know, typical sister stuff."

"I don't remember ever having that particular fight with my sister," I comment, "but I hear you. Go on."

"That's when Cami got the idea to make Jessy have a baby. She got all excited. It was going to be like a scientific experiment. She said the best way to do it was to make Jessy think Cami wanted to have a baby more than anything in the world and was worried she never would 'cause she'd be too busy with her job. She said if Jessy thought she could make her jealous she'd do anything. And damn, if she wasn't right. It took some time, but Jessy got pregnant."

She has a pleased smile on her face when she finishes.

"That's terrible," I say.

My opinion doesn't sway her own.

"What's the matter? Don't you like babies? It's no big deal. Cami was right about how Jessy's life would turn out anyway."

Our conversation is apparently over. Madison turns suddenly and heads down my porch steps, pausing at the bottom to look left and right, then takes off across the street at an unflattering jog that makes the roll of belly above her shorts shudder.

I go inside with my prize.

I'm not thrilled to hear about this side of Camio,

but I'm not all that surprised. She was a teenage girl, quite possibly the meanest creature on earth. Even the best of them can have their moments of brutality.

I check on Mason and his marshmallow. I estimate he's roasting his third one already. I give him a graham cracker and part of a Hershey's bar and tell him that's enough and that I have a little work to do.

He makes his final s'more and follows me inside.

I take a seat at the kitchen table and pull Camio's binder out of the backpack. It's the standard three-ringed kind that can be found in any high school or college classroom, filled with lined composition paper covered with neat, careful writing in blue pen. Photos have been taped among the words. Each is of a different family member. Madison was right in that there isn't much text and what is here isn't psychological. Instead, Camio's jotted down the observations of any layman, much of it anecdotal, some of it interesting, most of it innocuous.

There's Tug and Jessy. Her mom. Uncle Eddie. Her dad and Shane. Grandma Miranda. Derk. Some random aunts, uncles, and cousins.

I turn to the last few pages and there's a picture of an elderly woman I've never met.

She's standing in a kitchen in front of a stove with a wrinkled old hand resting on the handle of a tea-kettle, smiling pleasantly, wearing a pair of lavender polyester pants and a blouse with tiny violets sprinkled over it. Her hair is a cap of pewter curls.

"Great-aunt Adelaide," Camio has written.

I grab my nearest pair of glasses and begin to read.

I've never met Great-aunt Adelaide but I plan to soon. We've never been allowed to have anything to do with her because she and Grandma had a falling-out a long time ago and were never able to make up. I think this is very sad, since they're sisters. I want to find out what happened. I wonder if Adelaide was jealous of Miranda.

This is all she's written. There's no mention of why she decided to finally reach out to Adelaide, or if someone else was behind it, or if the meeting ever happened. I saw Camio's phone log and all the numbers were accounted for. She never called her great-aunt or received a call from her.

I peer closer at the photo. What I can see of Adelaide's kitchen is neat and clean but humble. I recognize the gray linoleum spattered with color like a few paintbrushes have been flicked over it as a style popular in the fifties. The curtains look homemade: a thin, partially see-through fabric of bright red apples trimmed in green eyelet. The refrigerator is an old model, a plain white rectangle with no signs of an icemaker or water dispenser.

Beyond her is a doorway to another room. I see the foot of a bed. I imagine the house is small like a cabin.

My heart almost stops.

I strain my eyes as much as possible, but I'm still not sure I'm seeing what I'm seeing.

I get up from the table and start throwing open drawers looking for the magnifying glass I confiscated from Everhart last summer when I found him and Dewey out in the station parking lot using it to burn ants.

It was a slow summer.

I find it and hold it over the photo. My hand starts to shake and I steady it with my other hand.

There's no mistaking what I'm looking at. The bed in Adelaide's house has a bed skirt and comforter on it from the Jessica Simpson Sherbet Lace collection.

chapter twenty

NOLAN AND I DRIVE in silence once again. He doesn't ask if I'm feeling any better after the Massey shooting. He doesn't give me an update on Zane's condition or the search for my brother. He doesn't wonder if I've looked further into opening a doodad shop and acquiring a bunch of cats. He doesn't express any concern for Shawna Truly and how she might be doing after confessing some truly horrible details of her life yesterday that she's probably never told anyone before and then going right back to that life. He doesn't praise me for my dogged perseverance and attention to detail that has led to discovering what might turn out to be the key piece of evidence necessary to solve the Camio Truly homicide.

He does practically rip my head off for not telling him earlier about my conversation with the ladies at the Sanctuary regarding Miranda Truly and her somewhat unhealthy relationship with her sister, Adelaide, and her nephew Eddie's attempt to kill her with an ax.

"You need to decide if you're a law enforcement

officer or a glorified babysitter who ignores the rules and does whatever the hell she wants," he told me roughly.

When he put it that way, I kind of preferred the second option.

In all fairness to Nolan, when I came out of the academy with commendations for sharpshooting and academic excellence I looked like I had all the makings of a dedicated, level-headed, proficient trooper and might be a prime candidate for his beloved Criminal Investigations Division.

Nolan was not quite thirty but already a supercop by then. Already in CID. Already had the presence and demeanor of a leader and possessed that rare combination of gruff empathy and subtle sanctimony that made witnesses and suspects alike want to earn his esteem if only so he'd be on their side; he was a bully with a conscience.

He took an interest in me, not entirely professional but mostly. For all his sexist bluster, Nolan is a big supporter of women's rights. He has three daughters who all graduated from college, moved away, have careers and families, and manage to continue to love him even though he wasn't the most attentive father in the world and their mother probably fills their heads with tearful tales of neglect and woe during her constant visits, but I could be wrong about that. I shouldn't judge his wife. If she does complain about him, she probably has every right to do so.

Nolan had high hopes for me. Law enforcement in general is still very much a boys' club, and if municipal police departments have the metaphorical equivalent of a chain-link fence around them to keep females out, the state police have ten-foot-thick, towering stone walls with a fire-breathing dragon at the gate. He thought I could be one of the first women to break through the ramparts. Instead, I let down myself and my gender in the worst possible way: I let a man get to me.

My feelings for Nolan had become a distraction and were causing me to act recklessly. Sleeping with John to arouse his jealousy was incredibly stupid, hurtful, unprofessional, and just the beginning. I saw a future where I'd end up screwing every trooper in my barracks because I couldn't have the one I wanted.

I've never told him why I left. I've allowed him to believe that I couldn't hack it and, in a sense, I couldn't. I let my female desires come before my public-servant duties, and I know he would never be able to forgive me for that, but I've often wondered if he would care about me at all if I put being a cop in front of being a woman.

I try to enjoy the drive as much as possible. I watch the green humped hills fly by my window while Nolan stares straight ahead, yet I know his eyes behind his glasses are darting all over the interstate searching for signs of motorists behaving poorly or strangely or in need of assistance.

It's another sunny day without a cloud in the hazy, Vaseline-coated empty blue sky. This weather makes it impossible for me not to recall childhood summer memories full of greasy, sweet county-fair smells, the lazy buzzing of bees, warm pavement beneath bare feet, and the promise each day presented no matter how badly the one before had ended. I was a kid but no longer a baby, old enough to know better but not old enough to know best: the recipe for hope. I miss that feeling.

I called Nolan the minute I discovered the comforter in the photo of Aunt Adelaide. There was no point in trying to begin a full-on investigation in the middle of the night. He decided to wait for daylight.

In the meantime he contacted the local barracks where Adelaide lived and found out her surviving daughter, Angela—now in her sixties, happily married, residing in Ohio, a grandmother of seven—had called the police recently because she couldn't get in touch with her mother. She said they talked frequently and she was worried because of her advanced age.

The cops found her place empty and her door unlocked. Her purse, wallet, and car were still there.

Nolan didn't uncover Adelaide's suspicious disappearance during his own investigation because she isn't a Truly and she doesn't reside in his zone. She was born a Thorpe and married Joey Bertolino, the middle child of another big, sprawling family, but this one made up of hardworking, hard-playing Italian miners. She was only related to the Trulys through her sister Miranda's marriage to one.

Despite these factors, and even though the missing-persons report was only filed yesterday, I know Nolan's beating himself up for not catching the connection, but because she's been reported missing, he's already able to have a team waiting here to search the place. There will be no more delays in discovering what happened to Great-aunt Adelaide if something happened to her at all.

The circumstances aren't looking good for her, though. Women in their eighties don't just disappear. They also don't usually kill teenage girls, especially not by swinging heavy objects at them hard enough to crack open their skulls. Even though Addy may turn out to be the owner of the comforter that was wrapped around Camio, it's doubtful she was her killer.

Since Nolan neglects to tell me anything about the search for my brother during our drive, I assume this means he has no news. I'm trying not to think about what will happen if we don't find Champ. I'm worried for his welfare, but I have to admit I'm worried about mine, too.

I'm fifty years old. I've never been married or had children. I've never even had a pet. I don't consider myself to be a good candidate for instant motherhood.

I used to wonder what kind of mother I'd be and the thought would often scare me. I wanted to believe I'd be a good one, but I didn't have a good role model.

Our mother always did whatever she wanted to do without giving much thought to what she should do. She only tended to our needs when they coincided with her own or she was bored, but I know she didn't think she was neglectful.

I once heard a boyfriend ask her as they were departing the house for the night if my siblings and I would be all right staying home alone. Mom flashed me one of her dazzling smiles that always made me want to do her bidding and kick her teeth in at the same time.

"Dove is smarter than any grown-up I know," she said sweetly and probably truthfully. "And besides, what's so hard about staying home? She knows how to change diapers and call the fire department."

I was eight.

But truth be told, being left alone to fend for ourselves didn't bother me as much as her disinterest in our lives. I had lots of friends and spent time hanging out at their homes starting when I was in elementary school all the way through high school.

I saw moms drop whatever they were doing to rave over a gold star on a spelling test or an art-class project. I saw them sit down at the kitchen table and ask about their daughters' days and listen to every inane detail. I saw them surprise their daughters with outfits they bought at Rankin's, and *Tiger Beat* magazines they picked up at the newsstand, and packs of silver- and gold-plated barrettes they grabbed on their way out of Woolworth's, with explanations that were given almost as afterthoughts but to me were astounding proclamations of intimate vigilance.

"I saw this when I was out shopping today, honey, and I thought it would look cute on you."

"Look who's on the cover! I know you love this actor."

"I picked these up for you; I remember you told me you lost a barrette in gym class last week."

My mother never could have done any of that for Neely or me for the simple reason she didn't know

anything about us. She went to her grave not knowing our favorite colors, favorite music, what we
wanted to be when we grew up, the names of our
friends, what scared us, what made us laugh, what we
did in school that day because she never asked.

She might come home one night with a whole
stack of movie magazines she wanted to read and
we'd all sit on the couch and look at them together, or
sometimes when she had an extra-generous boyfriend, she'd buy us an expensive pair of shoes or a
coat or a dress, but it was always stuff we'd never
wear because it wasn't what we liked.

From watching my friends at home with their
moms, I learned the most important aspect of a
mother's love was not the intensity but its reliable
consistency.

I don't know what kind of mother Great-aunt Adelaide was to her two daughters, but I'm willing to bet
she was a good one. I get a mindful, nurturing vibe
from her before we even set foot inside her home.

I was right about the size of her house. It's barely
more than a cabin. From the outside it looks like a
child's drawing: a square base, a triangle for a roof,
two identical-size windows with parted curtains sym-
metrically placed on either side of a red door. It's
painted yellow and has two rows of red tulips planted
in beneath the windows.

The only thing missing from the picture is a curli-
cue of gray smoke coming from the chimney and an
orange cat sitting in front of the door.

The paint is peeling. The windows need washing,
the flowers need weeding, and the driveway needs

patching, but the place doesn't look run-down; it exudes the honest shabbiness that comes from the passage of time and the owner's inability to keep up with repairs and maintenance, whether it be for financial or physical reasons or both. One glance at it and I know the owner cares.

I step out of Nolan's car and walk past a bunch of very bored troopers who are trying not to appear nosy but are soaking up every detail. I'm glad I decided to dress seriously today in a pair of navy trousers, navy blouse, and a cream boucle blazer. (Not real boucle but close enough. I got it for a song at T.J.Maxx.)

I join Nolan and we step into the house together. Two CSU guys are quietly going about their jobs gathering evidence. We turn to each other smiling, then immediately rearrange our mouths into frowns as we realize the inappropriateness of the expression under the circumstances, but on the inside we're both thrumming with excitement: the house reeks of bleach. Someone had something very messy to clean up.

We put on latex gloves and head in opposite directions.

The interior echoes the exterior. The furniture's upholstery is fraying, the throw rugs are old and worn out, and the wallpaper is an outdated paisley print yellowed with age, but everything is clean and neat.

I feel like I've stepped inside a life-size seventies diorama. The only thing missing is a wall phone and a TV set inside a huge fake wood console sitting on shag carpet. Addy does have a flat-screen, although a small one, and a cord-free phone. According to Nolan, she doesn't own a cell phone. She also doesn't have a computer or a microwave. An old-fashioned radio shaped like a toaster with knobs the size of halved Ping-Pong balls sits on a Formica-topped table in the kitchen. Copies of *Reader's Digest* and *Ladies' Home Journal* are stacked on an end table next to a lamp with a ceramic base shaped like a collie and a shade decoupaged with autumn leaves.

One wall is completely covered with family photos. She and Miranda may have been estranged, but the bad feelings on Addy's part apparently weren't strong enough to have made her want to forget her sister and her progeny existed. There are too many people from too many time periods for me to identify all of them, but I recognize some. She has photos of Camio, Jessy, and Shane long after they were taken from her.

I notice one photo is missing. A nail juts out of the wall above a faded square of wallpaper where the sun hasn't shown in years.

Next to this empty space are a few old-timey, sepia-shaded photos of two little girls I assume to be her and Miranda. She has photos of them in their teens and as young mothers with their first babies in their arms. Looking at the pictures I don't see any signs of ill will on either of their parts, not in their body language or expressions.

I find her wedding picture. She doesn't have a formal staged one. It's her and Joey standing at the top of a set of church steps. She's holding her bouquet and waving. He's looking at her, not the guests, and smiling broadly at her. I like that.

Not much can be seen of the church. It appears to

be a humble one. White wood with cement steps. The doors are propped open. It looks familiar to me, but all the churches around here do.

She has two more photos taken in front of the same church. In each one she's holding a swaddled baby in her arms and Joey stands beside her in a dark suit, still not smiling for the camera but smiling at each of his daughters in turn. I like this, too.

The baptisms, I wonder, then it strikes me what's out of place about the church. Surely the Bertolinos are Catholic, which means they would have attended the nearest Catholic Church, and back then that meant going all the way to Hellersburg. I know that church and it's an impressive gray stone edifice with marble stairs. Maybe this humble church with its weathered white wood had been the one Addy's family attended. Usually the father's religion won out over the mother's, especially if it was a battle between Catholic and Protestant, but maybe smiling Joey had loved his new wife more than his old religion. I bet that went over well with his mama.

There are plenty of photos of Angela and Layla growing up, every school photo from every grade, hung in its proper place in the progression of their young lives.

Layla was barely out of high school when she got pregnant with Shane. We've checked the records. Layla Bertolino had three children, Shane, Jessyca, and Camio, with fathers listed as unknown on their birth certificates that we've now been led to believe were the product of a union with her cousin Clark Truly. The three children went to live with Clark after a drunk driver in a Dodge Ram pickup T-boned Layla's car. There's no reason to doubt what Shawna told us. Why else would Addy have let them go?

What a triumph that must have been for Miranda when she told the sister she hated that her beloved grandchildren were freaks spawned by first cousins and the father was her own son. Or did this knowledge disgust Miranda even more than it did Addy? After all, she supposedly hated Addy. The feeling didn't seem to be mutual. Addy seemed to only fear her.

Regardless, Miranda took her grandchildren from her. She was the big winner. I can imagine her victory speech.

We're taking them, Addy. They're Clark's children. Don't make us prove it. We don't want to call outside attention to this and we don't want the children to ever know. It's for their own good. How much do you love them? Enough to let them go and never see them again and let them have a normal life? Or is your need to keep them so strong that you would tell them the vile truth behind their parentage and ruin them?

I take down one of the photos with the church in it and remove it from the frame to see if anything is written on the back. Nothing. I try with the other two.

Suddenly it comes to me and my head swims with memories of stained glass and Nolan on a respirator.

I hurry off, looking for Nolan, and find him in the guest room staring at a bed made up only with sheets. The comforter is missing but the incriminating bed skirt is still on it.

I hand Nolan the photo.

"This is the church at Campbell's Run," I tell him. "The family has a tie to the place where Camio's body was dumped."

He studies the picture.

"Good work," he says.

I'm momentarily stunned and equally thrilled by his praise, but my good mood only lasts a second as I consider the bed in front of me and what it's telling me.

"Look at this," I say to him, and grab one of the pillows off the bed. "She even has the matching throw pillows. She has the whole set, and it's not cheap. Whether she bought it for herself or someone gave it to her as a gift, she obviously loved it. There's no way she used the comforter to wrap up a dead body."

"What are you saying?"

"I'm saying if Addy were present and a willing participant in Camio's murder, she would've objected to using the comforter and used a different blanket. If she wasn't present or wasn't able to object . . ."

I don't finish the sentence. I don't need to. Both Nolan and I are holding out little hope for a happy ending to her disappearance.

I follow him into the kitchen.

It's one more small, spotless room that looks like nothing has been touched in it for the past forty years. I don't see a single modern appliance. Not even a food processor or a blender. The toaster is a shiny silver affair with a red-and-white-striped cloth cord that looks sturdy enough to drop from a ten-story building without putting a dent in it.

A set of canisters made of tarnished copper line

one counter. A drying rack holds one plate, one cup, one fork, and one spoon. A snarl of steel wool sits near the sink faucet. One of her dish towels has fabric sewn to a corner along with a button and is looped through a drawer handle and fastened. My grandma did the same thing with hers. She said it kept her from misplacing them.

The stove is an old gas range. Sitting on one of the back burners is a cast-iron skillet.

I walk toward it, slowly, softly, holding my breath as if the pan were a living thing that might bolt if it hears or senses me.

It can't be this easy passes through my thoughts. I'm still wearing the latex gloves I put on earlier. I pick up the skillet by its handle and feel the heft of it. I turn it over as a matter of course, not expecting to find anything. Flaky patches of orange rust speckle the bottom and a small dark stain near the perimeter catches my eye.

I don't have any glasses on me. I hold the pan away from my face at arm's length, hoping the mark will come into better focus.

"Holy shit," I hear Nolan say behind me.

He reaches around me, puts his hand over mine, and brings the skillet up to his face.

"What is it?" I ask.

"If I'm not mistaken," he says in a whisper, reinforcing the same sensation I had that our evidence might disappear if we spook it, "it's hair stuck to a clot of dried blood."

Within moments, our discovery is confirmed. Slowly

but surely every bored trooper manages to wander in and eyeball the weapon.

"Someone killed that girl by smashing her skull in with a skillet, then put it right back on the stove?" one trooper asks me. "That may be the coldest murder I've ever heard of."

I know of one colder, but I keep it to myself.

NOLAN DOESN'T DROP ME at the station until almost five. If I had been driving my own car, I would've left much earlier. After my discovery of the murder weapon, I felt pretty useless for the rest of the day. Nolan's team works together like a well-oiled machine; I'm a similar cog, but one that belongs to another team.

I gather my men for a meeting around the murder board the moment I get back. I called to let them know what was going on. Along with the discovery of the skillet, hair and blood were also found in the trunk of Adelaide's car, and microscopic blood evidence was found in the cracks of the kitchen linoleum along with a few tiny splatters the killer missed while cleaning up. None of it has been confirmed as belonging to Camio yet, but there's little doubt.

My four officers are strutting around, barely able to contain their excitement over our department breaking the case and besting the state police.

I also put Singer on the job of finding out what tied Miranda and Adelaide to the town of Campbell's Run.

I tack up Adelaide's photo beneath the word "motive" written in all caps in the middle of the board followed by a bunch of questions marks. I've run out of new marker colors. In black I write beneath her: *Missing, presumed dead.*

Next I draw an arrow between her and Miranda.

"A lot of bad blood between these two," I tell them.

Then I underline Miranda's alibi: <u>Home alone but too old?</u>

"We all agree she's too old to have done this on her own, but she could have been part of it."

I draw an arrow between Eddie and Addy.

"We know he tried to kill her once before, although it's only hearsay at this point from one source. He has no alibi, and now we also know he was at the scene.

"There were no usable fingerprints on the murder weapon but there were some on the driver's side interior car door handle and steering wheel that belonged to Eddie Truly," I explain.

"They were able to run the prints before they even finished clearing the scene. Eddie's prints were in the system from prior arrests. He's been picked up and Corporal Greely is interviewing him as we speak."

"Poor bastard," Dewey says with a grin.

"Singer, did you find out the significance of Campbell's Run?"

"Yes, ma'am," he replies eagerly.

The three other officers snort and shake their heads at his enthusiasm.

"The two sisters are originally from the Run. Their parents were some of the people who lost their homes. The sisters were already married and gone by then, but it still would've been rough watching the town where you grew up get bulldozed under."

I can easily see Miranda coming up with the idea of hiding a body there. She's well acquainted with the town's ability to swallow up lives.

"Excellent," I say to Singer.

He blushes. Blonski throws a pen at his head.

I turn my back to them and study the board for a moment.

"But," I announce when I face them again. "What does any of this have to do with Camio's murder?"

We all mull over the question.

"You told us she was about to go see her great-aunt," Everhart points out. "Maybe she was there when Miranda and Eddie showed up?"

"Okay," I say, nodding. "Good observation for a guy who was asleep at his desk when I came in."

He gives me an embarrassed smile.

"The Jakester woke up every couple hours last night. He wants to eat all the time."

"Isn't your wife nursing?" Dewey asks.

"Yeah but she wakes me up, too, even though I don't do anything. She says it's a matter of principle."

"Maybe Camio was collateral damage," Blonski interrupts, not the least bit interested in the woes of new fatherhood. "Maybe Eddie and Miranda killed Adelaide and Camio witnessed it? They had to take her out."

"They killed her?" Singer wonders. "That's cold. Couldn't they have convinced her to keep her mouth shut? They're a tight-lipped bunch."

"I don't know," Blonski goes on. "She seems like she would've been the kind of kid who'd want to do the right thing. Go to the police. She was the black sheep."

"Or she was the white sheep in a family of black sheep," Dewey comments.

"It would also explain why we've never been able to come up with a motive," Blonski adds. "Because there wasn't one. She was collateral damage."

I turn back to the board and stare at the word "motive" again.

"Why after all these years? Why do it in front of a witness?" I ask them.

"Crime of passion?" Dewey suggests.

"It's not a bad theory," I tell them.

They look even more pleased than when I arrived.

"Speaking of collateral damage, I'm going to visit Tug at Broadview tomorrow. We'll see if I get anything useful out of him."

I head for my office looking for some alone time to help me sort this all out. I find a stack of mail waiting for me on my desk. I pick up a manila envelope with no return address. The postmark is a town near the Pennsylvania-Ohio border. I shake it and something jostles around inside it.

There's a note. I can't say that I recognize my brother's handwriting but I recognize what can only be his words.

I put on my reading glasses and my vision swims into focus.

He used to put a birthday candle on top of a cupcake. When he was done, he'd let me blow out the candle and eat the cupcake. I still see those flames in my sleep. I know they're never going to go out.

I numbly turn the envelope upside down. Dozens of melted candles topple out onto my desk. Dainty things in pretty party colors. Their wicks singed black. I stop counting at twenty-two.

chapter twenty-one

I HAD A TERRIBLE NIGHT. What little sleep I got was plagued by nightmares; fortunately they were the kind I couldn't remember, but they've left me with a queasy stomach full of dread.

I stand in front of my bathroom mirror with a bad case of MOF and the first thought I have is of Champ. Did that envelope contain his suicide note? Or was he telling me something he'd never been able to reveal before and maybe it made him feel better? Or was it his way of saying he can't cope with the pressures of raising a child anymore and he won't be coming back for his?

I want to discuss this with Neely but I also don't. I'd be doing it only so I'd have someone to share my worry. There's nothing she can do.

I texted Nolan the name of the town on the post-mark last night. I didn't hear back from him until very late and then it was only to tell me about Eddie Truly. Despite the evidence against him, he wasn't talking. Nolan hadn't been able to get a confession, and he wasn't very happy about it.

I put off thinking about my face and go to my closet to pick out an outfit. I settle on my celery green seersucker suit. It's a lot more attractive than it sounds. The skirt hits above the knee. It's definitely not a mini, and I still have the legs for it, but I question its appropriateness for work now that I'm fifty. I don't know what it is about this number. I wouldn't have thought twice about this ensemble a few months ago when I was forty-nine.

Downstairs I find Mason and his Trapper Keeper in front of the TV already dressed, his neon orange toes sticking out of the ends of his sandals. I found a dozen pairs of the same socks in his duffel bag. When I asked him the significance of them he gave me the same answer he did before: "*Orange goes with everything.*"

"Would you like to join me in a bowl of non-fake Cinnamon Toast Crunch?" I ask him.

"Sure," he says, and follows me into the kitchen.

"I've got something I have to do this morning and Aunt Neely is coming along, too," I say as I pour him a bowl of cereal. "Would you be okay hanging out at the police station for a little while, then she can pick you up when we're done and take you back to her place?"

"I'm nine," he states flatly.

"I know."

"I can stay here by myself. I've stayed alone plenty of times."

I consider his position.

"Okay, but not for the whole day. I'm still going to have Aunt Neely come get you."

"What about Great-grandma?" he asks.

He pops a spoonful of cereal into his mouth and starts crunching.

"Great-grandma lives in a retirement home and she's also too old to babysit."

"When do I get to meet her?"

"Soon."

"Dad told me all about her," he goes on, his words coming out between crunches. "He said even after your mom married that rich guy and you had a housekeeper, your grandma still came over and cleaned for you because she liked cleaning so much and didn't trust anyone else to do it right. And she had her own room where she stayed over on the nights she drank too much of the fizzy wine your mom liked. And she took Dad to Pirates games and made puppets with him."

"Lysol, Mateus, Willie Stargell, a pack of tube socks and some stick-on googly eyes," I say with a sigh. "That pretty much sums up the great loves of her life."

I notice the time on my microwave.

"I have to get going. Don't turn on the stove, don't take a bath, don't touch any knives, don't go near any electrical outlets, don't open the door for anyone or answer the phone."

He throws up his hands and collapses on top of the table like he's been struck dead by exasperation.

He raises his head.

"I'm nine," he states again.

"Okay, I'm sorry. I don't know much about kids."

"Don't worry about it," he says, returning to his breakfast. "I don't know much about ladies."

ON MY WAY TO BROADVIEW to see Tug I stop by the salon where Camio and her friends had their nails done. My intention is to talk to her manicurist and see if she can embellish further on the argument the girls had last time they were in. It turns out she has no useful information, but she does manage to talk me into getting my own nails done as a sort of tribute to Camio. She even talks me into getting exactly the same ones.

I can't stop looking at them the entire time I'm driving. I can't decide if they're amazing or awful or if they make my hands look older or younger.

The Broadview juvenile detention center is brand-spanking-new. People around here were delighted while it was being built and staffed because it provided jobs. None of them stopped to think *why* it was being built. None of them noticed the irony, either, that the day it opened for business and dozens of hopeless kids in matching orange jumpsuits and handcuffs were bused and shuffled in from other overcrowded facilities was the same day our public library lost its state funding.

Fortunately for the coal and gas industries, our region is not only rich with natural resources but tons of shortsightedness.

This is my first time here since the grand opening, an event with an inappropriate amount of hoopla attached to it, including a ribbon-cutting ceremony by Mayor Sawyer, who stopped short at wearing a top hat and settled for an English tweed motoring cap.

As chief of police I was obligated to attend and expected to eagerly start filling it with unfortunate children who I couldn't help thinking might not need this facility at all if they had spent more time in the library that was currently being dismantled.

Then as now I marveled at the size of it and the absurd, sadistic design team who decided to distinguish the four different dormitories with structures that look like gigantic LEGO blocks in bright primary colors stacked on the roof. It would be a great idea for an elementary school.

Neely is waiting for me in the parking lot. Smoke is riding shotgun in her truck.

She's in a pair of skinny jeans, a lilac-colored T-shirt, and sandals. Her hair is down, and she's ditched the ball cap. If asked, I'd say she was at least ten years younger than her forty-eight.

We start walking to the entrance. She notices my nails right away.

"Are you kidding me?" she asks.

I hold up my hands and wiggle my fingers at her.

"Are you going through a midlife crisis?"

"I think they're pretty," I tell her.

"Sandra's inside," she quickly changes the subject. "She told me the good news. Do you know?"

I shake my head.

"Zane's regained consciousness. It looks like he's going to be okay."

My relief is so great and instantaneous, my knees almost buckle.

"That's fantastic news."

I've been trying not to think about Zane clinging

to life these past few days, but the feel of his blood oozing through my hands while I held him on his living room floor and the sight of his family's haggard faces at the hospital continually pushed their way into my consciousness.

"It's good news for Tug, too," Neely says.

"You realize this doesn't change much," I point out to her. "He committed a serious crime. He's not going to get away with a slap on the wrist."

"We'll see what Sandra can pull off."

"How are you paying her?"

"I have a secret money source I only allow myself to access in case of emergencies. Maybe someday I'll tell you about it."

I stop short at the doors before going inside.

"Before I forget again, I meant to tell you this the other day. Lucky went to see Grandma."

"That piece of slime," she says, squinting her eyes in disgust. "Bothering an old lady."

"He told her he's going to make our lives miserable. I don't know what that means exactly, but I wanted to make you aware."

"Consider me aware."

"Do you ever feel like it might have been wrong?" I ask her. "What we did to him?"

She gives me a look of reproof.

"If Lucky had been a swell guy instead of a creep, when the opportunity came to hang a crime on him he wouldn't have been the likely candidate. It would've never crossed our minds and no one would've believed it."

She reaches for the door.

"I concede he was an asshole," I say. "He was a good-for-nothing liar and cheat scamming his way through life living off some women and beating up others. But should he have spent his whole life in jail for that?"

"Maybe he should've paid more attention to whose path he crossed."

I follow her inside to the reception area where we check in. I hand over my gun, and Neely begins to be searched by a correctional officer.

"Even so, he would've never known to stay out of our way," I say to her in a confidential tone, continuing our conversation. "We seemed completely normal on the outside."

"We still do," she says back, and raises her arms to be frisked.

We join Sandra and Tug at a table in the visitation room. The space has the feel of a high school cafeteria given over on Saturdays to kids with detention. No one is smiling or saying much. We're in the blue section, boys between the ages of eight and fourteen. I can't bear to think of a child the age of Derk or Mason locked away from their family and friends, although during my career I've been privy to many of the homes these kids come from and life here may be an improvement for some.

Fortunately, the few inmates here along with Tug look to be in their early teens. They sit with women of varying ages and sizes who are doing most of the talking and trying valiantly to appear upbeat. There's a complete absence of men except for the two guards who stand unarmed at opposite ends of the room with a seeming lack of alertness only to be rivaled by a night-shift security guard at a petting zoo. They're dressed in dark-wash denim and blue shirts in an effort by the private company that owns Broadview to make them seem more accessible to the underage inmates if they have a problem. That would've been an entertaining meeting to attend: a bunch of old white guys in suits hypothesizing that juvenile delinquents would behave better and put more trust in men wearing jeans. Then later deciding the boys should be dressed like caution signs in crocs.

I wonder who's been here to see Tug besides Neely. Has his father crawled out of a bottle long enough to visit the little acorn to his oak? Shawna told me she's been here once. I doubt more than twenty words were passed between the two of them. Probably Jessy toting Goldie with her. She was at the station the night he was arrested and by all accounts was very distraught.

Sandra is explaining something to him when we arrive at their table. I'm relieved to see he doesn't look bad aside from the purple smudges of exhaustion beneath his eyes and redness on his earlobes where he's tugged them raw. It's not possible for him to get any thinner.

I don't see any signs that he's been in a fight. His crime is one that combined brutality and integrity. He tried to blow off someone's head, but he did it because he believed the guy murdered his sister. The hard-asses are probably going to avoid him and those with any principles left will admire him.

I'm also relieved to discover I'm not afraid of him.

"This is entirely off-the-record," Sandra announces before we can even greet the boy and take our seats. "Nothing he says here can be used in the investigation."

"There's not much of an investigation going on," I tell her. "He was apprehended in the act."

"You know what I mean," she replies, and levels the same kind of steely look at me I want her to use if anyone in the town council raises any questions about my competence.

"I suppose you've heard the news about Zane Massey. He's going to be fine."

"Yes. I just heard. How do you feel about that, Tug?"

"I'm glad," he says. "I didn't want him to die."

"It was an accident," Sandra assures us.

Neely nods her agreement.

"An accident?" I look skyward but stop short of actually rolling my eyes. "He accidentally ended up in the Masseys' living room with a rifle pointed at Zane's head?"

"He wasn't thinking straight," Sandra argues, already trying out her courtroom schtick. "He was overcome by grief and rage."

"Which describes ninety percent of people who kill other people."

"Chief Carnahan, you promised to behave."

"Counselor, I'm not a dog. Don't tell me to behave."

Neely and Tug glance at each other. Something like amusement passes between them.

Tug's face suddenly brightens.

"Your fingernails," he says. "They're just like Cami's. They even got the sparkles."

Sandra glances down at my hands, then up at my

face, and I know she's thinking if need be this can be used as further proof that my hormones are out of whack.

"They're sort of a tribute to her," I tell him. "I was talking to a few of her friends who said she had them done like this before . . ."

I don't finish my sentence.

"I remember," Tug says. "She and Jessy got in a big fight about it."

"A fight about her nails?"

"Yeah. They were always getting in stupid fights over nothing."

"How did the fight go?" I ask him. "Do you remember?"

He closes his eyes and lets his head loll back on his neck as if this is the only way he can conjure up memories of his home.

"Jessy told her they were ugly. Made her look like a stripper or something like that. Camio said she was just jealous 'cause she didn't have any money and her life was over 'cause she had a baby."

"Did they fight a lot?"

"I guess so. Things got worse between them after Goldie was born. Jessy started getting meaner to everyone. Mom said it was because she was tired and depressed, having a baby wasn't easy."

He opens his eyes and lowers his head.

"Jessy couldn't afford anything and here was Cami getting presents from her boyfriend all the time and working at Dairy Queen, buying herself fingernails and other stuff," Tug goes on. "I guess I couldn't blame Jessy for being mad."

He looks down at my hands lying on the tabletop with their bedazzled nails.

"She was really mad that night. I remember thinking if she had an ax, she'd cut Cami's hands right off."

A surge of excitement courses through me followed by a stab of sadness when I realize what I may have uncovered.

I flex my fingers. I can almost feel the splash of gasoline and the searing heat of the fire beginning to devour them.

chapter twenty-two

FOR ALL OUR supposed God-given common sense my churchgoing friends constantly reference or the obvious fact of our bigger brains and therefore superior reasoning abilities, I find humans to be even less capable of unlearning behavior than other animals.

I've seen my sister work miracles on dogs where abuse and neglect have elevated their fear to the point where they have become mindless feral beasts whose reaction to any creature is one of vicious self-defense. With incredible patience and persistence, Neely is able to return them to their trusting selves. They find loving homes and live happily without ever reverting to their previous aggression.

Yet abused children often grow up to be abusers even though their common sense tells them it's wrong and their big brains remind them how much pain they experienced and they know firsthand how damaging that pain can be. Time and again I've seen adults grow up to become the very parent who treated them badly.

We are what we know. Not what the world tells us

we should be. Not even what our own hearts want us to be.

Neely and I used to wonder if something bad had happened to our mom to make her the way she was, some cataclysmic trauma or even some insult given at the wrong time by the wrong person that changed her. We never knew her father, but from all accounts he was a decent, hardworking man. Grandma had her quirks, but no one could ever fault her in the doting category of motherhood. As far as we knew, Mom grew up in a normal home with normal parents and was cherished. She certainly wasn't ever neglected.

Over the years, I've been a keen observer of mothers. I'm sure some of this interest comes from the fact that my own fell short in the role and then was taken from me too soon so there was never any chance for her to ask for my forgiveness. I've discovered not all mothers provide the unconditional love that's supposed to be hardwired into their DNA. Some people simply aren't capable of loving anyone, even their own children, or what passes for love in their minds isn't what most of us expect.

With Miranda and Shawna as role models, what kind of mother is Jessy destined to be? I wonder. From the glimpses I've seen she seems to love Goldie. She appears to be taking care of her as best she can.

I don't like the suspicions I've begun to have about her any more than I liked hearing about Camio's manipulation of her and how ugly their fights could be, but I know I can't let my personal feelings get in the way of this investigation.

Jessy has an alibi. One of her friends swears she was with her at her apartment during the time Camio was murdered. Nolan never talked to the girl personally but apparently felt her statement was solid. Almost as important in crossing her off the suspect list, Jessy didn't seem to have a motive and appeared to be genuinely torn up over her sister's death. Maybe as important, it's hard to imagine a girl with a baby attached to her hip as a killer.

People lie. Nolan knows this better than anyone. For this reason I know he won't be upset if I interview Jessy's alibi witness myself. Even so, I decide not to tell him. For now.

After we're done talking to Tug, Neely swings by my place and picks up Mason. I swing by the hair salon Snips, where Jessy's friend Gina works.

She's happy to talk to me. She finishes adding a few strokes of hair color to a customer's head, sets her timer, and joins me outside in the sunshine.

I blink up at the turquoise sky and the two blindingly white clouds stuck to its surface. For the hundredth time this week I make the observation that this weather can't last.

She takes a drag off a cigarette and a slurp of a Big Gulp and nods her head in agreement.

She's wearing a long black tank top spangled in flat silver studs over leggings and a pair of sandals exposing yellow polished toenails, each adorned with a different character from *South Park*. Her shoulder-length hair is dyed a shocking shade of purplish red that reminds me of a time when Neely, Champ, and I were experimenting with condiments for our school lunch sandwiches and mixed grape jelly and ketchup together. It wasn't good to eat or to look at.

"How's Jess doing?" she asks me.

"I'd think you'd be better able to answer that question than me," I reply, a little surprised.

"I just thought if you're here wanting to talk about her maybe it's because you've seen her. I haven't talked to her since it happened. She's kind of gone off the grid. Camio's death really wrecked her."

"They were close?"

She blows a stream of smoke out the corner of her mouth.

"Sure."

"What about you and Jessy? Do you see each other a lot? Must be hard with the baby."

"She doesn't let Goldie get in the way of anything. She takes her with her everywhere. It's kind of sweet."

"And kind of something else?" I ask her.

She flicks some ash on the pavement and shrugs.

"She never gets a break from her. I still feel kind of bad I said no to her that day and wouldn't watch Goldie for her. But babies freak me out. I'm scared the whole time I'm going to break them."

"What day was that?"

She looks at me for a second, then her eyes flit away nervously.

"Did Jessy ask you to watch Goldie the day Camio was murdered?" I prod her.

She smokes and drinks, stares at the sky, then her toes.

She's already given away the answer. I just need her to realize this and say it out loud.

"Yeah. Sure," she finally admits. "I said no, so we just hung out together instead."

"Instead of what?"

"Instead of her going where she wanted to go without Goldie."

"Where was that?"

"I don't know."

"I think you know where she wanted to go. Can you tell me?"

"Why?"

"Because in an investigation like this, the smallest detail can end up being very important. Don't you think Jessy wants Camio's killer to be caught?"

She thinks about this for a moment.

"I don't see how it can help, but she was going to see Goldie's baby daddy. She was hoping to hook up with him and didn't want the kid around."

This is the first I've heard about Goldie's father.

"What's his name?"

"Kirk."

"Last name?"

"Don't know. He's a bartender at the Rusty Nail."

"Are he and Jessy serious?"

"Huh? No way. He was a one-time thing and she got pregnant. They don't have anything to do with each other."

"What about Goldie?"

"He knows about her. I think he offered to give Jess some money but he doesn't want to be a dad.

Sorry, but I've got to get back to work," she finishes hurriedly.

She takes a final drag off her cigarette and tosses it on the ground. I raise my eyebrows at her and she picks up the butt.

"I'd like for you to come to the station with me. I think we should talk further."

She runs a hand through her tomato-grape hair and lets out a deep, frustrated breath.

"Okay," she says. "She wasn't with me. Okay? She was with Kirk. She asked me to lie because she didn't want her family finding out. They hate the guy."

"I thought they didn't know him."

"The Trulys don't have to know you to hate you."

All the tension leaves her body. Like most people keeping a secret, the revelation has freed her.

She tilts her head back and smiles up at the sky.

"God, I feel so much better," she cries. "I didn't like lying to the cops, but I didn't think there was any harm in it. It's not like Jess killed her sister. She has a good alibi, she just doesn't want anyone to know its Kirk.

"Am I in trouble?" she thinks to ask.

"No," I tell her.

"Is Jessy?"

"No."

"I wish I could do something for her."

"You could help her with her roots," I suggest.

"Yeah, right." She laughs. "She likes them that way."

* * *

I CONTACT the Rusty Nail and get Kirk's last name and phone number. He doesn't respond to my calls throughout the day and leaves me no choice but to ambush him at the bar.

I call Neely and ask if she can bring Mason to my house after work instead of me picking him up, stay for dinner, and then watch him while I go talk to Kirk. She agrees.

I've often wondered at the wisdom behind naming a bar and eatery after something that evokes images of rotting boards and tetanus shots but apparently it never bothered anyone else. The Rusty Nail has been here forever and has always thrived. In my mom's day it was a dive—dark, dank, claustrophobic hole, devoid of women, and silent except for the sounds of empty glasses and bottles clacking on the bar top and the drone of a sports announcer coming from a solitary flickering black-and-white TV. In many ways it was reminiscent of the mines where most of the patrons worked, and many of them sat hunkered down over their drinks as if they were still toiling in the tunnels.

Sometime during the nineties, ownership changed hands. The two neighboring storefronts were up for sale, too. The establishment tripled in size and acquired a kitchen. Now it's a loud, slick sports bar like a thousand others across the nation.

For some reason, they kept the name and also attempted to keep some of the original spirit by covering the walls with a pasteurized mishmash of blue-collar manliness: sports memorabilia, brand-new parts of old-model cars, a length of shiny railroad track, a mounted deer head.

Now just as many women come here as men. The place reverberates with the sound of raised voices trying to compete with the noise coming from the twenty TVs. On weekends they compound the problem by having live music.

It's a weeknight and I arrive around seven, before it gets too busy.

As I walk in and glance at the bar's name etched on the door, I can't help thinking about Jessy noticing the scar on Camio's foot in the crime scene photo. She remembered it came from a rusty nail and the wound got infected. That kind of attention to her younger sister came from either truly caring about her or creepily chronicling everything about her.

Kirk is easy to spot. The other bartender working tonight is a girl.

I've changed into jeans, heels, and a champagne-colored silky tee with a little bling. I sit down at the bar near Kirk and immediately take out my phone so I blend in with everyone else.

He makes his way toward me.

"What can I get you?" he asks.

I ignore him for a moment while I finish my imaginary tweet: Getting hammered at the Rusty Nail. #get it?

He's not a bad-looking kid and he knows it. A few suitably defiant but basically nonthreatening tattoos. Carefully considered stubble. A crop of wheat blond, purposely mussed-up hair. An onyx stud earring and a woven leather choker.

"A sultry night like tonight makes me feel like I'm south of the border. I'll have a Corona and don't forget the lime."

"South of our border is Maryland," he volleys back.

I smile at him.

"You're a smart-ass. And you know your geography. I like both those qualities in a man."

He brings me my beer. I nurse it while he tends to other customers. He stops by a couple of times to check on me. We make a little more small talk.

I'm trying to decide how to bring up the topic of Jessyca when one of the blaring TVs does it for me. An update of Camio's murder flashes on one of the news channels. Fortunately, it doesn't include any of my interviews.

Kirk happens to be standing in front of me when we both catch the video.

"Did you hear about the murder of that girl?" I ask him. "Pretty awful, huh?"

"Yeah."

"I hear you're a friend of her sister's."

He gives me a startled look. I sip innocently at my beer.

"The dead Truly girl's sister? Who told you that?"

"The girl who does my hair," I explain. "She's friends with her. Jessy, right? When I told her I was meeting someone here tonight she said Jessy has a thing for the hot bartender at the Rusty Nail. I assumed that's you."

The stroking of his ego works. He drops his defenses for a moment.

"I might know her," he concedes. "I wouldn't call us friends, though."

"What would you call her? The mother of your child?"

His glib exterior cracks into a million pieces of panic. "Hey, whoa."

He lowers his head and leans across the bar. I do the same.

"Where did that come from?" he whispers to me.

"I'm the chief of police," I whisper back.

I reach for my creds and place them on the bar in case he doesn't believe me. It happens all the time, because I'm a woman and I don't resemble the eighties stereotype of a gym teacher or an Eastern European athlete; I also look exceptionally good tonight.

"Are you kidding me?" He keeps his voice lowered. "Is she getting the police involved? Can she even do that? I told her I'd give her some money but I'm not paying child support and I'm not changing diapers."

I think about my own dad having this same conversation with my mother. Or did he? I only have my mother's version of what went on between them as told to her mother, and she didn't provide many details. I also have no way of knowing how much of it was true. This is one of the biggest regrets of my life: having the master plan of my creation and the question of my desirability be in doubt. I don't care what Miranda Truly says about my paternal grandmother's feelings toward my mother and me. She could be lying, too.

"Legally, if Jessyca wanted to pursue this matter, you'd have to pay child support if the child is yours," I tell Kirk. "But that's not what I'm here about."

I fall silent for a second and let him stew.

"You don't seem to have any doubt that you're the father," I observe.

"I don't know for sure," he says, "but I figure why would she come and tell me this kid is mine if she wasn't going to shake me down or try and get me to marry her? She said she just wanted me to know I had a kid. That it was the right thing to do. So I figure she's probably telling the truth. But if she tries to get me to pay up, we're getting a DNA test."

"You're a real stand-up guy."

"It wasn't my fault," he insists angrily.

He walks away but returns almost immediately.

"I don't have to talk to you. Do I?" he asks.

"Nope," I reply. "How about another beer?"

This time, he doesn't rush back. He busies himself with other customers, laughing with a few of them, trying to seem blasé, but I know my presence here at the end of the bar is killing him.

He finally returns and sets another bottle in front of me. The lime wedge is missing. I know he did this on purpose.

"Why wasn't it your fault?" I ask him, and give him a sympathetic pout. "Did your daddy never have the sex talk with you? Were you absent the day they explained how babies are made in health class?"

"She lied to me," he says, lowering his voice into a whisper again and leaning into my face. "She told me she was on the pill."

"But you still used a condom?"

"She asked me not to. She said it felt better. I'm not going to argue with that. Why am I talking to you?"

He stands up and stalks off again but boomerangs back. His type needs constant vindication.

"You have no idea what it's like being a guy."

"You're right. Educate me."

"You want to have sex, right?"

"I'm with you so far."

"But every time you do you could end up with a kid."

"How is that any different from being a girl?"

He glares at me. I move on to something more relevant.

"You say you and Jessy don't have any kind of relationship, but last time she saw you, she wanted to hook up with you. What do you think that was about?"

"She didn't want to hook up with me. She wanted me to babysit."

"Did she say why?"

"She had somewhere to go and she didn't want to bring the baby along. She said it was going to be emotional or something like that. She said it could get messy."

"'*It could get messy*'? Those were her exact words?"

"She was upset about something. She even started crying. Then the baby started crying. Then they left."

"Upset about what?"

"I wasn't paying attention."

"So she wasn't with you this past Friday between the hours of five and eight?"

"I saw her for fifteen minutes, maybe."

I lean back on my stool, take a long swig from my beer, and give him my best disapproving stare. It doesn't take long for him to wilt under it.

"I had good intentions," he feels the need to explain. "She's not bad-looking but she's got some extra poundage going on. I was kind of doing her a favor."

"A favor?"

"I'm not a loser. I'm going to school. I got student loans to pay. I'm working. My whole life should be flushed down the can because I had pity sex one night?"

I've lost all patience with this jerk.

"Maybe you could try looking at having a child as a good thing instead of a bad one. Lots of people do. It's not all about bills and responsibilities. There are rewards.

"And if you were able to get it up, pity isn't what you were feeling, jackass."

I stare him down again.

"Now get me my lime."

I should leave. There's no reason for me to stay, but I do it anyway just to cramp the style of Mr. Pity Sex.

I'd like to tell him if what I've heard is correct, he shouldn't feel any pity for Jessy. She got exactly what she wanted. Her only interest in him was as a sperm donor. He did do her a favor but not the way he thinks.

Jessy shouldn't have even been in this bar or any bar. She was eighteen when she got pregnant. Even now she's still shy of twenty-one.

They're serving minors in here. I make a mental note to have one of my men look into this, then I make another note to stop being a cop and enjoy the rest of my beer.

I only last for one more beer before the noise gets to me. I'm ready to leave when a woman sits down beside me. I almost faint.

"What are you doing here? You hate bars," I say.

"You've been weird lately. Stressed out. I thought you might want some company."

Neely looks all around her, gets her bearings, then motions at Kirk who pretends not to see her.

"You mean you were worried I was going to get shitfaced and do something stupid," I correct her. "Those days are long past. I get drunk on two shots now and I'm so sick the next day I want to die. Where's Mason?"

"At your house, a couple blocks away, with Smoke, watching TV."

"I guess he's safe. The only guard I'd feel safer with would be Nolan, and that's only because he has opposable thumbs."

"Screw his thumbs. People are more afraid of a snarling German shepherd than they are of an old cop. Besides, why does Mason need a guard? What do you think is going to happen while you're gone? Aren't you the chief of police of this town? Don't you pride yourself on how safe it is?"

"It didn't turn out to be very safe for Camio," I say dejectedly, my three beers starting to make me feel sorry for myself. "And I don't like Lucky skulking around."

Neely makes a sour face and waves away the thought of Lucky with her extended middle finger.

"So how'd it go?" she asks. "I can tell you talked to the bartender by the way he's avoiding us."

"Helpful. I think. Camio's sister might've been with her when she died or right before. Same for her uncle. Same for her grandmother. They're all lying. I don't know why. I don't know how much they're lying. I still don't see any reason for any of them to kill her."

"Family members kill other family members all the time," she says.

"But not simply because they're family. There's always a specific motive. Something that the killer needed or wanted or set him off. Let's change the subject."

"Hey, kid," Neely says to Kirk in her best instructor voice. "Bring me a Jack and Coke. Now."

He looks her way and obeys, no differently than Sammy the golden doodle.

"The last guy I slept with I met at this bar," I announce as it occurs to me.

I'm not counting Nolan. I never count him.

"The guy who owns the sporting goods store in Hellersburg?"

I nod.

"How was it?"

"Eh."

"Why do you do it then?"

"Because I want to have sex."

"Don't you want to have good sex?"

"Of course. But good sex isn't always available."

"And eh sex is an acceptable substitute?"

"No." I sigh.

Kirk brings Neely her drink, asks me if I want another beer, then asks someone behind me what he's having. Neely and I turn around and find Lucky standing behind us.

"Speak of the devil," I say.

Neely hasn't seen him for more than thirty years. It takes her a minute to place his face. He knows her instantly.

"The high-and-mighty one," he coos, his voice sounding as oily as his hair looks. "Princess Neely. Too good to give me the time of day except for her bitchy little comments when her mama wasn't listening."

Neely turns around on her stool.

"Don't you talk about my mother."

"I'll talk about your mother all I want. She was the love of my life and somebody killed her and you're going to tell me who."

Neely gets off her stool and gets in his face. He's wearing a lot of cologne, and she blinks her eyes against the smell.

"We're not going to tell you anything," she says in a low, calm voice. "Dove says you've been running around threatening us and saying you're going to sue us. You even went and harassed Grandma. No one's impressed. You don't scare us. You can't prove anything, and you don't have the balls to try and hurt us.

"Come on, Dove," she says to me.

I'm pretty sure he's wearing the same shirt as when he came to see me five days ago but it's been laundered. Mingled with his noxious cologne is the cloying flowery scent of some kind of fabric softener.

I don't know where he's staying or how he's getting by. Life isn't easy for an ex-con and definitely not for one pushing seventy. I picture him living in a single rented room, empty except for a lumpy mattress on an old iron bed frame and a dresser topped with an amateurish flea market painting of a basket of kittens on black velvet, with one belt buckle and one going-out shirt to his name.

I start to get off my stool and he grabs me roughly by the arm.

"You stole my life. You think I'm just going to let it go?"

"You don't have a choice."

I meant for the words to come out sounding fierce and final, but they sound defeated and full of regret.

Neely pulls his hand off me and gets between us.

"I'm going to tell you this one time and one time only. You leave Dove out of this. I'm the one who convinced her to lie. I'm the one who came up with the whole idea."

He gives her a leering smile full of graveyard gaps and stained teeth like old headstones.

"Then you're the one who should buy me a drink."

"Let's go," Neely commands.

I reach into my purse for my wallet.

"Don't you dare," she warns me.

"I'm paying for ours."

She leaves first. I throw three twenties on the bar and hurry after her, not waiting to see Lucky's reaction.

I join my sister outside the bar.

"It had to be done," she says.

I'm not sure which crime she's talking about. I agree the first was necessary, but maybe we didn't need to falsely accuse Lucky. I tell her as much.

"We had to lay it on someone," she reasons, "and he was the best candidate. If the police had kept looking they might have found out the truth."

Neely is not a physically demonstrative person with people. I could probably count on one hand the amount of times we've embraced during our lives. Even now she doesn't hug me. She reaches out and cups my face with her two hands the way a mother does with a young child who she's trying to soothe.

"I know you think it was selfish but it wasn't," she says. "You didn't do it for yourself; you did it for me. There was no way I would've survived if they caught you."

I look into her eyes, our mother's eyes, and marvel at how I can't live without someone who so resembles someone I killed.

chapter twenty-three

I MANAGE to keep my emotions in check until we get back to my house and I'm alone in my bedroom. When I start crying it's because I'm overwhelmed once again by my sister's loyalty. I've never been able to cry over what I did to my mother. I've felt sorrow, rage, shame, and disgust since that night but I've never shed a tear or experienced a moment of regret. I don't know what this says about me. I do know what it says about her.

I found out about Gil and Champ innocently enough and have often looked back on that day and thought how easy it would have been for me to have not discovered what was going on and also how I had failed my little brother by not discovering it sooner. I don't know which feeling has been worse: the guilt over my dereliction of duty or the twinges of self-preservation that make me wish I'd never known.

I came home unexpectedly from school. After a dentist appointment downtown, I walked home instead of going back for my last few classes. My plan was to grab a bite, then convince Mom to let me borrow her car to drive back later for basketball practice.

It turned out she had gone shopping. I saw Gil's big cranberry Buick in the driveway but thought nothing of it. He came and went from his places of business whenever he felt like it. He was the boss.

Champ should've been in school. Gil had taken him out for what he called a family emergency.

He hadn't bothered to shut his door completely because he thought they were alone.

We all like to think we know how we'd react in a crisis. We've all watched plenty of tragedies covered on the news and thought, *I'd handle it differently. I would've gone to the authorities,* or *I would've taken that boy and run away,* or *I would've killed that son of a bitch right then and there and no matter what I did, I'd be on the side of the angels and when it was all over, I'd be able to put it behind me.*

The problem with this armchair supposing is that it's fiction even though it may spring from true outrage. Nothing shatters the reality of our good intentions like reality.

I was in a situation I could have never imagined in my wildest, most perverted dreams. It was inconceivable. I would have been less shocked if Gil had turned out to be a werewolf or an alien from another planet than a human doing what I witnessed when I walked by that door.

I didn't panic. I didn't scream. I didn't threaten. I didn't vomit or run.

I turned my head away and stood back from the door.

"Champ!" I called out, trying to sound strong and whole instead of the shivering, frantic bits I'd become. "Come here."

I never spoke to Gil. I would never speak to him again. He left. Later that night the police would find him at Rankin's with a half dozen of his employees going through inventory and able to give him an impeachable alibi.

I called Grandma and told her she needed to take Champ to her house and watch him for a while. I explained in a demented twist of irony that I had a surprise planned for Mom that just involved Neely and me and wanted Champ to be absent.

Grandma never questioned my story, and I never told her what happened to Champ. I didn't think she could handle it or that she could help. I've often thought since then, after a lifetime of knowing her, that I was wrong on both counts.

I waited until Mom was taking her bath. I knew I'd have her undivided attention that way.

She was settled deep in a cloud of bubbles, her golden hair piled on top of her head and drinking a glass of wine, when I walked into the bathroom to tell her.

I had no idea how to begin the conversation. I wanted it over. I truly believed once I told her, she'd fix everything. My heart swelled with love as I stood before her knowing she would be our savior. She would finally be our mom.

I took a deep breath and blurted out, "Gil's been messing with Champ."

I think I expected her to be in denial at first. Or thought she might even laugh. Or maybe she'd always sensed something was wrong. Maybe she'd be subconsciously prepared. Maybe she'd go directly to fury. Or collapse even deeper into her bubbles sobbing. Or jump for her robe and head for the phone to call the police.

She sighed and looked annoyed at me.

"It's not a big deal, Dove."

I was sure I hadn't heard her right or she hadn't heard me right. Before I could repeat myself, she went on with an explanation she seemed to feel was perfectly fine.

"He lives in a big, beautiful house. He has all the toys he could ever want. Food on the table. And he finally has a father. Gil has even talked about adopting you kids."

She knows, a voice screamed inside my head. *She's known all along and doesn't care.*

"He'll get over it," she assured me. "He's a boy."

Was it a swap? the voice continued screaming. *Did you discuss it calmly like a business deal over a nice dinner? Did he hold out the velvet box with the diamond ring sparkling inside it and tell you it was all yours if you gave him your son?*

I'd never find out the answers.

Once again I didn't fall apart. I didn't hang around to further discuss the situation. I didn't snap. I didn't lose my temper. I remained calm and sane. I knew exactly what I was doing as I walked to my little brother's bedroom and returned with his baseball bat choked up firmly in my hands. I was so in control and considerate that I remembered not to damage her face for Grandma's sake.

Neely is the only other person who knows the truth and even she doesn't know all of it. I told her about Champ and I told her what I did but I never told her what Mom said to me in the bathroom before she died. I knew it wasn't necessary.

Neely wouldn't care about the details and the depths of our mother's depravity. All she needed to know was the bitch failed to protect her pups.

THERE'S A TAP on my door.

Neely and Smoke have gone home. I left Mason downstairs in front of the TV. I tell myself he's watching too much TV. I need to find him some kind of day camp.

"Just a minute," I tell him, and head for a box of Kleenex.

I blow my nose, dab at my eyes, and check my reflection in a mirror. Along with MOF, I'm now also a victim of SOF, Sad Old Face. My eyelids are puffy, my face sags like Deputy Dawg's, my skin's sickly pale with patches of red. In my youth, crying made me look deliciously vulnerable and dewy.

"Come in," I call.

Mason enters clutching his Trapper Keeper.

"You look sad, Aunt Dove," he immediately confirms.

"I'm a little sad."

"Is it because of me?"

"No, definitely not."

I plop down on the edge of my bed and pat the space beside me.

"Come here. Let's have a talk."

He moves toward me, then has second thoughts.

"Wait a minute," he says.

He lays down his binder and rushes from the room.

He returns with a smartphone in a rosy glitter-frosted case and hands it to me.

"I was going to save this and give it to you as a thank-you present when Dad comes back but maybe you'd like it now. It might make you feel better."

"Where did you get this?" I ask.

"Derk. He traded it for these goofy paper umbrellas and toothpicks shaped like swords Dad and I collected on our road trip. And some other toothpicks from Manny's that have little Mexican flags on them."

I turn on the phone and slide my finger across the screen to access it. Up pops a photo of Camio and Zane.

Mason crawls up on the bed beside me and looks over my shoulder.

"I asked him why he had a pink sparkly phone."

He pauses while he grabs his binder and starts leafing through its pages. He seems to find what he's looking for.

"Derk said it belongs to an angel who dropped it from heaven," he reads from the page, then smiles up at me.

"I wrote that one down. Pure gold."

chapter twenty-four

I'VE ALWAYS THOUGHT of regret and guilt as salt and pepper siblings: the first a clean, straightforward, righteous emotion aroused by circumstances beyond our control or power to repair; the second a murky, confusing, selfish muck fueled by culpability, real or imagined, and kept bubbling by a sense of inadequacy.

Regret is spontaneous, but I believe we choose to feel guilt. This is the only way I can explain good people like Neely and Nolan who, while capable of admitting mistakes and taking responsibility for their failures, move past them and never seem to let them impact their lives.

I don't think I'm a selfish person and I try not to feel guilt, but sometimes I fail. Today is going to be one of those days.

It was a different time, I remind myself as I stand in front of my closet searching for an outfit. Pedophilia wasn't openly discussed the way it is now. Teachers, doctors, guidance counselors, even the police weren't trained to notice it. No one was ready to acknowledge it existed, especially in white-picket-fenced little towns. And if it did exist, the men committing this vile act had to be the unwashed, unsavory, unnoticed dregs of society.

Gil was rich, highly visible, from a good family, a pillar of the community. Our mother was a loose woman with three illegitimate children who married him for his money and was murdered by an ex-lover.

We knew we could never get anyone to believe what Gil had done to Champ. We also didn't want Champ to have to talk about it. He wasn't even able to talk to us about it. We naïvely thought he could forget about it and we could, too, if we pretended it never happened.

None of these suppositions help me to climb out of the guilt swamp I've found myself wallowing in this morning.

I realize I've lost a skirt and blouse, a sundress, and a shoe to this investigation, ruined by coal, dirt, blood, and chewing tobacco. All that's left is for me to get spattered by motor oil or the grease from a serving of hot wings and I'll really feel like one of the boys.

I know I'm bucking the odds, but I put on one of my favorite summer ensembles: a fitted robin's egg blue sleeveless dress, nipped fetchingly at the waist, with a matching jacket, and the taupe pumps I was wearing the day we found Camio.

Her phone is long gone, scooped up by a state trooper who was in the area almost instantly after I called Nolan last night and told him about my gift from Mason.

I also told him Jessy no longer has an alibi.

I've been invited to the state police barracks this morning purely as a spectator and once I arrive, I do feel like one. What unfolds before me is even better than attending a sporting event or a Broadway musical. Watching Nolan try to interrogate Derk is an unparalleled form of entertainment all its own, and my mood begins to lighten.

Shawna sits with me watching the proceedings on a computer screen. She didn't want to be present in the room while Nolan talked to her son, but she did agree to observe rather than bring in a representative from child services.

I watch her watching him looking for any signs of distress or anger. She reveals nothing, and I wonder if she's retreated again into her titanic detachment.

According to the troopers who escorted them here, Mrs. Truly cooperated fully with them when they showed up at her house, although it did take close to a half hour of her repeatedly going to the back and front porches and shouting for Derk before he finally appeared, but once he did, he surrendered peacefully after informing both officers that cops are a bunch of cocksuckers and showing them how he could throw his pocketknife hard enough to make it stick in a tree trunk. Their suggestion that maybe she wanted to give her son a bath and have him change his clothes was met by expressions of utter disbelief on both their faces.

"Has he always been this energetic?" I ask Shawna.

Derk is on top of the table jumping up and down, his fists clenched, his now bare feet hitting the surface in loud slaps, his head tilted back, howling, "Not telling! Not telling! Not telling!" in response to Nolan's latest attempt to find out where he found the phone.

"Even as a baby," Shawna says, her eyes never leaving the screen. "He was hard to control.

"But he's a good boy," she thinks to add.

"Of course."

Derk has been reacting to all of Nolan's questions in a similar fashion. He's hidden under the table. He's done a headstand in the corner. He's done a cartwheel-type maneuver by grabbing the back of his chair and throwing his legs up and over it. He took his sneakers off and chewed away big chunks of the soles and spit out the pieces at the wall before putting them on his hands and crawling around the room on all fours. He ran in place at an impressive speed while shouting "Dick!" at the top of his lungs.

There were no usable prints found on the phone. Derk is our only lead.

Nolan gets up from his chair without bothering to give Derk an explanation and heads for the door. Even after he leaves, the boy continues to jump up and down and yell.

The door to the small empty office where we sit with nothing but a laptop opens and Nolan steps inside.

"Mrs. Truly," he begins, and runs a hand over his crew cut, "is your son retarded?"

"You'll have to forgive Corporal Greely's political incorrectness," I intervene on his behalf. "What he meant to say is, is he special?"

Shawna doesn't respond to either question.

"He doesn't like to be confined," she states. "Makes him antsy."

"Maybe I should talk to him on a mountaintop somewhere," Nolan says gruffly.

"Or the surface of the moon?" I suggest.

He gives me an exhausted, frustrated look I'm not expecting.

He wasn't able to break Eddie, and I know this is weighing heavily on him.

Even though Eddie's fingerprints were on the steering wheel of Adelaide's car and on a few surfaces inside her house, and it's been confirmed that the blood in the trunk of the car, in the kitchen, and on the bottom of the cast-iron skillet belongs to Camio, he claims he visited his aunt recently and that she loaned him his car. Nothing more. He says he doesn't know anything about Camio's murder or his aunt's disappearance. He's sticking with this story for now.

"Do you want to try?" he asks me.

I don't want to steal Nolan's thunder, especially here in his own barracks. I also don't think I'll have any better luck.

"I think we should let his mother try," I reply.

"He don't listen to me," Shawna says automatically before Nolan can comment one way or the other. "I can't make him tell me anything."

"Don't make him," I say. "Ask him nicely. Tell him it will help Camio. He thinks she's an angel now."

Nolan and I wait.

"Just speak from your heart," I urge her.

She looks back at the screen where Derk's antics continue. I wonder how long he could do this.

A heavy sigh fills the room and she rises, seemingly pulled up by the release of air from her lungs.

Nolan nods at me. I accompany her, and he stays behind to watch.

Derk doesn't even look at us when we enter the room.

We each take a seat on either side of the table where he hops up and down like a frog still shouting, "Not telling!"

"Maybe you should tell him to stop," I say to Shawna.

"Won't do no good."

I get up and walk to the end of the table, put my shoulder under it, and heave with all my strength. The table tilts and Derk slides off onto the floor. He grabs the chair I was sitting on and swings it around while backing into a corner. Once safely situated, he squats down and sets the chair in front of him like a cell door.

"Your mother has something to say to you, Derk," I tell him. "I know you think you're pretty tough, but even the toughest guys in the world listen to their moms."

He puts his hands on the back of the chair and peers through the metal railings at Shawna.

"Go ahead," I say gently, hoping she might still feel a little of the empathetic connection we had the last time we spoke and still trust me.

The three of us sit in silence for what feels like an entire afternoon but is probably only a minute.

"This ain't a game," Shawna finally speaks.

Her voice is low and quiet, barely audible. She

doesn't look at Derk but stares at her hands clasped between her knees.

"Your sister's dead. And she loved you. You know how rare that is? To have someone who really loves you? It don't happen much. Now she's gone. Forever."

I know she's talking about Camio being gone forever but I can't help wondering if she's also thinking about herself before she met Clark and Miranda Truly and even Sugar, the sacrificial cat.

Derk watches her, fascinated.

She raises her head and stares back at him.

"Derk, I want you to tell us where you found that phone. I'm not going to tell you to do it for Camio. She's an angel in heaven now, like Grandma told you. She's happy. I want you to do it for me. Your old mom. Because I'm very, very sad."

He shifts around behind the chair but continues to hold the seat's back rails like they're bars he can't shake loose.

"I'm going to get in trouble," he replies. "I'm going to get kilt."

"Don't say stuff like that," Shawna tells him. "I won't be mad at you no matter where you were."

"You're not who's gonna kill me."

"I won't let anyone kill you."

His mother's promise appears to be the key that frees him from his corner. He pushes the chair aside and walks over to her.

"You will be the mighty good queen?" he asks with extreme gravity.

He's a slip of a boy, all wiry muscle and bone hidden beneath his dirty, ill-fitting clothes. He looks like he'd be easy to subdue, but I imagine trying to physically force him to do something he didn't want to do would be like taking on a rabid weasel.

"Yes," his mother answers him.

"I go in her house sometimes and take things and put them back later," he confesses. "I want her to think she's crazy. She locks her doors, but I know an upstairs window I can get in."

Understanding shines briefly in Shawna's eyes. She knows what he's talking about.

"You found Camio's phone in your grandma's house?" she asks him.

"On the table next to her bed with her Bible and her *TV Guide*," he confirms.

He moves closer to her.

"Now you can make me a knight," he states.

From his shorts pocket, he pulls out one of the novelty toothpicks Mason accumulated on his road trip that he traded with him for Camio's phone and gives it to her. She takes it and holds it delicately between her chubby fingers.

He kneels down in front of her and bows his head. She gently taps his skinny shoulders and all the burdens he carries there with the tiny plastic sword.

chapter twenty-five

NOLAN DOESN'T SAY MUCH to me after questioning Derk other than to ask if I want to hang around for Miranda's interrogation. I tell him nothing on heaven or earth would keep me from seeing that.

It makes no sense for me to drive all the way back to Buchanan, then back to the barracks. I find a nearby Dunkin' Donuts, have a coffee and cruller, and feel like a cliché.

Upon my return I find Nolan standing statue-still in the parking lot, his hands in his pants pockets, his Ray-Bans affixed firmly to his face, his shoulder holster and gun peeking out from underneath his suit jacket.

I don't know what this means at first, then I think I do.

I want to see Camio's killer brought to justice as much as anyone—sometimes I think I want it more than her own family—but the official investigation doesn't belong to me. I'm doing all I can to assist, but aside from listening to future grumblings from residents about the incompetence of the local police department and irate blogging and letters to the editor bemoaning their once idyllic community's loss of innocence, it's not going to impact my career.

Nolan is at the end of his, but this doesn't make a bit of difference. Every case has always been of equal importance to him. He works as hard now as he did when he first joined the force. In some ways, I think he works harder. He's no longer performing his duties with an eye toward advancement and glory but out of accountability.

A teenage girl from a small town brutally bludgeoned to death and lit on fire is a very big deal. He needs to close this case for his own peace of mind as well as for everyone else he has sworn to protect.

He's nervous.

I park, get out of my car, and walk toward him.

"She's here," he says.

I wait for him to expand on this narrative, or he might say nothing more and I wouldn't be surprised.

"I don't have to tell you how important this interview is," he finally continues. "Once she talks, Eddie will talk, too. I can't screw this up."

"You won't."

"Don't patronize me."

"I'm not telling you what you want to hear," I jump to my own defense. "I didn't say you will get the confession; I said you won't screw up. There's a difference."

We both fall silent. I know from experience that Nolan can remain this way indefinitely until he decides to depart without any explanation.

I'm getting ready to say something when he speaks again.

"We checked Eddie Truly's phone records and right around Camio's TOD he received a phone call from his mother on her landline. After what we've just learned from the boy, we were able to access her phone records, and before she called Eddie she received a call from Jessyca's cell. We already have her records, since her line is on a family plan under her father's name. Originally we didn't pay much attention to her calls."

He pauses. I know he's upset he let this get by him. He's feeling regret but not guilt.

"Why would you?" I reason. "A girl calls her grandmother. So what? Even if it happened around the time her sister was killed, there was no reason to suspect either one of them."

"Now we know what we're looking for," he goes on. "We checked the origination of the call. It bounced off a tower near Adelaide Bertolino's home."

My heart drops. I didn't realize until this moment how badly I didn't want Jessyca to be involved.

"Jessy was at the crime scene at the time of death," I state unhappily. "She called her grandma. Her grandma called her uncle."

"To help clean up and dispose of the body," Nolan finishes for me.

"Or maybe not," I argue hopefully. "When are you talking to Jessy?"

"I want to hear what Miranda has to say first."

"Can I bring Jessy in?"

"I guess you've earned that right if you want it."

Silence descends once again. I don't notice it this time because I'm busy coming up with alternative theories of the crime. Nolan is the first to talk.

"Last time you saw Miranda, you got under her skin. She got personal with you. Was inappropriate?" he asks.

I nod.

"Why do you think she did that?"

"There's the obvious answer: that she wanted to upset me and throw me off my game," I reply. "Or she might have done it to impress her family. Show them she wasn't afraid of the police. But the more I've thought about it, I think she was testing me. She wanted to see if I'd make a worthy adversary."

"When I talked to her she was polite as can be," he tells me, "the epitome of a little old lady who was dealing with a horrible tragedy in her family and using it as an excuse to tell me nothing."

He pauses.

"I want to go at her together."

An adolescent thrill rushes through me in spite of myself. He's impressed with me. He trusts me.

"Good cop, bad cop?" I joke with him, trying to sound nonchalant. "Or good cop, glorified babysitter cop?"

"From everything we know about her, she likes to control other people's relationships. If we need to, we can distract her with ours."

"Our real relationship?"

"Hell no."

He turns and walks into the station. I follow,

knowing full well we won't end up putting on any kind of act when we confront our suspect. We will be ourselves, only Nolan won't realize it. He's an expert at reading others but knows nothing about himself.

"I'VE ASKED CHIEF CARNAHAN to sit in on this interview," Nolan tells Miranda.

She maintains her composure and gives me a nod, not showing the slightest bit of surprise or discomfort.

Now that I've seen a few pictures of her from her youth, I know she's a woman who has aged from the inside out. Joy, pleasure, optimism left her long ago. Not all at once; like air from a punctured bicycle tire with the nail still embedded in the tread, her compassion atrophy was probably a slow leak.

Aside from the inevitable wrinkles and gray hair, she looks remarkably like the young mother I saw posing with her sister and their babies in the photo on Adelaide's wall, but the stony condemnation in her stare and condescension in her carriage is that of ancient gall.

"You don't mind, do you?" he asks while pulling out a chair for me on the opposite side of the table from Miranda.

I smile at him, not her, and take a seat, crossing my legs, and being sure to flaunt my girlishness.

I have a stack of folders with me that have nothing to do with this case and a legal pad with a bunch of nonsense I jotted down on it before we came in. I'm wearing my plainest reading glasses and carrying a cup of coffee I hand to Nolan like a doting secretary.

"Not at all," she says.

Despite the heat, she's costumed in a long-sleeved black sack of a dress that falls below her knees. If it weren't for the presence of her head and a pair of withered, blue-veined hands, I'd think the garment was still on its hanger.

She wears no jewelry of any kind, not even a wedding ring or a cross on a chain around her neck. Her hair has been cut since I saw her a few days ago. The style is almost mannish now, shaved on the sides but feathered on top like a grate full of white ashy embers has been dumped on her head.

The severity of her mourning is excessive.

"We appreciate you coming in to talk to us," Nolan says.

"I didn't have much of a choice," Miranda counters.

He takes off his glasses and levels a concerned gaze at her with his baby blues.

"How's that? The troopers didn't explain? I told them to answer any questions you might have."

"They don't always listen to you," I say snidely.

He makes a point of ignoring me.

Miranda is already watching us closely.

"They said it had something to do with my granddaughter's murder. That's all," she provides.

She doesn't know we've found the crime scene. She doesn't know Eddie has been detained and is in a holding cell in the basement of this very building. His phone was taken from him the moment he was picked up and since then, he hasn't asked to call anyone, including a lawyer.

"Is it true things have been disappearing from your home?" Nolan asks her, going completely off topic.

Miranda's eyes shift quickly from him to me. I raise my pen, poised to take notes.

"Yes. I mean, no," she stutters. "I misplaced a few things. Then I found them again. I'm an old lady. How do you know this?"

"You're lying," I state flatly. "You didn't misplace anything. You might be old, but you're sharp as a tack."

"Don't speak to Mrs. Truly like that," Nolan commands.

"Don't you speak to me like that," I snap back at him. "You were my superior eons ago. Not anymore. I know how to conduct an interrogation."

He leans back in his chair, puts his hands behind his head, and stretches out his legs.

"Fine. Go ahead. Conduct away."

"Mrs. Truly," I begin again. "Has something of substantial value gone missing from your home recently?"

She glances at Nolan. He's staring at the ceiling.

"I don't own anything of substantial value," she answers me in a prickly tone.

"I don't mean expensive. I mean something important. Like your dead granddaughter's phone."

I got her good. Panic dances in her eyes for a split second followed by the fight-or-flight reflex. Flight is impossible for her at the moment. She decides to fight. I'd expect no less from her.

"I don't know what you're talking about."

"Camio's phone was found in your house. We have it in our possession now and we have the testimony of the person who took it from you."

The seed has been planted. We know who invaded

her home and messed around with her stuff and her sanity. This is a piece of information she'd love to have.

"You have the testimony of a thief then," she responds angrily. "What good will that do you?"

"He's only a thief if he took it. So you're saying someone did take the phone from your home?"

My backward looping logic has her temporarily confused.

Nolan jumps in.

"We just need to know how you came to acquire the phone," he says conversationally.

"Your fingerprints are on it," he lies.

"Camio wanted to show me how it worked. That's why my fingerprints are on it," she lies, too.

We've got her on the hook. She's admitted she handled the phone.

"These are the freshest prints on the phone. They're on top of Camio's," Nolan continues feeding her a forensic fairy tale. "They belong to whoever touched it last. After she was dead."

"Yeah, but . . . ," I interrupt him, "whoever had the phone used it to frame Camio's boyfriend, Zane. They sent texts to him pretending to be her to lure him out so he wouldn't have an alibi during her time of death. That's pretty smart. I don't think Miranda here could've come up with that."

Nolan frowns at me.

"There's no reason to be insulting to Mrs. Truly."

He turns to her. She's having a hard time digesting everything and deciphering how much we know and how much we can use against her.

"Do you watch a lot of TV?" he asks her. "Crime dramas?"

Before she can answer, I continue with my musings.

"But you did hate Zane. So maybe it was you. That's a lot of hate to want to send someone to prison for something he didn't do. Or did it have nothing to do with your feelings toward Zane? Was he just a convenient scapegoat the police would buy into? You needed someone else to be found guilty so they'd stop looking for the real killer who you're protecting because . . ." My voice breaks off.

Nolan gives me a questioning look.

"Because you still love that person even knowing what they did."

"I don't have one of those phones," she tries. "I don't know how to work them."

"You just said Camio showed you how," Nolan corrects her.

"That's not what I said."

"It's not rocket science," I join in. "You know how many dumb people have smartphones?"

Nolan smiles at that.

"It might not take intelligence, Mrs. Truly, but it does take patience to write a text if you're not familiar with the device, and the person who sent the texts took a long time to write each one," he explains. "He or she wasn't very experienced at using one."

"Who gave you the phone?" she asks him suddenly.

She's lasted as long as possible. The inner workings of her family and maintaining control over the living, breathing cogs in the machine she created are of much more importance to her than trying to out-maneuver some questions from a couple of cops. She wants to know who had the audacity to wrong her and violate her home so she can begin to plan apt punishment.

"We don't have to share that information with you," Nolan informs her.

"But we might," I add, "if you tell us what happened to Camio."

"I don't know."

"Why did you have her phone?" Nolan presses her.

"The person who slipped into your home unnoticed and took your personal possessions did so with malicious intent and we believe will continue to harass you," I tell her.

Her internal struggle has to be intense at this point, but none of it shows on her exterior. I'm sure she'd give almost anything to find out who was in her house, short of her own freedom and that of her son's.

Nolan leans across the table.

"Mrs. Truly, we've arrested your son Edward for the murder of your granddaughter. We've found the site where she was killed and the vehicle that was used to transport her body. We think he may have also harmed your sister, Adelaide."

Her face grows pale and a small tic begins at the corner of her mouth. She refuses to meet Nolan's gaze and stares over his shoulder.

"If you have anything to tell us, you better do it now," he adds. "You're up to your eyeballs in this."

"You really think I'm capable of killing my own

granddaughter?" she asks, her voice trembling slightly. "Or that Eddie would be capable?"

"Shawna told us a few things you did to her awhile back," I answer her. "I think you're capable of just about anything."

She clasps her hands in front of her on the table, forming a fleshy ball of gnarled fingers and knobby knuckles.

"It's time for me to get a lawyer," she says. "I've watched enough TV to know that."

Nolan stands and nods at me. I gather up my folders and notepad. We didn't get exactly what we wanted, but we got enough for now.

"That stuff with Shawna," Miranda says.

We both pause at the door and look back at her.

"We only did it to get her to stay. It was for her own good. She needed us."

We step out and Nolan closes the door behind him. We look at each other and don't have to say a word. Sometimes during an interview you stumble into another person's view of the world around them and all you want to do is get the hell out.

Another detective joins us. He greets me and hands Nolan a report. Nolan pulls him off to one side for a private conversation. When he turns back to me, he only meets my eyes for a second, then stares off in the direction of the war room. My heart begins pounding at an unhealthy rate.

"We found your brother's car. Looks like he never left the state."

"Is he okay?"

"I said his car. There's no sign of him."

"Where?"

"Fayette County. Parking area near a boat launch on the Monongahela. Any reason for him to be there?"

"Not that I know of.

"What are you thinking?" I ask him, doing my best to sound calm and failing.

"I'm thinking there's no point in thinking anything," he replies roughly, doing his best to be kind, and failing.

"I'm thinking you should go get Jessyca Truly," he tries again. "Concentrate on the job. You got some control over that."

AFTER LEAVING THE BARRACKS I drive without giving much thought at all to where I'm going and end up at the cemetery where my dad is buried.

When I was a kid I used to come here on Father's Day, but once I became an adult, I started coming here on the anniversary of his death instead. The main reason was because lots of other people visited their fathers' graves on Father's Day and I felt like I was cheating. They came armed with true grief and bittersweet memories. I came with nothing except the knowledge that I never knew the man I mourned. All I really knew for sure about him was he briefly owned a cool car and his sperm was motile.

I haven't violated this schedule in thirty years and because of this, I'm never here in summer when the grass is green, the birds are singing, the trees are full of whispering leaves, and loved ones have left colorful bouquets of flowers on the graves.

I'm always bundled up in a coat and gloves. It's usually sleeting. The tombstones stand stark and untended with a moaning wind whipping through the bare, black branches reaching over them.

The cemetery sits on church grounds, but it's far enough away that people worshipping the Lord don't have to look at the place where their bodies are going to end up while their souls are at the pearly gates reminding him of all the time they spent in those uncomfortable pews.

My mother is buried in the biggest and most prestigious cemetery in town, the place where many of our wealthiest and most important citizens have been interred along with members of the middle class striving even in death to impress others with what they can afford. Statues of angels, engraved marble columns, massive headstones taller than the men lying beneath them, and the occasional mausoleum dot that landscape along with a smattering of small, unadorned, rock slabs belonging to humble folk who were laid to rest a hundred years ago before anyone knew this would be prime hereafter real estate.

Neely's the one who talked Gil into providing our mother with a marker worthy of her beauty. She did it to make Grandma happy. The negotiations took place during a succession of long-distance phone calls. Gil had already fled to Europe and wouldn't return for Mom's funeral, although he did return for Lucky's trial. Her headstone is made of pink marble shot through with veins of ivory and silver, and her name is carved within a heart. I saw it the day of her funeral. I've never been back.

Donny's headstone is a simple one. Donald Allan McMahon. Beloved Son. His date of birth and death twenty years apart.

I'm much older than he lived to be. He's young enough to be my son. I'm much older than my mother now, too. A strange time-traveler feeling comes over me when I look at photos of them. How am I supposed to think of that boy and that young woman as my parents? I don't. I can't. It's easier to believe I came from no one. The thought is freeing in some ways but also fraught with obligation. Since I owe allegiance to no one, I often feel like I should serve everyone.

I take off my shoes the same way I did out at the Run as I approached Camio's body, and I walk across the soft grass.

I arrive at Donny's grave. Old Hot Wheels cars are heaped up against his stone like a salvage yard of tiny auto parts, many of them no longer sporting their original flashy paint jobs and stickers that were weathered away long ago. Some have disappeared over the years. I don't know if kids have taken them or one of Donny's family members has removed them.

I used to like to think his mother saw them when she visited his grave and somehow knew the cars came from her unclaimed bastard granddaughter and she left them there with her blessing, wondering if maybe I wasn't that bad after all.

Grief stabs me all over but I realize I'm not mourning my father, but my brother. Was I drawn to a cemetery because I'm already envisioning putting him in the ground?

I see Champ as a boy in a dark suit with a single rose clasped in his hands waiting to place it on our mother's casket. I see Mason the same way with orange socks peeking out from between his pant legs and shoes, holding his binder, waiting to put a coupon or a novelty toothpick on Champ's casket.

I shake both images from my head.

I look down at my father's grave and wonder what I'm doing here. He can't provide me with solace, strength, or guidance. He can't inspire me with the memory of the love we once shared, since we never did. All I have is the assurance of Grandma that he used to pay me clandestine visits when Mom was out and hold me in his arms and tell me I was the sweetest thing in the world.

I will never be able to forgive my mother. I've made my peace with this fact. But I have forgiven my father for turning his back on me and driving his new Sunbird into a tree. He was a child, a reckless boy with an unyielding, overbearing mother, and if she were anything like Miranda, I couldn't blame him for his prejudices and fears.

"It's okay," I tell him. "It wasn't your fault."

I've never said these words out loud before. I realize as I do that my forgiveness is the only thing my dad has ever needed from me. Maybe giving it to him will help ease the loss of everything I needed from him but could never have.

I get back in my car and drive to the Truly house.

chapter twenty-six

DERK ANSWERS THE DOOR taking me by surprise. I didn't expect to see him corralled.

His face and hands are covered in red goo and for a panicked second, I think there might be another Truly to add to the body count.

He looks up at me, says nothing, and scampers into the living room, yelling, "It's the chief."

It's hot sauce.

Shawna's housekeeping hasn't improved since I've been here last, but she seems a little more aware. She's enthroned in her usual spot on the couch, but she's not alone. Derk is sitting beside her. They're eating wings and nachos and watching a Disney movie instead of the blathering talk shows and mindless reality TV she seems to prefer. Her hair looks washed and she's wearing a pair of earrings.

"Hello, Shawna," I greet her. "I hope you don't mind the intrusion."

"What's going on now? Do you need Derk again?"

She reaches for a roll of paper towels. The coffee

table is a dirty snowdrift of used ones streaked with hot sauce.

She gives one to Derk and takes one for herself.

"Derk did a great job. We don't need him again. You should be proud of him."

"So he wasn't lying? Miranda admitted she had Camio's phone?"

"We're still sorting some things out, but Miranda and Eddie were involved."

She pauses while wiping her mouth.

"I can't believe it," she says, shaking her head, her words muffled inside the paper towel.

"It's okay, Mom," Derk tells her, and pats her shoulder.

"Can we get her back now?" she asks, her eyes shining with tears. "Can we finally bury her?"

"Are we going to put her in the ground?" Derk asks, visibly upset. "Are we going to bury her like a bone?"

Shawna reaches for him and pulls him close. I almost expect the skinny little boy to disappear into the folds of her ample flesh, a reverse birth of sort, the mother reabsorbing her child and starting all over.

"I told you, Derk. It's not really her," Shawna assures him. "She's in heaven. It's just what's left over."

"Is Jessy here?"

"She's upstairs somewhere."

"I need to talk to her."

"Suit yourself."

I'm only supposed to escort Jessy back to Nolan. I'm not supposed to risk damaging an official interrogation by discussing the case and revealing any of the evidence we have against her, but Nolan knows I won't be able to see the girl again without having a chat with her. This is why he sent me to pick her up. Figuring out how much information he wants me to gather for him to use against her and how much of our hand I can show her in order to get it without obstructing our ultimate goal is the hard part. As usual, I'm going to wing it.

A chill runs through me when I find Jessy has already moved into her dead sister's room.

She's sitting at Camio's desk texting. The once neat, almost barren surface is strewn with makeup, jewelry, gum wrappers, and girlie knickknacks. The walls are covered with posters of actors and bands. The bed has a black comforter with fiery red swirls like comets streaking across it.

Country rock music blares from a speaker shaped like a softball sitting on the dresser, and a nauseating combination of smells ranging from apple cinnamon and sugar cookie to pine forest and tropical coconut waft from dozens of lit candles placed on windowsills and even the floor.

A crib is pushed against one wall. Goldie is sitting on the floor not far from an electrical outlet and a bag of potato chips. She's sucking on the lid of a deodorant.

I don't say anything to Jessy as I walk over to the baby and take the deodorant out of her hands. She starts to cry and I hoist her onto my hip.

Jessy glances over at me, her face displaying no emotion as if the chief of police breezing into her room and scooping up her baby is an everyday occurrence.

"Hi, Jessy," I say.

"Hey."

"Can we talk for a minute?"

Goldie grabs on to my lapels, then raises one tiny sticky fist to my lips, leaving behind a smear of orange grease on my jacket. I didn't notice she'd been eating the chips and they were barbecue.

I lick at her fingers and she laughs.

Jessy turns back to her phone and I use the opportunity to take a good look at her to see if anything major has changed since the last time I saw her.

She's in cutoffs and a cropped low-cut halter. I'm sure she thinks the amount of cleavage she's exposing is enticing, but the top also reveals rolls of the extra poundage Kirk the bartender found unappealing but appealing enough.

Her hair is still in desperate need of a touch-up, and her nails are even more chipped. It takes everything I have not to go forage in a bathroom for polish remover and cotton balls and force a manicure intervention.

Camio was prettier, thinner, smarter, had a good-looking boyfriend and a bright future in front of her. Could the motive have been something as common and biblical as simple jealousy?

Goldie continues grabbing my jacket. I look around for something to distract her that won't possibly kill her and I spy one of her stuffing-free dog toys. This one is a gray flattened rabbit. I give it to her and sit down on the bed with her.

Jessy finishes her text and looks over at the two of us. She isn't exactly glaring but she's annoyed.

"What do you want?"

On one level I feel for Jessy, but I also think there's a good possibility she killed her sister and maybe her great-aunt.

I don't think she needs someone to be saccharine nice to her. I also don't think she needs someone to be hard on her; she has Miranda for that. I don't think she'll respond to a performance or a manipulation. I think she needs someone to be interested in her.

"When did you find out?" I ask her.

"Find out what?"

"Who your mom is? Your real mom."

She flicks a hot glance at me. I didn't know for sure that she knew, but now I do.

"I don't know what you're talking about," she replies.

"Then you're the only one who doesn't. I even know and I'm not part of your family."

I make the rabbit squeak. Goldie smiles and grabs for it.

"Who told you?" I go on, giving all my attention to the baby. "Or, no, don't answer that. Who are you maddest at? Your grandma for lying to you all these years? Adelaide for giving you up? Your dad for being a pervert? Your stepmom for going along—"

"Shut up."

"Or Camio for finding out the truth?" I finish.

"Camio? Camio didn't know nothing."

This disclosure throws me off for a moment. I assumed Camio knew the truth behind her parentage, too. It gave her a reason to be at Adelaide's house with her sister, but then I remembered her project in the backpack, a treatise on her family and the declaration in her notes that she was going to visit her great-aunt soon. Maybe she was there to get more information for her book, and her sister and Adelaide continued to keep the big secret from her.

"How did you find out?" I try a different route.

She doesn't say anything at first. I know she's trying to decide how much she can tell me without admitting anything that can get her in trouble.

I give her time. She'll need to tell me eventually. People like Kirk have to explain their actions because they need everyone to think they're always right. Jessy will want to explain because no one ever asks her to.

"About ten years ago my dad was in a bad quad accident," she begins to answer. "Almost got killed."

I don't bother asking if alcohol was a factor. Riding around on ATVs while drunk is one of the leading causes of gruesome injuries around here.

"When he was in the hospital and thought he was going to die, he told Shane the truth. One of those deathbed-confession kind of deals, except he didn't die. Shane told me. We didn't bother to tell Cami 'cause she was still little."

"You miss Shane?"

She gives me a surprised and slightly pleased look as if knowledge of Shane is something magical and closely guarded like a clubhouse secret handshake.

"Yeah, I miss him a lot. He's never even held Goldie yet."

I look down at the baby in my lap, happily sucking on her dog toy. I stroke her soft curls.

"If Camio didn't know who your real mother was,

then what was she doing at Adelaide's house? We know she was there."

I stop short at saying we know she was killed there.

"And we know you were there. We traced a cell phone call you made from that area."

I don't know what Nolan would think of me giving away this crucial piece of evidence against her but I feel it's necessary.

This is the key moment when she'll either realize she should shut up altogether or think she can still tell me a little more of her story without beginning to dig herself into a hole, not realizing the hole has already been dug and already too deep to escape.

"I thought she was old enough to know now," she decides to explain. "She'd been asking Miranda questions about Aunt Adelaide lately and making her really mad. I wanted to keep the peace, so I told Cami I'd take her to see Addy. I thought she could meet her and see how nice she was and we could tell her together."

"So you've been in touch with Adelaide over the years?"

"I go see her when I can, but no one knows about it."

"And how did Camio react?"

Now she does clam up. I wait but nothing seems to be forthcoming.

"And hearing this long-kept secret devastated her," I try providing an answer. "This family Camio loved so much was damaged beyond all repair. She found out the poison wasn't in your hearts or your minds; it was in your blood. How do you get rid of that?"

She gives me an incredulous look.

"What are you talking about? You sound like one of my mom's cheesy romance novels."

"Your mom reads?"

"We're not stupid," she shouts. "We know how to read."

She wags a finger at me.

"Grandma told us all about you."

"I bet she did."

"You came from trash."

"I came from trash who kept her nails perfectly polished."

She looks down at hers, then over at mine that are usually bare but happen to be pink with bling today.

"I didn't mean any offense to your mom," I apologize. "I just meant she seems to be more interested in TV."

"She doesn't read a lot," she says, her anger fading. "She only reads these crappy old paperback romances. She has a bunch from when she first married Dad, and she finds them at yard sales and flea markets. It's the only time I've ever seen her get really excited. When she finds one of those old books for a quarter buried in a cardboard box on somebody's driveway."

By the look on her face this was a good memory for her, but the feeling doesn't last and the anger returns.

"It wasn't nothing like what you said. Camio didn't love us. She was writing a book about us. Some kind of psychological profile, she called it, about how dysfunctional we all were. She told me about it in the car on the way to see Addy."

"You shouldn't have let that upset you," I tell her.

"She was a seventeen-year-old kid. She wasn't going to write a book."

"She'd write it someday," she insists, her agitation growing. "Or even if she didn't, she thought all these bad things about us. She was going to leave and go tell everyone she met her family was a bunch of fucked-up rednecks."

She suddenly stops talking. I can sense her mind is racing, once again trying to figure out if she's said anything incriminating. It's one thing to talk about the biggest skeleton in her family closet but another to reveal anything that would tie her to her sister's death. She must realize she's just put herself and Camio and Adelaide together in the house where Camio was killed and maybe Adelaide, too. She must also realize she's admitted to being very mad at her sister.

I stand up from the bed. There's no reason for me to try and get more out of her, since she could deny all of it later. I need to get her to Nolan. My only reason for prying deeper would be to satisfy my own curiosity. I'm tempted.

I glance down at Goldie in my arms and notice a stain on the underside of one of the rabbit's ears.

"Has Goldie hurt herself lately?" I ask Jessy.

"No."

"Is this blood?"

I show her the dried reddish-brown blotch on the fur.

"Was Goldie with you? You tried to get Gina and Kirk to babysit but they wouldn't do it."

She looks shocked that I know this.

"Is this Camio's blood?" I go on. "Or Adelaide's? If we find out that it is . . ."

She walks slowly across the room toward me as if in a trance, her eyes glued on the plush rabbit in my hand.

"I didn't know she got it on her toy, too," she says distractedly. "She got some on her clothes and in her hair.

"Camio pushed her!" she suddenly screams. "An old lady like that. She pushed her. In front of my baby. She got blood on my baby!"

She rips the toy out of my hand and shakes it at me.

"She got so mad when Addy told her the truth. She yelled at her and said she wasn't some mutant hillbilly freak and she pushed her."

Her voice breaks and she begins to sob.

"When Addy fell against the oven and hit her head, Camio didn't even flinch. She didn't try to help her. I don't think she did it on purpose. I don't think she meant to kill her, but once she realized she did, she didn't care at all.

"I got so mad at her. How could she do something like that and not feel bad about it? She killed our grandma. She got blood on my baby."

My own blood freezes at the desperation behind her question. I know that free-falling panic. I see her hands tighten around the skillet handle searching for a handhold that would save her the same way mine wrapped around Champ's bat.

"Everybody thought she was perfect and nice," she says, calmer now, tears streaming down her face. "She wasn't perfect, and she wasn't nice."

I should place her under arrest, but I can't do it.

"Jessyca," I say quietly. "I need you to come with me."

She nods numbly and glances behind her at a framed photo on the desk. I didn't notice it earlier, stuck behind all the other clutter.

It shows a young woman sitting on a couch holding a baby with a little boy and a little girl on either side of her. I don't have to ask who it is. The picture was probably taken a few months or maybe even a few weeks before Layla died in the car crash.

"Grandma Addy had it hanging on her wall," Jessy explains. "I took it so I can remember. Is it okay for me to keep it?"

"Yes," I tell her.

She turns and reaches for her baby. I want to hold her forever, but Goldie smiles at her mom and reaches back.

chapter twenty-seven

THE REST OF MY DAY and night goes by in a numb blur. My only clear memory is of the fiesta I made for Mason. He asked for Mexican food, which happens to be one of my favorite cuisines, and since there isn't a good Mexican restaurant within a hundred miles of here, I've learned how to make my own.

Cooking helped me relax a little, but sleep tonight has proved impossible. I can't concentrate on a book. It's almost two in the morning. Mason is fast asleep and I've zoned out in front of the TV when I get a cop knock at my front door: three short, hard booms.

Nolan stands outside my front door with a bottle of Maker's Mark in one hand. Neither of us are big drinkers. I don't know if this means we're going to celebrate or drown our sorrows. He's unsmiling. I'm pretty sure he's been wearing the same suit for three days. His sunglasses have been retired for the night and his eyes look tired.

"It's done," he says.

His statement is a hollow fact; there's no joy, or pride, or even relief in it.

No one knows better than Nolan that solving a case like this one doesn't fix anything. Words like "closure" and "justice" will be thrown around, but they're only words.

He once told me the reason cops make such a point of referring to their profession as "the job" is because its vital to view it as a series of straightforward, attainable goals like writing out a ticket, canvassing witnesses, making an arrest, appearing in court, getting a confession, filing reports. If you allow yourself to dwell too much on the human condition and think you can make things all better, he explained, the futility of it will make you quit.

"Congratulations," I tell him.

He rubs at his eyes and the bridge of his nose and takes a strangely long time staring at a tiny cloud of dust-colored moths fluttering around my porch light.

"Yeah," he says.

He walks past me into my living room, taking off his suit jacket and even his tie. When he also kicks off his shoes, I wonder if this case was the one to finally make him lose his marbles and he's decided to move in with me.

"Do you have any food?" he asks.

"Chipotle pork tacos with grilled pineapple, chiles rellenos, arroz verde, a habañero salsa. Mason wanted Mexican. We have a ton of leftovers."

"You make good Mexican food," he says.

A compliment and a bottle of premium bourbon: he *has* lost his marbles.

I head for the kitchen.

"How's that working out?" he calls after me. "Having your nephew around?"

"I couldn't do it without Neely's help. She's been watching him during the days while I'm at work. He's a nice kid, though. No trouble really."

"Once school starts, it'll get easier."

I pause in my preparations and stick my head back into the living room, trying to appear calm, but my heart is thudding in my throat.

"What's that supposed to mean?" I ask him. "Why would he still be here when school starts?"

"You're the one who told me you thought your brother was leaving his kid with you for a while, maybe even permanently."

"Then you didn't find anything?"

"No."

I calm down and finish making a plate for him, nuke it, and return to the living room. I also bring some chips and salsa and two glasses with ice.

I set it all on my new coffee table. It was delivered today.

"I've spent the past sixteen hours interrogating Trulys," he tells me as he digs into the food.

I sit down beside him and tuck my bare legs under the oversize T-shirt I've been wearing to bed since Mason's arrival along with a pair of men's boxer shorts. I usually sleep in the nude and hang out in nothing but a shorty bathrobe before bed but I don't want to run the risk of Mason catching his fifty-year-old aunt in the buff. I can't imagine what kind of psychological damage that would do to the kid. He has enough problems.

"You deserve a medal," I say.

He looks over at me. "I deserve something."

There's not a hint of sexual suggestiveness in his glance but I don't take offense or lose hope. We have an unspoken rule that as long as we don't plan our hookups, flirt, or make out beforehand, the actual sex doesn't count.

I let him eat, then pour us a drink. We clink glasses and settle back into the couch. I don't ask him anything. I know he'll tell me the details when he's ready.

He's on his third drink before he begins.

"Jessyca Truly took her sister, Camio, to meet their biological grandmother Adelaide Bertolino with the intention of telling her the truth about their parentage. An argument ensued in Adelaide's home that turned physical. Camio pushed her grandmother, who fell and struck her head. The wound was fatal according to Jessyca. We have no one to back up her story and no evidence to corroborate it so far, but we're sending cadaver dogs out to Campbell's Run at daybreak. Eddie Truly told us where they buried his aunt's body."

"Near the church?"

"How'd you know that?"

"Lucky guess. Did Jessy admit to killing Camio?"

"The snapped defense. She claimed seeing her sister kill her grandmother made her fly into a rage and lose control. She picked up the nearest heavy object and hit her with it."

"But she hit her several times."

He sets his empty glass on the table and leans forward, his elbows resting on his knees.

"There was definitely more going on there than her simply reacting to what she witnessed, but there are also mitigating factors. If a lawyer like Sandra Goldfarb gets hold of it and it goes to court, she might be able to get her a lighter sentence, but she's going to be convicted."

A chill runs through me despite the warmth of the summer night and the spiciness of my salsa. He could be describing me and my situation thirty-five years ago if Neely hadn't convinced me to frame Lucky.

Neely said I shouldn't feel guilty, because I agreed to do what I did for her sake even more than my own. I wonder if Miranda was thinking of Goldie when she agreed to help Jessy cover up Camio's murder.

"What about the burning of the hands?" I ask. "The burn marks on the blanket?"

"The three of them are telling the same story. Eddie and Miranda were accessories after the fact. Neither knew what happened until Jessyca contacted them. Eddie disposed of the bodies on his own. Miranda and Jessyca stayed behind and cleaned up."

"Jessy wasn't there?"

"Eddie said he tried to put out the fire with the blanket once he started it. He said he couldn't stand watching her burn. The hands may have been badly burned, but I don't think it was done on purpose. It was probably just how the gasoline was splashed onto the body."

He looks back at my hand clutching my glass.

He hasn't commented on my nails yet. He doesn't now except to say, "But I guess that detail, whether it was a coincidence or not, helped you break the case."

Even though what he just said is true, and even if Nolan has always had a reputation for giving credit where credit is due, I'm not prepared for his blunt acknowledgment. I'm completely thrown for a loop. I don't know what to say or do.

I quickly change the subject.

"Has Sandra taken the case?" I ask nonchalantly.

"Jessyca hasn't asked for a lawyer yet. If Sandra does take it, she'd have to agree to do it pro bono. The Trulys can't afford her, and I doubt your sister is going to pay for Jessyca Truly's defense as well as Tug's."

"You know about that?"

"I know about everything."

His gaze strays back to me and lingers briefly at the outlines of my bare nipples beneath my T-shirt. I throw back the rest of my drink.

"Whatever happened to Lonnie Harris?" I continue to be casual.

"Came slithering home two days ago. I had a talk with him about the altercation he had with Camio at Dairy Queen. He said it was nothing personal. It was just his way of hitting on a girl."

"Swell guy," I comment.

"His wife took him back. No questions asked. I won't be surprised if someone ends up dead out there," he adds.

"But you won't be surprised if someone doesn't," I finish for him, smiling.

He kisses me and, before I can respond properly, stands and swings me up over his shoulder caveman-style, and stomps up the stairs to my bedroom.

He could have just as easily thanked me for the food and left mumbling something about an early morning and I wouldn't have been surprised or offended. I never know when he's going to want me and definitely not why.

Nolan doesn't have skills or finesse, but he doesn't want them and doesn't try to fake them. I've been with too many men who I felt had memorized a textbook before taking me to bed; I could almost hear them counting out the amount of times they were expected to rub a nipple. Then there were the ones who learned the art of love from pornos. And those who expected me to act like I was in one with them. And the talkers. The hackneyed sex scripters. *Yeah, I like that. Ooh that's good. Ooh you're wet.*

Nolan is a war machine; his battleground is me. He does thorough recon, invades, penetrates, withdraws, and leaves me in ruins. Every time.

Afterward, he wants to stay but can't allow it. I want him to stay but won't admit it.

I hear him getting out of bed and looking for his clothes in the dark. I pretend to be asleep to make it easier.

He's a sprawling sovereign empire to my lawless island nation.

chapter twenty-eight

SINGER SPENT TWO SUMMERS as the Buchanan Flames mascot, Milton Matchstick, running around in red foil long johns with a big, red, tinselly, fright-wig headpiece. He never showed his face on the field without being pelted with beer cans and ketchup-stained ends of hot dog buns. I didn't hold it against him when he applied for a job with my department. I thought it showed he had composure under fire.

Since then he gets into the games for free and has a seat of honor above the dugout.

I thought a baseball game would be fun for Mason after spending these last few days worrying about his father and being largely ignored by the two aunts taking care of him who have lots of other things to take care of, too.

I came up with the idea yesterday and invited the whole department to come along. Karla had other plans and Everhart's wife explained to him that it's not a good idea to take five-day-old infants to loud sporting events. He didn't understand why and argued over the phone with her before finally giving in and then arguing some more with her over why he couldn't go by himself. After hanging up he continued to complain until Dewey told him to SUDS.

I invited Dewey, his wife, Angie, and kids, and Singer and Blonski back to the house with Mason and me for an extension of our fiesta the night before. Neely and Smoke come for the meal.

My backyard is full of noise and chaos. Dewey's children climb my overgrown apple tree and throw a ball for Smoke.

Singer and Blonski are deep in conversation about a controversial call at third base. Out of their uniforms, wearing shorts, T-shirts, and red ball caps, carrying pennants and giant Slurpee cups, they don't look to be that much older than Dewey's oldest son, who's eleven.

Angie offers to help with the food, but Neely makes her sit and stay outside with a cold beer.

Mason is getting along fine with the Dewey clan but continues to pop into the kitchen now and then to see what we're doing.

I was able to convince him to leave his Trapper Keeper at home and not take it to the game. Since we've returned, he hasn't gone to get it. I think this is a good sign.

Neely hasn't asked me to elaborate on the few facts I gave her regarding the solving of Camio Truly's murder. She was glad to know it's all over and commented on the big notch it would be in Nolan's already well-scarred belt. I didn't tell her what he said to me last night. Or what he did to me. I do keep some secrets from my sister.

I'm surprised when she looks up from taking a

couple of baking dishes of chicken enchiladas out of the oven and says, "So after it's all said and done, what was her motive?"

Anyone else asking me this question and I'd reply that I already explained what happened: Jessyca Truly became enraged at the sight of her sister killing their grandmother and reacted violently, striking her with a heavy object and accidentally killing her.

But I know there's more to this story and Neely senses this, too. She isn't any more satisfied with this easy answer than I am.

Jessyca saw a side of her sister that others didn't. I think about how upset she was while telling me Camio showed no remorse over killing Adelaide and that she planned to betray their family by airing their stained, patched psychological laundry for the whole world to see.

How she got blood on her baby.

"There was something Grandma said not long after Mom was killed," I say while chopping tomatoes for a pico de gallo. "I don't know if you'd remember this but you were there. So was Champ. We were sitting in her kitchen eating dinner after we moved in with her."

I fall silent remembering how cramped we were in Grandma's small house after all the space in Gil's, and how deprived we were after all the excess at Gil's, and how deliriously happy and grateful we were to be there.

"Champ was complaining about kids at school asking him questions about Mom's murder. He was asking our advice about what to say."

"I remember," Neely breaks in. "I told him to tell

kids he didn't like to talk about it. You told him to tell kids he wasn't supposed to talk about it. You were already a cop."

"Maybe," I say. "Grandma was busy at the stove and I didn't know if she was paying any attention to our conversation when all of a sudden she said . . ."

I look up from my task and do my best Grandma impression.

"'. . . If you find a small fire in a back room, you don't let it spread and burn down the whole house. You put it out.'"

"I remember," Neely confirms.

"At the time I didn't know what she meant. I thought it was just one of the weird sayings she said sometimes like 'I'm about to have a come apart' or maybe she hadn't heard him right. But now I think I know exactly what she meant."

We exchange knowing looks.

"Jessyca was putting out a small fire," Neely says.

The back screen door opens and slams shut.

"I need my binder," Mason says breathlessly, and streaks past us into the living room.

Neely glances at the clock on the microwave.

"He's gone for four hours without it. That's not bad."

He returns almost immediately, empty-handed.

"Aunt Dove," he says. "There's a police car out front."

Neely and I follow him out of the kitchen.

I look out my windows and see a state trooper cruiser parked on the street. Nolan's car is parked behind it.

I take Mason's hand. Neely takes his other. We walk out onto my porch in a flesh-and-blood chain.

A rumble of summer thunder echoes in the distance and I peer up at the bank of ominous gray clouds gathering over my neighbors' rooftops. Our perfect weather is coming to an end.

Nolan gets out of his car. He bows his head and walks slowly toward the three of us.

I know what this means. Neely and I have a son.

angels burning

Tawni O'Dell

Introduction

Angels Burning tells the story of a small town that has suffered the tragic and gruesome murder of a teenage girl. Local police chief Dove Carnahan has been tasked with finding the girl's murderer but must navigate through a slew of defensive and hostile relatives and friends in order to determine the truth. In the process of this investigation, dark secrets of a similar murder in the town years earlier are unearthed and the trauma from her personal life competes for Dove's attention. Throughout the investigation, Dove learns that under everyone's tough exterior and behind all of the rumors that the locals spread, no one is who they appear to be—including those closest to her and even herself.

Topics and Questions for Discussion

1. Discuss the title of the book *Angels Burning*. How does the title relate to Campbell's Run's hardships with the collapsed mine and its "ability to swallow up lives" (pg. 287)? What is the physical and economic impact on the town's inhabitants?

2. Dove calls Campbell's Run a "poisoned ghost town" (pg. 1). However she and many others have chosen to remain near it. Discuss Dove's motivations for remaining in the town that has caused her so much pain. Discuss how your perception of her character and motivations changed after learning about her past. Was she really "on the side of the angels . . . when it was all over" (pg. 320)?

3. Discuss Dove's motivations for becoming a police officer. In what ways did she grow up to protect others from the horrific things that happened to her, Champ, and Neely as children? In what ways is she trying to cope with the murder of her mother and the cover-up?

4. Lucky, the man convicted of murdering Dove's mother, has been released from prison after thirty-five years. How has his release affected Dove? How does she react to him finding her? What is her perception of him and the past that they share?

5. How does Lucky's return affect Dove's investigation of Camio's murder? Dove observes that "One of the worst aspects of growing older is the

lengthening of hindsight. As it stretches, it becomes thinner and more transparent and we see things more clearly" (pg. 27). How does Dove feel about her actions in her mother's death at the end of the novel?

6. Discuss how your interpretation of Dove's investigative tactics changes after learning about her violent past. Has her personal history informed how she approached this murder investigation? Why or why not?

7. Dove observes that she gets "these flashes of irrational passion where [she's] willing to risk everything [she's] worked for in order to accomplish one thing [she] can't control" (pg. 94). Where do you see instances of this in the novel? Where does she lose her objectivity when reflecting upon Camio's murder and on her personal life?

8. Discuss how your impressions of some of the following characters changed and evolved throughout the novel: Dove, Champ, Shawna, Camio, Jessy, Zane, Lucky, and Miranda. Was your initial impression of these characters based on physical presentations and rumors? Did learning more about their backgrounds and experiences increase your empathy towards them? Why or why not?

9. Discuss the relationship between Dove, Neely, and Champ. How are they complicit in each other's lies? How do they distance themselves to avoid thinking about their past and their mother?

10. As the first female chief of police in Franklin County, Pennsylvania, Dove faces sexism at various points in her career and throughout the novel. How does she deal with being treated differently among her coworkers and with the men and women she interrogates? What assumptions do others make based on her age? As Dove notes: "I'm okay with my age, but nobody else is. Especially men" (pg. 20).

11. Dove observes, "We didn't know living nightmares don't ever go away because you can't wake up from them. The most you can hope for is to dilute them by spreading them around" (pg. 107). How does this quote reflect the lives of various characters in the novel?

12. Consider the parenting styles portrayed in *Angels Burning*. During the course of the novel, parents are portrayed abandoning their children, being disinterested in their well-being, putting them in harm's way, or defending and protecting them. Reflect on how these characters were treated as children and think about how that may have informed their parenting style. Dove observes: "I also know what it's like to have a mother who doesn't care about you. This isn't always the same thing as having one who doesn't love you. Love is a highly subjective concept; everyone has different standards for what qualifies" (pg. 92). How is this reflected in the various relationships portrayed in the novel?

Enhance Your Book Club

1. Read Tawni O'Dell's previous novel *One of Us* with your book club. Discuss how these two novels relate to each other. Both are set in mining towns. Discuss the significance of setting and locale in O'Dell's work.

2. Tawni O'Dell wrote an essay called "The Oprah Effect" for OfftheShelf.com detailing the experience of her book *Back Roads* being chosen as an Oprah Book-of-the-Month Club Main Selection. Read the essay here and discuss her experience: http://offtheshelf.com/2014/09/the-oprah-effect -tawni-odell-back-roads/

3. Visit www.tawniodell.com to learn more about the author, her other books, and read other essays she has written.